FINAL REPORT

"I can run just one test at a time," Kratzel said. He bent forward, holding the sword over the pale blue back of a report. The file bit into a spot about five inches below the handle.

The sound that George heard was like a fingernail on a blackboard at first, only louder and more piercing, with a background howl of rage and fury. Then there appeared to be a flash of light, and he seemed to behold a man, shaggy, bearded and gaunt with whitely burning eyes superimposed on Al Robinson, who had leaned close for a better look. All of a sudden Robinson grabbed the sword—or rather, the sword seemed to wrench itself from Kratzel's left hand, turn over in the air, and land in the young lawyer's hand.

"Hey, what?" Kratzel exclaimed.

Robinson, smiling, drove the sword into the metallurgist's neck!

THE
SEEKING
SWORD

JAAN KANGILASKI

BALLANTINE BOOKS • NEW YORK

Library of Congress Catalog Card Number: 76-13215

ISBN 0-345-25650-6-195

Manufactured in the United States of America

First Edition: February 1977

Cover art by Darrell Sweet

1

August 8, 1968

THE OLD MAN was making a genuine effort to remember, squinting his watery blue eyes and grinding his knuckles into his temples. "Let me see, now," he said, shaking his bald head. "There was the house, and then the fires on the hillside, and then . . . and then . . . then, all of a sudden, everything went black. Black." He paused as he reached for the cup of coffee; his old, gnarled hand with huge knuckles trembled on the red-and-white-checked tablecloth.

None of the other three people in the sunlit kitchen said a word. The woman, fortyish and blond, with the same straight nose as the old man, stared out the window. George Quinterus looked across at his lawyer, Harry Bradley, who appeared fascinated by the kitchen clock.

Yes, Quinterus thought bitterly, it was always the same: shabby kitchens (or living rooms), and men with vague, fading memories, tag ends of weird phrases, troubled eyes trying to recall scenes of violence and death. This one was no different from the others he had talked to since starting his wild-goose chase three years ago.

"Mr. Goltz," he said, trying to keep the weariness and distaste out of his voice. "Mr. Goltz, when you went to the Bergstrom house, did you have the knife with you?"

"Knife?" Harald Goltz sounded surprised.

"Yes, knife. Or did you think of it as the Seeking Sword?"

He hated the term: stupid, inane, ridiculous—but

1

that's how most of them seemed to think of the murder weapon.

"Yes," said the old man.

"Yes, what?"

"Seeking Sword . . . Of course I had him. Had to, otherwise Seppiyeh wouldn't have talked to me. I mean—" The old man shook his head. "I mean . . ."

"Go on, Dad," urged his daughter, chiding. "Do you want somebody else to go through what . . . you and Ed Bergstrom went through?"

"No, Eleanor. I don't. It's just . . . hard to put in words, and I just can't remember. I don't think most of it ever was in words, really—just occasional things, proverbs like . . . like 'Making spears, and reaching into range—those are things that every hunter must learn first. Striking hard enough, when close enough —that's simple.' "

"I never heard that one before," said the woman.

"Never seemed any reason to bring it up," the old man explained.

"Seppiyeh told you this?" asked Quinterus, unhappily certain of the answer.

Davidson's trial transcript had mentioned something similar; E. P. Yarness had muttered about Seppiya's (that's how he had pronounced it) sayings; and others had said similar things. He should be glad this one had been victimized by the same thing—or people— but he was not. He was merely weary, disgusted— and a bit frightened, because sooner or later the people behind the Seeking Sword would become aware somebody was prying into their affairs.

The old man was nodding his head vigorously. "Yessir. Yes, that's what Seppiyeh said to me. It made sense at the time, I recall, but now—well, I'm not so sure now."

"He's not sure about anything at all," the woman added. "I told you all he ever told us—and we asked him, many times, especially after he got out of jail and came to live here."

"Yes, Mrs. Radtke," Quinterus responded. In a way, he felt sorry for the old man, with his daughter and two strangers all staring at him and asking why and

2

how he had killed Ed Bergstrom one summer's day back in 1928.

"Ain't much to tell," the old man said in response to his daughter's statement. "I drove over, got out of the car and walked up to the house . . . listening to Seppiyeh's voice in my head. Old Lizzie came out and started barking at me." The old man rubbed his eyes. "Had to kill 'er, poor Lizzie. A good dog, she was, and I give her to Ed, myself."

"Did Seppiyeh tell you to kill Bergstrom?" asked Quinterus.

The old man shook his head. "He never told me to kill nobody, and I never killed nobody. All I done was put out a fire, but nobody ever listened, so they put me in jail." He paused. "Don't you think fires should be put out? I mean, before they cause damage."

"Of course," Quinterus said, trying to ignore Mrs. Radtke's scandalized expression. "Only—why did Mr. Bergstrom end up dead because you put out a fire?"

"That's what I been trying to figure out." The old man shook his head. "You tell me, mister. You tell *me*," he said, with a trace of belligerence.

"Bergstrom's wife and sons saw you do it. The sons took the knife away and held you till the sheriff got there."

"They kept beating me and beating me," the old man complained. "There was two of 'em and they kept beating me with a chair, and kicking me. It was no way to treat a white man."

Quinterus decided to let this pass. "After all, he was their father."

"I never killed him. Just put out a fire," the old man said sullenly. "I don't know how Ed ended up dead, but that was all right, too."

"That's how he talks about it, all the time," Mrs. Radtke put in while Quinterus and Bradley exchanged glances.

This too fit the pattern, they thought.

Quinterus smiled at Mrs. Radtke. "Thank you," he said, and turned to her father. "Whatever happened to the Seeking Sword?"

"They took it away from me. Mr. Gordon, he put it into evidence at the trial." Harald Goltz shook his

3

head. "Damned if I know why they put me on trial! All I done was put out a fire."

"You know, Dad, these men are not the law," Mrs. Radtke soothed him. "They don't want to make trouble for you, or put you back in jail. They're trying to find out what happened so they can prevent it from happening again."

"I been telling 'em what happened, but they don't listen, either," the old man flared up.

"We've been listening," said Bradley.

"Yeah," the old man agreed reluctantly.

"What happened to the sword?"

Harald Goltz shrugged. "They locked it up with the bloody shirt and the broken chair and the rest, I guess."

"You never saw it again?"

The old man shook his head.

"Did you ever hear from Seppiyeh again?"

"Dreamt of him, sometimes. I think I heard his voice, once or twice, but maybe that was my memory playing tricks."

"Do you have any idea where the Seeking Sword might be now?" Bradley sounded just like a lawyer. Sometimes this was a distinct advantage.

The old man rubbed his jaw. "Don't know . . . wherever the sheriff keeps things, I guess." He frowned as he saw his questioners' expressions. "I mean—you mean, it's gone?"

Bradley nodded.

"What happened?"

"Nobody seems to know. One day, it just wasn't there. Or so they told us."

"Who told you that?"

"Sergeant Ainsworth."

"Ainsworth? Must have come since my time." The old man looked puzzled.

Quinterus repressed a smile. Ainsworth was in his forties; he would have been a child when Bergstrom was knifed to death. "Never mind who told us . . . How do you feel about its being gone?"

"Dunno." The old man thought it over. "One thing, though, mister—I'm not surprised."

"Why?"

4

Mrs. Radtke decided to join in here. "Yes, Dad. Why?"

The old man turned to her. "Look, Eleanor," he exploded. "Look, there's a lot of things I can't explain how I know." He shook his head. "Next, you're gonna ask where Seppiyeh is. How would I know? I haven't heard from him in ages. I'm getting goddamned tired of it all, 'cause all I done was put out a fire and they —everybody—ganged up and threw me in jail like a common criminal, a murderer, or something."

"Dad . . ."

"I'm tired of all this." The old man threw his head back. "It happened forty years ago!" He paused. "Forty years, dead and gone. Forty years." He forced a laugh. "Now, then, let's talk about something interesting—like, you think Humphrey's gonna have a chance against Nixon?"

"I sure hope so," Quinterus said, steeling himself to try again—and wondering whether, right now, at this very moment, some other Harald Goltz was about to kill another Edmund Bergstrom with nobody knowing why.

2

August 15, 1968

As A MATTER of fact, killing somebody was the farthest thing from John Lambert's mind. He was swearing in most unteacherly fashion at the driver of the milk truck who was taking too long with a left turn off State Highway 87. What was wrong with him, anyway? Terminal lack of reflexes?

Lambert smashed his fist on the horn button. The truck blinked its side lights.

Screw him! Lambert leaned out the window, weighing his chances, listening to the rising tide of sound in the back of his mind, hoping it would not stop or start to fade as so many times before. Now! The blue Chevy *whoosh*ed by, the driver of the truck was still hesitating, Lambert jammed his foot down on the accelerator, zoomed past the truck, whipped into Sheppard Drive—

There! He thought of the truck driver's face and almost grinned, but this was no time for gloating.

Gradually, the excitement of the turn subsided, and as Lambert's hands relaxed, the torrent of sound in his mind increased in strength and volume. He knew there were words in it, but right now he was content to listen, let the waves of . . . Well, a pine forest on a windy autumn night sounded something like it— not much really, but the idea did convey the flavor: the bleakness and strength, with no hint of the underlying tenderness and concern. Anyway, there was the white frame house where he must turn right on Thirlway Drive.

For a moment, he wondered whether the cops would hear about his illegal turn. No matter. He could explain, and when they heard what he had done they would all line up to shake his hand. Line up for miles and miles; and Howie Dornbusch, the school's superintendent, would apologize for overlooking him almost twenty years; and . . .

There. No traffic on Thirlway Drive.

John Lambert's glance shot ahead, along the line of economy ranch houses in four pastel shades—lime green, deep coral, brick red, and azure gray—with identical lawns and three-year-old shrubs. *The* house was a hundred yards ahead, on the right, the green house this side of the red house with plaster flamingos in front.

The plaster flamingos were about to plunge their long, red beaks into a foot-high birdbath. A real sparrow fluttered up from it as Lambert pulled up in the driveway.

Hah! The waves of sound were still beating on his mind, at previously inconceivable intensity; his heart was beating madly; his hands were shaking on the steering wheel; his throat was dry . . . This would never do.

He willed his hand not to shake as he shut off the ignition, shoved the keys in his pants pocket, picked up and crumpled the *News-Intelligencer* on the right-hand seat; the headline said something about Senator Eugene McCarthy's chances. He tossed the newspaper on the floor, grasped the Seeking Sword, got out and— Yes, this was the day everything was working out, because there *he* was, coming around the corner of the house.

A sensation of thrilling, throbbing, almost sensuous warmth shot up from Lambert's fingers to his right wrist, elbow, all the way to the shoulder. He closed his eyes. The world was black, or most of it, anyway —all but the star-sprinkled sky and the hillsides dotted with fires, myriads of fires, right fires and wrong fires, and none wronger than the one closest at hand.

Lambert opened his eyes. The waves of sound were rising to a deafening pitch, so overwhelming he could hardly see *him*: a kid, really—a husky, tall kid with hairy legs and arms in his cut-off bluejeans, sneakers, and yellow T-shirt with "PEACE" across the chest in big black letters. A Gene McCarthy supporter, not that this made any difference.

Wrong fires must be put out.

Lambert walked around the car, his right hand behind his back, clutching the ribbed handle of the Seeking Sword. The kid was saying something, but the sound was just too damned loud. All of a sudden, the kid's eyes widened, he took a step back, Lambert leaped forward—really the Seeking Sword thrust forward, dragging his right hand and arm after it. The kid dodged, but not fast enough. A diagonal red line appeared on his chest; the Seeking Sword pulled back, leaped forward again into the kid's stomach. The kid bent over. The Seeking Sword pulled out, thrust in again, again, and again. The kid's knees sagged; he fell down on the blacktop driveway and rolled over on his back, and the Seeking Sword went into his chest, right through the final "E," grating on a rib, meeting a pulsating resistance, sinking through it, coming to a crunching stop on a pebble under the youth's back while the torrent of noise in John Lambert's mind rose to a deafening, nerve-wracking crescendo like a hundred fire sirens in an underpass.

The kid's mouth was open, he gasped something, his legs thrashed wildly, he closed his eyes. A trickle of blood ran from the left corner of his mouth. He tried to raise his head, opened his eyes, lay down again.

The Seeking Sword pulled out and thrust in again, this time under the chin. Lambert watched, fascinated, seeing the dark, crudely forged blade sink into the sun-tanned neck while he also saw—no, perceived, sensed, became aware—that the bright, menacing flame which had overshadowed everything was growing pale, sinking, fading out.

The kid's legs twitched. The sound in John Lambert's head stopped with a startling suddenness—so abruptly that a passing car made him jump to his feet. The Seeking Sword was still stuck in the kid's neck—and what did *he* have to do with fires on the dark hillside and, more particularly, with the fire now put out? The kid looked like a punk, had long brown hair, and if he was old enough for a draft card he had probably burned it. But, all in all, he was no different from the kids in Lambert's own classes at Marbury High.

Lambert got to his feet, wiping his hands. The reporters would be here soon, asking how he came to do this public service and who he was. And he would answer, loud and proud: John Edgar Lambert, 264 Maple Avenue, Marbury. One wife, Alice; two children, dead; one German shepherd, old and lazy. Profession: educator, teacher of English for seventeen years.

Soon they would be here. Any minute. Reporters and photographers and television cameramen. He would be a hero. No: *was* a hero. The heroic deed was done, the deed that must be done even if the whole world misunderstood—or so Seppiyeh had said, warning him that the world was full of strange, quirky people.

He knew that already. But no one could fail to recognize the worth of what he had done.

The door of the green house opened and a woman ran out, a fat, dumpy woman with brown hair and a flowered dress. She was shrieking, "Larry! Larry!"

She threw herself down beside the body, her hands suspended over the boy's chest, her mouth gaping.

John Lambert looked on in amazement. Part of his mind was still busy with thoughts of posing for the photographers.

The woman pulled the Seeking Sword from the boy's neck. Lambert stepped forward. What was she trying to do? She looked at him wildly and then haltingly handed him the weapon, blade first.

There was something comforting, reassuring, pleasing in the way the rough-forged blade felt against his fingers. The metal was cool and dry; no blood on it. He studied it, wondering what was delaying the photographers.

3

May 5, 1970

THE *Thrilling True Crimes* article had a lot of pictures: John Lambert; his wife Alice, a thin, weary brunette with "haunted eyes"; Lambert and his fat German shepherd; Lambert and his attorney, Joseph W. Carnett, tall and righteous-looking, with gray temples and Marine drill instructor haircut. And then the victims, young Larry Jacoby with shoulder-length hair, guitar, and open mouth; Mrs. Jacoby, trying to look dignified next to the casket, which was buried under flowers; all six Jacobys around the backyard grill, with Larry kneeling to pet a mongrel identified as his dog, Catnip.

George Quinterus found the pictures fascinating, more so than the story—after all, what could you expect in *Thrilling True Crimes?* The pictures of Lambert, especially: the man was short, slightly built, and dwarfed by the deputy sheriff, who looked ready to hit him with his nightstick. There was something owlish about the killer's face—pointed chin, the tuft of hair standing up above the wide forehead, and staring eyes set too close together. He looked almost like a cartoon character, Festus pretending he had saved Dodge City. The triumphant expression did not fit the rest—clothes, features, physique—especially since he had been caught literally red-handed at the site of a senseless murder. He had not even known the victim.

George shook his head. No doubt about it—another killing had taken place only a week after he and Harry Bradley had interviewed Harald Goltz. But he ought to be glad, because the location was only five hours' drive from Cincinnati. Glad? God, no! He felt sick inside, just sick, at the stupidity and terrible waste of human lives: the Lamberts, the Jacobys, their friends and all the other people whose lives had been touched by this thing.

The Seeking Sword. Its name made no sense, even though Harald Goltz and Wayne Hirschman and so many others kept repeating the words "Seeking Sword." Which implied purpose. But what could be the purpose of this apparently endless chain of murders, garbagemen killing mailmen and schoolteachers killing boys from another town? It made no sense, except possibly as a long-term exercise in viciousness. Sickness, really. What was so unusual about that, though, in view of the things going on in Vietnam? Still, the Seeking Sword, whatever it was, was a chillingly efficient weapon, magnificent in its evil way—though its wielders were something else. Picking obscure men as agents made sense; most successful assassins had been men of no stature or distinction, from Sirhan B. Sirhan—God, how that name grated on the nerve ends—to Lee Harvey Oswald, Jack Ruby, James Guiteau, Gavril Princip, and so forth. By their measure, such killers as Wayne Hirschman and John Lambert could serve just as well.

Their targets, though: a Bronx mailman and a senior at Culberton High School . . .

George Quinterus rubbed his eyes, hard, and lit

a cigarette before returning to the magazine. The picture in which John Lambert seemed about to get clobbered also showed the murder weapon—a knife stuck in the lawn near the deputy's left foot. The thoughtful editors had put a white circle around the knife, but it blended too much into the background. The text was not much help, either, stating that Lambert had committed his murder with a "large, crudely manufactured knife" he had bought from an antique shop three months before the killing.

Larry Jacoby had died almost two years ago, on Thursday, August 15, 1968. This meant Lambert had bought the knife in mid-May, while Bobby Kennedy was making his triumphal campaign tour and—more à propos—about two months after the Seeking Sword's disappearance following Jerome Zelaitis' murder trial in Camden, New Jersey.

Feeling queasy, George rose to his feet and went to the kitchen to get a beer. Lambert's trial had ended almost nine months ago, on Wednesday, August 20, 1969. If everything had run true to form, the Seeking Sword had probably vanished again, and right this minute, on May 5, 1970, some unsuspecting, humble, obscure individual was being slashed to death in the street, or on opening his door to a stranger, or God knows how—no use thinking about that now.

In the future, however, there was a chance: J. Edgar Hoover might be a bastard, but even he could not fail to see that the Seeking Sword and its manipulators or controllers had to be stopped. Bradley had coined the term "Kill-thinkers" for them; it was totally inelegant, but so were the faceless men who controlled the Seeking Sword. The only problem was getting to Hoover. They had tried, he and Bradley both, but the FBI men in New York only shrugged. Get some proof, they had said.

Proof? George had a list of murders over the years, but the FBI men had said these could all be coincidence, that thousands of people stabbed others every year and a lot of the killers turned out to be cuckoo —and how did he and Bradley intend to prove all sixty-two murders had been committed with the same crudely made knife? Had they any idea how many

11

crudely made knives were floating around? And what, exactly, did the description mean, anyway?

To hell with them. George drank to that and put the beer can on the end table next to his old armchair. He sat down heavily and reached for the phone. They wanted proof, eh? He'd get it for them! The article had said nothing about the knife vanishing, and that was the sort of thing to excite people who wrote for, edited, and read *TTC*. This meant the Seeking Sword might still be in the sheriff's property room, and once an electronics expert or mechanic, or someone with a screwdriver even, got his hands on it, there should be proof aplenty.

"Hello, operator," he said, after dialing the information number. "Could you tell me the Culberton County sheriff's department number?"

Four minutes later he hung up.

Still there! The wheezy-voiced sergeant he'd talked to kept an extra close watch on it because no dust would settle on its blade. He'd even marked the blade with black grease pencil once, just to see what would happen, and the mark had ". . . sort of crumbled away, you know what I mean. It was real peculiar."

Had the sergeant ever thought of using a file on it, say?

"Thought about it, but decided not to." There had followed a long, long pause before the sergeant muttered something about regulations that prohibited the damaging of evidence. George had said he understood, gave the sergeant his phone number, asked him to call if anything happened, and hung up because there was nothing else to tell the man.

Lambert's attorney had been made something like the legal guardian of his nutty client when Lambert was committed to the state hospital at West Carroll, Ohio. After another sip of beer, however, and another look at client and counsel, George decided not to call Joseph W. Carnett just now. Something about the severe, smug expression suggested that Mr. Carnett probably would not feel too friendly toward strangers interested in the Lambert case. Speaking of lawyers, though—George dialed Harry Bradley's number.

Mr. Bradley was not in his office, he was in court.

When was he expected back . . . ? Well, all right, could he leave a message? The name was George Quinterus, Q-U-I-N-T-E-R-U-S, and he would like Mr. Bradley to call him—collect, if necessary—because George Quinterus had a new lead involving the Seeking Sword . . . S-E-E-K— Hell, strike that, make it the Hirschman case. H-I-R-S-C-H-M-A-N. Yeah. Mr. Bradley knew what it was about. Yes, he'd be at this number for some time, until late in the evening.

George swore, slammed the phone down, lit a cigarette from the half pack kept at the ready on the little table. Some people . . . To hell with them!

He shook his head, glared at his wristwatch—more than an hour yet before Gloria got off work—got up, and went to the bracket-mounted bookshelves that stretched from foyer door to kitchen. He pulled out the battered old volume titled *Reminiscences of a Frontier Ministry: Forty Years Among the Pioneers* and flopped back on the armchair.

He was rereading, for the hundredth time, about the Reverend Amos Ward MacKenzie consoling the man who babbled about a Seeking Sword and strange voices, when the phone rang. He picked it up.

"Hi, there."

He had been expecting, hoping for, a call from Harry Bradley; still, Gloria was pleasanter to talk to, any time.

"Off already?" he asked.

"I've got another hour," she answered. "I just wondered if I still had a date tonight, since you never called."

"Sorry." A moment later he added, "Sure, you've got a date."

"Just checking." Then brightly: "Any clues as to where we'll be going?"

George winced. Was she really cheerful, or amused, enjoying his perplexity because, with one thing and another—including, even, work on his book—he probably had not given any thought to this traditionally important matter? As a matter of fact, she was right.

"Well . . ." He shrugged and said, "I came across another lead."

13

"Really?" She sounded politely interested.

"It's a real recent case and not too far from here. A couple of hours' drive. In fact, I'm thinking of going out there, but I think I'd better have Bradley come along."

"I thought you were all through with him."

"Something like that. But this is different. This guy committed a murder with the Seeking Sword six months before I moved here from New York, and the cops still have the sword."

He was becoming excited; for an instant he let the current carry him along, before picturing Gloria's face as she listened to him. Then, suddenly remembering her opinion of the whole thing, he said: "Look, this really is the best lead ever, so I've got a call in to Bradley and I don't want to miss it. How about driving up here after work and we can go out later?" He paused. "Anyway, this way I'll have a chance to think of a place and make reservations."

She laughed. "Okay."

4

May 5, 1970

GLORIA BARR WAS almost as tall as George Quinterus, five feet eight, and perhaps a bit on the chunky side in view of her relatively short legs. She was wearing a short orange dress and patterned hose, with open-toed shoes. Her light brown hair was straight and long, and she had beautiful eyes—gray, almost green in some light conditions. Long ago, she'd had trouble with her skin and now there were clusters of barely visible pits on both sides of the slightly turned-up nose and near the left corner of the full-lipped mouth. Standing in the foyer door, she was pursing her lips and wrinkling her nose so that her dimples blended into disapproving lines.

"I smell a cheap cigar," she said.

"You do. Jim's here. He's a sort of refugee who says the Kent State teach-in was fine, he agreed with every single sentiment expressed, but enough was enough."

"At least he stood up to be counted."

"Yeah." George nodded. "He did. Come on in."

She was muttering something about people who never took a stand on anything as she passed him. George shrugged, closed the door, picked up his beer from the end table while Gloria tossed her purse on the sleep sofa that faced the foyer door.

"Don't tell me nothing will come of it all," she said. "I get enough cynicism all day at work. I don't need any more now."

"I didn't say anything. I was going to ask what you wanted."

Jim Stanfield appeared in the kitchen door. "He's only got beer and cheap bourbon," he complained.

"Beer is fine," said Gloria.

George got her a can of "Cincinnati's Finest" and a glass. Jim, who taught German at the University of Cincinnati, sat on the sofa with Gloria, while George relaxed in the armchair. It was one of the few things he had kept when he and Betsy broke up; why did he think of her every time Gloria came here? She was gone, and good riddance. He forced himself to listen to Gloria and Jim, about teach-ins and strikes, whether any Ohio grand jury would get to the bottom of yesterday's Kent State murders, and what, if anything, John Mitchell's Justice Department might do. Nothing, most likely. They all agreed on that. Jim observed that the army that invaded Cambodia had again missed the Viet Cong Pentagon.

A few more minutes of significant conversation, and then Gloria asked George about his new lead. "Will it fit into your thriller?" she added.

"Maybe." He felt suddenly reluctant to talk about it.

"Did Bradley ever call back?"

15

"Yeah."

"And?" she prompted.

"I'm going to New York next week. I've got some things to peddle, anyway, and Nick Gobel's been after me." He paused, took a sip. "Actually, I want to look over Bradley's shoulder while he writes this man's attorney."

"Why his attorney?"

"Lambert has been declared mentally incompetent and the attorney is sort of like his guardian." George picked up the *Thrilling True Crimes* from the end table's bottom shelf. "Here. Start on page eight. I need a refill."

Jim Stanfield came along to the kitchen—he had already read the story—while Gloria looked at the cover and whistled.

"You sure read some crap, George," she said. "They'd flip at the public library if somebody gave us a gift subscription."

"I will, as soon as I'm rich and famous enough."

She chuckled. Her laugh was one of many things about her he liked—surprisingly throaty. Her voice was rather deep and he had really offended her once by saying she would make a fine baritone. That had been five months ago, right after they had run into each other again.

Jim went to the pantry, where George kept his liquor. "I suppose you've already made arrangements to have the sword examined," he said, pouring. "I'll bet you won't find a thing."

"There's got to be something."

"It may not be anything you can measure with a micrometer."

"I know. It's an accursed weapon. Siegfried's sword, or . . . What was that poem you recited at Lenore's party?"

That had been the night he and Jim met. Usually George did not care to talk about his private obsession, but the combination of old acquaintances like the MacDonoughs, unlimited booze, and a genuinely interested listener had caused him to speak at some length about the Reverend Mr. MacKenzie's book,

16

the curious and tragic fate of Mr. Osmond Pettigrew, and the long series of coincidences that had proved fatal to so many people on both sides of the Atlantic.

Jim had raised an eyebrow, knocked the ash off his cigar, and suggested that the trail might lead a long, long way back.

Really? Why?

Another party guest had wandered by, they'd got rid of him, and then Jim had said that George ought to look into Germanic mythology—read about the sword Tyrfing, for example. In the end he had quoted part of Konrad Meyer's poem about the sword of Attila, how Sir Hugo carried that ancient weapon into battle and how the sword just wouldn't quit until the weary knight called on it to stop, for God's sake, and then:

> . . . Es zuckt in grauser Lust.
> Der Ritter stürzt mit seinem Pferd,
> Und jubelnd sticht ihn durch die Brust
> Des Hunnen unersättlich Schwert.

The reciter had been a bit put out when George said sure, he could understand it, and had even provided a rough on-the-spot translation: " 'It throbs in gruesome joy. The knight falls down with his horse, and joyously'—actually, 'full of jubilation'—'it pierces his breast, the Hun's insatiable sword.' "

Nice image that, but metaphorical, not for real—though if Meyer had based the poem on folk songs or local tradition, it might well be worth looking into, by Stanfield or Quinterus, if the Ford Foundation or the Rockefellers, or anybody, decided to stake him. They'd both had a good chuckle, but the laugh had died in George's throat as he remembered the story of Osmond Pettigrew.

Mr. Pettigrew was born in 1832—a few years after Meyer's birth—in Connecticut, the fourth son of a retired ship's captain who had married the daughter of a ship's chandler in Hamburg. Young Mr. Pettigrew, after a few years at Yale, went to complete his studies in Germany, where, instead of listening to the lec-

17

tures, he started reading the Brothers Grimm and other German mythologues. In the spring of 1853 he had left Bonn to wander around Holstein and Mecklenburg, asking peasants about the *Suchen-Schwert,* or Questing Sword. Late that summer, he had suddenly rushed to Hamburg and posted one last letter before embarking on the *Amalie,* a Hamburg-based ship that ran into trouble and had to put into Hull, England, to refit. The *Amalie* reached New York on October 29, 1853. As Mr. Pettigrew stepped ashore, a roughly dressed man with long brown hair and a bushy mustache slashed him to death with a large knife and escaped in the confusion. Contemporary newspapers said the "stranger Dutchman" had made a habit of waiting for incoming ships; many people had noticed him since mid-September. He was never caught.

Jim interrupted George's thoughts. "You were just thinking of Pettigrew, weren't you?"

"Uh-huh." George focused his attention back on the here and now. He lit a cigarette. "Yes," he said, cautiously. "Poor Mr. Pettigrew."

"You had that particular troubled look on your face." Jim grinned. "You're sure it was a Seeking Sword case. Right? At the same time, if you accept that, you've also got to assume that Pettigrew died because he was getting too close to the truth about the Seeking Sword."

True enough. Very likely the killer had set out to follow Pettigrew across the Atlantic. But then the victim's ship was delayed, and this was another point in favor of Bradley's theory that the Kill-thinkers were ruthless, well organized, and had been around for some time. He told Jim so, yet again.

The other man nodded. "And now you're worried because you may be getting to the same point. Though Osmond's killer was exceptional in not hanging around for a prize . . . How does that fit in?"

"That's what I hope to find out."

Jim frowned, studying the level of whiskey in his glass. "I think you're still going about this the wrong way," he said. "That last letter from Hamburg said nothing about international conspiracies, which had already been invented before 1850. The kid was worried about something else entirely."

George nodded.

It had been quite a letter, as reprinted in a memorial "album" published by the dead youth's family, four pages of purple prose leading up to: "It seems as though this may well be a long quest, and a hard one, but I am resolved to see it through, especially since already I have an inkling of where it should lead. I am more certain now than ever that when we have finished following this monstrous myth back to its origins, we shall find that the Questing-Sword springs not from the sun-lit Greek or Roman lands of Classical Antiquity, or even fabled and mysterious Egypt of the many monstrous gods, but rather from some dank burial mound beneath the ceaselessly dripping skies of this barbarous North, the region whence is sprung our own race. Altogether, this is a prospect that, I must confess, gives me a distinct thrill while at the same time filling my heart with forebodings of nameless evil."

The letter seemed to speak for itself, even though it had been written in the real world—and even in 1853, accursed swords emerging from "dank burial mounds" were simply not part of everyday reality. The monk who wrote the *Beowulf* manuscript had, after all, died a thousand years earlier. Reality was monstrous enough, but in it there was no place for accursed weapons. And since real men had died through the Seeking Sword, its wielders must be real men, too.

"Well, what about it?" Jim was saying.

"About what?"

"Pettigrew's letter."

"The man was paranoid."

George wondered whether Gloria was finished with the article about John Lambert, Larry Jacoby, and the lawyer, Joseph W. Carnett—a stuffy, self-righteous bastard by his looks. Still, he must be a pretty fair lawyer, as Bradley had said, because Lambert had a

19

good chance of getting out in another couple of years.

"Paranoia is no answer," said Jim.

"I'm done," Gloria yelled from the living room. "You can come on back."

"Another beer?" asked George.

She said why not; she kept tapping her knee with the rolled-up magazine and looked quizzically at George as he sat down on the sofa after handing her the beer can.

"Well, what did you think of it?" he asked at last.

"It's everything you said."

She might as well have said, "So what."

George began to explain. "Lambert heard voices, too, and thought he was doing something to benefit the human race."

"If that's all you're hoping for, why bother? They've all told the same story."

"Only, Lambert should be more articulate than most, and this murder happened less than two years ago, so he should remember." He paused. "More than most, anyway."

"It still looks like a really nothing lead."

George started feeling annoyed. "Then there is the knife itself," he said. "We can get that analyzed."

"So what would that prove? None of the others have been tested."

"You still don't believe the murders were committed with the same knife?"

"Some of them may have been," she said. "I said some, and that's granting quite a bit. But neither you nor anybody else as far as I know has ever come up with any proof it was the same weapon." Her tone was firm, but a bit wearied; they had gone over this often enough since he'd told her of what they now called his "obsession." He used the word jokingly. She didn't.

"It's a lot of similar murders to be a series of *coincidental* killings," he said.

"For one series, yes. But how do you know it's one series? The victims ended up dead, sure, but that doesn't mean they were killed for the same reasons, even if most of the killers happened to be insane."

"All right. All right." It wasn't worth arguing about. "Whatever you say."

"I'm glad you're seeing it my way."

Gloria could look and sound awfully demure at times.

George snorted. "I don't see why you can't try and see it my way sometimes, for a change," he said. "Anyway, analyzing the sword will at least give us—okay, me, damn it—a point to start from."

"Temper," she said sweetly. "Temper."

He almost told her off but managed to stop himself. She meant well; too bad she found the whole idea mad —crazy, except perhaps as a source of ideas for *Thoughts That Kill,* the thriller that he hoped would make him rich and famous. If it came to a choice, he would rather be rich; he'd already delighted critics once years before, with *Bleak Hills of Death* (Andy Hardy in Korea), and all that had got him, besides Betsy, was a $500 raise in his salary from Ainslie College.

As for his vehicle to fortune, Gloria considered *Thoughts That Kill* a terrible title, but that's how the Seeking Sword might work. In real life people were constantly going around wishing that somebody would kill So-and-so. Suppose the Seeking Sword were a telepathic receiver–transmitter (never mind its origins, for the moment) and that some people were more attuned, or susceptible, so they would go and pick up the weapon and then go and kill So-and-so, often after a long zeroing-in process both times. But why did the murder have to be committed with the Seeking Sword? There could be several explanations. The radar echo from somebody like Lambert, so to speak, might activate a recorded message in the sword to the effect of "Use me, use me," a message that became louder as the susceptible person approached —and the recorded message might also provide the killer with some sort of justification in his own mind, as suggested by some of the murderers' ravings about how they should be rewarded.

Anyway, that was one possible explanation: the

"random deaths" variation of the Kill-thinker hypothesis. There were other possibilities, such as the one favored by Bradley: that the Kill-thinkers knew exactly what they were doing.

The very thought made George shudder. Suddenly, he noticed the cigarette in his hand and stuck it in his mouth.

Gloria, who had been watching, smiled and shook her head.

George looked around for an ashtray, ended up flicking the ashes from the cigarette to the marred linoleum. Then he smiled back.

"I was going to ask about your book," Gloria said. "That is, as long as you aren't going to bite. You aren't, are you?"

"Of course not."

"Well?"

"I'm where the hero returns to his hotel room and finds the maid dead. He doesn't know what happened, but actually the bad guys were zeroed in on the room, knew somebody was there—and, well, they just didn't know it was the maid, rather than Foster."

"I see." She thought it over for a moment. "So what's Foster going to do?"

"He'll try to dispose of the body so the police won't suspect he killed her."

"I see." A pause. "Did the poor lady get to do anything at all?"

"Not really. She just said good morning as Foster went out."

"And that's all?"

He shrugged. "Probably. There are people like her in every novel—people who are victims and nothing else." He noticed the gleam in her eye, and added hastily: "Some of them are male, some female. Sex has nothing to do with it."

She grinned. "Glad to hear that. But you still ought to change the scene. You've never seen the Riviera, so how is Foster going to know his way around the place?"

"Novelists do things like that all the time," Jim put in.

"Sure," said George. "So maybe I'll switch the locale to Marbury, because that's why I'm really going there. Who cares about Lambert and this guy Carnett?"

5

May 19, 1970

THE SEEKING SWORD had always had a predilection for simple, unglamorous surroundings and Marbury (1970 pop. 18,654, est.) certainly fit the bill. County seat (wet, thank God) in a rich agricultural area, with light industry, lots of farm machinery and automobile dealers, a free municipal parking lot, two movie theaters on opposite sides of Long Street and drive-ins on each of the three highways converging in the city, with its proper Gothic courthouse and Civil War monument, cannon and all, across from The Embers Steakhouse, where George Quinterus was emptying his glass of beer while contemplating the remains of a fine steak and wondering about tomorrow—Wednesday—and his scheduled interview with Mr. Carnett. This was a time for preparation, a time to fortify oneself and find out everything possible about one's opponent on his home grounds. Harry Bradley had not been able to spare the time to help, and the hell with him.

George caught the eye of the waiter, a short, thickset, egg-bald man reclining against the bar.

The waiter walked over, slowly and painfully. "Yes, sir?"

"I'm ready for another."

The waiter turned to go. No doubt he'd been around for years, listening to the customers and warily sizing up strangers in town. He might have gone fishing with John Lambert. Maybe his wife and Lambert's wife were sisters, or maybe they lived next door to each other. He would probably know Carnett, too.

For a moment, George toyed with a fantasy: the waiter would be Carnett's father, who had put little Joe through Harvard Law, and now the son came in every Saturday for a big steak and left a $1.25 tip . . . Dumb. He had not even met the man. So why dislike him already?

So why not? His parents had told him and told him about Carnett's sort of people.

The waiter came back.

"Thank you," George said, and asked as the waiter turned away: "Say, do you know Mr. Carnett? Joseph Carnett, the attorney."

A flicker of interest appeared in the watery blue eyes as the waiter turned and nodded. "Yeah," he said, displaying bad teeth. "Comes in every once in a while. Mostly for lunch."

"What's he like?"

"Good-looking gentleman. Distinguished-looking."

"I mean as a lawyer."

"As a lawyer . . ." the waiter repeated to himself. "Oh, I suppose he's the best you can find around here. You fixin' to hire him for somethin'?" he asked with more interest, after a long moment.

"Maybe so."

"Well, mister, I don't think you could do any better for local deals." The waiter leaned against the edge of the booth. "You see, he usta be prosecutor, and a good one. Then he decided to run for the State Legislature. More money in it, I suppose, though with the gal he married he ain't exactly hurtin', not that he ever was." The man was warming up to his subject, speaking faster, gesticulating with his left hand. "I'm positive he woulda been there yet, workin' his way up to run some committee, maybe even in Washington, if it hadn't been for Goldwater."

For a moment, the lined old face looked perplexed. "Damned if I know why they ever let that one run, since the farmers like their price supports and every-

24

body's got relatives on social security, but they did; and so Mr. Carnett come back home and picked up practicin' law again because Mr. Northridge had got the prosecutor's job all sewed up by that time. Besides, I once overheard him say in the Wyandotte Room that a man could get pret-ty disgusted with prosecuting."

"I imagine so. Say, what's your name?" George held out his hand. "I'm George Quinterus."

"Pleased to meet you, George. Call me Mack."

"Look, Mack, I said I might . . . er, retain Mr. Carnett. That's not exactly true." For a moment he wondered whether to continue. But why not? "Actually, I want to talk to him, but it's not exactly a legal matter because it's about the John Lambert case."

"Lambert?" Mack made a face. "Oh yeah. Lambert . . . He's the high school teacher went and cut up that kid back in sixty-eight." A brief pause. "Yeah. Sure."

"You knew him?" Shades of fantasies!

Mack shook his bald head. "Not to talk to, not really," he said. "He may have et here, or at the Central Hotel, a few times for outside-school banquets, but he wasn't the kind to stop off for a drink on his way home."

"What did the kids think of him?"

Mack was older than Lambert, who would be about fifty. Still, scores of Lambert's former students must have ordered meals and drinks from the bald-headed waiter.

"Mmmm." Mack scratched his left jowl, studied his fingernails, shrugged. "Mmmm. Nobody ever said much about him, matter of fact. He was . . . sort of dry as dust, you know what I mean. Usta drill them on grammar—you know, adverbs, objects, that stuff." Mack grimaced at a memory from his own school days. "Nobody much liked him, nobody much hated him. One thing though, mister, for sure; everybody sure was surprised."

"Why?"

"He just wasn't the type, you know what I mean. Sure, he'd call some kid on the carpet, time to time, and he wasn't one who'd let 'em get away with diddly-squat. But he'd do it icy cold, sarcastic, sort of. The way one of my cousins described it, he'd really make 'em feel creepy inside. Know what I mean?"

George nodded. "Yeah."

"You see what I mean. Now, far as anybody knows, he didn't keep grudges. And anyway, he'd never even met that kid. So it just didn't make sense."

"Maybe he didn't want the kid messing around with his daughter or something?" Banal as it was, especially these days, it was always a possibility.

"The Lamberts had a couple of kids, but they died young, years ago."

So much for that. "How about nieces or cousins?"

Mack thought it over and shook his head.

"I see. What does Lambert look like, anyway?"

Mack twisted his mouth, trying to recall. "Oh, he's a bit shorter than me, sort of scrawny, really, with a face like a prune, with big round glasses and not much hair. Ha-ha. Don't think he ever had much. Somebody told me that, during his trial." Mack shook his head again. "One thing puzzled ever'body: how he managed to kill that kid to begin with. Because the kid had a good bunch of inches on him, and good reflexes, too. Usta play forward for the Trojans basketball team and screwed all their cheerleaders, or so I heard." He shrugged, with a gaping leer. "It sure was weird as hell, for sure, and Lambert was lucky Mr. Carnett took his case."

"Nobody ever came up with a motive. Even afterwards?"

"Nyah. And not for lack of tryin'." Mack grinned, horribly, exposing the gaps among his upper teeth. "The *News-Intelligencer* ran an editorial, trying to be funny, about how the poor election turnout wasn't because no one cared about Nixon and *Humph*-rey, but because everybody was still arguin' about Lambert." He shook his head, chuckled, then shrugged again. "May be something to it."

Lambert and his victim had never met. So much for that theory. What about the kid and Mrs. Lambert?

The question evoked another hideous grin from Mack. "Oh yeah, everybody thought of that—and I

26

mean everybody. You'd be surprised at what your leading citizens and their wives come up with. Only there wasn't nothin' to that, either. The kid was getting enough around home, so why should he drive twenty miles this way? And besides, Mrs. Lambert ain't hardly the type."

"Oh. What about still waters running deep?"

"Been watchin' daytime shows, hey?" Mack grinned. "I tell you, mister, no one ever come up with anything that made halfway sense."

Too bad, because if the neighborhood experts—unhampered by formal rules of evidence and the like—had come up with zilch, there probably was no plausible explanation. Meaning that since the Seeking Sword was involved, it had been accidental, another of one of the world's long series of Seeking Sword coincidences. Or the result of some other kid wishing somebody would kill Larry the Stud, or—

All of a sudden George became aware of the silence in the dimly lit dining room. He had felt superior, looking at the imitation wagon-wheel chandeliers and proverbial, maroon, flocked, whorehouse wallpaper with silvery fleurs-de-lys. The jukebox had lost its voice. No one seemed to be speaking to anybody, except Mack, who was bending over, perhaps too casually, to ask, "Why so concerned, mister?"

George clenched his fists under the table, wondering, worrying, before reaching for the cigarette smoldering in the ashtray. "I am a writer," he said, trying to keep his voice level and noncommittal. "A crime writer."

"I see." Mack knit his brows. "Yeah, this would make a good story, only it's been done already." He nodded. "Ever hear of *Thrilling True Crimes?*"

"Their story is how I found out about Lambert."

"Pret-ty good story," said Mack, nodding again. "Real good. Too bad Doug Sleighton never got to read it."

"Doug Sleighton?" George asked, trying to dismiss his forebodings.

"He usta be a writer for the *Gazette* in West Carroll, and he used a pen name, Hardy Douglas, for this

27

story." Mack shook his head sadly. "Poor guy wrapped his car around a pole, back in March. He and his wife, they had their seat belts fastened and burnt to death."

"Hell of a way to go," said George, shuddering.

"Sure is." Mack turned and strolled back to the bar.

6

May 20, 1970

WEDNESDAY, MAY 20, had been a beautiful day and now the big grandfather clock (real English, dated 1803) showed 4:37. Joseph Wright Carnett looked at the clock and then past it, out the window with its view of the courthouse and the red brick façade of the Hotel Marbury. That New York lawyer, Harry Bradley, had written and asked whether he and his associate, George Quinterus, could call on him about the Lambert case. Carnett had suggested 4:30 today. So where were they? He glanced at the clock, shrugged irritably, put the letter from Washington in his coat pocket, and then, with another shrug, turned back to the latest of John Lambert's letters:

". . . furthermore, the food is too bland for words, and I'm getting tired of this place. Tired, I tell you! Oh yes, you'll say Death Row would be worse and John E. Lambert is a lucky man to be an inmate of West Carroll State Hospital. Oh yes, oh yes, oh yes. Oh yes, that would be true, were John E. Lambert guilty of something. But he is not, and you know it!

"How many more times will you have to be told, you, Dr. Jankel, Dr. Drews, and all the rest: I am not guilty of anything. All I did was put out a fire, an evil and dangerous fire in the forest that would have swelled to a real blaze with the passage of time. If young Jacoby got in the way of my doing my civic duty, that is regrettable. I regret it from the depths of my misfortune-ravaged heart, but I cannot perceive any justice or logic in my being locked up here with all kinds of criminal and mental cases.

"I know you are working on my release, and I have every confidence in your legal abilities; but in the meantime I must ask you for a favor. Get me assigned to some other psychiatrist besides Dr. Jankel! She has a nice smile, and tries hard, but she is not the right person to listen to my dreams. It is even hard for me to recall my dreams for her. In any case, she does not have enough time; she is supposed to see fifteen of us every working day, a total of seventy a week, including the ten foreseeable emergency sessions, computered on the basis of some incomprehensible formula. You can see where that leaves me.

"But I digress. About my dreams, now: According to the subject index I prepared at the suggestion of Dr. Semelhoff when I was still working on Notebook No. 3, and which I have now brought up-to-date, approximately two-thirds of them had some bearing on the Seeking Sword. (I know you don't care for Seppiyeh's term.) I rarely have dreams of the actual occurrence, and this is another reason why the official version must be all wrong. I can't see any reason why my subconscious mind should flinch from dwelling on the performance of something that had to be done. I have nothing to be sorry for. You, and all of Society, do, and some day soon this fact will be generally recognized because Man, after all, is still by definition a rational Being. But I'm digressing.

"As I just said, the dreams fall into seven different categories according to the index, apart from dreams that are clearly irrelevant or have a bearing on the matter only in a quackish Freudian or a Jungian sense. That is one of the points of disagreement between me and Dr. Jankel, and another reason why I believe Dr. Savigny would be much better suited to bear with me in my adversity. He is in any case a better conversationalist, and a man. Certainly, the sword could be a phallic symbol, or a symbol of justice, or the symbol of my conviction of ultimate vindication; and a dream of happy hunting grounds where Seppiyeh, sword in hand, comes out of a cave could have any number of interpretations, psychoanalytically speaking. But these won't wash, I tell you."

The buzzer rang. Carnett put the closely written sheet—third of five—down and pressed the button. "Yes, Miss Lefton?"

"Mr. Quinterus to see you." She did not approve of the visitor.

"Send him in."

Better late than never. But ten, fifteen more minutes and he would have walked out past the man. It had been a tough day; every time he expected court to adjourn at noon, something would come up to drag things out—and then, his Washington friends still couldn't tell him anything certain about the job with the space agency; the FBI must still be checking him out. Ah well, as Lambert said, ultimate vindication was most encouraging. And speaking of Lambert—too bad the little man hadn't started writing letters earlier. This particular one would have cut jury deliberation time by ten minutes. No, make it five—

And there was the door, opening.

Joseph Carnett stood up and walked around the right-hand corner of his mahogany desk, keeping his hand by his side as he sized up Mr. Quinterus: close to forty, about three inches short of six feet, 185 pounds or so, with a broad nose, wide mouth, and fair-sized jowls. Brown eyes and light brown hair, newly cut. Rumpled brown suit, off-white shirt and narrow green-and-white-striped tie. Scuffed black shoes and a bulging old briefcase.

Miss Lefton's look as she closed the door summed it all up—trouble *sí*, bucks *no*. But then there had never been any money in the Lambert case; he had taken

30

it because everybody was entitled to counsel and the man had done a good job teaching Carnett's children.

"Mr. Carnett, I'm George Quinterus." The handshake was fine and firm.

"How do you do," said Carnett. He led the way to the corner by the window with a view of Main Street and indicated the leather sofa and two stuffed chairs next to the low antique table. "I think we'll be more comfortable here."

"Harry Bradley couldn't make it," said Quinterus, who had remained standing while Carnett sat down with his back to the window.

The visitor sat on the sofa; while the writer arranged the briefcase on his lap, Carnett reached for the briar pipe on the ceramic ashtray that Debbie had made in crafts class. When he looked up, he noticed Quinterus studying the floor-to-ceiling bookcase. The two men's eyes met.

"It's late," said Carnett, glancing at his gold Bulova wristwatch.

It said 4:45. Should he call Helen and tell her to hold dinner?

"I'm sorry, but talking to people in Culberton took longer than I expected." Quinterus opened the briefcase, rummaged among the folders and binders, and extracted what looked like a trial transcript with dark blue covers. "If you'll look at this, sir, especially on page sixty-seven, I think you'll find some interesting parallels with your own case," he said. "There. The significant part starts at the red pencil mark."

Carnett took the transcript, wondering, while his visitor muttered something about being sorry that he'd never been any good at small talk. He sounded Midwestern, most likely from northern Ohio.

"That's all right," said Carnett, lighting his pipe. He took a leisurely drag and braced himself for a dreary half-hour. The case was *Illinois* vs. *Goltz;* he flipped it open to the marked passage:

DEFENSE COUNSEL: Mr. Goltz, the gentlemen of the jury would like to hear it straight from your own mouth. So go ahead and tell them.

31

DEFENDANT: All right. But there ain't much to tell, don't say I didn't warn you. [Rubs his eyes.] I went around the front cause there wasn't no secret about what I come to do, but I didn't see any fire through the window. So I went around to the back. Old Lizzie, that's the dog, she come at me and I had to kill her. That was a pity. Then, what with all the racket, I had to hurry and I ran up the kitchen steps . . .

The judge interrupted here, and after a rather strange exchange, the defendant was allowed to proceed:

. . . Let's see now, I'd said I ran up the kitchen steps. Old E. J. Bergstrom was standing right at the door where the fire was and I just put out that fire. That's all I done. I don't rightly know what happened to E. J. then. He was lying on the floor, and his sons, they started to beat up on me. Mrs. Bergstrom, she was crying and I can't blame her for that, but the way young Pete kept hitting me with a chair, that were something else again. [Rubs his shoulder.] My right shoulder's still all sore and two of my ribs got broken, all for putting out the fire before it could spread.

DEFENSE COUNSEL: You said you saw a fire. Describe that for the jury.

DEFENDANT: Ain't nothing to describe. Fire's fire and that was a bad one I had to put out, and that's what I done. [Waves hands in air.] Listen to me, everybody. I had to do it, because Seppiyeh showed me it was a dangerous fire that could spread all over the county, and he told me how to do it.

DEFENSE COUNSEL: How?

DEFENDANT: With the sword, of course, because a special fire takes special equipment like Seppiyeh says. "How to make the tools, how to get in tool-reach—that is the important thing. Striking hard enough, when close enough—that's simple." Something like that. I had the tool, even if I hadn't made it myself, and I was in tool-reach, so I done it. I never meant to hurt anybody and I'm sorry.

DEFENSE COUNSEL: You mentioned Seppiyeh. Who or what is that?

DEFENDANT: Can't really tell you.

DEFENSE COUNSEL: Why not? I'm sure the gentlemen of the jury would be interested.

DEFENDANT: It's none of their business. [Rubs his eyes.] Anyhow, I've forgotten. All I can say is he was right about everything—the fire, and about saying that people no longer appreciate it when you do the proper thing. It's no longer like when he used to hunt with everybody.

Carnett turned the page, wondering what was next, and at that moment his visitor leaned forward. "They get off the subject, next," Quinterus said, sounding genuinely regretful. "The prosecutor never followed up either, and when we asked the old man about Seppiyeh in 1968, he said he couldn't remember."

"He got a real railroading job," Carnett exclaimed angrily. "I hope this counsel—what's his name, Naismith?—got disbarred."

Quinterus shook his head. "It reads awful, but actually Naismith did a pretty good job. The dead man's sons caught Goltz with the knife still in his hand. The prosecutor argued that Goltz only pretended to be crazy, but that performance in court convinced the jury he was. Eventually he got out of the state mental hospital, and . . ."

"I see," said Carnett. Actually, Naismith's strategy had not been too different from his own, but Goltz had committed his murder in an earlier, cruder time. And, yes, the case offered several parallels to that of John Lambert: putting out fires and performing a service for mankind, the trance in which the murder was committed, the absence of any attempt to escape, the strange name of Seppiyeh, and the awkward aphorisms.

Of course, there were also differences. Goltz and Bergstrom knew each other, for example. "What kind of a sword did Goltz use?" Carnett asked.

Quinterus had been waiting for that. "It was described as a large, heavy knife, probably forged by a blacksmith, and with its handle wrapped tightly with old rawhide."

While speaking, the visitor reached into his briefcase again, pulled out a manila folder and handed Carnett some 8-by-10 photographs. "When we talked to Goltz back in 1968, he said his sword looked exactly like this."

The photographs depicted a large knife on a light-colored tablecloth next to a ruler. An index card in the corner of each picture read "Wentworth Police Department 1961" and listed some vital statistics: "length of blade 15 1/4 inches, length of handle 5 5/8 inches, width of blade 1 11/16 near the handle, not quite 2 3/4 inches at the widest spot; thickness of blade 9/16 of an inch near the handle, thinner towards the point; weight of knife . . ."

"Well?" Quinterus asked.

"Hmmm." Carnett puffed his pipe, slowly and leisurely. He needed time to think. This looked exactly like the knife Lambert had used: the same elongated leaf-shaped blade, almost like an Indian arrowhead, and the same handle, leather laces wrapped tightly around a spike or tang hammered from the same piece of metal as the blade, with the spike's rounded tip protruding half an inch or so. The workmanship was crude—the hills and valleys on the blade showed up even without magnification—but for all that, the edge was razor sharp.

One of the Culberton County deputies had told Carnett this; he had taken quite a fancy to the weapon. As for Lambert, he had said dirt and dust never stayed on the blade. But then Lambert said a lot of things. He also maintained that the blade was warm to the touch and that he could feel a sort of pulse, or vibration, along the groove running down its middle. Nonsense. Carnett had touched the weapon several times.

He put his pipe down and looked at his visitor with new interest. What was his game?

Carnett felt almost resentful; defending Lambert had been a duty and good deed as well as a challenge, and he had done a reasonably good job of it. He had not bargained for Lambert's weekly letters, but he could live with them. Pushing for the man's release —Lambert was no more of a danger to society than he himself—was a chore, but it was part of the job, a job that had been basically simple, a classic case of temporary insanity. He had saved his client from prison and was seeking his release from West Carroll in Mrs. Lambert's custody. Alice Lambert was a real jewel and would straighten her husband out if anybody could, or at least she would take good care of him.

But now, suppose Lambert's crime had not been an isolated event. Suppose it fit into some wider pattern. That could mean (A) that he, Joseph Carnett, had done a sloppy job, and/or (B) that maybe there had been something to Lambert's assertions about some higher purpose. Of course, there was no point in jumping to conclusions until he knew more. Still, Illinois wasn't far off, and he *should* have spotted *Illinois vs. Goltz.* That hurt. It hurt, and he would have to be careful not to take out the hurt and annoyance on the stranger bearing the bad news.

All right. He clenched his teeth once, and then asked about the Wentworth Police Department.

"That's Wentworth, Oklahoma," said Quinterus. "The police took the pictures . . . I'm not sure why. But it's good they did, because the knife disappeared before the trial."

"What trial?"

"Oh." The visitor thought for a moment. "Davidson's. Yeah. A man called Joseph Davidson found the knife in front of his house trailer. He grew moody and irritable, and one day in 1961 he jumped from a truck stopped for a red light, ran into the A&P parking lot, and killed a total stranger named Jack Thomas."

Another one. Damn! Carnett kept his voice carefully even while asking about Joseph Davidson's fate.

"He committed suicide while waiting for his trial."

Carnett heard a tremor in Quinterus' voice. The man was sitting on the edge of his seat, apparently trembling with excitement. He had even forgotten to finish the cigarette smoldering in the ashtray.

The lawyer tried to sound casual as he asked whether

his visitor knew about any other similar cases. The answer came quickly.

"We have copies of testimony in fifteen cases, and we've found references to a whole lot of others."

"Why do you think these cases are all related?"

"All the murders were committed with the same knife. Almost all the killers called it the Seeking Sword, or something like it. They usually said they had put out a bad fire and should be rewarded. Most of them, as far as I know, heard voices telling them what to do."

"I see. And how far back do these murders go?"

"The oldest trial record is from 1923, but they started earlier. There are two very detailed descriptions from books, one from 1867 and the other from 1853, and then—"

"That's enough for now." Carnett picked up his pipe again. The way its stem felt, smooth and comfortable, helped him collect his thoughts. All right, so there had been a whole series of similar murders, all of them committed by emotionally disturbed persons who had got hold of a large old knife. Wait a minute: Quinterus had said it was always the same knife! How could that be—and how could he know?

He asked both questions.

"We . . . I have no absolute proof, of course. But we're convinced of it."

"Oh, come now." This was ridiculous. How could they know?

"There are at least eight fairly detailed descriptions and all of them agree. Besides—"

"Even if it *was* the same knife, how could it always end up in a murderer's hands? It must get around awfully selectively."

"It does, sir," said Quinterus in a heavy voice.

"How, for God's sake?" Carnett was starting to feel ridiculous.

"It keeps disappearing from police property rooms. Sometimes the police can account for that. It's been sold at auction a few times. But usually it just disappears."

"Really?" He could see it happening thirty, even ten years ago, because procedures used to be pretty

36

sloppy, especially in small towns. But now? Ridiculous. "I'll bet the knife is still in Culberton," he said.

Quinterus nodded grimly. "Yes, at least as of this afternoon. I saw it." He wiped his forehead. "That's fine, but in 1968 it vanished from the police headquarters basement in Camden two months before Lambert bought it from the junk shop. A grocery truck driver called Jerome Zelaitis received an indeterminate sentence for murder in Camden on February twenty-second. He had killed a plumber, naturally a total stranger, with the Seeking Sword in September of 1967, and he'd found it in a vacant lot about mid-August. The sword had vanished from a police station in Palmyra the sixth of August. The Palmyra police knew the exact date because they were still questioning witnesses about a series of earlier murders."

He had been speaking faster and faster. Now he had to stop, flushed and out of breath.

Carnett looked at him with some distaste. He'd never cared for people who couldn't control themselves. Whining defendants, blustering police officers, orators who broke down and cried while promising pie in the sky to voters—like Humphrey, for instance, or that charlatan, Truman, with his phony rages and bad language.

Beside the point. Regardless of his opinion of George Quinterus, the man had information important to his client, which he should take and consider. Quinterus' story was fantastic, but a lot of strange things happen in real life, as Hamlet had pointed out to Horatio. Nevertheless, he could see that this would take time. It was already 5:02.

"I take it you'd like to tell me the whole story," Carnett said.

Quinterus' eyes lit up. "Fine. Only let's do it somewhere else. You name the place."

"All right. Let's see, now . . . How about The Embers?"

It was in walking distance, the food was tolerable, and he really didn't feel like taking his visitor to the country club, where he never knew who might decide to butt in.

"Okay."

"Very good." Carnett stood up. "I suggest we adjourn this discussion for the time being."

He walked over to the door and let the man into the outer office, where Miss Lefton was still sitting, reading a magazine. They exchanged glances. He nodded; she got up, said good night, and left. She was a treasure. Carnett asked Quinterus to wait a moment while he made a phone call. Helen might as well go ahead and eat; this could take time.

Going back to his own office, he was almost glad of the visit. At worst, it would take his mind off worrying about when those characters in Washington would make up their minds on whether or not the procurement branch of NASA needed another legal advisor, a Republican this time. At best . . . well, he felt a small shiver of excitement.

7

May 20, 1970

THE HOSTESS AT The Embers had an extra-warm smile for Carnett as they entered the restaurant and old Mack winked at George when he took their order for drinks. George asked for a draft beer, Carnett for a dry martini with a twist.

The drinks arrived in double-quick time. Carnett took a sip and leaned back comfortably. "I hope I can borrow some of these transcripts," he said. "There are several things I'd like to check out, too, if you don't mind."

"Sure." This was better than George had expected; in fact, he felt slightly ashamed of being so ready to dislike this small-town patrician—the very sort that his mother had always held up as an example for her children.

Carnett put the transcripts George had suggested —Goltz, Davidson, and Yarness—on an empty chair and leaned slightly forward. "Mr. Bradley said in his letter that he once defended a client accused of a similar crime. Would you mind telling me what happened?"

George had a long sip of beer. "The man's name was Wayne Hirschman. He was convicted and sent to Attica prison in upstate New York." The lawyer looked disapproving and George added, "Hirschman died in prison, supposedly of pneumonia. He was a mailman and very inarticulate. That's why we—I thought that Mr. Lambert might be able to help us."

"I doubt that." Carnett sounded extremely dubious.

"Why, if I may ask?" demanded George.

"I doubt Lambert knows anything of value. Furthermore, I'm not sure it would be good for him to talk about this with strangers, in view of his mental condition."

"I would expect you to be present at any interviews."

Carnett smiled. "I would be," he said. "I assume you know he's been made my ward for all practical purposes, for the time being."

"It's an unusual arrangement," said George, trying to reassess his feelings about the lawyer—a stuffy bastard, but obviously dedicated to his duties.

Carnett nodded in agreement. "Yes, it is unusual. You see, Mrs. Lambert had a nervous breakdown during the trial, and since there were no living relatives, I was appointed guardian of his interests. Mrs. Lambert is all right now and even has a job in the bank, but she asked me to continue the arrangement."

Wonder why . . . ? But George kept silent.

Carnett looked at him and said: "Now that I've told you about my involvement in the case, Mr. Quinterus, I'd like to hear about yours."

"Fair enough." George took a deep breath. "I'll try to make it as short as I can. The Seeking Sword is a menace and should be stopped. I know this sounds like something on the late show, but that's what I—Bradley and I are trying to do."

"Don't you think it's more a job for the police?"

George had him there. "Do you know of any policemen who would take me seriously?"

Carnett looked noncommittal and did not change his expression as George said, with heat, "I've tried. I've gone to police, to the FBI, prosecuting attorneys and defense attorneys." He grimaced at painful memories. "That's how I met Mr. Bradley. I'd read a *Daily News* story of how he was defending a New Yorker who had senselessly killed a subway motorman. Bradley's about the only one who ever listened. As for the others—some of them asked me to leave politely, and some threw me out."

"Yes, I see your point." Carnett paused, then asked George whether he was an attorney.

George shook his head. "No, I'm a writer. A freelance writer. Used to teach at Ainslie." He could see what was going through the other's mind: cool exteriors couldn't fool him any longer. He'd been around too long. "Yes, I write crime stories," he said after a quick sip. "I've always been a sort of crime buff, and at first I thought I'd write this up for a good magazine." He paused. "It's become more of an obsession, or 'cause,' than anything else. It's a menace, something that must be stopped."

"Most assuredly."

A pause followed while George, breathing heavily, told Mack to bring him another beer. The waiter asked if they were ready to order.

Carnett shook his head. "Not yet. But I'll have another drink, too."

Old Mack brought the drinks, and when he had shuffled halfway back to the bar Carnett asked George how he first heard about the Seeking Sword.

The story had acquired a certain polish from repetition. "Back in 1961, I was still teaching at Ainslie College, and my wife and I drove to Philadelphia for Christmas shopping. She was rummaging around the dress racks in Gimbels and I was next door at Leary's Book Store, wondering where I could find an ashtray. Well, I saw one volume called *Recollections of a Fron-*

tier Ministry, by the Reverend Amos Ward Mac-
Kenzie, published at Chicago in 1892. I don't know
why I picked it up or why I opened it to page 98,
but that just happened to be about the murder of
Curtiss Laxen. Shall I go on?"

"Please." Carnett was puffing his pipe and maintaining the noncommittal look.

"Laxen is described as a respected citizen of Armistead Junction, Nebraska, though the book doesn't say
what he did for a living. Be that as it may, on August
19, 1867, he was walking past the general store when a
newcomer to town, a man called Frank Bohnau, attacked him with a large knife. Laxen was carrying a
stout stick, and broke his assailant's arm. Then the
town marshal arrived and shot Bohnau twice.

"So far, there wasn't much to it, if you know anything about Western history. It was Bohnau's death-
bed confession that got me. He'd been a store clerk
some place near York, Pennsylvania, but one morning
he found what he called the 'seek-sword' on his doorstep and shortly afterwards a voice told him to go to
York. He wandered around the streets of York until
he came to the house of the widow Schirmer. He
butchered her and her four children, starting with the
fifteen-year-old twin boys. The voice, or song, in his
head then told him to go to Weigelstown, and there
he knifed an old man and his son.

"This was soon after the Civil War, and I guess
there was a lot of confusion all over the country, including the North. In any case, the law never caught
up with Bohnau. He couldn't understand why he was
killing all these people, while feeling he was doing a
public service."

George took a sip of beer. "Bohnau kept wandering
and committing more murders—he had no idea how
many. Reverend MacKenzie got him to name some of
them, but since Bohnau had never cared about his victims' names, he wasn't much help. You see, he kept referring to them as fires he'd had to put out, especially
in view of the recent tragic conflagration that had
engulfed the nation. I trust that term sounded familiar."

George paused, drank more beer, cast a quick look

41

at Carnett, who still looked expressionless. Oh, hell! Why couldn't they ever realize how serious this was?

He continued, grimly: "Sometimes Bohnau would go to a railroad station and buy a one-dollar ticket in any direction. MacKenzie doesn't say where Bohnau got his money. I suspect he started robbing his victims, because he told MacKenzie that the world owed him compensation for his labors and that putting out fires sometimes paid quite handsomely. By that time he may have been delirious as well as mad.

"Anyway, Frank Bohnau died on August 19, 1867, saying he was grateful to the marshal who shot him before he killed another innocent man. He added, with his next breath, that no good would come of leaving Mr. Laxen alive, and began raving about vengeance even far past the seventh generation."

"Men used a lot of Biblical phrases in those days," said Carnett. "Go on."

George was beginning to feel annoyed. "Okay. Bohnau died on August 19, 1867. On August 26, a man called Gunderson, from just across the Kansas line, drove his buckboard into town. The marshal saw him loitering around the jail and scratching himself. The marshal—his name was Whaley—told Gunderson to move on. That night Gunderson broke into the office, stole Bohnau's knife, and slashed Laxen to death as Laxen opened his door."

George paused. Carnett said nothing; a moment later, he started filling his pipe. Some people really picked roles that became them well!

George took a long drink and continued, "Well, Mrs. Laxen screamed and the neighbors came running up. Gunderson didn't even try to escape. A Mr. Jameson told MacKenzie he just sat on the ground, caressing the knife. He was all spattered with blood, but there wasn't one drop on the fatal blade. Gunderson had a fair trial, as they used to say, and was hanged on September 17. They let him speak from the gallows, of course, and he made a rambling speech about not killing anybody but putting out an incipient prairie fire, and how a voice started singing in his head five days before he hitched up the gelding for his trip to Armistead Junction." He paused. "By the way, the town's name was soon changed, because even though the Founder was no kin to the Rebel general, the names were the same."

"Hmmm," said Carnett. He had just lit his pipe; now he put it down, took a gentlemanly sip of his martini, and said, "Maybe Mr. Gunderson had the itch because he'd forgotten to change his underwear for some time?"

8

May 20, 1970

A LONG, PAINFUL moment later, Carnett felt rather ashamed of his deliberate attempt to bait George Quinterus. The writer had been asking for it, though, with his ham-handed posturing. Of course—and mere admission of the possibility was disquieting—there might be something to it.

"I'm sorry," he told Quinterus, who had furiously downed the rest of his glass of beer. "I really am. I apologize." He leaned forward. "I promise to be a better listener. When I was defending Lambert, I assumed it was all in his mind and paid no attention to the weapon. It looks like I was wrong. Just what do you suppose there is about that knife?"

"That, sir, is something we hope to find out in the next couple of days," said Quinterus angrily. "I hope to have the knife checked out by a metallurgist."

"I see." Carnett wondered what the writer had told Jerry Wald over at Culberton—but that really wasn't any of his business. "What do you expect to find?" he asked. "A tiny transmitter?"

"I don't know," said Quinterus heavily. He paused and licked his lips before continuing. "You see, I've talked and talked about it with Harry Bradley, and crazy as it may sound, the only way it makes sense is if the . . . sword operates by some sort of mental telepathy." He swallowed. "I know it sounds insane, but let me finish." He plunged into a long discourse about so-called Kill-thinkers, operating either by chance or design and concluded with: "I know this is hard to believe, but it's the one explanation that seems to fit the facts. Of course, it may be all wrong." He paused and forced a smile. "A friend of mine keeps saying maybe it's an accursed weapon, like the Nibelung treasure. But goddammit, a telepathic receiver–amplifier–transmitter is far-out enough for me. I'm not ready to buy the supernatural yet."

"I see." On this point, Carnett and Quinterus were in complete agreement. As for telepathy—that was unlikely too, Carnett thought.

"Just what do you expect to find under those leather strips?" he asked after a long, thoughtful pause.

Quinterus spread his hands. "I don't know. A bunch of little transistors maybe, but I doubt that, because the sword has been around so long. More likely there'll be some crystals, because if one kind of crystal reacts naturally to certain wavelengths, why couldn't others react to thought waves? Those involve electromagnetic energy, too."

"You mean the killers and victims have different brain wave patterns and that's all?" The writer was right: this *was* far-out.

Quinterus looked at him with some surprise. "Yes. Possibly."

"That leaves one very important question."

"I know. Who made it, when, and why?"

Carnett nodded. "So who made it?"

"It's been around at least a hundred years. As far as I know—and I read up further on the crystal business a couple of years ago—no one is thinking even halfway seriously *now* about making such gadgets. But the only explanation I can think of is that somebody, somehow, got hold of this type of crystal and put some into the knife. But who he was, and why . . ." Quinterus' face was red and his brown eyes glittered under the heavy lashes.

Carnett suppressed a smile; an afternoon's diversion

44

was turning into serious business because he found himself inclining toward beginning to believe the insane story, perhaps even the telepathy part of it; after all, there had been all these scientific experiments in recent years. In any case, the knife should be studied more closely—and it was hopeless to expect the authorities to do it. In fact, maybe *he* shouldn't get involved because of the NASA job he was hoping for. No. He owed it to John Lambert to check this out, because if Lambert had been under external influence, or "hypnotized" . . . The psychiatrists had ruled out hypnotism, but they had not known about this possibility involving the knife.

Quinterus was repeating that he had no idea who had made the sword, but that it might have been constructed as a sort of fiendish booby trap, a way to have an enemy killed by a bystander. He mentioned the Kennedys.

Oh? All right, maybe, but it was silly, theorizing without sufficient facts. Carnett decided to interrupt the torrent of words. "You said something about more than a hundred years. How do you know?"

"The earliest detailed account I've found is from 1831, from a place called Wismar, a seaport in East Germany. The circumstances were a lot like those of the Lambert case, but this schoolmaster was hanged. His name was Schiefer and he had just moved to Wismar from Elbing, a town in what used to be East Prussia. It's called Elblag now."

"All right, all right. But what's that got to do with it?"

"I was just leading up to another point," said Quinterus, a note of triumph in his voice. "I told you about a series of murders in this country, but they have also been going on in Europe. Most of the descriptions I've seen are pretty sketchy, and I haven't got the money to go and look up German court records, but they seem to refer to the same thing: people who buy or find an old knife or sword, start hearing voices, and kill some stranger, claiming that they are putting out fires."

"Good God!" This was appalling; Carnett wished his visitor had presented the case in a more organized way instead of sticking an as-yet-unread transcript in his hand and then feeding him the story piecemeal.

"Yes."

Quinterus signaled Mack to bring another beer. While Carnett exchanged nods with the waiter, the writer fished a sheet of ruled notebook paper from his battered briefcase.

"A list of the murders. And a summary. The Lambert case is here, on top of the list's left-hand column. Here are the European murders, over to the right." Carnett let his eyes run down the list of unfamiliar names while Quinterus' voice went on: "First there's a series of murders in America, a few quiet years, and then a series in Europe. Then another year or two without a murder, and a new series. That's one reason I think there is only one Seeking Sword. Also, most of the involved people have German- or Scandinavian-type names and most of the killings in Europe happened either in North Germany, Denmark, or along the eastern Baltic coast."

Carnett nodded. "Yes. All right. Now, what does that mean?"

"That's something else I'd like to know. In a way, though, this supports our Kill-thinker theories, because people might inherit a, well, susceptibility to certain wavelengths."

"There's no scientific proof of this, is there?"

"Not that I know of, but on the other hand I don't think anybody has ever set out to study the problem. Anyway, I only said this seemed to be possible."

Carnett was trying to recall what he knew about the Lamberts and the Jacobys. Lambert's family had lived around Marbury for generations; he had no idea where they might have come from, with a name like that. As for the Jacobys, there had been something about the dead boy's great-grandfather coming from Germany and one of the boy's great-uncles had been murdered around the turn of the century.

"Do these killings run in families?" he asked.

Quinterus nodded. "There are several cases, including one where a man killed his son. Another man was shot dead trying to knife his eldest brother."

"What happened to the survivor?" Carnett felt ashamed of his reluctance to ask.

"A stranger killed him two months later," said Quinterus inexorably. "I don't know much about the details. It happened in what used to be called Russian Livonia, back in the 1700s."

"That far back . . . ?"

The writer nodded. "I told you it's been around a long time. One of the old German lawbooks in the New York Public Library had a marginal note that the weapon used in these senseless killings could have some connection with a so-called *wode swertstosz* mentioned in some texts of the Lübeck Law Code of medieval Germany. *Wode swertstosz* means something like 'crazy sword thrust.' "

"Do you speak German?"

"I read it pretty well."

"I see." Carnett looked at the writer with new respect. Obviously the man had done a great deal of work.

"Sometimes I think I'll die before I find out anything," Quinterus was saying without the least trace of humor. "That's why everything can be helpful— talking to Mr. Lambert, testing the knife, anything you may think of."

Carnett said nothing. It sounded sensible enough —and yet, what would be the effect on Lambert's mental equilibrium if Quinterus went in there and started expounding about the Kill-thinkers? On the other hand, the ministrations of Dr. Jankel and Co. didn't seem to be doing much good, either. He would have to think it over. In the meantime, testing the knife wouldn't hurt and he might as well tell Quinterus all he knew about Larry Jacoby's great-uncle.

As it was, the writer already knew about it. Carnett then offered to help him with Jerry Wald, the Culberton County prosecutor.

"Thank you. He wasn't in today, but I talked to one of his assistants, a Mr. Robinson. He seemed to like the idea of testing the sword."

Al Robinson would. A nice young fellow, but someday his enthusiasms would get him in trouble. Still, Carnett saw no harm in it.

"If Jerry has any objection to your borrowing the knife, tell him it's all right with me," Carnett affirmed. "In fact, I'd like to watch the tests, if I can."

"That's fine," said Quinterus with eagerness. "Thank you. The only trouble is, I haven't found an engineer yet."

"Try the state university at Addyston," suggested Carnett. "It's only fifty miles away and they have a good engineering department." He finished his martini, glanced at his watch—7:20—and stood up. "I've got to go now."

"Sure," the writer said with a smile.

9

May 20, 1970

IT WAS CLOSE to midnight Wednesday, when Carnett finished rereading George Quinterus' thirty-page summary of Seeking Sword murders and the three trial transcripts. He shook his head and started to refill his pipe, after jotting down notes on one of the dreary cross-examinations.

Ridiculous; he was still looking for a motive behind all the fantastic events. That, in a way, was the worst weakness of the case as presented. A Seeking Sword must be, ought to be, used for worthier or at least more serious purposes than these apparently random murders: teacher killing student, bum killing storekeeper, fireman slaying bartender, one farmer doing in another farmer. It just didn't make sense for anyone to manufacture such a weapon, and then use it in such banal ways. And yet . . .

He smiled, telling himself to beware of excessive romanticism in his old age. Leaving a solid practice for the second time to go to work for the space people should be enough quixoticism for any professional man, especially one who had volunteered for destroyer duty against the Japanese. Crusading was for the likes of George Quinterus; the man seemed a real fanatic, with all the tediousness and lack of humor that accompanied true conviction. Crusading? Watch it, man, or you'll end up looking at this ugly knife as an Excalibur out of some crazy Camelot, with a special meaning for the romanticist buried under all your layers of defensive propriety. Tch, tch.

Carnett lit his pipe and sat back, studying the toes of his slippers. Whatever the Seeking Sword was, it was not Excalibur; there wasn't the slightest hint of moral purpose, any purpose, behind the killings. As magic weapons go, it was more like the spear of the Gaelic god called Luagh—a weapon that literally thirsted for blood and had to be stored with its head in a jug of poppy juice between battles.

It was all insane. Perhaps Quinterus was trying to set him up. But why? He wasn't starving, but he certainly didn't have the kind of money to make such an elaborate confidence scheme worthwhile. Blackmail? Same objection—and there had been no suggestion of anything unlawful, or even embarrassing. Testing the knife was perfectly reasonable in view of the possibility that it might have been used in other crimes. In any case, he owed it to John Lambert to explore every possible avenue. He'd let the poor man down once already: citing Goltz or Davidson probably would have made no difference, but this did not eradicate the fact of his failure to find these cases to cite.

Damn it all. He'd been proud of his handling of the case, and had taken such pleasure in the congratulations. He shook his head. Pride goeth before the fall.

But he should bear no ill will for the man who had jarred him out of his complacency. George Quinterus was not likeable. True. And irrelevant; George Quinterus was doing something worthwhile.

That is, *if* Quinterus was telling the truth—he'd admitted starting out to write a trashy magazine story and he might do it, yet.

49

Carnett sat up straight. Aha! Perhaps this was the reason for Quinterus' anxiety to talk to John Lambert? Could be. In any case, it would behoove him, Joseph Carnett, to be more careful. Why, he had all but decided already to accommodate his visitor!

He stood up, shaking his head, and went to the kitchen for a glass of milk. It would help him sleep; as it was, it would probably be an hour before his churned-up mind calmed down enough.

Helen was already in bed. Both Debbie and Roger were still away at school; some colleges had been closed because of the riots and demonstrations after the Cambodian campaign started—too little and too late as usual—but both his children's schools had been relatively quiet. Thank God for that. It was painful to even think of either of them marching against the cause for which Joe Junior had given his life eighteen months ago.

George Quinterus was sitting on the edge of his hotel bed, watching Dick Cavett talk to some actress or other. The name didn't make any difference, they were all interchangeable heads on one luscious bod, talking about what a challenge their next role was going to be.

He finished the bourbon and water in his glass and set it down. If learning new lines qualified as a challenge, what about the task he'd set for himself? He could see the reaction of the producer of the Cavett show—any show—as he presented himself with his bundle of transcripts and offered to talk about his latest challenge.

At least the lawyer had listened, and taken the transcripts home to read. That was the best he had any reason to hope for. The man was stuffy, self-righteous, Establishment personified—but he just might help.

The Cavett show ended. George heaved himself off the bed, picked up his glass, and headed for the bathroom. On the way, he turned off the sound. He let the cold water run as he poured more bourbon into his glass. The faucets were right out of a museum, but the glass was real, not plastic. Fine. Walking back to the bed, he thought about calling Gloria. It was late, sure, but she liked the show and would probably still be up.

She'd be wondering how he was doing, but she would probably make some crack about his obsession and he'd heard enough wisecracks today already. Still . . . He picked up the phone and put it down again. He really didn't have anything to report, so far —and he was under no obligation to check in. Or was he?

"Let us review the situation," he said aloud, sitting down. Here was George Barry Quinterus, and there was Gloria Barr, who had signed up long ago for one of his classes at Ainslie College, just before his marriage with Betsy fell apart. Afterward, of course, he and his student had gone their separate ways, he to New York to write. And then after he'd decided to chuck the New York trade press scene to return to Ohio, whom should he find working in the public library? Gloria, of course. Not the same Gloria— neither of them was the same. He'd had his years of grinding out trash, and she'd had a short-lived marriage she didn't talk about—but there they were. Since last February they had been going out practically every week, and for a month he had been wondering where it was all going to lead.

To bed, of course. To bed. Well, he was good and she was good, but that was not the point. They'd both gone that route before. The whole world was developing relationships. He'd had a few; he even had a thirteen-year-old daughter to show for his longest-lasting, most-meaningful relationship—and he damned well wasn't any too sure about trying that sort of thing again. Besides, if he got married, it would have to be the real thing, kids and all, and there was no way he could support that habit without a 9-to-5 job. And where would he find one? Cincinnati had fine scenery and fine beer, but the jobs he could endure were pretty scarce around the Queen City. Columbus? Cleveland? Toledo? Worse; even the Detroit beers they sold in his old home grounds could not compare to Schoenling. New York? He'd tried that, a novel under his belt and all, but he wasn't so young and promising anymore. San Francisco? Hell, dream big: $50,000 a year—1970 through 1979—to study changing cloud patterns above the Riviera, a job that would even enable him to delve into local color, for his new book, so that good old Foster Graves would be able to find the shortcut from St. Tropez to Bayal and the ruined lighthouse that served as the Kill-thinkers' headquarters.

Yeah, sure. But until then, or unless *Thoughts That Kill* made a bundle, he'd better just carry on. Travel cost money; seeing Bradley in New York had set him back $174—the equivalent of a month's child support —and visiting scenic Marbury would cost nearly as much, even though the hotel charged only $14 a night. The little nest egg from his parents was finally almost gone—mostly for wild-goose chases—and he would really have to get his nose down to doing articles for the house organs when he got back home. That would have to be Monday, at the latest; *Tractionator Tidings* were a pain in the tocus but they paid for rent and ground chuck. The writing and layouts were not so bad, actually. Getting accounts was worse, having to act polite and eager and respectful. Too bad Lenore MacDonough's husband's ad agency didn't have more accounts they could steer him to.

Anyway, it was free-lance work, grinding out house organ copy, or 9-to-5, and the latter hadn't worked out in New York either. Sometimes he thought he should have taken the re-enlistment bonus even if it meant another eighteen months in Korea. By now, he would be almost ready to retire—or, with his luck, dead under some jungle bush with his leg swelled up from stepping on a stake dipped in shit.

Sometimes it all seemed to be so useless— Ahhh! The triangular-faced college graduate, probably the local Cronkite apprentice, faded from the silent screen and was replaced by a bulgy middle-aged man with a loud tie and his left hand on a 1968 Chevrolet, his right on a 1965 Plymouth. No, George said to himself. I would not buy a used car from you. Or vote for you for President. Instead, I'll just try to get to sleep, because I'll have to find an engineer tomorrow.

10

May 22, 1970

ON FRIDAY MORNING, George Quinterus was wearing the same brown suit, but with a green shirt and a brown-and-white tie. He had worked up quite a sweat on his way over and had loosened the tie. Miss Lefton, ushering him in, looked even more disapproving than on Wednesday afternoon.

The two men shook hands. Carnett led the way to the leather sofa and sat down. Quinterus followed suit, fishing out a new package of cigarettes.

"Just finished making the arrangements," he said, hunting for matches. Carnett held out his lighter. "Thank you. Yeah. Thanks." Handing the lighter back, he repeated: "I just finished with the arrangements. Al Robinson will take the sword over to Addyston tomorrow and a metallurgist named Kratzel will run the tests. Thanks for the tip."

"You're welcome."

Today, Carnett found the man's enthusiasm engaging; any kind of enthusiasm, properly controlled, had something heartwarming about it, though this was something he might not be prepared to admit in public. He nodded. So Jerry Wald had gone along with the idea? "Did you have any trouble?"

"Not really. I don't think Mr. Wald really cares, and I was lucky to see Al Robinson first."

"You certainly were." Jerry might have thrown Quinterus out on his ear, but Al's father and Jerry played golf every weekend and Al was the ideal person to talk Jerry into trying something off-beat. "What did the metallurgist think of it all?" Carnett asked.

"He thought it's a crazy stunt, but since he has to

work Saturday anyway, why not? He's not even charging much." Quinterus paused. "By the way, are you coming?"

"Hmmm." Carnett was free Saturday. He really hadn't given it much thought; perhaps because he had been trying to avoid the issue. An annoying thought: suppose Kratzel found something strange, as he probably would. Almost inevitably, then, Quinterus would talk to John Lambert. Should he go, for Lambert's sake? This, in turn, brought up all the old insoluble arguments about worthy ends and unworthy means, and this was no time to get sidetracked into bad puns. Jokes never solved anything. He had written to some people for confirmation of Quinterus' information, but that was more or less for the record. Like it or not, he was hooked. He might as well be gracious about it.

As for driving over to watch the tests—why not? The kids were still at college, Helen would be busy in the garden, there was still no real reply from Washington . . . Hell, he'd be better off going to Addyston than driving over to the club. Joe and Barney could beat him at golf; he could beat Big Ed, Jim, and Walt; he and Bill, Casey and Little Ed were roughly even —there really wasn't much sense going through the motions Saturday after Saturday.

He glanced at Quinterus, who was trying hard to act indifferent. The man was no dummy; he knew how Kratzel's tests, especially with Carnett watching over them, would affect his chances of talking to Lambert.

"All right, Mr. Quinterus," Carnett said, doing his best to sound duty-bound and reluctant. "I'll be there. What time?"

Quinterus' eyes brightened. "Fine. Two o'clock," he said eagerly. He nodded at the pile of transcripts on the table. "How do you feel, now that you've read them all?" he asked, sounding rather self-confident.

"Not quite sure I remember things right."

Quinterus agreed. "I know. I still wake up some mornings and wonder why I ever got mixed up in this." He shrugged. "Somebody once told me any cause is better than nothing, but I'm not sure I agree."

"I wouldn't either," said Carnett warily.

"Do you have any specific questions?"

"What was Harald Goltz like when you talked to him?"

"An old man with shaky hands and a weepy voice. He and his daughter didn't get along. And he'd never realized how much he had forgotten. It really tore him up to read his own statements and the things he'd said at the trial. In the end he started crying and said he must have been crazy after all." Quinterus paused. "I felt rotten. Talking to him didn't help me much and didn't help him at all."

"So why are you so anxious to talk to John Lambert?"

The writer took a moment to think this over. "Several reasons," he said. "He's better educated and probably more articulate than any of the other victims I've seen. The killers are just as much victims as the people who die, and sometimes I feel sorrier for them, actually. Then, Lambert is the most recent killer. They do forget, but it's a gradual process and Lambert may remember some important things."

"Such as?"

"What made him buy the sword in the first place."

"Why is that important?" Something about the writer's earnest, plodding manner made it hard for Carnett to resist prodding.

"None of the others I talked to remembered how they found the sword, even though they might have mentioned this in testimony."

Carnett nodded. Then he asked, "What did they say about it?"

"All four of them thought it had always been around. When I prompted them with those details from their testimony, Goltz said he couldn't remember, Hirschman and Zelaitis accused me of lying, and Koskenkyll said I was trying to mess him up. He punched me, too," Quinterus concluded ruefully, rubbing the left side of his broad nose.

"It hasn't been all fun, has it?" A moment later Carnett wished he hadn't said that. Damn it, he didn't usually have problems like that controlling his reactions.

"Koskenkyll's psychiatrist said I had endangered an elaborate construct, partly based in reality, which his patient had built up to explain the lacuna in his memories," said Quinterus with great earnestness.

"And what do *you* think?"

The writer spread his hands. "Who knows? Sometimes I think they make sense, and sometimes they don't. But then, who am I?"

"Of course." Carnett had felt the same way. Many times. But people who were supposed to know believed in psychiatry, or said they did. However, back to the point: "Would Lambert know who, or what, Seppiyeh is?"

Quinterus looked startled. "You think it's a person?"

"What else would it refer to?"

"I've been thinking it might be a code word, an acronym—something like 'Headquarters.'"

The idea—quite reasonable—had not occurred to Carnett, who now leaned forward. "Do you have any idea what the acronym might stand for?"

"One of the German killers mentioned 'Seppie,' too, so I'm pretty sure it's not English," the writer said with a shrug. "The dictionaries I've gone through aren't much help—Sepp is the German equivalent of Joe, as in Sepp Dietrich, the SS general who had the GI prisoners killed during the Battle of the Bulge. In a way, that's appropriate, because the word stem has to do with sepulchers and taking care of the dead. Or so it says in a book on Indo-European languages that Gloria found."

"Indo-European, eh? Think the knife goes that far back?" He could ask about Gloria later.

"God, I hope not," said Quinterus. "I don't mind brushing up on my German, but I don't want to start studying linguistics."

"Maybe it will be all settled after tomorrow," said Carnett. Might as well sound encouraging. "By the way," he added after a pause, "has anybody else ever come up with an explanation of this series of murders —other than your friend's Kill-thinker hypothesis, of course?"

Kill-thinkers—grotesque name and crazy hypothesis. Unprovable, and yet it did seem to fit the known facts. *Known* facts. Still, there must be other, so far unknown, facts that would provide a reasonable explanation.

Quinterus thought it over. "People in the old days didn't have as much trouble," he said at last, sounding tentative and ill at ease. "Some of them thought the Seeking Sword was cursed—like a negative rabbit's foot, you might say. One clergyman ventured that it was the sword Cain used to kill Abel."

"Come on, now!"

This was really too much. Carnett barely kept from laughing out loud. Nowhere in the Bible did it say that Cain's weapon was a sword. There had been no swords until . . . until much later, the time of Tubal-Cain or somebody like that. Quinterus had no doubt looked up the references, being the type to spend days checking out citations.

Carnett looked at Quinterus. The man was perfectly serious, almost grim. True crusading type. Even as he filed that decision—revocable, of course, if contradicted by later developments—in a back compartment of his mind, the lawyer decided that the interview with John Lambert was in order, most likely on Sunday.

11

May 23, 1970

BERNARD J. KRATZEL was in his early thirties, short and wiry, with drooping blond mustache and longish hair. He was wearing a dark green knit shirt, khaki trousers, and brown loafers. The first-floor office, which he shared with somebody called Burleson, was large and untidy, with exposed overhead pipes, institutional green walls, and tall windows. The afternoon sun, shining through the elms and maples, made pools of light on the splotchy red concrete floor. The Venetian blinds were battered and dusty, raised to accommodate piles of reports and journals on the window sills; Kratzel had shoved other heaps aside to sit on his dark green metal desk.

George Quinterus remained standing, his back against a filing cabinet.

"Sounds like quite a gadget," Kratzel was saying, tapping the floor with his left heel. He pointed to one of the two beat-up office chairs. "Have a seat there; this'll probably take a while. I never yet knew a lawyer who was on time."

"It's okay," said George, just as glad to be standing. Maybe it was the long drive—and all these hours spent in his car the past week—but his legs felt odd, sort of itchy. That could be part of the general feeling of uneasiness that had been building up inside him. Same old thing: butterflies before action. He'd felt the same way climbing aboard the troopship, and then, four days out, they'd heard of the cease-fire at Panmunjom and his butterflies and general agitation had been all for nothing. This might be more of the same.

Sure it might. Sure.

"Say, are you sure this sword isn't going to explode?" Kratzel asked.

"Why should it?"

"Anything as sophisticated as you make it out to be might be booby-trapped."

Another thing to worry about. George dug out a half-crushed package of cigarettes and lit one. "It's awfully old," he said. "Goes back before blasting caps, even."

"So you say." Kratzel sounded thoughtful. He muttered something about crystals and lattices and looked at the clock. "I wonder where they might be," he said. "Maybe I'd better borrow Roy's counter." He looked at George. "Think it could be radioactive?"

"I don't have the slightest idea."

"I'll go get the counter," said Kratzel, leaving

George to muse about the events of the past days, his conversations with Joseph Carnett—not such a bad guy, really—and the neighbors. Not that he'd learned much.

Larry Jacoby had been quite a stud—somebody's father had beaten him up in 1967—and had spent his final summer enjoying himself and pumping gas at a filling station. He had been accepted by a college. His great-uncle had been murdered on March 22, 1901; the killer was never caught. Mrs. Lambert worked for the Marbury National Bank. John Lambert had been a martinet, a person who was forever complaining about his neighbors' garbage cans and the way they burned leaves in the fall. Some neighbors had noticed a change, in the month preceding the murder. Others had not.

A car pulled into the gravel-covered parking lot— a 1969 Porsche, bright orange, with dented left front fender. Yes, it was Al Robinson. He parked next to George's old Ford and got out with a flourish, brandishing a long narrow package wrapped in brown paper. Robinson was a large young man with long brown hair, short sideburns, and sunglasses; he wore a yellow, open-necked shirt and rust-red slacks. Carnett, also getting out of the Porsche, wore a blue sports coat and dark trousers.

George knocked on a window and pointed toward the entrance door of Engineering Annex B. Robinson nodded and said something to Carnett; at that moment, Kratzel returned with the Geiger counter.

"They're here," said George.

"I heard the car." The metallurgist put the counter on his desk, opened a drawer, and took out a horseshoe magnet. "The sword is probably iron-nickel alloy with some peculiar impurities," he explained. "Chances are, if it's that old, it might be meteoric iron. Some of those meteorites are very interesting, from my point of view."

"I'm sure they are," said George.

Carnett and Robinson arrived, and Kratzel seemed a bit amused by Robinson's excitement.

"I doubt we'll find anything all that exciting," the

engineer said. "George tells me it's been around several hundred years. That means we won't find circuitry—there just wasn't anything like that back then."

"What do you think it is, then?" asked Robinson. He put his parcel on Burleson's desk and started to rip open the end flap.

Kratzel shrugged. "My guess is that its special qualities, if any, are due to crystals that are present as contaminants." He lifted his hand. "Hold it—I don't know a thing yet, really. But let's have it, now." He took the weapon from Robinson. "Not much bigger than a chef's knife, is it?" the metallurgist commented as he brandished the sword and put it down on his desk. "Really heavy," he said, reaching for the Geiger counter. "No doubt about it, though—it's old. Real old. Hmmm." He listened to the clicks of the counter and announced that the sword seemed to be radioactive, but only slightly.

"That raises several points of interest," he added. "Some meteorites are radioactive and some iron ores contain radioactive elements as contaminants. There are even six radioactive isotopes of iron, but all of them together make up less than a twentieth of one percent of the iron found in nature and five have very short half-lives. Nine minutes to less than three years, if I remember right. The sixth is something else, with a half-life of around 350,000 years. Fe-sixty—but that's beside the point. Let's see, now."

He touched the magnet to the sword and swore while pulling the two apart again. "Iron, all right," he said, grunting, and put the magnet back in his desk drawer.

"What happens next?" inquired Carnett, who had not said a word since the introductions. He looked almost as fascinated as Al Robinson.

"Any one of a number of things." Kratzel studied the blade closely. "Jeez. Crude," he said, largely to himself. He ran his thumbnail along the cutting edge, whistled, looked at Robinson. "You sure nobody's been sharpening it?"

"Not that I know of."

"Some killers were surprised at how sharp it was,"

said George, reaching for his briefcase. He halted, a bit annoyed, when Kratzel shook his head.

The metallurgist had shown no great interest in the gory details during their cafeteria lunch, either. He had some kind of experiment going, something he had to check on every couple of hours, and as a result he had to spend his afternoon at the Annex. Running the tests was just a diversion to him; his interests were in the war and sports, rather than crime.

Now Kratzel was holding the sword in one hand and a triangular file in the other. "The next step is going to be X-ray diffraction," he announced. For a moment his face became solemn, befitting an assistant professor. "I don't know if you're aware of this, but the way various crystals bend X-rays is a good thing for some of us, because it gives us a way to identify them. The diffractometer is back there." He gestured with the file. "Now, since the impurities may not be evenly distributed, I'd better take samples from several places."

"The handle would be a good place to start," George suggested.

"Yes." Kratzel nodded. "Only, I can run just one test at a time, and so let's start with the business part." He bent forward, holding the sword over the pale blue back of a report. The file bit into a spot about five inches below the handle.

George had expected the sound of metal on metal. Carnett said later it was like chalk on a blackboard; the sound that George heard (or felt) was like a fingernail on a blackboard at first, only louder and more piercing, with a background howl of rage and fury, but he did not have much of a chance for contemplation. Later it seemed to him there had also been a flash of light, somehow milky white and reddish at the same time—and as one hue flashed into the other, he had seemed to behold a man, shaggy, bearded, and gaunt . . . with whitely burning eyes that were first directed at Kratzel and then seemed to turn toward himself.

The weird image appeared to be superimposed on Al Robinson, who had leaned close for a better look, smiling in anticipation. All of a sudden, now, Robinson grabbed the sword—or rather, the sword seemed to wrench itself from Kratzel's left hand, turn over in the air, and land in the young lawyer's hand.

"Hey, what?" exclaimed Kratzel.

Robinson, still smiling, drove the sword into the metallurgist's neck. Kratzel raised his hands and tried to step back; the other man withdrew the blade and moved forward, slashing Kratzel across face and chest in a curious, complex pattern, winding up with a thrust in the stomach. Kratzel doubled over with a groan and crumpled to the floor. Robinson turned and ran out, sword in hand. His smile was unchanged.

Carnett was the first to move. He tried to tackle Robinson, missed, and went sprawling in a rectangle of afternoon sunlight.

George looked around for a weapon. At times like this it was best not to think, just let the reflexes take over . . . He found an iron bar, rather heavy—but it would do—and set off in pursuit. When he got outside, Robinson was gone, vanished among the trees.

George stood clutching the bar, wondering how the Kill-thinkers had sensed their peril and taken quick action, and—he started shaking—all it had taken was one twist of the file and the closest bystander had become a zombie, a mindless robot pulling the Kill-thinkers' chestnuts out of the fire.

He leaned against the Annex wall, his knees suddenly weak. He'd been lucky . . . But then there had been those pale eyes that turned his way, changing expression somehow—why? And why, oh God, why had he ever got involved in this? If it hadn't been for his obsession, Bernie Kratzel would be going home to his wife and three children.

Meanwhile, where was Al Robinson? George had a chilling vision of a smiling madman, sword in hand, slaughtering passers-by on the wooded campus. No, the Kill-thinkers didn't operate that way. More likely, Al Robinson would return and kill the witnesses. George shuddered.

Or—and again the weight of his responsibility hit

him—Robinson might be returning the sword to its masters, wherever they might be. Presumably close —it stood to reason they would want to keep an eye on their instrument, and their swiftness in bringing Robinson under control argued for that, too.

"What the hell have I done?" said George, shutting his eyes and shaking his head as he pressed his back against the concrete-block wall.

As he opened his eyes, he heard Carnett's footsteps. The lawyer was carrying a red fire axe. His pants were torn at the right knee and his leg seemed to be bleeding. He looked at George and was about to speak when he suddenly turned his head.

Al Robinson stepped from among the trees, his clothes spattered with blood, eyes wide open and a baffled expression on his round young face.

"Where's the knife, Al?" demanded Carnett.

"Knife? What knife?" Robinson clapped bloody hands to his face. "Oh my God," he said. "You mean, I really . . . ?"

"Where is the sword?" asked George.

"Oh my God . . . I don't know." Robinson started to sob aloud. "Oh my God, what's going to happen . . . ? How is he?"

12

May 23-24, 1970

WHEN THE AMBULANCE arrived, Kratzel was still alive—and then the police came rushing in. Campus police, city police, sheriff's deputies . . . They all searched for the sword, in vain, and asked questions, the same questions, over and over.

Without Joseph Carnett, who was on first-name

terms with Addyston's police chief, it might have gone badly with George. As it was, they didn't get away until after 8 P.M. Carnett then went to the house of a friend with whom he had served in the Pacific in World War II. George found a room at the Addyston Highlands Inn, got something to eat, a few drinks, watched television to calm his nerves, and tumbled into bed and oblivion.

Now he lay sweating, terrified, for some reason staring at the neon sign flashing on and off beyond the window shade, and listening to cars whoosh by.

Come on, he said to himself, reaching for his wristwatch. Nightmares are for kids. You're too old to wake up whimpering, even after a truly lousy day. Your lousiest day ever, in fact, since you caused the death of one man and ruined the life of another.

He looked at the watch: just after 11:30, still the same day. He sat up, had a swig of bourbon, and lay down again to watch the red flashes and to wonder about the feeling of helpless dread—and vague, incongruous, faint overtones of regret at something that he could not have helped.

He must have fallen asleep for some time, to dream about racing down endless corridors and . . . now what? When he seemed to awake, the sign was still flashing, but faintly and far away because the moon was so high. The whooshing sounds were still there, but they were trees sighing in the night wind rather than passing cars. Yes. Trees—black shapes against star-filled sky dotted with clouds. The wind was from the southwest, warm and moist, the sort of wind that makes ice break in rivers and flowers bloom on exposed hillsides within a span of the last, rotten snow of wintertime. Nice wind, good wind.

Good trees, too, elms and maples and old mountain ash with feathery leaves, as well as the others —the trees that were not altogether right, though that was of little consequence because trees are trees. The same for the grass. Some of the grass was right and some of the long, slender blades were different, strange, not quite right. But they all had roots buried in the moist dark earth, with beads of dew gleaming above on stalk and leaf.

Strange: it was a dream, and yet no dream, despite George's strange impressions of the night—trees, grass, insects crawling on the ground, field mice scurrying about, an owl gliding by overhead on silent wings, partially obscuring the moon as its luminous white face broke clear of clouds. In spite of this sensory input and his appreciation, or rather relishing, of it all—never before had he realized how concerned the squeak of a field mouse could sound, and how akin to a human voice, both as a sound and as a means of expressing concern—in spite of all this, a part of George was still standing aside, or back, wondering about the sounds and sights, or rather about what they all meant. For instance, the point of view. It seemed to be extremely low, almost ground level, but there was no front or back—his field of vision encompassed the full 360 degrees and that didn't make sense. Then he perceived footsteps.

The mice, both of them, scurried off to their den, off toward the highway. The female was pregnant. Weird—not her condition, but rather that he, with his D in high school biology, should know for sure from a fleeting glimpse of tiny, darkly glowing shapes in the tall grass.

What was this? Dream? Nightmare? Vision?

The footsteps sounded closer. A moment later he saw what made them: from his viewpoint, they appeared as tall, hulking, dark forms that shut out large portions of starlit firmament, and which were vaguely human-shaped but terribly elongated.

Adults must look like this to small children, George thought. At the same time, he became aware of something else. The heads of the two people, apparitions, or whatever, appeared to be illuminated from within; in other words, they glowed—or that was as close as he could come to describing their appearance, or the *impression* they made. There was a distinct difference in the two glows; somehow he knew one was male and the other female, though that really wasn't important. Some kinds of glow were highly significant while others were not, but everything alive glowed—the mice and the owl, crickets and other insects. The realization was sudden, and then he was shocked to realize further that trees glowed also, and grass, dirt . . . even pebbles! But that was beside the point. The important thing was that two people were approaching the spot where he was lying.

He? Why? George Quinterus wondered, and suddenly became aware that wonder was permeating another mind as well, accompanied by vague resentment: Darlene had been ready enough, back where the car was parked—so why was Jimmy dragging her toward this gnarled tree standing sort of alone in the moonlight? She hadn't said anything, she was still pressing her hip against Jimmy's leg whenever they halted; but George could tell from the way she was moving that she was starting to wonder.

Twenty steps from the tree Jimmy stopped and gathered her in his arms, dropping the blanket he had carried along. One level spot was good as another . . .

Ahhh! He crushed her to him, and she pressed against him with a sort of desperation—or relief, George said to himself, a bit ashamed of his cynicism. Their tongues met, his hands ran down her back, over the bra hooks and on, down over her buttocks, cupping them, and back up—while George, now flat on his back, writhed on the bed wondering whether this was going to be another wet dream. That was all he'd need, a soggy ending to a messy day. Weird, though—this didn't feel like a dream; he'd had spectator dreams before, but never with this much of a sense of being an observer.

Jimmy's hands were back up now, under her blouse, working at the hooks. George shared his exasperation. Ahhh . . . There. The hands moved on, around the smooth-skinned body while the young lovers kept up the kiss that by now must be well into its third minute, mouth to mouth and belly to belly, pushing and straining together.

George tried to snap out of it, to wake up before he made a mess of himself. No use. In a way, this was like the dreams where one ran through corridors or whatever, never moving; in this kind of dream one tried to wake up, to put a mental distance between himself and the action, to no avail.

The young lovers were sinking down upon their blanket on the dew-moist grass, and now . . . now they were down, had been for some time. He'd got off her flowered panties—no panty hose or girdles for Darlene Ridenour—and now, after long minutes that had brought George to the end of his endurance, young Jimmy Soyers brought up his right hand to grasp her shoulder. Darlene's hands slid down his flanks and . . . and then, just as the boy again thrilled to the touch of her fingers, his own fingers encountered something in the grass.

Something akin to a cramp racked the muscles of George's legs, causing his painful erection to subside.

Jimmy was puzzled, wondering what his hand had closed on directly before hard-earned fulfillment; but George knew, mostly because of a curious kind of two-fold perception, in the last moments, a vision of the blackness of an outstretched hand, encompassing networks of glowing lines, huge against the stars, closing in—and a sensation of rough, stiff, solid, ancient tendons partly obscuring the view.

Again George tried to wake up, but something in the back of his mind suggested that awakening would only cut off the transmission—or whatever—and he had no way to help, because he did not even know the location of the young lovers.

Why was he condemned to be the helpless bystander—? No, he'd better thank his lucky stars, because now Jimmy was getting on his knees, Seeking Sword in hand, brushing off Darlene's eager fingers.

"What's the matter?" she was saying. "Jim? Jimmy!"

Jim didn't answer. He was staring at the sword, even though she was there, beyond it, sitting up, her white blouse unbuttoned and the brief skirt of wet-look vinyl up to her hips, shapely white thighs spread apart on the blanket. He sent a message to his fingers: throw this away, man! But his nerve fibers would not obey. Even his head was turning, of its own accord, forcing him to follow. As for the sword, it, too, moved and ended up pointing half-left, dragging his hand and arm along. George watched, equally baffled, though Jimmy felt his loss more keenly and less philosophically.

Goddam it! George said to himself, both relieved and disappointed. Now what? And what would Freud, not to mention Krafft-Ebing, make of it?

Never, never, never had he dreamt anything like this. If this was a dream.

Ugh. Maybe this was how Kill-thinkers made their initial contact, while a man was half asleep, drifting off into an erotic reverie, all his defenses relaxed? He closed his eyes. This made no difference, of course.

Jimmy was still following the sword, making his way between trees, occasionally stumbling over roots and bushes. The beetles and crickets, not to mention mice, fled long before he'd come within two fathoms. Once in a while, he lurched against a tree. A couple of times, he fell. The first time, Darlene screamed but Jimmy paid no attention, and a few seconds later George had a glimpse of her standing up, brushing down her skirt, buttoning her blouse, looking after Jimmy for a while . . . But the lad kept stumbling along while Darlene turned, with an angry shake of her shoulders that sent long, ash-blond hair, silvery in moonlight, swirling about her head. She stamped her foot, kicked the blanket, and walked away.

Jimmy just kept going. Eventually, as his feet grated on gravel, he looked up—and how did he, George Quinterus, city boy, know it was after midnight from a glance at the goddamned stars? Once more he tried to wake up, really tried, straining at whatever was keeping his mind chained to the scene before him: Jimmy Soyers crossing the parking lot and trying to pry open a padlock.

In the end, with a weary sigh, George relaxed, the muscles in his arms and legs loosening—weird, how he could be aware of so many things at the same time—and let the sensations associated with lock pick-

ing wash through his mind—in some ways not unlike prying bits of popcorn from under the gumline.

Click! The padlock gave way. Jimmy's relief was
obliterated by the pleasure—of whom? The Kill-
thinker at the controls? But why? To some extent,
everything made sense. The Kill-thinkers had attracted Jimmy, who for some reason—bad genes?
moral infirmity?—was more susceptible to an order
to move the Seeking Sword. Since the Kill-thinkers
had to be sadists to begin with, it also made sense
for the controller to pick on somebody in Jimmy's
particular state. But now what?

Perhaps it was all a sort of mirage, something
meant to lull George to sleep while the murderous
swordsman or swordsmen closed in. But if so, why
bother? A show like this took energy and imagination, and whatever the Kill-thinkers might be, whim-
sical they weren't. Ten hours ago, George thought,
he would have agreed that Kill-thinkers might act in
ignorance, that the Seeking Sword was like a pistol
with safety off, lying in a second-grade classroom
where one and then another kid would pick it up
and pull the trigger and yell *Bang!*

Not now. Not after this. And in any case, regardless of whether this was an effort to deceive or a
sort of telepathic leakage, what he was seeing now
proved indisputably that there was method in the
Seeking Sword's madness.

Meanwhile, Jimmy Soyers had entered Kratzel's
office and turned on the light.

The room looked unchanged. The report with blue
covers lay under the desk and there were chalk
marks on the floor—an oblong for Kratzel, crosses
where George and Carnett thought the metallurgist's
feet had been planted, circles to mark the positions
of Robinson, George, and Carnett, and a line where
the file had fallen from Kratzel's hand.

What now?

Jimmy was dropping to his knees, more or less where
Al Robinson had stood. He moved the sword back and
forth across the red-painted floor. George could see
the file mark now—an angry, shiny scar on the back
of the blade. And now . . . Jimmy's hand stopped,

with the swordpoint next to a dustbunny containing some glittering particles of metal—and these started to move, down and across the floor to the sword and along the blade, slowly, in unhurried and inexorable fashion, up to the file scar. There, they tumbled over the edge of the tiny crevice and into it. Meanwhile, Jimmy had again started sweeping the sword across a different sector of the floor, under chairs and desk, seeking, seeking. George's scalp prickled; he began clenching and unclenching his fists. Other glittering particles emerged from the dust to crawl up the ancient blade as far as the rapidly fading scar.

Just in case, George tried whispering the Lord's Prayer. Nothing; more shiny particles crawled up the blade and remerged—if that was the word—with the Seeking Sword. Jimmy finished the area before the desk. Now he ran the sword along the front of the desk, with particular attention to desk drawer handles; then, along the desk top; and after that he got back on hands and knees and crawled out into the corridor.

Of course—some of those particles might have adhered to Robinson's shoes.

By now, George was drenched with sweat, trembling —and no longer because of any conviction that assassins were closing in. This vision, or whatever, must be telepathic leakage. Somehow he and the sword must be on the same mental wavelength; and this raised all kinds of possibilities, none pleasant.

But meanwhile . . . meanwhile, Jimmy Soyers had finished his vacuum-cleaner act, out in the parking lot. Some of the last particles recovered had been close to infinitesimal in size—but all had been equally mobile. Now Jimmy stood up, sword in hand, and started walking toward the highway. He went through the trees—elms and black walnuts—looking neither right nor left, until the strip of asphalt. There he paused, raised his head as if to sniff the wind, and walked across, dropping the Seeking Sword, none too gently, near the white line. He kept going; George's last glimpse of him was beneath one of the sodium vapor lamps, shaking his head and scratching himself.

Two cars whizzed by, coming from the direction Jimmy Soyers was headed; then, a car coming the other way, from the north, stopped with squealing brakes. An old car, with no front license plate. The driver—elderly and heavy-set—got out with painful slowness and looked around. He stared at the sword, nodding, and bent down to pick it up—no easy operation since he must have weighed close to 300 pounds. As he lifted the weapon, George got a look at Fatman's ruddy, bulgy-cheeked face. The man must be in his sixties: . . . button nose, pointed chin lost among the jowls and rolls of fat . . . wire-framed spectacles, little beady eyes . . . dressed like a farmer or factory worker, in coveralls and a gray shirt.

Fatman seemed to reach a decision.

For just a moment, a sensation like that of a searchlight turned directly upon George's mind, almost causing the writer to scream aloud. Then he clenched his fists at the stomach-churning sensation that the world was spinning around him, before ceasing to turn, with a jolt he felt in every fiber of his body, as the sword landed on the car floor among old cigar butts, dust, and flip tops from beverage cans. He could make out the faintly glowing outline of Fatman's knee, part of his glowing arm, the dark steering wheel, and the numbers on the odometer.

The car started with a jerk. Country music came blaring from the radio and the odometer numbers started turning over. Once in a while, Fatman hawked and spat out the window and from time to time the car came to a halt. There were turns, several of them, and George realized he must be out in the country because there were no more streetlights; and, finally, everything faded out as a burst of static roared out of the radio.

He found himself truly awake at last. He was covered with clammy sweat, shaking as he lay in the tangle of bedclothes, listening fearfully and flinching every time the red sign flashed on or off. His watch said 12:09.

A car went by. Another. Then . . . was that the sound of a laboring, rickety engine?

No time to waste. He had picked up the phone when he realized what the police would say and what

Carnett would say. Damn. He'd got himself into this mess; he'd see it through by himself.

The thought made him feel better, almost serene, as he wedged a chair under the doorknob, turned on the television—sound off—and began writing an account of his dream or vision in a notebook. He would call Carnett in the morning, after checking with the police—and even if the Kill-thinkers got him, they might overlook the notebook.

Somehow, though, he didn't think he was in any danger—a thought disturbing in itself.

13

May 24, 1970

JOSEPH CARNETT WAS still a bit annoyed at George Quinterus' insistence that they should get together, immediately, regardless of his hosts' plans about breakfast and church services. All right, so he'd had a sleepless night too, but what could they do now about Kratzel's death?

The writer was prone to see things in melodramatic terms, even if yesterday's events had left no doubt the Seeking Sword was real, dangerous, and strange. Carnett's first look at Quinterus in the coffee shop of the Highlands Inn only confirmed his earlier opinion. The writer had cut himself shaving and had dark shadows under his eyes. His ham and eggs were half finished, his handshake desperately eager, and he overdid such gestures as showing Carnett the Sunday paper.

A waitress arrived, a matronly woman with champagne-colored hair done in cow-plop bouffant. Carnett ordered coffee and two sweet rolls. "I'm sorry to hear about Mr. Kratzel," he said after she had left.

"Me, too." Quinterus sighed, shaking his head. "I wish . . . Hell, it doesn't make any difference what I wish. I just hope that someday I'll forget his face." He reached for his cigarette.

"I would like to forget it someday, too," said Carnett. He could not resist adding: "It's always the innocent bystanders who get it in the neck."

"Yeah. First Sleighton and now these two. Poor Al."

Carnett nodded. Yes. Poor Al Robinson. Also, poor Bernie Kratzel, poor everybody . . . Incredible. He could just see the gang at the country club shaking their heads over the fiend who went after Joseph Carnett with Lambert's knife. Sure, that's how it would look to them. What the hell did they know? It was the same thing Quinterus had complained about all along, and after last night's conversation with Chief McEwen, he knew exactly what the writer meant.

Right now, though, the writer was blathering about moral responsibilities. He'd opened the subject with his remark about poor Al and he was still at it when the waitress, whose badge identified her as Ruby, arrived with rolls and coffee. Carnett suddenly felt famished, and went to work, nodding whenever encouragement appeared necessary. After a while he steered the conversation to Quinterus' dream.

The writer changed subjects in mid-sentence. "Oh yes," he said. "Sorry. Here." He took a spiral notebook from the seat beside him, flipped it open to a closely written page, and shoved it across the table. "I hope you can cope with the handwriting," he said. "And now—pardon me—gotta go to the men's room."

Ruby returned, coffeepot in hand. "Please," said Carnett absent-mindedly, eyes skimming the self-conscious narrative. ("The grass appeared to teem with life and I even seemed to perceive feelings in the bugs.") But gradually it engaged his attention so that he was hardly aware of the writer's return.

After a time he looked up. "You wrote this last night?"

Quinterus nodded.

"Perhaps . . . How about going over it again for me, just in case you think of something else?"

"Okay. If you believe it'll help." Quinterus paused. "What do you think of it?"

"It's the weirdest document I've ever read." That was the truth; and listening to Quinterus' narrative would give him time to think.

"Does it remind you of John Lambert's statements?"

"Not really."

"I see." Quinterus sounded disappointed. He had some coffee, lit a cigarette, and began telling the story. A couple of times he almost got stuck, perhaps due to embarrassment that seemed natural enough, even for a writer. Carnett listened, coffee and second roll forgotten, making mental notes: What phase of the moon? What lights were visible from the place of rendezvous? Then, after Quinterus had come to the break-in, the writer's flow of words became a veritable torrent—especially where he described in detail how the metal fragments crawled up the blade and how Fatman picked up the sword.

"I was really starting to expect him to come pounding on the door, when I realized the scene had been fading and, all of a sudden, it was gone," Quinterus concluded. He ground out his cigarette and reached for the coffee cup. "Any questions?"

"What happened to the boy?"

"Oh yes." The writer grimaced. "Here comes the confirming evidence. I called the cops about nine this morning and the desk sergeant told me Car Four had picked up a juvenile. I revealed some of my inside information and learned that, yes, it was about 12:25, his fly was open, the cops asked him where she was and he said he only wished he knew. He told them everything had been groovy until he had put his hand down and found this rusty knife, and next thing he knew he was busting this padlock. I don't know how much reliance we should put in his statement about the rust." The writer shook his head. "The cops checked up and found the lab had been broken into, so they booked him for breaking and entering, being under the influence, and indecent exposure. His folks bailed him out at 4, even though the cops were a bit reluctant because he wouldn't say who the girl was and what had become of the knife."

"Had anybody been reported missing?"

"No." Quinterus shrugged. "If I'd been poor old Jimmy," he added thoughtfully, "I'd have told them I made up the part about the girl because I was embarrassed getting caught while taking a leak." He paused. "Everybody would have been happier."

"No doubt about it."

The writer nodded earnestly. "Any other questions?"

"Let me think." Carnett decided he'd better continue acting judicious. He contemplated his cup; Ruby came to check on them and Quinterus said they both could use more coffee.

"Do you have any idea of precisely where Jimmy dropped the sword?" Carnett asked after a pause, appalled at his readiness to accept the whole preposterous story. Quinterus answered his question negatively. It didn't make sense, Carnett thought. The Kill-thinkers could have recovered the metal fragments in a less spectacular way, if they needed them —and Kratzel had not even taken his sample from the cutting edge. Surely they knew the filings would be swept out and dumped in the trash. So why go to all that trouble? The fact they had done so, however, was in itself interesting, suggesting a tightly organized bunch of psychopaths who did things by the book, an appalling, monstrous book to be sure, but a firm set of regulations nevertheless. Fine, real fine. This attempt to erase the evidence had widened the spoor considerably.

Presumably the man on the job had been an apprentice monster, whose zeal exceeded good judgment and who must be catching hell. Carnett restrained his impulse to gloat. Not worth it. Instead, he asked Quinterus if he could recognize Fatman again.

"I doubt it. You know people really look different from that angle." He paused. "Maybe that's why psychiatrists talk so much about traumatic memories of childhood."

Could be, but irrelevant. "What about this—feeling of rapport you mentioned?" asked Carnett. Quinterus' oral account, facial expressions, and language, rather than the descriptions, had given him some idea of this strangest of all aspects of the case, but he still wanted to hear—and watch—the man say it in his own words.

A shadow crossed Quinterus' voice and he squinted his eyes. "It's hard to explain," he said in a faraway voice. "It was a feeling—no, really, an awareness— and part of it, now, is a belief that I'm not sure there are any Kill-thinkers. Because the sword . . ."

"Is what?"

"An eye, camera lens, something." The writer frowned, rubbed his nose and lit another cigarette. "I'm not sure there is a word for my vision."

"How about visualization?" Carnett asked, drawing on his memory of scientific papers he'd read during a malpractice case involving a radiologist.

"It's as good as any, I guess." Quinterus blew smoke straight at Carnett. "I'm sorry. Really. Also, I don't think Fatman was a Kill-thinker," he added suddenly. "I think . . . I'm sure I would have sensed it if he had been."

"Really?"

The other man spread his hands. "This is going to sound ridiculous, I know," he said, glancing around. "What I'm trying to say, now, is that there was a sort of tone—yeah, tone, about my visualization, and this tone was disdainful—no, detached— where Jimmy Soyers was concerned." Beads of sweat had appeared on Quinterus' forehead; he wiped them away and continued: "Well, there was no change when Fatman appeared—putting him in the same category as Jimmy and probably Al Robinson, too."

"You can't prove that, can you?" asked Carnett, feeling a bit reckless.

"Prove it? How would you prove anything?" Quinterus snapped. He bit his lip, ground out the cigarette with a savage gesture, lit another. "Only Bernard Kratzel is dead, and Al Robinson had an

attack of temporary insanity. That we can prove."
He bit his lip again, and rubbed his eyes with the
back of his right hand.

"I'm sorry. I really am," Carnett said contritely.

Quinterus made perfectly good sense, anyway: any
radio operator would swear there was a definite
feeling about Morse transmissions. the rhythm of
pressing the sender key—the operator's "fist"—something about the pauses—not just the duration, which
could be measured by stopwatch, but the feeling of
the pauses, and many an intelligence operation had
been aborted because of this during World War II
—by both sides—and no doubt later. There was just
no way to remove every trace of the human operator, or hadn't been, back when he was dealing with
gunsights and the like. That might no longer be true;
but he doubted it. And—hopefully—in six or seven
months he would be in a position to know.

Meanwhile, Quinterus was still mauling his lip,
staring at the fake-marble table, savoring his sin or
whatever . . . Yes, he had caused two human dis-
asters, but gestures of sincere remorse wouldn't make
the slightest difference as far as future victims of the
Kill-thinkers were concerned. Action would.

"All right," said Carnett. "So Fatman is not a Kill-
thinker. Was he taking the sword to the Kill-thinkers?"

"I suppose," said Quinterus in a dull voice.

"Which way did he go?"

This touched off a long, labored discussion over a
road map and a street plan Quinterus had ripped
out of the phone book and marked with a red
pencil. It was a bit pointless, though. Straight . . .
how far? Then left . . . how many yards? Straight
again? The only facts were the odometer readings from
46,805 to 46,834.

"You'd like to think that fixes the Seeking Sword's
range—right?" the writer asked, and shrugged. "Maybe. But maybe I woke then because a truck went
by, or maybe because Fatman passed a microwave
tower." He shrugged again. "There was a burst of
static just before the fadeout."

"What was the station?"

"How would I know?" Quinterus knitted his brows. "What's the difference?"

"Every little bit may help." Carnett was beginning to feel strangely excited, as he'd felt at the start of his big cases, the first time he ran for office, the first time he seriously thought about the space agency. And a few days ago he'd been afraid that from now on life would be a long afternoon's stroll around the courthouse square.

He had been wrong, because this—not project, but adventure—had promise, more even than his running for Congress. That had been a quest for promotion, but this . . . William Bolitho, in *Twelve Against the Gods,* had said every man tries to be the hero of some book he read as a child. True enough. So what was his role here? Lone Ranger? Don Quixote? Somebody out of Kafka? Yeats' Oisin?

No matter. Quinterus was clearing his throat—and what role was *he* playing?

If he'd picked one, he was not in a confiding mood. All he said was, "You are very right about every little bit. So—I suggest we go and talk to somebody else who may remember. John Lambert."

"Of course." Carnett nodded. "As soon as you're ready."

14

May 24, 1970

THE ADMINISTRATION BUILDING OF West Carroll State Hospital was a nineteenth-century Gothic stronghold surrounded by a cyclone fence, a tangle of scraggly evergreens, and acres of gravel-topped parking lot now almost empty. There were also some dismal flower beds. George stayed in the car for a moment, studying the vast ivy-covered building that seemed to combine aspects of the Houses of Parliament and the Cincinnati Workhouse.

Carnett was twenty steps ahead, almost at the massive door with its leaded glass. George followed the lawyer into the large, gloomy room where Carnett asked him to wait as he walked through an AUTHORIZED PERSONNEL ONLY door.

George sat down, lit another cigarette, and looked around at the other visitors who were waiting, too, with furtive glances at each other: an elderly couple with a shopping bag, two middle-aged men studiously trying to ignore their surroundings, a lost-looking teen-aged girl, and two women who were trying to make polite conversation.

The writer leaned back, wondering about the sword —and there was Carnett, with a lovely brunette he introduced as Dr. Jankel, who said they could see Mr. Lambert, of course. He was in Wing C, the day room, likely enough.

"I know the way," said Carnett. "You don't have to put out the cigarette."

"Fine," said George, getting to his feet, while Dr. Jankel began a brief description of how Lambert was doing.

The day room was long and narrow, ten feet high, with narrow windows and walls that had once been bright orange. Now they were faded, unevenly; afternoon suns over many years had left angled tracks on the wall opposite the windows, and even one of the battered couches bore that same brand of passing time. The trellised pattern had been worn off the linoleum, except here and there, under card tables and along walls and beneath the ancient table now bearing a color television set. The dozen or so patients watching the Tigers–Senators game all turned their heads suddenly and fastened their eyes on George as he stepped on one of the patches.

"What do you suppose that means to them?" he asked in a half-whisper, stepping aside. His face felt red hot.

Carnett shrugged. "Perhaps it's part of a game," he said, looking rather uncomfortable himself.

79

The middle-aged woman attendant who had gone to fetch Lambert returned with a small man in a faded green shirt with a frayed button-down collar, wrinkled khaki slacks, and dirty-white tennis shoes.

"Here they are, John," said the attendant, who then nodded and departed.

"Hi, John," said Carnett.

John Lambert nodded, a curious look on his face. "Is he from the governor's office?" he asked in a hopeful, cultured voice.

"I'm afraid we haven't got that far yet."

"We—that is, you—haven't? Then why did you bring him to stare at me?"

The little man—five-feet-two at most—reminded George of a ruffled owl. His face came to a point, he had close-set eyes behind round glasses and tufts of hair stuck up and out from his temples. He was literally hopping mad, skipping from one foot to another, repeating that his mother hadn't raised him to be a tourist attraction. Finally he settled down on his left foot and began smoothing down his sparse reddish-brown hair.

Carnett launched into a long explanation of why George might be able to help and how he had become interested in the case.

"I see," said Lambert from time to time, sounding like the commanding general commenting on a so-so report on logistics.

This didn't appear to bother Carnett, who began describing yesterday's events.

"Served him right!"

"Eh?" Carnett had not anticipated this comment on Kratzel's death. Neither had George; John Lambert was not quite what he had expected. The little man's serene self-confidence was unnerving, especially this soon after hearing the psychiatrist say that his physical and mental condition were deteriorating rapidly. Dr. Jankel said he scorned table tennis and volleyball as kid stuff and naturally wouldn't play basketball. He looked pale, coughed frequently, and kept rubbing his left ankle with the side of the right foot. It was hard to see, sitting around one of the card tables, but George was certain Lambert had a callus on that ankle. The little man's whole demeanor fit in with the photograph in the crime magazine, and George wondered whether he'd always been that way—or had the Seeking Sword given a final, irrevocable shove to a rigid, inflated personality? Also—would it do more good than harm to challenge his attitude?

Carnett beat George to it. "What do you mean, served him right?"

Lambert raised his eyebrows. "What right had he to lay hands on Seppiyeh?" He leaped to his feet and sat down again, grinding away on his ankle so hard that George flinched. "Let us forget Kratzel, or whatever his name is." A crafty look passed over Lambert's face as he inquired: "Rather, how is Mr. Robinson behaving in his hour of glory?"

"Hour of glory?" Carnett sounded as though he had lost control of his voice.

Lambert nodded, a peaceful smile on his face.

Carnett and George exchanged appalled looks. They'd had quite an argument about Kill-thinkers in the car, and regardless of yesterday's events George still felt people like Lambert had been misled and kept up appearances out of silly pride. Looking at Lambert, however, he decided he might have been wrong.

"Al is trying to figure out what happened to him," ventured George. "I'm not sure how he's bearing up, but I doubt he considers this his hour of glory."

"He ought to."

"But he's in jail."

Lambert crossed his arms on his chest. "Sooner or later, he will be vindicated," he said, raising his little pointed chin. "Please tell him that and warn him it may take time. After all, I'm still waiting," he added, with a glance at Carnett.

"Okay," said George, feeling there must be something better to say.

Lambert smiled, revealing even white teeth. "Please tell him not to worry about people saying he's in jail. It's not really true, no matter what his counselor may say. Pharrgh!" And Lambert spat on the floor.

"It's not just his counselor who says he's in jail," George added after an uncomfortable pause.

"Some people would say that I am imprisoned."

What could one say to that?

After a moment of silence, Lambert smiled. "They are mistaken," he said. "This is no prison, but a sanatorium, and I am here to recover from nervous strain brought on by overwork." A shadow passed over his face; his eyes glinted moistly. "Sometimes I don't think that is exactly right, either, because I am by no means certain that my wife may not be behind this. She never really cared for Gertrude, and the fact they won't allow Gertrude here militates as a point against all their protestations. Gertrude is not a mere dog!" His gesture took in the whole world, Carnett included. "On the other hand, it may be a bureaucratic mistake," he concluded with a magnanimous smile.

"Of course," said George hastily, trying to get in ahead of the frowning lawyer.

"Of course, what?"

"Of course, it's all probably a mistake." George spread his hands to emphasize the point. It was in a good cause. "All of it, everything. Everything from the very beginning."

Lambert looked at him suspiciously; but after studying George's face, he beamed. "I'm glad you think so."

"Sure." On a sudden inspiration, George pulled out his package of cigarettes.

"Thank you," said Lambert, carefully selecting one.

"How about a light?"

George fished out his matches, put another cigarette in his mouth and lit both, Lambert's first. The little man leaned back and blew a perfect smoke ring, looking blissful.

"You never did this for me," he told Carnett.

"I've always brought you cigarettes," protested the lawyer.

"It isn't the same. There is a great difference between being offered a smoke from somebody's pack and having a carton bestowed on one."

Carnett inhaled sharply.

Don't! thought George, and he said hastily, "Now then, Mr. Lambert—"

He had been totally unsure what to say next, but the little man took care of that. "Call me Johnny," he said, adding: "You are George Quinterus?"

He pronounced it right, with the accent on the second syllable.

George nodded. "Right. Just call me George." Both men stood up and shook hands, properly; Lambert's handshake during the original introduction had been of the limp halibut variety.

Now what?

But Lambert took care of the problem once more, saying with a wide grin: "You're a writer, eh? Ever do any teaching?"

"A little."

"Found out it's not your cup of hemlock, hey?" Lambert sounded very smug.

George nodded. No doubt about it. But what should he say now? From the corner of his eye, he saw Carnett go to work on his pipe.

Lambert wrinkled his nose. "Wonder what they make that from," he said. "It smells funny."

"For the most part, it's just good burley tobacco," said George.

All right, this was off the subject but they had a sort of rapport and should keep working on it. He began describing a long-ago trip to Kentucky and Virginia, tobacco barns and auctions, how the drying sheds looked and smelled and what a cigarette factory looks like. Lambert listened with obvious fascination.

"I never had a chance to see such places," he said, looking downcast. "They don't grow any tobacco around Fort Sill. Nor did I have a chance to see our country after I finished serving it. I came home, went to college and began teaching. That is, until . . ." His voice trailed away; he swallowed and said, "You'd think they would know better."

"Yeah," George offered, uncomfortably. He could see Lambert's point: after the years in harness, pulling on cue, the authorities should have given him the benefit of the doubt. Reasonable enough—except that John Lambert had been arrested, literally red-handed, for a senseless murder; and, unlike the perpetrators of many homicides, Lambert was capable of killing

83

again and again, as long as the Seeking Sword was anywhere within its undefined range, even if the authorities would scoff at the idea.

They looked at each other. Lambert smiled. "Yeah, *what?*"

"Ummmm . . ." This called for quick thinking. The wrong answer might send Lambert back to his room, sulking. "I thought you might be able to help me."

"Help you? In what way?" Lambert's voice was suspicious; so were his eyes.

"I need some help with a writing job."

He lit another cigarette while Lambert thought it over. After what seemed an hour, the little man leaned forward, a gleam in his eyes. "This writing job —it wouldn't be about Seppiyeh, now, would it?"

Some instinct told George to say "Seeking Sword" rather than "Seppiyeh." He was right: Lambert nodded gravely and settled back to puff on his cigarette. He was rubbing his ankle—very briskly, to judge from the jerking of his body. After a while, he said George was going about things properly.

"I'm glad to hear that," George said, wondering.

"The discussion of the instruments of the hunt is the task of the prose writer, while the explanation of the reasons is work for the poet." Lambert paused. "You may think yourself a poet, but you don't have the proper flashing eyes."

"Thank you," said George. Oh, hell! On a hunch, he asked: "How are you coming along with your explanation?"

"My poetry . . ." Lambert frowned and shook his head. "English really should have a word, a good short transitive verb for 'composing poetry.' Seppiyeh says languages proper for men possess such verbs. But I digress." He shook his head with a sorrowful expression. "As far as my poem goes, it's becoming more and more difficult. There was a time I'd awaken ten times a night with waves of wind-sound all around and throughout me." He smiled wistfully. "Back then, it was a matter of finding a private place with light, and copying everything down, and later putting it in code." He paused. George heard Carnett inhale sharply. Lambert finished his cigarette and dropped it in the tin ashtray. "Now, however, I hear the sound only once a week, or at even greater intervals, and even so the words I distinguish tend to be extremely repetitious. I can't understand it." His voice dropped to a low, tragic half-whisper—and, judging from his wincings, he must have really dug in with that foot.

George made what he hoped was the proper sympathetic sound.

Lambert shut his eyes, opened them, and leaned toward him with a timid half-smile. "You'll help me, won't you? You've got to tell the governor."

"Of course . . ."

"Can I have another cigarette?"

"Uh . . . sure." He extended the package to Lambert, who carefully chose one—fourth from the left—and put it in his mouth with trembling fingers. His nails, George noticed, were chewed to the quick.

"You've got to get hold of the governor," Lambert repeated.

"I'll do my best." Suddenly George had an idea. "Maybe if you showed me the poem, I—we could get a better idea of the right approach."

"Impossible."

"I don't see *why*," he protested, but Lambert cut him short with an imperious sweep of his hand.

"It would take too long to decode what is fit for publication, and in any case I can't bring out the text now. You can never be too careful." He looked closely at George, who nodded, hoping he would appear simpatico. Lambert continued, in a whisper, nudging George's knee. "You're all right, I know, but Mr. Carnett . . . Well, sir, I don't always know whether he's working for me or my wife."

"Come on, now!" Carnett said sharply.

"He's working for both of you," said George. "I'll vouch for that."

"Well . . . if you say so."

Now what? George decided to try and steer the conversation back onto its original course. "Just what is the connection between the Seeking Sword and this . . . Seppiyeh?" he asked, pronouncing the name exactly as Lambert had done. "And what is Seppiyeh?"

Lambert burst out laughing. He laughed so hard

that his cigarette fell on the table, where it lay, smoldering, while his visitors looked, first at each other, at Lambert, and each other again.

"What's so funny?" demanded Carnett.

"Everything." Lambert started coughing, and George pounded his bony back, hard, until the coughing subsided and Lambert sat straight, gasping, wiping at his mouth. George handed the cigarette back to him.

"Thanks," said the little man, and he sat back, puffing frantically.

"I'm sorry I asked what must have been an idiotic question," George said, trying to sound apologetic. Lambert was worse than Wayne Koskenkyll with his bluster and ready fists. He took a deep breath. "I told you I need your help because I'm trying to write a technical history of the Seeking Sword. So, please bear with me."

He had finished more sharply than he'd intended, but Lambert didn't seem to mind. He smiled brightly and asked what George thought the Seeking Sword was.

This was something else George and Carnett had discussed at length in the car. They had decided to take a chance that the Kill-thinkers were not monitoring Lambert.

"It's . . . a long story," George began, starting with Frank Bohnau.

Lambert listened to the end without interrupting once. At one point, he indicated he wanted another cigarette; George handed him the package.

When George was done, Lambert closed his eyes, squirmed, and said: "This is extremely ingenious and not funny at all."

"We didn't think it was funny, either," said George. "Why did you laugh?"

"Couldn't help it."

Did the man sound just a little bit defensive?

"Asking about Seppiyeh seemed perfectly reasonable," said George, not trying to hide his annoyance.

Lambert looked penitent. "I couldn't help it. I couldn't help laughing because—because I had never thought about it in these terms."

He squirmed again, scratched his nose, adjusted

his glasses. George got the impression Lambert was looking for a sign that they were both in this together, whatever this might be. He'd probably do best looking blank.

"On the other hand," Lambert went on eventually in a small, subdued voice, "my laughter may have been a defensive reaction, to use Dr. Jankel's terms."

"Oh?"

"You see, sir, because if you're right, there is no way I could vindicate myself. All I could do is sue for a pardon." Lambert's voice rose, to a near-shriek. "A pardon! That can't be! Can't and won't. And so I laughed to demonstrate I knew you were joking, to take you off the hook, so to speak." He paused, looked beseechingly at George. "Don't you understand?"

George said nothing, trying to follow the train of thought. A long minute passed, during which one of the Tigers hit a double and the television audience cheered loudly.

"What's the matter, you stupid or something?" Now Lambert was sounding like the schoolmaster, a stern schoolmaster addressing a dim-witted pupil. "I tell you and tell you, but . . ." He paused. When he spoke again, his voice was completely changed. "I should have known. Truly, I should have."

"Known what?"

"That it was stupid to hope somebody might understand." Lambert's lip was quivering; he arranged his features in what he must have considered a tragic, heroic expression. "Seppiyeh told me and told me it was too much to expect anybody to understand, in this degenerate age we live in. No one cares about the principle anymore—see?"

Hmmm. Visions of right-wing fanatics flashed through George's mind and he could see, looking at Carnett, that the lawyer's thoughts were along similar lines. Lambert began to open his mouth, but then shook his head and reached over to pluck more cigarettes from George's package, even though his cigarette was only half-finished.

Somebody had to say something.

George took a long pull on his cigarette, exhaled,

and asked whether Seppiyeh was a code word or maybe an acronym.

"Not really," said Lambert. His hand had almost reached the cigarette package; suddenly he burst out laughing again, grabbed the package, and ran.

"Hey, come back here!" yelled George, more startled than angered.

The reply was a small child's: "Try and catch me. Yaaachh!"

George had half risen to his feet and so had Carnett. Their eyes met; they sat down, more heavily than necessary, still looking at each other.

Somebody cleared his throat loudly. George looked over his shoulder.

One of the baseball fans, skinny, middle-aged, with a gigantic hairy Adam's apple, had got to his feet. "Don't pay no attenshun to him," he advised the visitors in a gravelly voice. "Weekends is allus his off days, on account he misses his dog so much, and the Sunday paper crossword ain't near good enough for him."

"I see," said George, standing up too. On a hunch, he asked: "Have you ever heard John say anything about . . . Kill-thinkers?" It was Bradley's term, but he could think of nothing else.

Baseball fan closed his eyes, opened them—they were gray, almost colorless, with fine blond lashes—and shook his head. "Naw," he said. "Kill-thinkers, unh? Never heard of 'em. Only nutty thing I ever heard him say was about this here Seppiyeh gonna set him free." A sly smile came over the face. "Allus thought only prune juice could do that."

"Do what?"

"Prune juice shall set you free." The man grinned, cackled loudly, turned and sat down to face the screen, where the bottom half of the inning was about to start.

15

May 24, 1970

NO SENSE SCREAMING about spilt milk, Carnett kept repeating to himself as George Quinterus backed his decrepit car out of the parking space. Both men were grimly silent after the fiasco. But what could they have done? Proper procedure would have entailed a qualified, trained interviewer, somebody thoroughly briefed on the Seeking Sword, who had the skill to gain John Lambert's complete confidence. But, where would they get the interviewer, and wouldn't such an approach make Lambert even more skittish and suspicious than he was already? No way to tell. Besides, they had neither the resources nor time, because the Seeking Sword was on the loose again.

John Lambert might not know anything worthwhile anyway, but on the other hand, it was just possible he did know and might know how to get in touch with the Kill-thinkers. And in that case, all they could do was hope they were so far off the beam that the Kill-thinkers wouldn't consider it worth coming after them: a lot to hope for, since the Kill-thinkers had gone to a lot of trouble—and risk—to retrieve metal filings from Dr. Kratzel's laboratory floor.

Carnett felt hairs stand up on the nape of his neck. "I hope Lambert is as far out of it as he sounded," he said.

"Out of it? What do you mean?" asked Quinterus in a sullen tone.

"I mean, I hope he's really crazy."

Carnett didn't want to say what he thought, perhaps because of some half-remembered grisly fairy tale, but it would all come out anyway, eventually, and he was starting to feel ashamed of his fears. Still, one lapse a day wasn't so bad. He reached for his pipe, cleared his throat, and said he couldn't envision Lambert as an Oswald or even a hired killer who'd do a few years as part of his contract.

"Me, too," Quinterus remarked. "He's got the same innocent, hurt look as the others." The writer paused. "I wish he'd let us see his poem," he added with a sigh.

"You can see his letters."

Half a mile farther on, Quinterus said: "I wonder how they go about listening to conversations—or thoughts."

"Anybody who put that sword together . . ." Carnett did not finish the sentence.

"Yeah."

Neither of them said anything for the next three miles, during which Carnett found himself watching other cars, especially cars emerging from gravel-topped private and county roads between the lush green fields. Occasionally, he wished he'd had the foresight to bring his deer rifle, or the .38 he'd bought when Jack Tryon swore his brothers would get him, no matter what. That had been in 1959; he'd never heard from the Tryons since. He was not even sure where he had put the revolver when he brought his belongings home after he and Barry Goldwater suffered their respective trouncings at the polls.

In any case, even if the Kill-thinkers did maintain contact with John Lambert—perhaps monitoring the poor man's thoughts—it seemed unlikely they would want to zap this car, now.

He relaxed at the thought, for a moment, because if the Kill-thinkers monitored Lambert's thoughts—an idea that no longer appeared outlandish—then, presumably, they might also monitor his mind—and Quinterus'. No, damn it. He refused to consider himself whipped before he even saw the bad guy's silhouette. Likely, establishing contact would be rather difficult—and he hadn't picked up any strange objects lately, or had strange dreams, or heard voices . . . though George's dream was something else again. All he could do was wait and see, and hope the weekend hadn't cured the writer of his obsession.

Several miles flashed by. Then, just as they passed the sign saying that Hotel Marbury was five minutes ahead, George Quinterus chuckled. "Hell! At least I may get something out of this," he announced.

"Indeed?"

The writer took a deep breath. "I've been working on a thriller. Something on the Kill-thinkers theme. It hasn't been going so well, but now I think I've got it." He paused, passed a beat-up blue Chevy, and said: "My problem was I'd set the scene on the Riviera, and it would fit much better in the Midwest."

"Let's hear more about it."

"It's mostly junk, but let's hope it sells—amen—because then I could really start hunting the bastards."

"Go ahead."

The writer did, at some length. To begin, there was this shy high school senior with thick glasses who was a real whiz in electronics, and his girl fell for the football hero, and . . .

George's disclaimers had been justified but, yes, it would probably sell. And it might make a movie, with Paul Newman and—possibly—Cher.

The suggestion made George guffaw. "Yeah," he said. "Since I haven't got either money or fame, I'll take whichever I can get. Preferably money. I've already been a 'promising young writer.' "

"Good luck to you."

"And what's next on your agenda?" the writer inquired.

"Mine? I'll keep my eyes and ears open," said Carnett, after a pause. "I doubt Lambert knows anything and I doubt the Kill-thinkers are watching him. They seem like the kind of operators who throw their tools away after each use."

Carnett took a deep breath. "Chances are I won't be around Marbury much longer," he said. "But I'll keep in touch. I meant to follow through on Lambert's appeals anyway, and now I'll have to come and testify for Al Robinson." He paused. "You, too."

"Sure," Quinterus said. "God, I really feel bad about him and Kratzel. Especially in view of what the widow said on television, about forgiveness and all that, if she meant it," he wound up with real feeling. A moment later, he asked, "Where'd you say you were going?"

"I'm trying to get a government job."

"In Washington?"

"Yes."

"Oh."

Quinterus' tone of voice spoke volumes to Carnett. Well, that was the writer's privilege, that was what America was all about and why Joseph W. Carnett had volunteered to risk his ass on a tin can in the Pacific, etcetera. He and Richard Nixon might even have had a beer and a few hands of poker together on Z Island—not that it mattered. Nixon was no Goldwater, but he'd do—maybe. At least he didn't run around grinning from ear to ear, and yacking about fundamental goodness—though all that was beside the point and Quinterus, probably a Gene McCarthy supporter, was entitled to his own opinions, wrong as they probably were. Carnett could imagine what Quinterus thought of the Cambodian campaign and the Weathermen who had cocked a snoot at the wrong Ohio Guardsmen, though he had his own doubts about that, and the shootings down South. In any case, George and he had a common goal: stop the Kill-thinkers.

George apparently felt the same way. "Lots of luck," he said. "Let's keep in touch."

16

May 27, 1970

AGREEING TO WORK together had seemed only logical back in Marbury. Explaining it all, here in his Galway Place living room three days later, was something else again. Both Jim Stanfield and Gloria were frankly dubious.

"Bradley copped out and Carnett saw it his duty to sign on. Nice of him, ain't it?" Jim was saying with a thoughtful puff on his cigar. The news stories about Kratzel's murder had diminished his spirits somewhat, but he was still trying.

"I can't figure him," said Gloria.

George shrugged, took a sip of beer, then put the can down. His cigarette was in the ashtray in the kitchen. Better get it; the trip had set him back more than $310 and he might lose another account. Too bad.

He'd arrived home at 3 P.M. and had barely had time for a shower when Jim dropped in and Mrs. Lyndell came down to talk about plants. Plants! She was the widow who owned the house and lived upstairs. In a way that had been lucky, because Mrs. Lyndell left just minutes before Gloria's arrival, and thus George had to tell his tale only once, filling in the blanks in the *Enquirer* and *Post Times-Star* articles before settling down to discuss Joseph Carnett's character and motives.

Quite a job, that—especially since he didn't fully understand his own motives. But he was glad the lawyer had been around. Talking with John Lambert had been a waste of time, but there had been no way to know that beforehand. Furthermore, Carnett had been worth his weight in gold after Kratzel's murder and on Sunday night, when every bit of encouragement was welcome. Mrs. Carnett was nice, too. George concluded by saying it was lucky that Lambert had taught Carnett's kids, and that Mrs. Carnett made such good beef sauté.

"Did you meet the kids?" Gloria wanted to know.

"No. The eldest was killed in Vietnam and the other two were away at college."

"What does he say about them?"

"They seem to get along okay." Carnett's attitudes —about Cambodia, the war, the campus bloodbaths— were indefensible; and had upset George, too. The man was an Establishment fink, but he had his good points and George was in no position to refuse aid. He took another sip of beer. "Let's drop the whole subject. Okay?"

"Some things are not to be questioned, I see." Gloria made a face and said, "Never let real life interfere with avocation."

He'd expected something like this—the more they went out together, the more they seemed to quarrel, as if both were fearful of losing hard-won positions of independence.

Too bad. He got to his feet, muttering about a refill.

"Saved by the bottom?" she called after him and he just managed to swallow a retort about maybe dropping his least pleasant hobby. Instead, he nearly cut his right forefinger on the flip-top ring.

"Well, what's the verdict?" he asked, returning to the living room.

"I've been trying to explain to Miss Barr that allies need not be soulmates," Jim said, gesturing with the cigar. "As I was saying, Hitler's boys built good rockets, and—"

"Oh, sure, Carnett's just using me!" George flopped angrily down in the chair. "Pray, inform me."

"I don't know, yet." Gloria's voice changed. "Look —the reason I worry is, I do care about you. I wish you'd understand that." She would not meet his eyes.

George sought shelter behind his beer can. Jim asked whether he should go. Gloria told him to shut up.

A long moment passed. George cleared his throat. "Okay. You disapprove of this tactical alliance. I'm sorry. You don't like the guy's politics and neither do I, but—"

"The moment he goes a-hunting swordies he becomes a 'nice guy,'" she said.

"You're being unfair," protested George. "Anyway, I don't care whether he's a good guy or not. We're trying to accomplish something. That's all."

"Oh."

"Yeah. Look, you've never seen the Seeking Sword in action. I have, now, and I'm not putting you on— it's something that should be stopped, regardless."

"Like a Martian invasion?" asked Jim.

Before George could answer, Gloria got hers in, too.

"You're sounding like the man who wants to stop Godzilla."

"Oh, Christ."

"I'm only trying to suggest that maybe it's more a matter of gullibility than actual danger." She stuck her rounded jaw forward.

This was almost too much. "You read the newspapers, didn't you?" George paused and picked up his beer. After a swig, he said: "All I can say is, I've got one hell of an imagination and I'll never know why my first novel never caught on. And now—nature calls!"

He stamped his feet, hard, on his way to the john.

When he returned, Gloria was saying earnestly, "There's got to be a rational explanation, something not as far-out as the Kill-thinkers—and I don't mean an ancient curse, either."

"Your prejudices are showing, lady," Jim said.

George sank down in his chair. "Come on, Jim. You don't really believe that."

"Runs in the family," said Jim with a crooked grin.

"You just went to school with Lenore MacDonough and her nutty brothers. That doesn't make you related."

"Birds of a feather flock together."

"Shut up, Jim." Gloria turned to George. "Forget Carnett. Let's get to the nitty-gritty. Conspirators or curse?"

Oh, hell. All right: there was such a thing as having your feet planted too firmly on the ground, never wondering what might lie beyond the horizon, ten miles away. And, damn it—even common sense was relative. Back in the 1600s, your shrewd hardheaded businessmen and erudite scholars would have agreed that curses made sense, even if they would have regarded the idea of Kill-thinkers as too far-out. And yet those people, that much closer to the primeval darkness, would have felt that Jim's theories—regardless of his degree of facetiousness—were worth serious consideration. The people of the late Middle Ages might have been dumb and benighted, but it would have been easier to rouse them, than their present-day descendants, to the danger the Seeking Sword posed to all mankind.

The Seeking Sword was an accursed weapon. Fine. Okay. Only who had accursed whom—and why?

George shut his eyes, visualizing the crumbs of metal crawling on floor and blade. The memory was unbelievably vivid and it really didn't fit in with the Kill-thinker hypothesis, for all his and Carnett's talk about tiny supermagnets turned on by remote control. And why would the Kill-thinkers take such stupid chances to get rid of evidence no one was likely to examine? No. Something didn't fit, but he had no choice except to keep working on the basis of the Kill-thinker hypothesis because the alternatives were, as Gloria would say, totally unacceptable. His mind was probably more open than the next guy's, but supernatural vengeance and literally undying hatred (whose and why?) were too much to swallow. Period.

So—no, no, and no, once again—regardless of what Jim might insinuate about Excalibur, Tyrfing, and other magic weapons. One nice thing about having friends over was that it could be like watching a late movie the eighth time: A would say X to B and B would respond with a resounding Z. Jim continued to expound on the subject of the accursed sword Tyrfing and Gloria kept rebutting him, never raising her voice. Jim did not seem to mind. Hearing his own voice often seemed to be all that was necessary for his well-being.

Yeah. Gloria was right, there. Supernatural was nonsense, even if a Seeking Sword operating on supernatural principles would be infinitely easier to deal with: all one would need was a competent exorcist. Or could any duly consecrated individual, Protestant parson or Jewish rabbi do the honors?

In any case, if exorcism worked against the Seeking Sword, presumably somebody would have done the job long ago. And now Jim was getting to his pet subjects: the God–Devil dichotomy was simplistic, scholars of mythology said blah-blah, why mightn't there be non-Christian magic resistant to priestly exorcisms . . .

"Nuts," said Gloria. "Come on, Jim, you can do better than that. I've *heard* you do better than that."

Amen, to Gloria. Jim was entirely too much concerned with the weird and occult. 'Twarn't healthy. George leaned back and let his thoughts wander. Jim was saying something about rhymes and the magic influence of words. Yeah. Sure. Long-range persuasion, as in the Barbra Streisand movie called "On a Clear Day You Can See Forever" and, more to the point, one of Heinrich Heine's ballads to which Jim had introduced him:

> *Herr Peter und Bender sassen beim Wein,*
> *Herr Bender sprach: "Ich wette,*
> *Bezwänge dein Singen die ganze Welt,*
> *Doch nimmer bezwingt es Frau Mette."*
> > *Herr Peter sprach: "Ich wette mein Ross*
> > *Wohl gegen deine Hunde,*
> > *Frau Mette sing ich nach meinem Hof,*
> > *Noch heut, in der Mitternachtstunde."*
> *Und als die Mitternachtstunde kam,*
> *Herr Peter hub an zu singen . . .*

(Sir Peter and Bender sat at their wine, and Sir Bender said: "I'll wager, even if your singing compels the whole world, it will never compel Lady Maisry." Sir Peter said: "I'll wager my steed against your hounds, I'll sing Lady Maisry into my hall tonight at midnight." And when the midnight hour came, Sir Peter started singing . . .) Then came several verses about his song's effect on all nature, and as for the poor lady:

> *Frau Mette erwacht aus ihrem Schlaf:*
> *Wer singt vor meiner Kammer?*
> *Sie achselt ihr Kleid, sie schreitet hinaus;—*
> *Das ward zu grossem Jammer.*
> > *Wohl durch den Wald, wohl durch den Fluss*
> > *Sie schreitet unaufhaltsam;*
> > *Herr Peter zog sie nach seinem Hof*
> > *Mit seinem Liede gewaltsam.*

(Lady Maisry wakens from her sleep. "Who sings outside my chamber?" She steps into her gown, she walks out the door—and this led to dreadful sorrow. Through the forest, through the stream she walks, and no one could have stopped her: Sir Peter drew her to his hall with his mighty song.)

And next morning when she came home with her gown torn, Sir Bender put her through a long, blustering cross-examination at the end of which she admitted where she had been, and why:

> "Sein Lied ist stark als wie der Tod,
> Es lockt in Nacht und Verderben.
> Noch brennt mir im Herzen die tönende Glut;
> Ich weiss, jetzt muss ich sterben."

("His song is strong as death, it lures into night and destruction. Its resounding—no, melodious—blaze still burns in my heart; I know I must now die.")

And so she did. Sir Bender was a bastard, capable of regretting the loss of wife and hounds in the same breath, in the final verse. George took one last drag on his cigarette and ground it out, listened to Jim expound on swords and curses—nice of him to keep Gloria occupied, giving him a chance to think about a difficult point in *Thoughts That Kill*.

Yeah. That should do it: the other school's coach wishing that Superback would drop dead or break a leg. Sure.

George smiled as he got up to get another beer. *Thoughts That Kill* should put him on easy street— and give him a real chance to go after Kill-thinkers, if he had decided right . . .

17

December 22, 1970

SEVEN MONTHS AFTER the Marbury trip, George was sure he had been right. Everything had worked out, far better than he had dared to hope, in view of past experiences. Wemble & Simon probably wanted the book. He was sitting at his desk and waiting for the phone call from Nick Gobel. In view of the publisher's interest and the way similar books were selling, George was sure the news would be good. As long as it paid for the investigation, he'd be happy.

This was a day for pleasant thoughts and an occasional sip of bourbon—not serious thinking. He even had three whole shopping days left until Christmas.

Wemble & Simon's editors would no doubt suggest changes. He could live with that. Rework some of the chapters? Okay. Add some nostalgia? Why not—after all, there was that pot of gold at the end of the rainbow; and the gold, 90 percent of it at any rate, would go for a good cause. The pride of the craftsman—what did that matter in such a context?

George shrugged, took a sip of bourbon, held his breath as an old lady almost fell on the icy sidewalk. At the last moment she managed to regain her balance and tottered off around the corner. George sighed with relief. He was glad for her—and just as glad he would not have to run out to pick her up. Winter in Cincinnati was just as dreary as winter in New York —or Ainslie, Columbus, wherever. Still, the rest of this winter should be something else again.

He lit a cigarette and took three luxurious puffs before putting it down. Not a bad life, this: Jim might be off work, skiing, but Gloria was searching out books in the stacks and other people were busy with their jobs while George Quinterus sat at his desk, gazing out, warm and snug and full of eager anticipation as he listened to "Das Lied von der Erde" and worked himself up to open mail that had arrived a full hour ago. He was even caught up on the free-lance stuff—and the work had helped him to keep from fretting too much over how his agent Nick was doing, trying to sell the book.

He took a long drag on the cigarette, went out to the foyer, returned, dumped the envelopes on the desk, picked up the first one. The little printed label said Thayer; he put it aside—they'd worked together on trade magazines and Jack would be concerned about job opportunities, a subject George didn't want to think about.

He looked at the alarm clock on the left-hand filing cabinet: 1:14. Nick wasn't going to have lunch before calling, was he? That wouldn't be fair. He turned back to Christmas cards from people he hardly knew, from his sister Lucille and from the MacDonoughs. A bright green envelope made him catch his breath—yes, postmarked San Diego, the annual message from dear old Betsy.

He refilled his glass in the pantry. What the hell was he so shaky about? He muttered to himself as he sat down and started opening the envelope with his thumbnail. Aloud, he added: "Just another form letter about the Herricks' little joys and sorrows. Nothing from Rita, but Betsy will have some gripe about her behavior." His daughter Rita never wrote anymore, not since his birthday in 1967, but then his heart didn't throb anymore either as he mailed the child-support checks. It had been different, sure—she'd been such a cute, cuddly girl. But now it was just another monthly payment.

"Yeah," he said a moment later. He had been right: form letter, with family picture and the old standard "greetings" and series of requests at the end. He winced, finished his bourbon, and stood up. The hell with it, especially those closing words about things

100

tending to work out for the best. Yeah, sure. In the long run, maybe; in the short run, the way things had worked out had been pure unadulterated hell.

He went to the kitchen, rinsed out the mug, made a cup of instant coffee, and strolled back into the living room. This time, he picked the easy chair. For a while he looked at the clock, but the phone remained obstinately silent.

Damn it. Every time he tallied up pros and cons, Gloria won out so easily. But letters from Betsy would still get him shook. When was he going to let bygones be bygones?

He stood up and stretched. Well, he might as well put the day to some use: get back to the books. His *Seeking Sword* studies had languished while he ground out *Thoughts That Kill,* pounding away on the typewriter madly, trying to meet the self-imposed Halloween deadline. He'd missed it, of course, but not by much. Nick had received the complete manuscript on Wednesday, November 18, and had called that night to say the change of residence must have done him some good. It had taken George two weeks to calm down enough to even start thinking of rereading his notes. The critics had liked the Korean War novel. The public hadn't paid any attention. Maybe, this time— Whoa, boy! Don't get your hopes too high!

Good old Nick. In a way, George would not have blamed the man for letting him stew a while or even for telling him to go get lost, years ago, when it became clear George Quinterus was not ever going to flesh out those gorgeous, glittering, resplendent plot outlines he'd brought along from Ainslie. Plot outlines, like talk, were cheap. Nick had cursed George some, but in the end he'd come around to just shrugging, treating George to an occasional drink or even lunch every now and then, muttering at last that he could afford to carry one or two long shots—within reason, that is.

"So here's to you, Gobel Associates!" George said, raising the coffee mug.

He looked down at the phone—unresponsibe as ever —then he moved to the desk. The alarm clock read

1:26. He shoved the rest of the mail off its left-hand corner and reached for the magazines that Jim had brought over before he left on vacation.

These were old German periodicals, things like *Königsberger Zeitschrift,* published in the 1840s in what was now called Kaliningrad, and *Inland,* published about the same time in Tartu, in what had then been Dorpat in Russian Livonia and was now Tartu in the Estonian S.S.R. And then there was also *Preussische Heimatskunde.* The hell with them. Sure, he should do some Sword-work, but right now he couldn't face any nineteenth-century German essays. Later, maybe. Meanwhile there were also the books that Gloria had brought over as a sort of Christmas present, perhaps hoping that the more he read about it, now, the quicker he would get it out of his system. She meant well. And the books were in English.

George took a long sip of coffee, waited a minute for the phone to ring, and then picked up the first book: an 1888 edition of John Martin Crawford's translation of *The Kalevala,* also called "The Epic Poem of Finland." Gloria had marked several places with paper clips.

"I wonder if that means she's getting converted to the Stanfield viewpoint," George said aloud. "God, I hope not."

He waited another minute, sipped his coffee again, and turned resolutely to page 578 in the second volume. Hmm. Somebody named Ilmarinen, a wizard, wanted to kill a girl, but . . .

> Quick the sword feels his intention,
> Quick divines his evil purpose,
> Speaks these words to Ilmarinen:
> "Was not born to drink the life-blood
> Of a maiden pure and lovely,
> Of a fair but helpless virgin."

Kill-thinkers were bad enough, and so was the idea of thoughts that could kill—but a sword that literally had a mind of its own was too much. The Longfellowish meter didn't help either, but he read on grimly, about how Ilmarinen changed the poor wench into a seagull; and, later, about Kullervo, "born in sin and raised in folly," who ultimately killed himself with his own sword—after an argument with the weapon, for God's sake!

This was really too much.

The implications were worse, because Finnish was a tough language to learn, and if George knew anything it was to mistrust literary translations. Still . . . He shook his head. All he could do was hope it wouldn't come to tracking the Seeking Sword through mythological swamps; assuming that it went back that far was almost as bad as really believing in curses. Sometimes, admittedly, the supernatural explanation might seem simplest—but this was the twentieth century, not fifteenth!

And yet the Seeking Sword was real—old, but real —and somebody had made it out of real iron. Maybe the swordmaker had come to be regarded as a god— Volund?—by later generations. But, whatever the explanation, it should pertain to real life, not magic.

He'd had enough of epic poems. His mug was empty. On his way to the kitchen he dropped *Kalevala* on the shelf reserved for current reading. Now, if the phone didn't ring within a minute, it was on to the German magazines. He sighed and added some bourbon to the coffee.

He got no further than *Königsberger Zeitschrift,* whose Spring 1838 issue contained a long poem titled *Die Klage der Wittwe des gehenkten Ackermannes.* Ugh. The poet's name, Hermione Trauttewin (1791– 1875), was as bad as the title, whose translation was "The Lament of the Widow of the Executed Farmer."

The clock said 2:05. George checked the electric cord; maybe the Wemble & Simon people couldn't decide whether to offer half a million or a whole million?

He sat down again, stared at the rain—more like snow now—and picked up another of Gloria's books, a stained and battered volume reeking with the dust of library stacks. Little wonder. James Colegrove was an English merchant who had spent a quarter-century in various Baltic Sea ports and had published his

Recollections in 1844 as "Usable Advice for Young Merchants."

Dull as hell, more than likely, but in English. And James Colegrove—judging from the subtitle—had taken a healthy disinterest in the supernatural. Good for him.

An hour later, George looked up and shook his head. There was a certain anesthetizing quality to the book, even though Colegrove provided an unusual glimpse at an obscure corner of Europe a generation before the Crimean War. His descriptions of sleepy ports like Memel, Libau, and Reval were interesting, in a way, but up to page 149 there had been no mention of anything like the Seeking Sword. George assumed the mention would be of somebody's murder.

He had almost given up hope on the phone; but returning from the kitchen once more, he did sit and stare at his darkening window for a few seconds before picking up the book again.

Chapter XII was titled "Journey into Hinterlands." According to the synopsis it would deal with "Pernau, its location, trade and appearance. Cholerus morbus in the sea-ports. Differences in mast-pines according to types of soil. More about flax-grading. Decaying customs-officers. Captain Borthoff worries about his Estates. Unrest amongst the tenantry. A journey inland, muddy roads, forests, swamps, hovels, parsonages, and *chateaux*. Low prices, wretched horses, sullen countrymen. The parson's explanation of the country's condition, and the sword upon the land."

Sword? George's blood rushed to his face. Pernau —Pärnu in Estonia, according to a gazetteer he had found—was not far from Luchefer, or Luhvri, the parish where the Seeking Sword had gone on two murder sprees in the eighteenth century. He shut his eyes, trying to remember . . . Yes, Mr. Colegrove's visit to Pärnu must have been in the 1830s. By then, Pastor Tiedemann, who had compared the Seeking Sword to Cain's own weapon, must have been dead. Even so, Colegrove must have heard something.

George skimmed over the pages until Mr. Colegrove had indeed arrived in the parish of Luchefer. No mention of Wilhelm Tiedemann; the incumbent parson's name was Johann Freimuth von Gleisch. He had excellent taste in cigars and spoke good English. He also sold Colegrove eight loads of flax and invited the Englishman to dinner with some friends. During the sumptuous meal, the classically liberal Mr. Colegrove's remarks about wretchedness and hunger among tenant farmers were brushed aside. "Your Irish be worse off, *mein Herr,* by all reports," said a Mr. Raushampf. Thus the conversation got around to unrest among the peasantry:

A foppish young gentleman from the nearby Schloss Wolschiel (which countrymen call Wolsia) expressed the opinion that the current troubles were caused by the severity of the authorities, who had had three spokesmen for the tenantry caned to within an inch of their miserable lives. Indeed, I saw one of these men dying in the tavern at Puckas only two days earlier, and one of his fellows had already died. One of the older gentlemen spoke up and said that a firm hand on the reins was the only way to keep the Beast under control, so to say, with a hundred strokes administered without fail whenever the Beast became obstreperous. Another said two hundred strokes would be better because the heathenish louts had calloused backsides, for all that they had been made in God's image. I suggested that bettering the tenants' conditions, by loans or otherwise, might reduce their obstinacy but Mr. Raushampf said the lazy, unregenerate wretches had nothing to be aggrieved about now, insofar as it had been otherwise twenty years past, with the Tsar's troops quartered on the countryside to counter the pernicious influence of Buonaparte. Then, they had had something to complain about!

The conversation continued in this vein a while, eventually returning to the natural viciousness and ignorance and although Mr. Wolschiel and I tried to dispute the assertions, this availed nothing. In the end, Pastor von Gleisch said in tones of bitter solemnity: "The willful spirit of this that the rabble call Freedom, in their hearts, is as stubborn and unmovable by Reason as that Sword in which some of the wretches profess to believe, the Sword that is said to go about monstrously requiting an ancient wrong."

"What ancient wrong have they to requite?" asked Mr. Raushampf. Mr. Wolschiel said that, after all, the Germans had taken the land of the natives from them, by the sword, and at this Mr. Raushampf made a jest about the Sword going about avenging the wrong wrong. Pastor von Gleisch said then that something should be done about this so-called spirit of Liberalism and to make the rabble realize that the benefits of Christian civilization outweighed by far any wordly pleasures, such as not having to pay rents. He was right in that, because duties do, indeed, develop character, not to mention mental faculties; but inasmuch as . . .

Mr. Colegrove embarked upon a long discourse about duties and justice, quoting various Prophets, the "Psalmist" in particular. George skimmed through the remaining pages—to no avail, as Mr. Colegrove would have said. There was no more mention of the "Sword that is said to go about monstrously requiting an ancient wrong."

Monstrous vengeance—the only new piece of real information.

James Colegrove obviously had heard and recorded a reference to the real sword George had held in his hand. Big deal. Whoever had made the Seeking Sword apparently lived at a time when Europeans had blood feuds. All of a sudden, George thought of *Kalevala* swords and shuddered. Good God!

He glared at the silent telephone, tired of sitting, tired of looking at his walls and books, tired of thinking about Wemble & Simon, Nick Gobel, Betsy, Gloria, the Seeking Sword, everything, especially personal relations and leads that petered out until a man could really believe in some monstrous age-old conspiracy involving generations of faceless killers who hid their tracks by sending a Jimmy Soyers to pick up crumbs of metal. God! It was hard to believe that had hap-

pened, even though he'd seen it with his own eyes—
just as he had seen Al Robinson kill poor Kratzel.
Joseph Carnett had the same problem in believing
he'd really seen those things. They had talked about
that during Robinson's trial. Poor Al had ended up
in the same state hospital as Lambert; and his lawyer
was working on an appeal, too.

As George put on his old red-and-black-plaid lumberman's jacket, he wondered how the lawyer would
react to *Thoughts That Kill.* Carnett had unearthed
a copy of *Bleak Hills of Death* a few weeks ago and
had dropped George a note saying he liked certain
things in it.

The phone rang. George turned, dashed back,
picked it up.

"Mr. Quinterus? Mr. Gobel would like to speak to
you."

Nick's news was good, so good as to be disquieting.
Wemble & Simon definitely wanted *Thoughts That
Kill,* but they would require some rather extensive
revisions . . .

Okay. Great! He would make the revisions, at
home, in New York, wherever.

18

April 21, 1971

FOUR MONTHS LATER, George was no longer
certain he should have given his consent so easily. He
had spent almost six weeks in New York now, in five
installments, wondering whether bestsellerdom was
worth it—arguing about changes, making the changes,
now and then snatching a few hours in the public library. Gloria thought he was making too much of
minor alterations in a book he didn't regard highly

to begin with. What did she know? What did any of them know, including himself?

Ever since last Wednesday, he had been dreaming of fires: scary fires in the night, on hillsides, beneath starlit skies. The fires were not alike. Many were like this match he had just used to light his cigarette, essentially meaningless phenomena accompanying the process of combustion. Others were something else entirely. The vocabulary of English was utterly inadequate to describe them, the malevolence of the twisting flaming tendrils, fires that would spread if not put out . . .

A shiver ran down George's back as he ground out the match. Damn and double damn! Here he was, with midnight almost here; soon he'd be lying down to sleep alone and the nightmares were preying on his mind even before he left the hotel bar for his room.

He shook his head and began to study the labels on the back bar. When he noticed the red-coated bartender beginning to look conversational, he turned his back. No conversation, please! He'd had enough of that tonight, first at the cocktail party Wemble & Simon threw for another author—somebody called Blaxton, with problems of identity. His problems were altogether different, involving . . . well, like Francesca.

Francesca Billings, red-haired, stacked, worked for some ad agency, and was a frequent guest at literary parties. Tonight, he had left the Blaxton party with her early, for her place. And right after he had helped her strip off her purple-and-green pantyhose, he'd had a premonition of impending murder.

This had put a damper on the proceedings, but—considering Jimmy Soyers' experience—he had acquitted himself creditably enough, plunging on ahead . . . And then, just as he was lighting her cigarette, he suddenly found himself thinking of fire, again, and theater marquees. Next thing he knew, the phone rang and Fran's roommate was saying he had caught an early flight and was at LaGuardia. Success could turn to ashes fast.

And here he was, trying to decide whether to call Gloria . . . and tell her what? And why? Theirs was supposedly a no-strings relationship between adults.

He finished his drink. The red-coated bartender was right there as he put his glass down.

"Another Jack Daniel's. On the rocks. Double."

"Yessir."

George picked up his cigarette for a luxuriant drag. So this was what success tasted like? (The marquee again intruded on his thoughts but he put it out of his mind.) He had wondered about that taste many times, back when he was living aboard a brick battleship of an apartment building near the Queensboro Bridge approach ramps, right where the airport cabs went by. His two windows had faced Manhattan, bright lights and all, beyond the East River. He'd dreamed of a night like tonight then, and of working for some other trade magazine—appliances rather than lingerie. God!

To success—sweet, succulent, sublime! Drinks in hotel bars, picked-up tabs, literary cocktail parties, girls with snub noses, rounded hips, and flaming red hair . . .

He shook his head. There had been this image, just now. Neither Fran nor Gloria, but a tall pale female with black hair and black coat, standing motionless among other female figures. A mannequin? Mannequins in a shop window. Why?

Sometimes a man's subconscious mind made no sense at all.

He waited, smoking; his eyes fell on the mirror—and instead of the Biarritz Room, there it was again: a street scene. Store window with mannequins, viewed from an alley he knew somehow was in the vicinity of 43rd Street and Seventh Avenue. But that was only the beginning. The whole scene was weirdly clear, down to the smallest, most insignificant details like the outlines of stains on the pavement, the surface contours of corroded bricks on either side, smudges on shop windows as well as the miasma of smells, of days-old urine, food scraps in the alley's allotment of trash containers, not to mention automobile exhaust fumes and fresh vomit. Each car that went past had its distinctive, distasteful, repugnant sound. He almost thought he could hear the pistons whooshing . . . And every set, or whatever, of footsteps sounded distinctive; he could even hear, or sense, the pigeons flying overhead and . . . communicating with each other on their perches a hundred feet and more above the droppings-stained pavement.

George's hands closed on his glass—cold, with many ridges, rightly made for clasping. It was a whiskey glass, wet, smooth, not quite thick enough—there, enclosed by his fingers, rising toward his mouth. And yet the other set of sensations persisted, superimposed on normal, everyday sensations. Well—not quite.

Now, all of a sudden, his fingers were again feeling the *other,* whatever it was, and the surface of the glass had become something half remembered, barely recollectible by the fingers of the man standing in the alley, listening to footsteps.

George knew who the man was: Lewis P. Neumann, born on February 12, 1935, in Hamtramck, Michigan, accountant, resident of Manhattan since October 1970 —six months ago. And there, too, was the incendiary —stocky, fiftyish, navy-blue coat, square jaw, bright white shirt and black bow tie, his whole being somehow illuminated from within by shiny veins of evil fire glowing behind the features of his face and under his hat. As for the woman—couldn't she tell how dangerous, nay, loathsome he was?—she was slight, not quite up to his shoulder, with grayish hair, beige coat, large brown purse. She pointed at one of the mannequins, looked at the incendiary, and smiled.

"Oh, my God," George exclaimed aloud.

Fortunately the piano player had just started "Goodnight, Irene" and all the enthusiastic off-key singers raised their voices so that even the bartender noticed nothing, even though he turned his eyes in George's direction for a moment.

George's back stiffened; he sat, fists clenched on top of the bar, repeating "No, No, No" under his breath despite knowing somehow that it would make no difference at all.

Neumann suddenly dashed from the alley, through the bumper-to-bumper traffic. He reached the other side of the street just as the man in the navy-blue coat and the woman turned from the store window, chuckling about something. George wanted to scream, yell a warning. But what good would it do? The Biarritz Room was many blocks from the scene.

And now Neumann's left hand fell on the stocky man's shoulder. George caught a glimpse of a flat nose, a half-opened mouth—*and* of a heavy-set black policeman with his head half turned his way while the right hand—Neumann's? His? Whose?—came from under his tan raincoat, clutching the Seeking Sword.

First, a streaking metallic arc in the air. The point of view switched abruptly from—wherever, maybe Neumann—to someplace where most of his field of vision was filled by a square jaw, half-opened mouth, thin lips, capped canines, some gold-filled molars, and a bobbing, jerking Adam's apple that disappeared suddenly, blotted out by a satisfyingly thick red line. Then the neck and welling red line across it receded, and the incendiary seemed to focus on a spot a hand's breadth below the bow tie. The Seeking Sword's point hit the third button, slipped through the shirt fabric, touched skin, and sank on until grating against a rib in thrilling exultation—

George managed to unclench his fists and to bring his hands to his face. He dug his thumbs in savagely beneath his cheekbones in an effort to banish, not so much the vision, as the associated feelings.

The treatment worked. Pain blotted out exultation, and even the vision faded momentarily, with George just catching a glimpse of the black cop, eyes wide open, mouth clamped shut, nightstick raised high. And then, as he relaxed his thumbs, there came a sudden intensification of pain and Neumann was falling, face-down, the nightstick against the back of his skull.

The stocky man was lying on the sidewalk, a broad stream of blood pouring in a crack between concrete slabs. Flames faded, went out . . . while the woman in the beige coat knelt by the man's side, screaming. People, crowding close. Too many individual details . . .

The pavement, its irregularities, spots and stains, somehow was etched clearly in George's mind, so clearly he knew he would never forget the faintest splotch, and if he only had the requisite artistic skill he would always be able to reproduce every one of them.

All movement ceased. George beheld shoes, all around, while street lights continued to glare far above. Lower, the undersides of people's chins and bellies loomed. A hand swept down—a thin, skinny hand—and all he could see were dark brown slacks, Wells Fargo belt buckle, black duffel coat, unbuttoned. Then all sights were gone, the Seeking Sword snug, hidden from light, even though George perceived movement, someone . . . Wayne, Wayne Rantzy, sidling through the throng because he had to catch the next train north from Grand Central Station.

George buried his face in his hands. The red-jacketed bartender, who had been studying him, started in his direction.

19

April 22, 1971

WAKING UP AFTER too many drinks could be hell anywhere, including a fancy New York hotel. George sat up and rubbed his eyes. Suppose that murder had been real?

He turned on the television set without moving from the bed, wincing at a raucous commercial that faded away to be replaced by an officious voice that said the accused, Lewis P. Neumann, age thirty-six, continued to insist that he deserved a reward—and that if his sword had not been stolen, everybody would realize this in no time. ". . . And you can make of that what you will," the newscaster said, half smiling. The victim had been Michael J. Hahmeier, age fifty-seven, an aeronautical engineer from Connecticut who had brought his wife to New York for dinner and a show.

Mrs. Hahmeier, now under sedation, had never seen Neumann. She did not think her husband had any enemies. There was no suggestion of any official concern about the disappearance of the murder weapon.

Naturally, George thought angrily, closing his burning eyes tight and shaking his head—too hard.

The Seeking Sword had killed, and vanished—and no one cared. Neumann would go on trial and disappear into a cell, puzzled and hurt because society had failed to recognize his merit. Wayne Rantzy would either drop the sword somewhere or murder a stranger. George Quinterus would sit and rub his eyes, rack his brains, and wonder about being a good citizen and calling the police.

He'd gone that route before. With Carnett's help, now, he might even talk to Neumann—but what difference did it make where the poor schmuck found the sword? Besides, if he called Carnett now, the lawyer would make a big fuss about Kill-thinkers. And there were no Kill-thinkers—none of his half-remembered impressions about whatever had caused Neumann to commit murder fit in with organizations and control boards and contingency plans.

All right, George, let your mind wander now, past the loneliness and solitude and resentments to . . . yes, it was a pity there were so few trees, not single trees, but clumps of trees and bushes, in Manhattan outside of Central Park. What did that signify? George shook his head; maybe he should find a shrink to listen to his crazy free-association sequences. Gloria, bless her, had actually suggested something like this back in March, only half in jest. He probably should start writing his thoughts down, though.

His working lunch with Nick Gobel was less than three hours away.

George got up, stretched, and scratched. He padded over to the dresser and took the thick three-ring notebook from the top drawer, threw it on the so-called writing table, and headed for the bathroom as he suddenly became aware of a painfully full bladder. Later, he stood splashing cold water on his face for several minutes.

George sat down, squirming because the chair's

edge felt cold against the backs of his thighs, picturing Carnett's face as the lawyer read his copy of the report. Carnett had insisted he make two copies of his notes, mailing one set to him and the other to a post office box in Chicago. It was straight out of a spy movie, but in a way it made sense—always supposing the organization of Kill-thinkers actually existed.

He stared at the blank page, wondering how he should start. With the marquees? Or trees? Or dirt? Dirt reminded him of the German poem about *Die Klage der Wittwe des gehenkten Ackermannes*. He had finally read it after Jim Stanfield brought him an article about a medieval allegory called *Somnium sancti Anscarii*, or The Dream of St. Anscar—or Anskar or Ansgarius. The *Klage*, by Hermione Trauttewin, had impressed George so much he'd copied parts of it in his notebook:

> *Die Scheide leget bei ihn nieder, lasst mich*
> *   sein!*
> *Mein Mann ist tot, doch seine Klinge kehrt*
> *   schon heim.*
> *Klinge geschmiedet aus himmlischen Glut,*
> *Klinge die durstet nach irdischem Blut.*
> *Suchende Klinge, geschaffen aus Erden,*
> *Was soll aus uns werden?*

The lady's—that is, the widow's—use of the German language was idiosyncratic, even if the poetess was a parson's wife from Koebelbude in East Prussia. Roughly, the widow lamented: "Put the sheath down by him, let me be! My man is dead, but his blade shall soon come home again. Blade that was forged from heavenly fire [or glow], blade that thirsts for earthly blood. Seeking blade, made of earth [or dirt], what shall become of us?"

This didn't make sense: how could the seeking blade be made of both dirt and heavenly fire? Furthermore . . . But the *Klage,* or *Lament,* was extremely long and its forty-odd verses provided no details of the murder. There were far too many verses describing the gibbet and only one, a sort of aside on the start of the farmer's troubles, was helpful:

Vor Tagswend, aus der Flurstreife,
Die Klinge rief ihn an.
Die sprach von was sollt verborgen sein
Dem seligem Ackersmann:
Von Leid, und Lieb' und Leben,
Wie Gott es einst gegeben
Waldumtreiber ohne Sorgen,
Ohne Pflicht und ohne Fron,
Waldumtreiber, den die Klinge
Sang nachtsdurch mit süssem Ton.

(Before daybreak, from a furrow in the field, the blade called him. It spoke of what should be hidden from a blissful farmer: woe and love and life, as God gave it to forest vagabonds without sorrows, duties, or feudal dues, forest vagabonds to whom the blade sang all night in sweet tones.)

Cryptic, to say the least, and yet this message—according to a final note—had caused the farmer to go and murder a Herr von Rauchzampf and his teen-aged son, visitors from Kurland. The note gave no date, and of course both East Prussia and Kurland (West Latvia) were now under Russian rule.

About furrows, though, and dirt . . . this brought up the subject of, well, burrowing, barrows and, next, Tyrfing. Good old Tyrfing, Jim Stanfield's favorite accursed weapon, one that anybody could look up in a good dictionary of mythology and legend.

Tyrfing was an invincible sword out of the Scandinavian epics. Dwarfs were supposed to have made it for a hero named Angantyr. It performed a number of terrible slayings, and seemed to have a curse on it, since once drawn, it could not be put back in its sheath until it had shed blood; eventually, it was supposed to bring death to whomever wielded it. The sword was buried with Angantyr when he died; but later his daughter Hervör called him from the dead and begged the sword from him.

It was harder to discover anything on Angantyr, but George had persisted, much as he hated getting bogged down in mythology. It seemed that Angantyr and his brothers had been killed on Samsö—or Samsey—by Hjalmar the Brave and Orvar-Odd—or

Arrow-Odd—a character with a magic shirt that no weapon could penetrate from the front. That made it just another mythological battle, especially since Odd Brother also had three arrows that never missed and went through any shield or armor. Angantyr, with his sword, never had a chance. As for his daughter— and Gloria had looked up Hervör with enthusiasm— she had done well as a Viking, even if she never reached Valkyrie rank. There was quite a bit about her in the *Hervararsaga* and in that same "late saga," as quoted by Paul Du Chaillu in *The Viking Age,* eventually King Heidrek inherited Tyrfing, got p.o.'d at Odin in a riddle contest, and took a swing at his god. Odin changed into a hawk and flew away, but was nicked by Tyrfing "and therefore the hawk has a short tail forever after."

Mythology was a bog without bottom. Where would it end? Nothing that George remembered from Virgil, Thomas Aquinas, and the like, had anything to do with the Seeking Sword. As for the Norse myths, some of them were fascinating, others amusing, and some plain dumb. Even Genesis made more sense, being more poetic and less ploddingly crude and earthbound. Still, George was beginning to see how the Seeking Sword, in the seventh or eighth century, or thereabouts, might have inspired some of these myths that were first written down around 1200 or later. Tyrfing, for instance, supposedly meant "The Ripper," "Tyr's Fang," or "Tyr's Snare." As for Angantyr, some scholars thought it meant "Dedicated to Tyr."

Tyr, Tyr, tir-rrr-rrr.

Now then, good old Tyr. Also known as Tiu, Thy, Tiwaz, Zeus, Theus, Jupiter, etcetera, Tuesday's god. He had been the ancient heaven god of the Indo-Europeans. This Tyr had a wonderful sword, as a god ought to. Being in charge of seasons, he had always been a deity of regularity, and no one could call him a cop-out. When the gods decided to chain up Fenris, the big bad wolf with jaws stretching from earth to sky, Tyr was the one who undertook to convince the monstrosity that the Aesir, or gods, were kidding: he thrust his right arm, up to the shoulder, between the monster's jaws; and when Fenris realized he'd been tricked, and chomped down, Tyr wiped the stump on his godly golden beard and said, "That's how the ball bounces."

As a reward, Tyr became divine supervisor of good faith and contracts, while the top job was usurped by an entirely different god: Odin, also called Othinn, Woden, Wodan, Wuotan, a divine CIA type, Wednesday's god, one-eyed and slouch-hatted, a treacherous and sorcerous wanderer.

More to the point, the varying ways to spell the gods' names were reminiscent of the many ways to spell the source of the modern killers' inspiration: Seppiya, Seppiyeh, Seppi Yech. George had searched the dictionaries and encyclopedias with Gloria's help and had come up with damn little, from the likes of German nursery rhymes about a grasshopper called Wurzelsepp to a nineteenth-century Dutch religious historian, a Bavarian painter, some other so-and-sos, and—another thing, Gloria had brought to his attention—morsels like the fact that *sepp* means something like "craftsman" in the Finno-Ugric languages; plain *seppa* or *sepp* means blacksmith in Finnish and Estonian, but there are also *kingsepp* for cobbler, *kullassepp* for goldsmith, *pütsepp* for potter, and *ratassepp* for wheelwright. Apparently Sepp was also a fairly frequent family name in the northern part of Seeking Sword country.

There had also been the *sepa* insect, a sort of incarnation of Osiris, and the *sepa* tree . . . But the very idea of the Seeking Sword being connected with ancient Egypt was all wrong. Osmond Pettigrew had written that the Seeking Sword belonged to the North, to the dripping skies and dank barrows, to the vicious semi-divine smith Volund or Wieland, Tyr and Odin, who carried a spear, and loitered around grave mounds. On the other hand, some scholars described Odin as an ancient shaman, or wonder-worker.

George ground out his cigarette and lit another, almost without thinking. Now then: most of this was nonsense, but Aesir sounded like *"ääs,"* the Estonian and Finnish word for blacksmith's forge. And some of the stuff on shamanism was suggestive. Shamans allegedly had the power to possess others—humans, nymphets,

117

vegetables, animals, minerals, whatever, since the people who believed in shamanism were thoroughgoing animists who believed everything was alive, literally, from the Pope of Rome to every dandelion and on to every pebble on every beach. A shaman could send his soul—or rather, one of his souls—out to take over people, trees, even swords, thus providing a neat explanation of demonic possession, werewolves, and the Seeking Sword, all at once. Sure. Admitting that there might be something to all this crap about shamanism and multiple souls would explain some things—but where would it end? Old Adam of Bremen had probably been right in the eleventh century when he said the way to Odin leads to madness.

All right. George Quinterus should keep his head. George Quinterus was not about to give up trying to solve the mystery of the Seeking Sword. So what should he do?

He could call Carnett. He could even catch a shuttle plane to Washington and tell the lawyer about his fears and visions. Well, he might ask Carnett's advice and help, but he wasn't going to run to him like a goddamned scared kid, especially since there was no immediate danger—at least as far as George Quinterus was concerned.

He could not have explained how he knew this, but he had no doubt about it.

20

April 28, 1971

JOSEPH CARNETT HAD his doubts about the wisdom of this trip to Cincinnati to see George Quinterus. He was not altogether sure what to make of the writer's request for a meeting after the Seeking Sword murder in New York a week ago. The writer's phone call had been something about magic weapons, weird visions—and shamanism.

Shamanism, for God's sake!

According to what he'd learned from Quinterus, shamans were possessed of some kind of supernatural power identified with spirits, animals, even inanimate objects—a sort of totem thing. But the power was born into them; sometimes it was considered hereditary. Apparently they didn't belong to any formal body of religion; they might develop their power either by buying it from or serving under another shaman, or by revelation through fasting and other ordeals.

Mostly they seemed to go in for some kind of animism in which they believed that everything was infused with individual spirits with which the shaman could commune.

A pity he had not had a chance to read up more on shamanism, if only so he would not have to depend on Quinterus for information. George meant well, but that phone call Wednesday afternoon had been a lulu, a real winner.

Carnett shook his head as he told the hotel doorman to get a cab. Sometimes he wondered whether George still had all his marbles. Maybe it was dangerous to get too close to the Seeking Sword; look what it had done to poor John Lambert.

Lambert had died of viral pneumonia in January, and no one knew what had happened to his notebooks. Carnett's own theory—and Dr. Jankel agreed—was that as the little schoolteacher lost hope of vindication, he destroyed his notebooks, possibly hoping that as he destroyed this link with his past, he might escape the influences of that past.

The doorman opened the door of the cab. Carnett nodded, put a quarter in the man's hand, and climbed in. The driver said he knew the way.

"Good," said Carnett, and he settled back to enjoy the ride. He had always liked the Queen City; he and Helen had tried to get here a couple of times a year, for the symphony, maybe Playhouse in the Park, shopping, and shop talk with other lawyers and

Republicans. The Grand Old Party had a fine organization here, always had. Last November had been a fluke. The party in the White House always lost percentage points in the mid-term elections.

The battered houses and drab bars along Vine Street north of Central Parkway made Carnett wonder about Quinterus' place and how it might have changed. Of course it would be months before the book was published, but George would have received an advance. The address was unchanged—but inside? Carnett had a momentary vision of waterbeds and a sideboard loaded with liquor bottles.

"This is it," said the cab driver, turning sharply to the right.

Galway Place had trees on both sides. Good. Residents were still taking care of their properties, with flowers just beginning to bloom and neatly trimmed lawns and hedges. Carnett caught occasional glimpses of backyards with swing sets and fences along the edge of the hill; from there, people would have fine views of downtown directly to the south.

Hmmmm . . . Number 659 could use some paint, but that would hardly be Quinterus' responsibility as a tenant. *The* tenant, really.

Fare: $2.70. Carnett handed the driver three singles and a quarter, nodded, then walked briskly up to the three concrete steps in front of the house. Two windows looked out on the left; the shade was down on the farther one, and a Venetian blind shut off the other. George Quinterus evidently valued his privacy. Carnett rang the bell at exactly 2:18.

Thirty seconds passed, forty, fifty—enough for him to begin wondering again . . . George Quinterus was playing with fire—and so was Joseph Carnett—but the danger to George would be more immediate and deadly. Suppose the Kill-thinkers, however they operated, had already got to the writer? And if so, how would Carnett be able to tell? They would be smart enough, with enough experience, so their puppets would not look like robots. Farfetched. But so was everything about the Seeking Sword, and Carnett was glad he had mailed a full account to Harry Hughes in Chicago. That was all he could do at this point, and if he did not call Helen by six this evening, or nine at the latest, she would call Harry, and all hell should break loose by midnight.

Aha. He clenched his fists, automatically, as the door opened. His first glimpse of Quinterus was reassuring: the writer had gained weight. It showed in his jowls and around his belt line. Otherwise, he was unchanged except for dark circles under his mournful brown eyes.

"Well, hello," Quinterus said. "Come on in." His voice sounded the same.

"Hello. Nice to see you again."

The sad eyes were particularly reassuring. Most of the sayings about looking into a person's eyes were superstitious bunk, but anything taken seriously by a lot of old policemen, bail bondsmen, schoolteachers, and merchants couldn't be all moonshine, even if pupilar movement—to use the proper scientific terminology—was only one of the components of assessing an interpersonal situation.

"I hope you had lunch," the writer said. "We've got a lot to talk about before Gloria comes over. Then I thought we could all go out for dinner."

"Fine with me," Carnett agreed, following Quinterus through the foyer. A staircase, no doubt to the landlady's apartment, went up along the right wall; Quinterus' door was to the left, perhaps eight feet from the street entrance. As for the apartment . . . yes, he'd done Quinterus an injustice: reasonably good carpet—Helen would not have cared for the lattice design in yellow and red, but Carnett did not mind—a fair amount of light, white-painted walls, pictures: a map of the Baltic Sea region and Scandinavia, a Shakespeare portrait print, a couple of abstractions in unexpectedly bright colors, probably gifts from Gloria. As for the furniture, it was serviceable, used, not part of a set but not junky either—with the possible exception of the brown corduroy armchair. The black vinyl sleep sofa opposite the entrance looked fairly new, and so did the typist's chair by the massive old desk. Tall filing cabinets stood at either side of the desk and Carnett saw quite a few plants on the cabinets and even on the desk itself. And books—books piled on the desk and cabinets and crammed on shelves between kitchen and entrance door.

"Beer or bourbon?" Quinterus asked, turning around.

"Beer will be fine."

Carnett stood, studying the books, until Quinterus thrust a tall pewter mug into his hand. They sat down, Carnett on the sofa and Quinterus in the old armchair.

He had imagined the beginning of the conversation several times when not wondering how shamanism could possibly be fitted into a twentieth-century context. Perhaps there was a way, with the new studies of the brain's alpha and beta waves . . . but that was *really* reaching for it.

Quinterus might look tired and downcast, but he was certainly not embarrassed. His apologies for interrupting Carnett's normal work week were strictly perfunctory. Then, before Carnett could say it was all right, the writer leaned forward.

"Did you hear about the latest murder?" His voice quivered a bit with eagerness.

"You mean . . ."

His sentence was lost as Quinterus launched into an account of how two men, cousins, had been killed last night in some Massachusetts town just west of Worcester. The names were Wolff and Neisman. The *Post Times-Star* story had been sketchy, but the murder technique had been the same. And no arrests.

"Oh, no!" What else was there to say?

Quinterus looked shaken, too. "I told you I don't feel personally threatened," he asserted. "On the other hand, this . . . well, this doesn't really fit my latest theory."

"Why not?"

The writer frowned. He had lit a cigarette; now he took a long drag on it and shook his head. "Hell, the way I figured, operating the sword was a kind of proficiency test. Something an apprentice shaman had to do before he qualified for the next stage." The words started spilling out more and more rapidly. "I told you how shamans were supposed to be able to possess other people, and even objects. That's nonsense, of course, but suppose—suppose the sword really goes back a thousand years, to when a Finnish or whatever witch doctor discovered some weird crystals." He paused, took another drag on his cigarette, and wiped his forehead.

Carnett took a judicious sip of beer. Possible; plausible, rather. And better expressed than in the phone call.

"All right," the writer was saying. "Suppose all this happened. The witch doctor put the crystals in the sword, and discovered he could control the tribesmen by sending . . . hell, *thinking* orders through the sword. His name might even have been something like Seppiyeh. That would make him a sort of super-shaman and stories about him could develop into the sort of thing you read in mythology." Quinterus paused; an avid gleam came into his eyes. "Okay so far? Well, the super-shaman would pass the secret, probably to his children, and they would hang on to a good thing. That's only human, right?" He held up his hand. "I know. You'll say it would have come out because the Order of Assassins couldn't keep their secret and so forth. But I'm talking about a family enterprise. You see, the ability to control others by means of the sword might even be hereditary, and maybe the crystals could also be used to tell people to . . . umm . . . make certain investments, or vote a certain way. The possibilities are limitless."

Indeed they were. They were appalling. The Kill-thinkers had been bad, but this, in a way, was more revolting, like the Hindu castes of thieves and murderers—Thuggees, they had been called. Though, in a way, it was less dangerous to humanity at large.

Not that this changed anything. Murder was murder.

The writer was speaking again. "I said the possibilities are limitless, and if the super-shamans were all men who like comfort but don't need millions, and who don't care about ruling the world and telling everybody what to do . . . hell, they could stay more or less out of sight indefinitely, especially after

123

people stopped believing in possession and things like that. There might be only a few dozen of them at any given time, and the murders would occur only when it was time for little Johnny to take his exams, so to say. At some point of—let's call it a rite of initiation—he would have to make one stranger kill another." George paused. "That particular test might come either before or after he had used the sword to put some people through some other kinds of paces. It might be repeated several times. Does that make sense?"

Carnett nodded, sipped his beer, and nodded again. The scenario just outlined by the writer was a definite possibility. Improbable, yes. But not really less probable than the existence of the Seeking Sword itself. Carnett had persuaded an engineer, a black named Frank McCullough, to make a computer run-through on the problems associated with the Seeking Sword. The odds were astronomical against all of them—as well as against the existence of the damned thing.

"I see," the lawyer said in his most judicious voice. "I see. Now why doesn't this fit in with the latest murders?"

Quinterus looked troubled. "It's hard to say, really. But I keep getting this leaked information, or insight, or whatever you want to call it." He looked both troubled and defiant. "That's why I don't think I'm in any physical danger, for instance."

Carnett nodded. What was the writer leading up to?

"But these two murders—they'd only make sense if there are several super-shamans operating the sword at the same time, maybe trying to show each other up. And, goddammit, that just doesn't fit."

Hmmm. Carnett could see the writer's point. But what if one of the—all right—super-shamans, was a practical joker? He suggested the possibility.

The result was rather unexpected, because George Quinterus was almost totally humorless. Carnett had expected him to flare up. Indeed, since George had his share of the human tendency to dissemble, baiting him could be a shortcut, something to be undertaken from time to time as a calculated risk.

Instead of blowing up—he came close, but literally clapped his hand over his mouth halfway through an expletive—Quinterus suddenly looked distracted. "Hmmm. That crazy article . . . that's what I was trying to think of."

He got to his feet, muttering an excuse, headed for the right-hand filing cabinet, and pulled a notebook from the second drawer.

"What's that?" asked Carnett, surprised at the writer's reaction.

"Something I found in a German scholarly journal. Let's see . . . Yeah, it starts out with Siegfried's sword, naturally, and how Wayland the Smith got his revenge. Right . . ."

Quinterus' voice almost died away as he leafed through his notebook, somehow reminding Carnett of John Lambert. What if the Kill-thinkers—or supershamans, a term every bit as ugly as Kill-thinkers—had taken over the writer's mind? Carnett felt his muscles tense, but a moment later he relaxed, realizing that Quinterus was far too concerned and anxious to find the right page to be a man possessed. He had to repress a smile as George handed him the notebook and got up again, this time to fetch more beer.

Carnett had been a faithful reader of the notes—about the sword Tyrfing (a real weirdie), the vicious Wayland the Smith, the invincible weapons of ancient Ireland—"the sword of Nuada, out of Findias, and spear of Lug, out of Gorias"—and the rest, some of them slightly familiar and others completely new.

The notebook was opened to where Quinterus had copied out and translated passages from an article by one K. W. Bohrocke, in the Spring 1931 issue of *Neue Zeitschrift der Völkerglaube*. Bohrocke had been fascinated by the talking swords of some heroes —if that was the word—of the Finnish *Kalevala*, and by the sword of Kalevipoeg. *Kalevala* was Finnish for "Land of Heroes," and Kalevipoeg meant "Son of the Hero" in the language of the neighboring Estonians. Anyway, Kalevipoeg's sword was accursed, or perhaps just resentful, because Kalevipoeg had used it to kill the Finnish blacksmith who had made it. The sword had a mind of its own. A demon stole it, but dropped it while crossing a stream; when Kalevipoeg arrived in pursuit, he could not pick it up from the water. Bohrocke's explanations, or Quinterus' rendering of them, left something to be desired. Apparently the sword considered the hero untrustworthy, even if it was already tiring of the company of mermaids. They had an argument, hero and sword, and in the end Kalevipoeg went his way after telling the weapon:

> . . . *Kui aga juhtub kõndidessa Jalakanda pistma jõkke,*
> *Kes sind enne ise kannud: Siisap, mõõka, sõbrakene,*
> *Murra jalad tal mõlemad!*

The strange words were translated (Estonian to German to English) as "But, if he who once thee carried happens to put his foot in the water, then Friend Sword: break off both his feet!" Kalevipoeg meant the demon, of course. But as it turned out, he himself passed that way years later, started to wade across —and *zap!*

Uh-huh. Some practical joker, that demon—though Quinterus indicated that the joker would have been the super-shaman who had talked back to Kalevipoeg through the sword.

Perhaps. The idea made Carnett feel uncomfortable, but more proof was in order. He read on, about the Estonian proverb that *"Surmamoek ja suovisormus, samast munast hautati,"* when the writer returned with two cans of beer.

"What do you think?"

Carnett cast one last look at the page, searching out the translation: "Death-sword and wishing ring, from the same egg were hatched." He considered his reply carefully. The German scholar could be right in maintaining that gruesome tales cluster around weapons because of the inherent frightfulness of "tools," whose only purpose is to shed blood and rend soul from body. Bohrocke was not the only one to say this. Quinterus believed that at least some of these stories had been inspired by Seeking Sword murders, which seemed likely enough. Still, there had been no suggestion of a practical joke in the story of Kalevipoeg's misfortunes, no suggestion of any demon gloating on the riverbank while the hero lay thrashing wildly in Kääpajõgi—"River of Grave Mounds," according to a footnote.

"Well?" Quinterus asked.

"We have to psych out the Kill-thinkers." Carnett found some of his daughter Debbie's expressions useful. "But I don't think this article proves anything about their nature." A pity, really, because practical jokers needed to demonstrate superiority—and betrayed areas of weakness by succumbing to the urge. Kill-thinkers or super-shamans with that kind of weakness were too much to hope for.

Evidently the writer had hoped for a different answer. "You may be right," he said stiffly. "Still, it would be nice, wouldn't it—sort of a glimpse behind the mask."

"I know." Carnett refilled his mug. "But then, those telepathic leaks serve the same purpose, don't they?" He asked the writer to tell him all about the Hahmeier murder, with special emphasis on his own thoughts and the various impressions—those he had felt at the time and those he had remembered later.

"Okay," said Quinterus. There was a trace of reluctance in his voice as he went on. "I didn't mention this before, but I was in this young lady's place and . . . Hell, there we were and all of a sudden I was thinking of this theater marquee . . ."

21

April 28, 1971

GEORGE'S ACCOUNT OF Michael Hahmeier's murder led naturally to more theorizing—and certainly no shortage of possible explanations. Perhaps the sword was really supernatural. But then was it God's instrument? Satan's? Just plain accursed? (And what did that mean?) Perhaps it was all a series of coincidences, or something from outer space; or maybe the sword was somehow alive and conscious. Somewhere, George had discovered that the scheme of things worked out by Gottfried Wilhelm von Leibnitz, one of the seventeenth-century fathers of calculus and other forms of higher math, had included so-called "monads"—sentient atoms, in modern terms.

Too many theories!

George agreed. "I might—just might—be able to buy the thing-from-outer-space idea," he said, shaking his head. "I mean, how the hell do we know what the Martians, or whoever, might have? The sword could be a sort of robot, and there might be some people whose minds work on the frequency that controls it. Right?"

"It could be," said Carnett, trying to remember whether any of the science-fiction writers had come up with that one.

He wondered when Miss Barr would arrive. He'd decided earlier to ask no questions, and George, carried away, had hardly mentioned her. Carnett saw no indication that she was living in, for all the writer's occasional bitter laments that her skepticism was most distracting. For instance, there was a medieval book (Aha! every good mystery needs a musty manuscript!) called the *Somnium,* which George was trying to get, going so far as to advertise, while Gloria . . .

George had fetched more beers from the refrigerator, and somehow by way of Carnett's suggestion that the sword might be the first of its kind, the world's first sword, they got back to Wayland, or Weland, or Volund, or Wieland—the vicious, supernatural blacksmith.

Apparently the stories about the "Norse Vulcan" went back to really dim prehistory. One proof of their antiquity lay in the means for obtaining steel used by the smith. Once upon a time, Wayland had an order for a super-sword, and his procedure, according to the *Thidrekssaga,* was to take an everyday regular-issue sword, break it into small bits, and toss these to the chickens; in Wayland's day, swords were made on the farm instead of in factories. Now, the chickens would pick up the glittering bits of metal. The gizzards of the birds contained gravel, and the calcium of the stones, in presence of loose carbon atoms from bile acids, or whatever, would combine with the iron to form what could now be called medium-carbon steel—a far cry from modern saw blades but a lot harder than a tenth-century B.C. standard sword. The way George put it, Wayland's apprentices spent weeks policing up droppings; and when he got pressed for time, Wayland just caught the chickens and ripped up their gizzards to get enough "steel" for a sword that could cut the other man's blade in half at one stroke—

"Hi! Hope I'm not interrupting something important."

Carnett had not heard her unlock the door. Almost automatically, he jumped to his feet while George began the formal introduction.

Item: Quite nice, at first glance anyway, and he had faith in his initial judgments.

Item: Pleasant-looking face; he liked the slightly upturned nose and full-lipped mouth. From rounded chin on down, she looked nice, too. Longer, slimmer legs would be an improvement since she was about five-eight and maybe one-sixty. But, all in all, everything was where it ought to be.

Item: If George was a wishy-washy, from all he

had heard from the writer, *she* was a doctrinaire liberal. The term was a misnomer, sure, but it had a certain validity for purposes of classification.

". . . and I think we've covered most of the bases," George was saying.

Carnett nodded. Gloria Barr hesitated a split second and moved to sit on the right side of the sofa. George headed for the kitchen without asking what she would like—naturally enough—and Carnett moved to fetch the typist's chair.

"You can sit on the sofa, Mr. Carnett," she said. "I haven't got anything contagious."

Carnett halted, caught off stride in spite of his preparations, more by her cheerful, almost amused, tone than by the words. "Fine," he said. She had picked up his mug and was holding it out, smiling. "Fine," he said again, settling on the other side of the sofa. The coolness of pewter felt pleasant. "Thank you, Miss Barr. By the way, why don't you just call me Joseph?"

"Okay, Joseph." She made a face. "I know what you mean—I think nicknames are awful, too."

Her smiles and changes of expression became her, adding just the right amount of animation to a face in some peril of looking too wholesome. Carnett relaxed; then her voice put him back on his guard.

"You know, you're one of the first commanders I've had a drink with. What's it feel like, sending others into danger?" Her voice was low and throaty, very pleasant but with clear intimations of how steely she could sound.

Well, Miss Barr was entitled to her views, but at the same time there were certain things of which she ought to be reminded.

"I'm not sending George into anything," he said.

"I know. You didn't put him up to it. He went nuts about the sword all by himself." She paused, then continued a moment later: "All I'm saying is, he is doing the work and risking his life against the super-shamans —or whatever they're called today." She finished on a note of frank disgust.

Carnett shrugged, feeling suddenly sympathetic to George. With all the girls in Cincinnati, he had fallen in love with one who thought he was half out of his mind. Helen thought George was trying to prove something to himself. Could be. On the other hand, maybe George had realized subconsciously that he might get in too deep, and had hit upon Gloria to keep himself from going too far. Of course, they had first met long ago, while he was still teaching—but probably after he had found the Reverend Mr. MacKenzie's book.

Carnett became aware that she was looking at him very intently, waiting for an answer. "I'm not so sure about the super-shamans, myself," he said, making his voice sound formal. "Kill-thinkers is at least descriptive, if that is the way the murders are brought about."

"You didn't answer my question," she said sweetly.

"True. All I can say is, George doesn't think he's in real danger and he ought to know."

"That's a good cop-out—sir," she said.

Carnett braced himself, but at that moment George appeared from the kitchen with a wineglass half full of dark red liquid. Gloria looked at him, smiling, and Carnett swallowed his angry retort.

"Here's the burgundy," said George, emphasizing the last two words. "Excuse me, now."

Gloria took a hearty sip of her wine. At the sound of the bathroom door's closing, she looked at Carnett. "Well?"

"Well, what?"

"The danger. You've seen it in action, haven't you —Joseph?" He nodded. She had obviously expected that. "When George first told me about the sword, I thought it was a real crock," she went on. "Still, the way he put it, he might make a thriller out of the idea. At that time, I thought— Never mind. It now seems to be a question of whether he's cracking up, or putting me on, or whether there is something to it." She paused. "He thinks there is. You, too. Right?" She thrust out her rounded jaw.

Carnett thought for a moment. "The sword exists and there's definitely something weird about it," he said in an even voice.

"So why don't you do something instead of leaving it all up to him?"

Her vehemence caught him by surprise.

"Do what?"

"You've got some influence. Call the district attorney." She paused. "Well, why not?"

He nodded. Certainly. Go to the police, tell them—what? He picked up his pipe and began to puff.

"Believe me, we've thought about that," he said. "The trouble is, we have no evidence. And George will tell you it's best for me to preserve my . . . credibility for the time being, so that when we've found them I can get the police to move in."

He took a long drag on his pipe. Neither he nor George were characters out of a thriller. Even if they found themselves in the goddamnedest mess, it still did not render them capable of commando tactics. The best they could hope for was to call in the specialists after they had found Seppiyeh's headquarters.

Gloria, of course, would not see it this way.

She didn't. She shook her head and took a deep breath. "I see. Yes, of course." Carnett did not like the tone of her voice. "Now then, either the sword is a relic of the Dark Ages, which I doubt, or it's of more recent manufacture." She took a ladylike sip.

"Uh-huh." What was she getting at?

"I know how George's mind works and what he's been working with," she said. "Legends, myths, sagas —and he didn't make these up. The same goes for the court cases and tales about blood revenge." She thrust her chin out again; the steely note came back in her voice. "I don't know how the legends got started, but I suspect that somebody who had the hardware might see that the old stories would be perfect to help cover it up."

She stopped, her beautiful mouth scornful.

Carnett bit his pipe stem. All right. She had a point. That kind of suspicion was only natural in a world where Palestinian commandos and James Bond types got all the hisses and applause. You might expect such suspicions when thousands of transceivers disguised as seed pods and what-not were dropped along the Ho Chi Minh Trail to spot Cong by the stink of their sweat or by ytterbium isotopes that Agent W had slipped into the Swedish-made dye on their Russian-made shorts and ammunition pouches. So why not a secret sword?

All right. As far as he knew, the government had nothing to do with the Seeking Sword. Gloria might think so; or maybe she was just baiting him because they seemed to have a natural antipathy, the kind sometimes explained on the basis of body chemistry.

"I suppose you can't say anything because of national security," Gloria prodded.

"Not really . . ." He took the pipe from his mouth. "As far as I know, the government has nothing to do with it." He smiled. "Besides, I deal with people who make parts for spaceships—not people who design weapons."

"I thought five or six companies had most of both kinds of business."

"Sometimes it seems that way. That bothers me, too." He didn't care for the retired military men working for these companies, either, but she was not the person to discuss this with. He narrowed his eyes. "The point is, you think the sword is a secret weapon. I don't."

"I think that's the explanation that makes most sense—it's a secret weapon being tested at home, under closed conditions, so to speak."

He shook his head. "I'd say you're wrong." He injected a touch of amusement into his voice.

Her face turned slightly red. "Why?"

"Several reasons. First of all, I've met Mr. Laird, and I don't think he'd allow anything like this. Neither would the President, or Mr. Helms, or anybody—"

"I'm not so sure. After all"—she leaned toward him—"all the people on George's lists don't add up to the score of a single B-52 raid." She paused for effect. "That is, even if you only count women and children."

Carnett winced. Well . . . all right. But war was war —the things the Cong had done in Hué during the 1968 Tet offensive weren't nice either, and over the years they had killed a lot more of their own people by disemboweling and cutting throats from ear to ear than the total of those who had perished as a result of bombing. She was right in one area, though: Governments should not be judged by the same standards as individuals, because whenever one person became responsible for others, he or she became a monster. Altruistic principles, by definition, necessarily supersede ordinary human impulses.

"What do you say to that?" she demanded.

"I didn't come here to argue politics. I thought we were going to discuss the sword."

"You still haven't said anything to convince me it couldn't be the CIA."

"So why kill a government engineer—and that Air Force colonel, back in the 1950s?" He tried his ironic best.

"Maybe they were spies. Maybe it was an attempt to mislead people like George. Or the colonel's death could have been coincidence, or an accident." She was obviously enjoying this. "Maybe the victims are picked at random. That is more scientific, isn't it?"

He wondered what was taking George so long. Most likely he was standing in the bathroom, listening. Carnett felt another momentary wave of sympathy for the writer, followed by resentment.

"If we're going to play games, your guess is as good as mine," he said. "Still, I don't see why a weapon that's been around for centuries needs any more testing."

"Who knows what bugs may lurk in the swordwork?" she asked with an expression of childlike innocence.

Carnett had to laugh. "The Shadow, of course," he said, and she grinned, obviously without wanting to.

That was the moment George chose to return.

"I see she's trying to make you tell national secrets," he commented.

Gloria looked annoyed.

Carnett shrugged. "There are at least three things wrong with her theory," he said, using his pipe as a pointer. "First, I don't think our government would test weapons on civilians, especially our own people picked at random. Second, I don't think we've got the technology to make something like the Seeking Sword. I've asked around, and people look at me like some kind of nut." He had done so, too; the bureaucrats would look dumfounded and the scientists usually intrigued, probably because of his own position in the scheme of things. "Third," he added, "I don't think anybody on our side would give the go-ahead on a weapon like the sword."

"Oh, really?"

She had not expected this. Good.

"Certainly. It's not bulky enough to impress reporters, there are no dials on it anywhere, it wouldn't look good on TV, and no official would go out on a limb about something involving telepathy." He paused. "You don't get anyplace in Washington, supporting nutty ideas. No sir. Besides— You've seen the pictures, haven't you?"

She nodded, puzzled.

"No experimental weapons plant here or in the Soviet Union would turn out anything that crude-looking for testing under field conditions. I don't care whether you believe me or not, but any chief engineer on either side would die before he let junk like that out of his plant. After all . . ."

"It could be camouflage," Gloria suggested. George smiled, seemingly enjoying the exchange.

"There's no way to prove a negative. There's really no way to prove anything until we get hold of the sword—and the people behind it."

"I see." A dangerous edge was in her voice. "The only reason you came here was to give George a pep talk, tell him the whole wide world depends on him, and all that crap—like, if he dies, it's in a good cause. Right?"

"Wrong." Carnett had decided not to lose his temper, but some people could be awfully exasperating. He had sounded curt to himself. The gleam in her eyes showed she had heard the tone, too. Damn her!

"I mean, you're wrong on both counts," he said hurriedly. "For one thing, I am lousy at pep talks. I wanted to talk to George, hear what he saw and heard that night in New York, and talk about how we should go on from here."

"Sure. I trust you brought along more stamped and addressed envelopes."

This was too much for George. "Why don't you

quit it?" he broke in. "It was my idea, damn it. He's just somebody I dragged in."

She turned on him, eyes blazing. "He's encouraging you. He's telling you to go ahead while he sits in Bethesda and gets his kicks out of your progress reports." She paused. "You don't see that, do you?"

Carnett almost made a remark about different strokes for different folks, but stopped in time, realizing that wise men stay out of lovers' quarrels. Instead, he reached for his mug, almost relishing the thought that it was now George's turn.

He had expected the writer to flare up; but George only shrugged.

"So, I'm making a fool of myself, and he's egging me on. Why get all worked up about that?"

"Why should you take all the risks?" Her voice was bitter.

"What risks?"

"Oh, hell," she said in exasperation. "What about the poor guys in New England? They never even heard of the sword—and now they're dead."

George nodded gravely. "I know. They're dead and that's another reason I've got to keep working on this, because— Damn it, I never was any good at sounding noble. But somebody should stop them." A quick grin flitted over his face, making him look almost schoolboyish. "Let George do it." He raised his hand. "Yeah. And I'm uniquely suited for the job, because I get these leaked visions and because I'm safe. I've told you and told you—I'm in no physical danger whatsoever."

"Sure," she almost jeered, and then shook her head. "Sometimes you don't make good sense."

"I know." George sounded thoughtful. "I know this doesn't make sense, love—but I do know, like I knew the fat man was not a Kill-thinker."

Gloria shook her head. George looked at Carnett. The lawyer shrugged—what could he say?

It didn't make sense to him either; but according to what McCullough and other scientists at NASA had told him, the very existence of the Seeking Sword didn't make sense. The thing ought not to exist, not only as a matter of morality but also as a

136

matter of mathematical probabilities, physics, wave mechanics—you name it. Anyway, he was glad George agreed with him, though he was not so sure the writer was in no danger. This peculiar telepathic link was their best hope of bringing the killers to justice, but it was also a potential source of deadly danger—and Gloria was right in suggesting he should feel guilty about staying safe. *He* did. But what could he do?

They looked at each other until Gloria smiled brightly. "I'm famished," she said. "How about Lenhardt's?"

22

June 19, 1971

THE SEEKING SWORD stayed idle all through May, but then came another murder: a farmer near North Adams, Massachusetts, was killed Thursday, June 3, 1971. George did not hear of it until two weeks later, when Nick Gobel enclosed a newspaper clipping in a letter announcing that a movie company wanted *Thoughts That Kill*—and would George want to work on the screen play?

Hell yes. For one thing, the job would start in August and get him out of Cincinnati during the worst weeks of summer. He had invested in a window air conditioner, but the apartment needed at least two and he didn't know how long he would stay here. Once big money started rolling in, or he and Gloria . . . He had decided, weeks ago, to stop worrying about super-shamans. If worst came to worst, he could always get himself committed.

Getting out of Cincinnati for a while would also be helpful for another reason; it would give Gloria and him a chance to make up their minds about strings and no strings. For a moment, he wondered what marrying her would be like. Then he banished the thought by looking at the letter, the strange letter that had arrived yesterday, after he'd given up expecting an answer to his advertisements in *Antique Bookman* and the rest.

The letter was short and to the point, even though it was written with a script typewriter on heavy, cream-colored paper adorned with a crest and the initials TPR. The writer had signed the letter only with these initials.

I write to you in response to your advertisements in the various publications. You have been expressing interest in rare and old works dealing with accursed weapons and superstitions concerning these, in particular with the so-called *Somnium sancti Anscarii*, or "Dream of St. Anscar" or "Vision of St. Anscar," in either manuscript or printed version. I believe I may be able to be of service because recently I came into possession of a large part of the book collection of a motion picture director, now deceased.

In your advertisement, you did not mention the reason for your interest in these works. This is only sound practice, and I do not intend to pry into the grounds of your possibly sorrowful interest.

Allow me to conclude by saying that I have in my possession a copy of the version printed by Meister Brandis, dated 1520, and you may write for further particulars at . . .

The return address was a Los Angeles post office box. George looked at it again, closely, and at the crest, which depicted a stylized column with a plume of smoke above it. To the left was half an eagle and to the right, a broadsword with the point up. The whole was surrounded by a wreath of oak leaves with acorns pendant and another eagle—whole—perched on top of the total assemblage.

There was no mention of price—and no wonder. The thought of the haggling ahead was most unpleasant to George, even though he had more money than ever before in his life. After all, the *Somnium* was a rare work, not even listed in van Beughem's great *Incunabula typographiae* of 1688. A later catalogue said the *Somnium* had been printed as part of an anti-papist pamphlet by Brandis, who had also translated it into "common German." Copies of the pamphlet had been burned in 1524 at Mölln and in 1525 at Lübeck, Copenhagen, and Greifswald. Several North German preachers that Jim Stanfield had discovered referred to things like *"unglaubliche Seppiesenwerck"* ("unbelieving Seppius-work") from 1528 on; and in 1544 a man called Clement Hasencleaver had been whipped out of the bounds of Segeberg in Holstein for assorted heresies, including a declaration to the effect that Jehovah would not punish sins of fathers even to the second generation, because that would make Merciful God a sort of associate of the "wicked wizard Seppius, whose story is told by Master Brandis in his book about the journey of Anscarius through the bounds of Hell."

A clan of early printers named Brandis had existed, and many of them had worked in North Germany. George wondered what this Master Brandis had thought, while printing the book, about hereditary curses. Printers had always been a radical lot. Had Brandis equated Seppius with the Pope? With Antichrist? (The language of religious debate in the early sixteenth century had been pretty rough.)

He shook his head and smiled. Just what was his obsession with blasphemy, now—another attempt to drift off the real subject of his worries?

Anyway . . . the Seeking Sword's documented history provided suggestions that heredity was involved, in some way. But that wasn't much help, because only kings and some rich, or rabbinical, families had pedigrees going back nearly a thousand years. The Seeking Sword had not crossed the path of anybody in either category, as far as he knew. Or had these been the shadowy people who wielded the sword through the hands of others?

Now it looked conceivable that even he, George Barry Quinterus, born March 5, 1934, might be conscripted as super-shaman, or Kill-thinker, though as far as he knew, all his ancestors had been good, clean-living, lower-class gentile bigots, with no fatal taint of any kind. Even his father's radicalism had only been par for his type of German heritage, limited to unionism and telling his children not to pay too much attention to the Jesuits. He'd agreed to let the children be raised in the Church, but that didn't mean they should ...

All of a sudden, something—perhaps only a subtle change in the light outside the living-room window with its blinds closely shut—caused a shiver to run down George's back. For the ten millionth time he wished he had never heard of the sword. A moment ago the possibility of his recruitment had caused him to smile. There was nothing funny about that. He hadn't said anything about it to Carnett and had done his best to avoid discussing it with Gloria, but the idea was really horrible.

Horrible was too anemic, pale, meaningless a word to describe the situation.

All right: he was in no physical danger. On that point, he had no choice except to trust his feelings. He had no immortal soul to worry about. Most likely, he was not headed for any trouble with the law either, because none of the John Lambert or Lewis Neumann types had any "leaked" visions like his. That left one possibility: his mind was somehow akin to those of the super-shamans, and even though they might be unaware of his existence so far, once they found out they would co-opt him into their ranks. The things he'd read about shamanism made that all the more likely because the "spirits" —or super-shamans—often literally forced a person to join. The reluctant future shaman might be literally struck by lightning, but more often he saw visions, became ill—and either died or became a shaman. A few people recovered and resumed normal lives, but they were decidedly exceptional. Most of the Chuckchi, Eskimo, Voguls, and other whoozises had grown up believing in spirits and shamanism, that whole ball of wax. He hadn't. This meant the super-shamans had less of a hold on him; or rather, would get less of a hold on him. Right?

Maybe. That, however, was suspiciously like trying to cheer himself up with the idea he was safe because shaman recruits usually started out with imaginary trips to the Other World. Literature was full of such accounts, from Black Elk to St. Fursey. Even Dante. The key word was *usually*. There was no shamanistic dogma. Maybe no medieval chronicler or modern anthropologist had ever gained the confidence of a super-shaman.

George got up and kicked the frame of the bedroom door, hard. There was no future in this brooding. Either he was relatively safe, because the idea was so alien to modern American thought—or he was lost, helpless, because he had never learned how to keep his own mind.

Still, he would find out. He had grim satisfaction in the thought. In six weeks, he'd be in Los Angeles; he could call on "TPR" then. In the meantime he had better get started dickering with him by mail—and never mind the super-shamans.

23

August 20, 1971

GEORGE GOT LOST twice on the hillside roads on the way to where "TPR" lived before he finally parked in the driveway of the Spanish-style building with its little grove of dusty palms. Air conditioners chugged in most of the visible windows, which were draped to shut out the fierce midafternoon sun. There was an air of neglect about the place, from the patchy brown lawn to dying shrubs and the cracked driveway and walk to the grandiose front door. A crack in one second-story window had been taped.

For a long moment, he sat in the air-conditioned comfort of the rented Pontiac. The decrepitness of the place made him uneasy, even though it was hard to imagine efficient Kill-thinkers or maniacal super-shamans—"You pays your money and you takes your choice," as Carnett had put it back at the end of July, three weeks ago—operating out of a place like this. Headquarters should have revolving antennas on the roof, or else it should be a ramshackle Victorian mansion, right out of the Munsters. Not . . . this.

Well, whoever was inside probably had his eyes on George right now. A large dog was barking. The corner of one first-floor curtain moved. George shivered, imagining himself in somebody's gun sights.

Hell. Nobody was going to shoot him like that. He had valuable information. He got out of the car, swallowing, and walked gingerly over to the carved front door, moving awkwardly because the .32 Police Positive he was carrying was pressing against the small of his back. He swallowed again. Odd that his throat should feel so dry. He pressed the doorbell marked with a small enamel crest. So TPR stood for Theodor P. Rauchampé. The red of the smoking column and the gold of the background both looked faded by the sunshine.

The chimes, which he could just barely hear, touched off a frenzied paroxysm of barking.

Vaguely, George wondered whether the big dog was running loose; then, to keep from worrying, he made himself think about Nixon's order freezing prices and wages—he wouldn't have thought the fool had that much sense, with those Chicago economists around him. Then he heard footsteps.

A voice, melodious and slightly accented, boomed from the intercom under the peephole. "Who is it, please?"

"I'm George Quinterus. I've come about the book."

"A-ha."

In the ensuing half-minute, George became aware

of sweat pouring down his face and back. He wiped his cheeks and forehead with the back of his hand as several heavy bolts shot back and the door opened to emit an icy blast of air.

The room beyond was large and dimly lit, with no dog in sight. The barking seemed to come from a closed door behind Mr. Rauchampé and George sighed, involuntarily, in relief.

The book dealer was a small man, perhaps an inch over five feet, fine-boned, with a beaky nose and white wisps of hair above slightly protrusive ears. He had a receding chin and a wide, thick-lipped mouth with startlingly white teeth. George thought he might be wearing violet contact lenses.

Mr. Rauchampé smiled. "Pardon my precautions, Mr. Quinterus, but you know the times we live in." His handshake was surprisingly strong. "Come on in. I trust your trip was uneventful?"

"Yeah." There seemed no point in admitting he had been in Los Angeles for ten days and expected to stay until mid-September. By then he should be sick—sick of story conferences and ready to hit the road.

"Sometimes visitors have difficulties finding my home."

By now, George was inside, out of the blasted sun, and he felt nothing ominous about the sound of the door closing behind him, especially since Rauchampé did not bolt it. His earlier fears appeared silly. One thing was sure, however; he, George Quinterus, was not cut out to be a secret agent.

"Please follow me." Mr. Rauchampé glided around George, past the door behind which the big dog was baying and snarling. The host was clad in dark purple polo shirt and violet, slightly flaring slacks, with little silver buckles on plain black sandals. His feet were bare and bony, of a kind with his hairless arms and hands. "Everything is ready in the library," he murmured.

The room was on the other side of the house, facing east; to get there they passed through three others, all large and dimly lit, crammed with antiques, with dark red Persian carpets. Gray dust lay thick on ornate tables and sideboards. The walls were masked by pictures: satyrs dancing in moonlight among trees, chained Andromedas confronting monsters, a large icon showing the flagellation of Christ in metallic gold and deep maroon.

The library was long and narrow with three muslin-shaded windows. Its inside wall was lined with books, many of them in ornate bindings. Near the far door sat a huge desk—not unlike Carnett's—and next to it a four-foot gilt-bronze Apollo on a black marble pedestal. Beyond the desk, three old-fashioned beige leather armchairs, comfortably stuffed, stood in a semi-circle around a low, oval greenish-marble table with gold inlay. Next to the table was a stand exactly like Apollo's—George recognized it as a miniature Corinthian column—surmounted by a black enamel tray with a dark green glass decanter and two goblets of gold-veined crystal.

"Have a seat, have a seat, Mr. Quinterus," Rauchampé said, indicating one of the chairs, on his way to pick up the decanter. "It's been on ice—not the genuine, *echtes* Krambambuli, you must understand, but I must say it does make a reasonable facsimile." He handed one glass to George, who was still standing, and raised the other. *"À l'honneur."*

"To honor," said George, puzzled. The liqueur was strong, pungent with the taste of unfamiliar herbs, quite pleasing in its sharpness and coldness. He praised its taste, then confessed his unfamiliarity with— Karambamli? Was that its name?

"Krambambuli," Rauchampé corrected him with an indulgent smile. "I am not surprised you have not heard of it, Mr. Quinterus. Even the . . . commercial version was not widely known beyond the borders of Liefland, and only a few households, before the *canaille* came to power, were still preparing the *echtes Nektar, Trank der Götter.*"

The accent was Teutonic, though different from that of other Germans George had encountered. In the next few minutes he found out why. Rauchampé's family had lived in the Tsar's Baltic provinces until the deplorable uprising of the *canaille*. It had been *schrecklich*—dreadful. George could not quite make out whether the old man—he must be over seventy—

was referring to the Russian Revolution or the nationalist wars of independence. At one point he said the English were as guilty as any for not having clamped down to save Riga in 1919.

George had worried about what he should say, but that was no problem; the problem was to get Rauchampé to shut up long enough so they could get to business. The man's perspective on history was strange and fascinating, but he'd come to buy the *Somnium*.

Rauchampé had fought for right and honor, but after the Western politicians sold truth and honor down the river—the phrase sounded odd in his accented English—he had come to America, where his family had certain investments. Somehow—George managed to speed him through this part—he had come to live in Beverly Hills, where he kept busy, despite his age, with many, many interests in music, rare books, art, his financial interests in the art gallery, two boutiques, etcetera, etcetera. Rauchampé must be a lonely man.

He and George had two more glasses each. George lit a cigarette and Rauchampé accepted a light for an oval, pungent cigarette in a long holder. While George was endeavoring to get back to the subject the older man suddenly said it was a pity no one appreciated old books—really old books—anymore, even though the work of the best sixteenth- and seventeenth-century printers had rarely been equaled. He had an edition of Aretino, for example.

"Youth has been an especial disappointment to me, especially in recent years," said Rauchampé. "So few of them are interested in the genuinely artistic, the true things of the spirit. All they care about is surfing and music—if you can call *that* music."

George agreed wholeheartedly, adding that all this was very pleasant but that he had another appointment in ninety minutes. He was still trying to remember the name of a suburb that would make the lie authentic when Rauchampé stood up with a heartfelt sigh.

"This pace," he mumbled. "This pace. It will yet kill me."

George could not understand the rest. He sat back and had another cigarette going when the old man returned with a black enamel tray under his arm. He handed it to George.

"Yes, yes," said Rauchampé abruptly. "Put it on your knees. Yes."

He refilled their glasses and walked to the bookcase. George heard things being moved around. Then Rauchampé returned with a thin book.

"*Violà*." He dropped it onto the tray on George's knees and returned to his chair, where he took a long sip of Krambambuli.

Neither man said anything for a long moment. George glanced at the book. It didn't look like much: no covers, 5-by-7 inches, a quarter-inch thick, title page all but obliterated by a reddish stain over which several people had scrawled their names, sometimes adding dates; he made out "*1622*" near the lower right-hand corner under an undecipherable signature, and a bold "*1650*" in the middle behind the name "*Theschenius*." There was also a dark blue rubber-stamped, "LASSETTE ET CIE., NANCY" in the upper right-hand corner.

He opened the book: The paper was creamy white, amazingly soft and clear in spite of age. Actually, of course, nothing was amazing about this. Sixteenth-century paper was made almost entirely of linen. The pages were unnumbered, closely covered with black Gothic letters known as "Fraktur" in America. Nine-point type on eleven-point slugs.

The place where George had flipped the book open seemed to deal with a violent denunciation of false shepherds, with wolves' teeth on their staffs. Hmmm. Everybody agreed that Master Brandis' pamphlet had been an anthology of anti-papal polemics, some contemporary and some much older, dating back at least to the Hohenstaufen emperors' struggle with thirteenth-century popes.

"I was interested in the story of St. Anscar's vision," George remarked.

"*Bestimmt*. Begin, yes, about five pages before the middle," said Rauchampé, who had been regarding George with avid curiosity.

The writer turned pages—yes, that seemed to be the vision section, with no pages missing. Now all he could hope was that these hundred pages would be worth $1,500. Fortunately he had the whole weekend to himself; the people at the studio thought he would be going back to Cincinnati.

He looked up. Mr. Rauchampé looked away.

"This looks all right."

"I am gratified you think so." The old man took a deep breath. "I have a question for you, if you don't mind."

"Sure."

"I would like to ask you for the reason of your interest. Swords are fascinating, but . . . your letters seemed to indicate a more personal concern." He sounded almost pleading.

"I am merely acting as an agent." George and Gloria had agreed on this line. He felt slightly foolish—once he had thought it might give him a few seconds' edge, like leaving the key in the ignition, but right now he just wanted to pay and get out.

"I had thought so," Rauchampé said, sounding disappointed. "I had thought so—but do you think he, your employer, might still be interested in a discussion of concerns?"

"Could be," said George, thinking fast. "You might write him directly about this." And he gave Rauchampé Nick Gobel's post office box number in New York.

"Thank you." The old man wrote it down. "And his name is?"

"I am not at liberty to reveal that." It sounded like a line from a bad movie.

"Bestimmt." Rauchampé was right on cue. "Of course. You may tell him, Mr. Quinterus, that my forebears have had some bad experiences with Seppié and his sword, both of which are described therein." He appeared to shudder. "I came in possession of the book quite recently, and now that I have read it, please allow me to say it is not unpleasant for me to get it out of my house. At a good price, too, I might add."

Oh my God, thought George.

Rauchampé smiled, his teeth flashing very white. "Might I ask you about the size of your commission?"

George took a deep breath. Mr. Rauchampé smiled.

"Now that I know how to contact your employer, it would be a simple matter for me to inform him that your . . . shall we say, boorishness, queered the deal." He paused. Thirty seconds clicked past, one by one. "Your commission?"

"Fifteen percent," said George, gritting his teeth.

"I see." After another, longer pause Rauchampé stood up. "Don't take it so hard, Mr. Quinterus. After all, it is not your money." A pause. "You have the traveler's checks, I assume."

"Yeah." George no longer tried to hide his annoyance—and yes, he would go through with it. He pulled out the blue American Express checks and stood quietly, seething, as Rauchampé compared his signature on them with the signatures on his Ohio driver's license and a couple of credit cards. "Do you want me to sign them over to you?" he asked, seeking to keep his voice under control.

"That will not be necessary. A rubber stamp I have." Rauchampé winked in what was no doubt meant to be a confidential manner, and added, very smoothly: "Now, about commissions. Don't you think I deserve one . . . Fifty percent of yours?"

George swallowed—always advisable before smashing somebody in the face. But the little bastard had doubtless taken precautions.

"I am sure you can make this up on expenses," the old man said, trying to sound ingratiating.

"I guess so." George didn't even feel like trying to bargain; he might lose control. "Look—can I write you a check?"

"Certainly. I trust you are a man of honor."

"Yeah."

24

August 22, 1971

ONCE, GEORGE HAD looked forward to celebrating when he got hold of the *Somnium,* but the taste in his mouth was too bad. Instead, he ordered a pizza sent to his furnished kitchenette apartment and started working, first transcribing the text and then translating the key passages, hardly stopping to think what the words implied. Forty hours went by in a kind of blur. And here he was on Sunday afternoon, rubbing his eyes and staring at the dusty palm trees outside his window.

Done!

His eyes fell on the heap of typewritten sheets on the table, thirty-eight double-spaced pages with many corrections and strikeovers. There might be other references to the Seeking Sword in the book, but he could hunt for these later. Right now, he couldn't face any more of the violent diatribes; and he even felt perversely glad that the pamphlet's six signatures had come apart when he fell asleep Friday, lying on the sofa-bed with clothes on. George Quinterus wasn't a book collector in the same sense as most of T. P. Rauchampé's customers. He'd bought the *Somnium* to read.

In a way, the book had been a disappointment, like everything connected with the Seeking Sword, everything connected with this trip—maybe he should now visit Betsy and Rita in San Diego? No. Not yet, anyway. He was supposed to be here to work on the screenplay.

All of a sudden he felt angry—at himself for letting his hopes build up, at Seppius, as it was most often spelled in the *Somnium*, Kill-thinkers and super-shamans, at Gloria for probably being right, at the book's author. Why couldn't he have used plain language instead of crappy Biblical metaphors and roundabout paraphrases? Of course, hoping for a guidebook had been stupid, but this was almost enough to make a skeptic believe in widespread conspiracies.

"Damn."

Here he was, on a hot bright Sunday afternoon, two weeks before Labor Day, a cup of instant coffee in his hand, a slight headache and general feeling of malaise, facing the worst: reading his damned translation and seeking to make sense out of it. He had tried to function as much like an automaton as possible, earlier; otherwise a job like this could take weeks, and he had a sort of 9-to-5 job again, for a change.

The coffee tasted as he might have expected it to. Ugh.

He turned on the FM part of the motel console radio-television set, recalled the bottle of Jack Daniel's he had brought along to celebrate, shrugged, sipped some coffee, lit a cigarette, and sat in the armchair, grimacing at the commercial for a boutique. The sounds of something by Mancini filled the room as George started to read.

The first five or six pages described the voyages and deeds of Anscar, ninth-century missionary, first bishop of Hamburg and probably the first to preach the Gospel in Sweden if not Denmark. A diatribe followed on how bishops were no longer what they used to be, and then:

Anscar, also, was favored often with visions of what to sinful man is hidden as a matter of course, glimpses of the bright golden meadows of Heaven and of the Fiery Pit. Often did the venerable man wake as though from a faint and recount to his fellows of what he had seen, his discourses with saints and angels, men and animals in other places, demons and the damned, and among these latter the renowned Seppius, the wicked, evil sorcerer and spellcaster who loosed yet another curse on this sin-laden world. And mightily did he howl, this Seppius de Perditio, when despite all his curses and spells, also called *woimenesannatzet,* he, the aforesaid Seppius, was dangled head-foremost in those same flames that forever play along Phlegethon Stream. He who had often boasted that the feeblest of his grandsons was yet able to turn himself to a salmon to swim swiftly beneath the Styx, or the River of Fire, to and from the castles of the spirits. Yet nothing availed then Seppius his boasts, not his curses either, and well would it behoove all men, Holsten, Wagren, Wilzen, and others of the Wendish nations, and Pruzzi as well, to keep this in mind. Of all *waideleren* was Seppius greatest, and yet the holy man saw him thusly, hanging with head-hair streaming among ever-burning yet never-consuming flames, for ever and ever. And let the same be said to the others also, the men of Funen and Liefländer, Kurs and heathen men of Leal and Ösel, warriors and farmers, *waideleren, noiten* and *sannaszeppen,* that no words of power are there save the name of the One True God, All-Merciful, nor swords of power either that might prevail against Him . . .

A peculiar passage, full of both classical and contemporary allusions. The Norse god Loki could change himself to a salmon and so did the heroes of the Finnish *Kalevala.* (In recent months, George had read a lot of mythology.) The Styx—spelled Stichs—might be the River of Tuonela; or it might not. Most mythologies featured rivers of fire. Wends were Western Slavs who lived mostly in sections of present-day East Germany before the Germans conquered the lands east of the Elbe River. Wilzen and Wagren were Wendish tribes, but the Holsten or Holsteiners were not Slavic. The Pruzzi had been the natives of East Prussia; the Kurs had lived in Latvia; Liefländer or Livonians, in both Latvia and Estonia; Ösel and Leal were part of Estonia, according to George's old German gazetteer; and Funen or Fyn, most incongruously, was one of the Danish islands. A German book that George had read in June referred to *waideleren* as

151

heathen priests—shamans, possibly—of the Prussians; *noite* was Lappish and Finnish for "sorcerer" or "shaman." The other two words—*Sannaszeppen* and *Woimenesannatzet*—he did not know, but they seemed to be somehow related.

So much for the first passage. Then, after a digression about the Red Sea and Israelites, the misdeeds of Moslems—at which point George went and fished out the bottle of Jack Daniel's—and mighty deeds then recently done in the Holy Land by Heinrich Walport and Heinrich von Salza as well as King Richard of England, and in Livonia by "Winne the Pious" and "Volkewein the Brave," the author got back his subject after still another incredible digression about certain Roman emperors.

. . . Even worse than the aforesaid magicians at Julian's court was the aforesaid Seppius, also called Tautewoimateyn, most malignant and intractable of sorcerers, fiery of breath and deathly of eye-cast, who was wont to travel through aerial realms on the back of a demon—Apolinara by name—with batlike wings and a member of solid brass, and who did compel this aforesaid demon, then, after strife, to enter into the swordblade in a steamy, fiery, flaming pit whereafter the said demon would bring about his goal of stirring up strife among men. Ever since has that strife raged, on earth and in Hell, beginning with the deaths of the false kinsmen of the aforesaid Seppius, as the vulgar say, and more recently the aforesaid strife has consisted of the hunting down and slaying of the sword-cursed folk. Now, it is written: The LORD says He will punish the sins of fathers even unto the seventh generation; but in the nighted regions of the North, by the shores of Moremarusa this so-called avenging of alleged wrongs has gone on, men say, for seventy times seven generations. And so strong is the might of the demon, Seppius, and so sinful the ways of men that even the coming of the holy religion of Our Lord, Jesus Christ, has made no difference perceptible in the broadest daylight; for the Dithmarscher's hand is as swift to draw the sword as ever, and the Holsteiner's only slightly less so. [Dithmarschen: the western part of Schleswig-Holstein, roughly from the Elbe River to the Danish border.] Even as the self-willed and fore-ordained immolation of himself by Sir Jesus sufficed not to purge the hearts of men of gruesome wickedness, manifested among other things by the adoration and worship of wooden idols of demons more loathsome than Nero, Julian, or Caligula, and of the accursed flaming eggs [or testicles; *flammendeeier* might mean either] from out of which was engendered the Death that stalks these lands by day and night. Indeed, a special curse is laid upon these lands, a sign of the wrath of the LORD, for no good does it do to lay the evil sword on the holy altar, or to burn him [*sic*] in fire; and when Ingalangues, a pagan but still concerned for his immortal soul, for good reason, gave the accursed seeking blade to the venerable Willibrortus, that aforesaid saintly man did cast this sword into the ocean sea, half a day's sailing from the Hadeland. Yet barely had a single generation passed to rest in the name of the LORD before, for their sins, Seppius came forth again from the black and dark green waves, to the white sandy shores, to bloodily rage among them who dwell in the *Wurtten* of Hadeland . . .

Hadeland was the German coast between Bremerhaven and Hamburg and *Wurt* must be local dialect for "village on artificial mound." Willibrortus—there had been a St. Willibrord, an Englishman trying to convert what the eighth-century English called Old Saxons—must have thrown the Seeking Sword into the North Sea. Half a day's sail must be at least twenty miles, probably more, and George had no idea of that sea's depth. Were there lobstermen, pots and all, back then? Anyway, in thirty years or so, the Seeking Sword was back ashore and Seppius had conducted another massacre of the ignorant by the unknowing.

But how had the sword reached land? Had successive storms shoved it along the sea bottom? If not, what happened? Had Seppius sent people to dive for it, somehow knowing the right spot? Incredible. But then, what about the Seeking Sword wasn't?

George took another swig of sour-mash whiskey, skipped two pages devoted mostly to homilies, and stopped at a particularly intriguing passage:

> Some say that, even though prayers and relics avail not at all in this regard, there are men whose very presence, by grace of the LORD, can cause a slumber to overcome the steely eyelids of the aforesaid Tautewoimateyn, who speaks with those of sword-cursed blood who allow him to, to ask for a place where he may rest. And so it is, sad to recount, that exorcism by a properly consecrated priest of good life and family antecedents in a church pure of all pollution have had no effect whatsoever upon the evil sword that hunts men to their deaths in their own courtyards, even on their own dungheaps. Beyond any doubt whatsoever does the LORD manifest His purposes in ways too wondrous to recount. A forebear of the Abbot Berthold, Minferth by name, kept the aforesaid sword in his house, and forty years the accursed blade slept in peace, all slaughters in the land ceasing. And of this Sir Minferth was it said, as of Ingalangues, and that Dudileaf mentioned in vulgar song:
>
> > Long slept the sword-blade in his home,
> > snugly under warm hearthstone.

The final couplet had been in a kind of Early Low German, barely comprehensible; in fact George was only one-third certain of his translation. And then, after five long sentences about Minferth's piety and three interminable sentences praising the martyr's crown that Berthold had earned on a crusade to Livonia—undated, but presumably around 1200—the narrative continued:

> Soon after the glorious news [of peace proclaimed by the Emperor Friedrich I, presumably

about 1156], Minferth died and was buried in St. Martin's church at Huimal; but not a single year went by before an impious, godless evildoer, terrible to relate, broke through to beneath the tombstone in the aforesaid house of the LORD, and took up the sword and ring that had been laid in Minferth's sepulcher as a result of the sinful pride of his kinsmen. The malefactor was never since seen, nor heard of, though no doubt he came to a dreadful end. Pray for him, and other sinful men, including those deluded by Seppius. We cannot say now what has become of the sword of the aforesaid Seppius, it being altogether too possible that the Enemy of Mankind, baffled and angry and dismayed at how the true doctrine has spread, lighting up the former realms of deep darkness, has removed for a time his worn-out handiwork for reforging in the flames of the Pit for the further tempting and testing of men who willingly and joyfully have taken upon their shoulders the sweet yoke of Sir Jesus.

In addition to these, dozens of other passages dealt with Seppius, Sepio, Theotechse-Wannach, Tautewoimateyn, Apolinara, Seppihizonna, and other oddly named people and their doings. None of that was very clear, though they all had something to do with Seppius—the most frequent spelling of the name. In between were dreary passages about local history, mostly of Schleswig-Holstein, Mecklenburg, and the feuds of various country squires and the city of Lübeck, but the author had paid no attention to chronology, skipping from the times of Emperor Heinrich IV (1056–1106) to those of the pretender Alfonso of Castile in the 1260s. Repeated hints were made that the murders ascribed to Seppius were part of a blood feud—and in that region of Europe blood feuds continued almost until the American Revolution. (Corsica and the Balkans were not the only areas where ancient customs endured despite Enlightenment; not to mention the Hatfields and McCoys, and others, even later.) Depending on the page, Seppius controlled the Seeking Sword, or the demon—Apolinara or whatever—

155

that handled the sword; or Seppius was the demon, or sword, or the curse. The contradictory statements were maddening.

His $1612.50 had probably been money wasted, George thought bitterly. Worse yet: the super-shamans' current North American branch manager might be showing his contempt by taking George's savings for a copy of a work of obfuscation produced to put off some long-dead investigator.

Hell. He shook his head, drank deeply from the bottle, and rubbed his eyes.

Okay. Maybe he was taking the excessively gloomy view of the situation. If the bastards behind the Seeking Sword had bothered to produce the *Somnium,* that alone meant they were not invulnerable. The very fact of his getting a copy of the *Somnium* from the super-shamans—if Rauchampé was on that team—meant that George was at least somewhere close.

So cheer up, old buddy.

He took another drink, wondering whether he should call Gloria. But what could he tell her besides "I miss you, darling," and "Very likely I got took?" He could call her tomorrow, after finishing this, a decent dinner, and a day's work at the studio.

The story about Sir Minferth was followed, eventually, by an account of bloody rites that had been practiced before his time at Assachwenmaege, a cluster of old collapsed buildings somewhere in eastern Holstein. Assachwenmaege was a place where "the vulgar" had formerly brought sacrifices to the *Suchendeschwerdt,* or Seeking Sword because once upon a time Seppius had rested thirty-one years in the main building. The *Somnium* didn't say when, or for how long, but it must have been well before 1100. In any case, the country folk didn't want the curse of the sword to return upon them, according to the *Somnium,* and so they sacrificed game, ducks, and geese, and later sheep and pigs, even though the area had been officially Christian since the 900s. Anyway, one day a man was slain with the *Suchendeschwerdt* and thereafter the country folk took to making greater sacrifices: cows, horses, and finally three-year-old children while Seeking

156

Sword murders went on and on, even after "a pious valiant lord, Eigo" razed the buildings.

Sir Eigo did not just burn the hovels of Assachwenmaege; he also hanged half a dozen peasants for sacrilege and murder. The author of the *Somnium* described the proceedings in detail, approvingly. But that did not stop the murders; the book listed four additional victims by name and implied there were others before the sword "came to rest underneath the hearthstone" of Sir Minferth's hall some time around 1120.

As George Quinterus read all this, he saw that the author and other presumably well-informed contemporaries did not think of the killings in terms of any organization. The author, in fact, seemed to regard the sword as somehow set apart from the whole Christian scheme of things. Apparently no one had suspected Sir Minferth of consorting with the powers of evil in the forty years he kept the sword in his house. The killings stopped in that time, sure. But on one occasion Minferth forced another squire to back down in a lawsuit by threatening that he "would take the aforesaid sword to that village wherein live the Aiseipelinger, to cast the sword down before the church door, and see what fruit might sprout thereof." The implication, clearly, was that Minferth knew the sword "rested" at his pleasure—or in his presence.

Further on, the *Somnium* mentioned people whose *Heyll*—an old German word meaning "virtue," "holiness," "good fortune," half a dozen other things including "mana"—apparently neutralized the sword's evil. The author now seemed to take it for granted that the killings were part of the aforementioned blood feud.

George shook his head in wonder. Assuming thirty years to a generation, seven times seventy generations would amount to 14,700 years; even assuming a then common sixteen years per generation, the feud would have started at a time when much of Europe was covered with glaciers. More likely, though, the figure came from the Bible or some medieval numerologist, as nutty as his modern counterparts.

One more point: the sword had been an object of worship. Seppius had regarded the worshippers as expendable, just as present-day men who killed with the Seeking Sword appeared to be expendable. The attitudes of the super-shamans had remained unchanged —the *Somnium* recorded no attempt to avenge the execution of two Seeking Sword killers and apparently Sir Eigo had never worried about being slashed to death.

So where did all that leave him, now?

How could he know? He got to his feet, upsetting the chair, and went to the bathroom. Okay, he wasn't worried about being killed, the way he once had been. On the other hand, he wasn't easy in his mind. The visions—he shuddered at the half-feelings of rightness —implied he was neither killer nor victim and, goddammit, he didn't want to be a Seppius or Minferth either. All he could do was wait, hope for the best, try to get over brooding about the moral implications of sending the sword forth to kill and nurturing—recharging?—the sword in between times.

25

November 1, 1971

As THINGS TURNED out, he got over his worry sooner than he'd expected. First, there had been work on the screenplay and then publicity tour No. 1, brief stop at home, tour No. 2, another trip to Los Angeles, tour No. 3 to Minneapolis and environs, home for five days, tour No. 4, an L.A. encore, tour No. 5 and here he was, home again.

The cab driver was voluble, with a raspy voice, full of opinions about the lousy war, the louse in the White

House, and what some louse musta done to the ten-year-old girl whose corpse had been found in the brush near Highland Heights, just across the Ohio River. The body was decomposed, sure, but it hadda be a sex crime, right?

Naturally. It hadn't been a Seeking Sword murder because, regardless of what you might think of Seppius, he apparently didn't go after women or children. On the other hand, George mused, there hadn't been any Seeking Sword murders in Cincinnati for decades—not that this meant anything.

"That sure was a shame about the little girl," he said while the cabbie was clearing his throat. "I hope they catch the guy and fix him, good. By the way, there haven't been any other sicky murders lately, have there?"

The cabbie thought it over. "Just the usual," he said. "Niggers and hillbillies, shooting and stabbing each other."

"I see." He sat back, relaxing, feeling lucky and uneasy at the same time.

The cabbie took the oblique left turn up Clifton Avenue, pulling around a panel truck that was having trouble with the 30 degree incline of the street. George smiled; it wouldn't be long now.

"Here we are," the cabbie said.

He had kept up his barrage, mostly about tomorrow's election, but George had hardly heard a word. That was probably just as well. He paid up, and carried his suitcase into the apartment.

It smelled a bit musty, but obviously Gloria had been around. The thought crossed George's mind that she must really care—maybe he was her neurosis—because it would have been easier for her to haul all the green stuff to Mount Adams in her little blue Saab. He wouldn't miss the philodendrons. But knowing she had not been around, in these rooms, since he left on October 15 would have cast a blight on homecoming.

He tossed his suitcase on the sofa.

Okay, maybe it sounded too rah-rah, but the hotel rooms certainly hadn't been home. For one thing, the old Royal was here, in this room. He'd written *Thoughts That Kill* in this room. The beers that inspired him had come out of the refrigerator in the kitchen, there, to his right. He went and got one, a Coors that had survived as a souvenir of his last homecoming. He flipped the tab on the floor. Hell, man, he was home!

She wouldn't get off for a half-hour, so there was no point calling; she was usually busy just before closing time. He'd better call Mrs. Lyndell, though, and tell her he was the person moving around downstairs. The dear old lady worried about burglars, with some justification. He took a long draught before flopping down in the old armchair to dial the landlady's number.

Five painful minutes later, he stood up and stretched. Ahhhh . . . and the can was almost empty. Hmmm. Light rain was beating against the window when he walked to the desk where Gloria had stacked the mail, neatly in five heaps. The typewriter was covered; the dimestore ashtray was clean, and next to it lay an unopened package of Winstons and a matchbook from a hotel in Portland. George was glad she had been here, that she had a key, that they had met.

The letters from his agent and publisher could wait. They were unopened, something that Betsy— He shook his head. Forget Betsy.

Remember Gloria. G-L-O-R-I-A. Okay, he couldn't call her and chitchat, not right now. She had work to do and that was one of the things he liked about her. She had her own life and would continue to. It was better so, because this way neither would have to spend too much time thinking about the other. They both had lived by themselves too long for the you-are-the-world-to-me bunk to work out, anyway.

He shook his head at his thoughts. Neither of them had said anything out loud about renegotiating the no-strings-attached relationship—and here he was, building castles on air like a teen-ager. Hmph. He did not even know whether the lady would care for any change in the present situation. Her first marriage, after all, had been a bad trip—partly because of the bum's attitude about having a family.

"At least that's the way I've got to keep looking at it," he said aloud, smiling. So-o-o, if each of them would stick to their respective worlds, he might as well get to work in his.

There was an envelope with German stamps. Yes. From Jim, over there on a fellowship. A nice, fat envelope.

George went to get another beer. He might as well read in comfort, in the old armchair. Its seat was starting to feel lumpy. But so what? He skimmed quickly over the badly typed pages about fall weather, beer schmecking gut after dusty hours, etcetera. Yeah. Then: Jim's hopes that Zacharias Werner (1768–1823) had known more than he let on were unjustified, and ditto for other Romantics. In the case of Hermione Trauttewin, however, Jim had struck pay dirt. A thin vein, more than likely. An editor of the periodical that published her poem had written that the lady's home territory abounded in traditions of accursed swords and rings of good and bad fortune.

"This got me to thinking," Jim added. "I'd bet half the folks who got hold of wishing rings ended up in bad trouble; and some of the Grimm brothers' disciples, like Schermerberg, even have a special category of tales about a 'stranger with a sword acting as agent of divine vengeance.' Some of these 'sinister divine swordsmen' (I'll save you the German thereof) don't kill the grandpa who abused the ring, but only his son. Sch. even has an Estonian proverb in a footnote, about the sword of death and the ring of wishing being hatched from one egg. Figure that out."

George turned to the letter with renewed interest, but after several more pages he put it aside with a sigh. At best it might make some footnotes to the *Somnium*. Anyway, it was 5:45 and he'd better call Gloria if they wanted to go to a good restaurant . . .

Gloria was glad he was back, but she couldn't come over or go out because there was a political meeting, and she had promised, and—

"Oh, all right!"

"Look, it won't last all night," she said, sounding hurt. "Besides, you didn't tell me when you'd be back today. So I thought . . ."

So he'd thought, too. He had missed her more than

he would care to admit—much more than he'd expected, to the extent of making him go around antique shops looking for gifts.

"As I was saying, the meeting should be over before ten, and I could come over afterwards. Or we could meet someplace." She paused. "Where?" she asked softly.

"Fine with me," he said.

"What do you mean?"

"I mean . . . why don't you call me after the meeting and we can meet halfway, or something." He was prepared to be gracious.

"Are you sure?" He said nothing. "About meeting halfway, I mean," she added. "It's a lousy night, and you might not want to be out driving."

"Out driving by then, you mean."

"I didn't say that!"

True. But it had been in the back of her mind that by ten o'clock he would be in no shape for the rain-slick streets, probably too drunk, period. Memories of some past occasions flashed through his mind. She had a point.

"Of course, you didn't say that," he told her.

Her tone revealed her uncertainty; and that, in a way, was worse than a scolding. "Then . . . I'll call you after the meeting is over," she decided.

"Fine."

"Are you sure?"

"Yeah. Fine. I won't be drunk, either."

"Oh." A pause, and she came back, brightly, about things that didn't matter: the performance of Saabs on icy hillsides, and dumb things the Citizens' League for Decency had come up with, and a poem she had come across at work—something by an African writer named Birago Diap—and how she wished writers didn't have to go through this ordeal of local talk shows and associated crap.

He agreed, almost apologizing. She cared, too! When they hung up, he barely resisted the impulse to make a kissing sound over the telephone.

"Let's see, now," he told himself after a minute of pleasant reverie. "Plenty of jug wine, but beer's getting low."

Okay, since he was going to be good, he might as well replenish the larder. He would need beer, fresh bread, luncheon meat, milk, orange juice, and bacon to replace the hideous gray-streaked strips in the refrigerator.

By the time he got back it was close to seven, and dark. He kicked off his wet shoes, wiggled his toes luxuriously, stowed the supplies, took the next-to-last can of Coors, and sat down.

Ahh . . . Let's see, now. Before he called Gloria, he'd been doing something— Yeah, he'd been reading Jim's letter, something about swordsmen, strangers clutching swords, swordhilts like—

He could almost feel one in his right hand, the comfortable roughness of old, petrified leather thongs around the solid, heavy, dark, iron tang. Exactly right for a man's hand, unslippable, the best-made swordhilt of all time, all the world.

Swordhilt?!? Oh no! Not again!

He tried to fight it, to banish the fearful sensation of feeling the sword in his grip—after all, he was right here, in his living room, sure as hell, without any sword in his hand. He could see it, though, almost . . .

He might even be able to tip off the cops while there was still time. Lewis Neumann had lurked in the alley for hours, waiting for Hahmeier. Neumann's thoughts had been full of clues, only George had been half-drunk and hadn't realized what was happening. This time would be different, because he knew what was happening.

Rain was blowing in his face—in his eyes, too. Leafless trees were groaning in the northwesterly wind. Why didn't the cheap bastards put up more street lights . . . ? Every house in the development looked alike, except for their TV antennas—but it was too damn dark to see these, anyway. All he could do was trudge on, on wet feet, his eyes bleary, probably catching a cold like real-life firemen did at this season, and . . . There! Somehow the knowledge seeped from swordhilt to hand, up his arm, shoulder, neck, into his mind: around the corner to the left. Hah! He could cut through the backyards— No, better not. Old Joe surely didn't want to end up with a blasted dog chewing his ankle. Old Joe had work to do—real, important work. Those fires. Why did there have to be so many? He stayed on the sidewalks. When a dog barked, somewhere, he crossed himself with his left hand because the right was clutching the sword under his coat.

A sign was on the corner but Old Joe never raised his eyes. Didn't wipe them either; he'd just get more water in them, and there would be plenty of time in a moment or two, right at the firehouse (heh, heh) door!

Damn! George bit his lip. Why couldn't Old Joe have looked? But even if he had, it wouldn't have helped much, because which suburb was this? Not grand enough for Amberley Village, but anywhere in a twenty-five-mile radius in Ohio, Kentucky, or Indiana would be a good guess.

The house for which Old Joe (Peiten? Paytna? Paitnas?) was headed stood fourth from the corner. It looked like the others, but as far as Joe was concerned there was a special, malevolent glow to the light shining through a gap in the picture-window drapes, in the slanting roof dimly visible against the cloud cover, the way the parked car loomed in the driveway. A sense of desperate urgency overcame Old Joe and he broke into a run, stopped, and started up again, while George kept screaming "No! No! Don't!" in his mind, heedless of possible danger—because if he could pick up Old Joe's thoughts, the Killthinkers might be picking up his, as well.

Coldly, grimly, desperately, George began thinking at Old Joe and his controllers, telling them to stop, for God's sake!

Joe halted a few feet from the door. George became conscious of a welling-up of reluctance—a crappy expression, but it seemed to describe the feeling involved —in the mind of the wet, cold man; and then gradually—he must have stood there for almost a minute —a sort of steely resolve prevailed over his thoughts that murder was wrong. But what did putting out a baleful fire have to do with murder? Old Joe's feet started moving once more, step after slowly taken step, until his toe bumped the welcome mat. He reached out to ring the bell with stubby forefinger, wiped his face with his damp sleeve.

George caught a glimpse of him in the storm-door glass as chimes sounded and the overhead light came on: heavy-set, square jaw, bulbous nose and heavy eyebrows, dark shadows under the eyes, battered hat pulled forward, short navy blue coat soaked through the shoulders. He almost gasped at the man's thoughts that maybe, at long last, it would be all over, and he could sleep long—sleep, sleep, and go home to his family. Old Joe Paytna's thoughts about his wife, two married daughters, and grandchildren sent a pang through George's mind; he had not expected the Kill-thinkers' zombies to retain any human feelings.

The front door opened, and it was all over. Old Joe pulled the storm door open and then, with incredible speed, his right hand came out from under his coat. The Seeking Sword flashed.

The victim was slight, thin, balding, with horn-rimmed glasses and bad teeth. His mouth opened in a soundless scream, his thin hands came up an instant too late to keep his throat from being slashed literally from ear to ear. Dropping a bit, the Seeking Sword, which really seemed to drag Old Joe's hand and arm along, also put a gash on the thin man's left forearm, withdrew, and then plunged forward into the solar plexus, halfway up to the hilt.

George's mind reeled under the onslaught of gleeful, relieved, unqualified rightness and the ensuing welter of mental images that somehow explained all: evil fires turned to rain-sodden ashes, dogs licking up evil blood and vomiting, nightmare monsters, women and children waiting among burning buildings—And all of a sudden, there was Old Joe walking away, bent over, with rain beating on his head. This had been okay, and maybe the last one, but a man never knew because fires kept blazing up. A man had no choice really. He'd tried running, he'd tried throwing it away —but Seppiyeh always caught up. "Do your duty, your duty as a man," Old Joe said savagely to himself. "Yes. Do your duty and get hung for it." Not this man. He had obligations to his family, the fault wasn't his, he was a plain working man without money to buy fancy lawyers, so he'd best keep his big nose clean . . .

George Quinterus' final memory—impression, rather—was of a mid-1960s sedan parked near a street light. Except that he had no idea how far and which way the firehouse was. Firehouse? Anyway, as Old Joe drove away, his eyes flicked over a street sign: Paddystow Road.

Paddystow Road? Now where—? George got to his feet, wondering why he felt halfway relieved when he ought to be utterly appalled. The feeling was frightening. Anyway, he should find Paddystow Road so he could call the right cops.

Call them—and tell them what?

He stopped, his left foot in the air. What could he tell them? That the killer's name was Joe . . . Paytna, Paitnas, Peiten, Beiden, in his fifties, Catholic, mechanically inclined—and how had he learned that?—a family man who had unwillingly committed several murders. The police would ask him how he knew and . . . Shit! He smashed his fist against his right thigh, hard, hoping it would leave a bruise.

A man was dead and there wasn't a thing he could do! He probably wouldn't recognize Old Joe in the street.

Suddenly George realized how earnestly he hoped never to see him again, and recollections of what he'd tried to do while the door opened made him feel cold all over. Listening in was one thing; there were circumstances under which eavesdropping had merit. But yelling out loud at such a time was dumb. Real dumb.

How long would it take Old Joe to drive here? Or, rather: how long would it take the Kill-thinkers? Almost three minutes had already passed since Joe was standing in front of the door and George was trying to warn the victim. Three minutes. At this hour, a car could cover a mile in three minutes.

George dashed to the bedroom for his plaid jacket. Let's see, where was the gun? Yeah. There. Smyser's was a good place, in walking distance, and dark enough so a man sitting in the back would have a certain advantage. Only, he'd better not think about the tavern in terms of its name or exact location. And thank God for Gloria's political meeting.

26

November 2 to 8, 1971

DRINKING HIS COFFEE Tuesday morning, George felt deeply ashamed of having panicked and run, without warning Gloria. But how could he? Besides, she had said she would call, not come over.

When she took her break from being an election judge and called—about 9:30—he decided, on the spur of the moment, to play it cool.

"I called last night," she said. "Several times."

"Uh-uh." He was trying to think of how to begin.

"Sitting at home . . . Oh, hell, George, what happened?"

"I—I had another vision, about a murder out in Urban Grove. And I thought maybe I should get out of the house for a while because the leakage may be two-way, and—"

"You mean you saw the Ashley murder while it was happening?" She sounded incredulous and he could just picture her face.

He nodded, then realized she couldn't see it, and said: "Yes, I saw it."

"Did you nod just now?" she asked.

He said: "Yes, why?"

"I just wondered." Gloria was calm but she was clearly concerned as she asked just what he had seen.

He told her in some detail, finishing with descriptions of the dark, rain-wet street as he hurried to

Smyser's and the way everything had looked when he came slinking back after midnight. "I thought of calling you, but I didn't know where the rally was. Later, I decided you could use a good night's sleep."

"You were right, there," she said, her voice sort of tinkly. Then, more gravely, she asked whether anything he'd seen might help the police.

"The killer's name, maybe," he said. "Only I'm not sure how it's spelled and I get the idea he's from some other city. I don't know where."

"How do you know that?"

"It's part of the package, like the way I know my life isn't in any danger but my—hell, call it my personality—may be." He felt his face turn red.

"That's been in danger for years," she said, trying to make light of the situation.

"What do you mean?"

"Nothing," she told him with a chuckle. "What I mean is, you have a tendency to get carried away and then you tend to . . . well, fall for people who seem to agree with you. Speaking of that, have you called your high-placed helper yet?"

"No." He thought about it. "I'm not sure he could contribute anything at this point, even though . . . well, talking things over with him, I might recall things I don't know I remember."

"If you say so." She sounded lighthearted again. "Well, back to work! Don't do anything I wouldn't do."

Now what did that mean? He shook his head in wonder and in the end he didn't call Carnett but instead spent three hours writing a report on the murder and how he felt about it.

The victim's name was Lorenzo Jewett Ashley and he would have been forty-six years old Tuesday, December 14, 1971, six weeks after he opened the door at his home, 862 Carnaby Street, Urban Grove, almost precisely on the county line. He drove a truck for a delivery service in Middletown, Ohio, and had owned the house since April, 1970. No one, including his widow Marilyn, had any idea why somebody might kill him. He liked harness racing and an occasional game of poker; he and his wife had been watching Roller Derby.

Mrs. Ashley described the killer as taller, heavier, and older than her Jay, with a big nose, bulging eyes, square face, and fixed grin. She said the killer had wiped his knife on her Jay's shirt before he ran away.

That's what the *Enquirer* said, basically, and the *Post Times-Star* added little, because the week's big stories were the election and the malfunctioning of Hamilton County's electronic vote-tabulation machinery. Something went wrong with it almost every time it was used, but this time the problems were worse than usual, and by the time George got on his plane for Los Angeles Sunday afternoon the election results were supposed to be published by 1 A.M. Monday for sure. He was still struggling to wake up Monday, when the phone rang next to his sofa-bed in the kitchenette apartment.

He picked it up, clearing his throat. "Ungh-huh?"

"Hi there!" yelled Gloria, and bleary as he was he could detect the malicious overtones. "Wake up, sluga-bed. We won!"

"Oh." This wasn't a presidential year, was it? And even so . . .

She laughed. "They're out on their asses. Tom Luken came in first, and the best any Republican did was fourth. That was Gradison."

She must be talking about the Cincinnati City Council. Okay. "Good," he said, attempting to put some feeling into the word.

"You're still asleep," said Gloria.

Very perceptive of her. Anyway, George was glad the good guys had won, both because his heart was in the right place and because they had gotten pretty snappish, and partly because he was tired of discussing how the vote-tallying system might have been rigged and how the Republicans would win at any price, not to mention who might have made how much on what sort of a deal.

"Hey, you!"

"You don't have to break my eardrum," he complained.

That made her laugh. "Just testing. You see, I've got news and I wanted to make sure you could absorb the information."

He ground his knuckles into his eyes, dropped the phone, picked it up again. "Go ahead."

Another Seeking Sword murder no doubt, or Old Joe caught by police. It should shock him, upset him—would, in time—but right now he didn't care.

"I've been looking through the Dayton papers," said Gloria.

"And you found more murders."

"How did you know?" She sounded disappointed.

"Getting psychic." He was starting to enjoy this; he must be waking up.

"Psycho is more like it."

"Come on. Let's have it." George sat up, swung his feet to the floor, and picked pencil and pad from the end table. "Who, when, what, where?" He paused for effect. "I know why. But what about wherewith, whenceforth, whither?"

"Better ask how many?" she said.

He traced a huge one in the air with his index finger before clearing his throat to ask her to proceed.

She beat him to it. "All right, George. There are two. No arrests, as far as I know."

The victims' names were Ambrose Eberhart and Bengt Rycksman. Eberhart farmed in Darke County, Ohio, near Union City; he had been found dead in his dairy barn on Tuesday, October 26. He had $23 in his wallet, untouched, and an Omega wristwatch valued near $200 in his pocket. Rycksman was attending Havener High School, not far from Union City but on the Indiana side, on a 4-H fellowship program; his home was near Borrby in south Sweden, and he'd come to America in August; on Thursday, October 21, he was walking out of the school with some friends when a stocky, elderly man ran up the steps, slashed him viciously, and escaped. The young Swede's wounds were not considered serious at first, but on Saturday afternoon he suddenly became comatose and died at 11:30 P.M., approximately forty-eight hours before Mrs. Eberhart found her husband dead, forty miles away.

Neither of them said anything for a while—a long while—after she had finished. Eventually George asked whether there was anything new in the Ashley case. She said no.

"Hmmm."

"Come on, George."

"Yeah?"

"There's a sinister, hidden meaning behind it all. Let's hear it."

After thinking it over—the two, three murders made no sense unless somebody was showing off, or an awful lot of young super-shamans were being initiated—he said he hated to disappoint her.

"I've got a theory," she countered. "It's all part of a plot to ruin American agriculture. You see, Ashley worked for a dairy company before—"

"Oh, come on!"

"That's what I like about you: your zany sense of humor."

"Yeah."

Next she would say it all went to prove the murders were a series of coincidences. But she didn't; instead she said she was sorry, but sometimes she couldn't resist the temptation.

"In case you're not all booked up already, we've got an invitation for Thanksgiving," she added.

"Who?"

"Mrs. Lenore MacDonough." He could tell she was making a face. "Well? How do you feel about it?"

"Okay by me. But how about you?"

Gloria and Lenore had never gotten along, even though she thought Sherm MacDonough was all right.

"I suppose I could stand it a few hours." She paused, started to say something, took a deep breath and then asked when he was scheduled to get back.

About November 24th.

Fine. Have fun.

You, too.

She hung up.

27

November 26, 1971

By Thanksgiving the "skein of killings," as the newspapers called it, had grown to five—Eberhart, Rycksman, Ashley, Kerr, and Grauman—and an *Enquirer* writer had suggested they might all be connected. The police had their doubts. People had all kinds of theories; and quite a few had been aired at the MacDonoughs' party. George was in the thick of it for several hours; when Gloria gave him the special wink that meant let's depart, he did not mind at all.

It was a raw, foggy night, reminding George of the night of Ashley's murder. The MacDonoughs' place was a good ten miles northeast of Galway Place and only three miles west of Stone's Grill in Silverton, where the latest Seeking Sword victim, Andy Grauman, aged thirty-eight, had died Wednesday night.

They'd come in Gloria's blue Saab, and he made no objection when she said she would drive on leaving. There was no traffic on Section Road, and almost none until McMillan Avenue, with the bars letting out. By then, they were almost home.

"Care for a nightcap?" he asked as she turned onto Galway Place.

"Why not?" She had seemed thoughtful, almost sad, but now she was smiling again.

The car's headlights caught a man's broad back as they topped a ridge; the man was wearing a dark coat reaching to mid-thigh and walking head down. For a moment, George wondered, half-fearfully, but then they were past him. The man had no hat.

"What's the matter?" Gloria asked. "You looked

awfully strange for a moment." She paused. "You don't think he's Old Joe, do you?"

"Nyah. Somebody walking home from a saloon."

"Let's hope so, anyway."

"Yeah."

She parked in front of Mrs. Lyndell's Skylark. The sky was clearing and a bitter wind blew straight from the north, causing her to shiver as she came to stand in the curve of his arm for a moment, before they went up the steps. Mrs. Lyndell's windows were dark. A dog was barking off to the west and they could hear cars on Vine Street, east and downhill.

Once inside, she handed him her dark red coat and headed for the bathroom. He put the coat on the typist's chair and shucked his lumberman's jacket. Let's see, now . . . a toddy for the body? He went into the kitchen, ran hot water, put sugar cubes in the mugs, added a little water, then stick cinnamon, cloves, grated nutmeg; the john flushed as he went to get the brandy. He finished the toddies, carried them into the living room, looked around—and the doorbell rang.

What the hell? He hadn't seen headlights, hadn't heard any cars go by. Okay, the lonesome walker had had time to arrive, probably to ask directions. Let's hope so.

Buzzzzzz!

George put the toddies on the bookcase, spilling a dab, and dashed to the bedroom. The gun would be —yeah, right there, in the top drawer, under clean shirts. As he hurried toward the door, he tried to remember: Was the safety on *this* way, or *that*? He stepped into the foyer, his right hand behind his back.

A single sixty-watt bulb burned over the stairs. In the past, this had made no difference, but now he wished for more light. The outside door was open, and . . .

He recognized the coat, and the over-all shape; the nose was bulbous and reddish and the jaw square, and the eyebrows thick and dark. Brownish teeth showed behind half-opened lips that were curling in something that might be called a smile.

He heard Gloria's footsteps coming from the bedroom. In a moment, she would ask what was going on.

Meanwhile, Old Joe—who else?—pulled a brown paper bag, the kind wine bottles go into, from under his coat. George pointed the gun at his middle, but Old Joe didn't even blink; he just held the bag out at George, sort of waving it in the air until the younger man reached out with his left hand, wondering why there should be no hint of a vision. As his fingers closed on the paper bag, a strange feeling—warmth? coldness?—shot up his arm. Old Joe let go, George's fingers loosened, and the bag fell and hit the floor with a loud clank. The two men's eyes met for a fleeting moment before Gloria demanded: "Who are you?"

That seemed to break the spell.

Old Joe shook his head, looking half dazed; then he nodded. "It don't matter, ma'am." He looked hard at George, with a hint of pity in bloodshot blue eyes as he said, "Well, got to be going, now. Good luck, mister."

"Hold it!"

The tone of his own voice surprised George; maybe that's what pointing a gun at somebody did to one's vocal cords.

Old Joe was midway in turning to go.

George waved the gun, remembering to flick off the safety, and almost screamed. "Goddamit, stop there, Joe, or I'll shoot you!"

The man did halt, for a long moment, during which he looked puzzled. Then he shrugged. "Go ahead, mister, and shoot. It would be a goddamned act of mercy."

He lowered his head and went down the steps, turned without looking around, and started walking west, toward Clifton Avenue. George stood, pointing the gun at his back. Then, realizing Joe was gone, he put the safety back on, shook his head, closed the door, and turned to where Gloria was standing in the apartment doorway.

"What was that all about?"

George looked down at the paper bag. Of course. He shuddered.

"Old Joe just gave it to me," he said, his voice oddly

dull in his own ears. "That's it, there. The Seeking Sword."

"Let's get out of here," said Gloria. "Let's go to my place."

"I can't leave it there." George picked up the bag gingerly, put it on the bookcase, and turned out the lights. He couldn't decide whether he felt glad or terrified.

"I'll drive," said Gloria.

28

November 27, 1971

CONFESSION SEEMED TO be good for both soul and appetite, even though George had done a lousy job of it, omitting to tell the priest one crucial point—the reason why. After all, the priest would have been duty-bound to dissuade him from possible suicide and that would have held up the condemned man's last big brunch.

A good one it was, too, and he ate with gusto, savoring every morsel to the utmost and studying Gloria's face as she played with the rahmschnitzel on her plate. She had called in sick. When he finished eating, he would walk home and she would drive back to her place in Mount Adams, where they had spent the night.

"I could come along," she said, for the fiftieth time.

"But what could you do?"

"I don't know." She bit her lip and grinned, suddenly. "Maybe I could hit you on the head when you get that twisted expression on your face. Remember what they said about driving out Beelzebub."

He held up his fork with a piece of Dover sole on it. Sometimes she could be damned exasperating. Here he was, headed for God knows what and— Okay, this was her way of releasing tensions and she had a right to it, the same as he had a right to his idiosyncrasies.

Put in those terms, he could almost make his smile convincing as he said: "If Beelzebub had a hand in this, the exorcists would have taken care of him."

"Oh, crap."

"Remember what Jim says about neither God nor Devil," George told her and put the fish in his mouth.

"So why did you go to church?"

"Why not?" He chewed and swallowed. "It makes me feel better. I think," he added, reaching for the wineglass. "That's half the battle, right?"

She poked at a mushroom in her creamy sauce. "Remember in that medieval book about the man who neutralized the sword . . ."

Of course he remembered Sir Minferth; that gentleman of Holstein had been on his mind all day. He'd got up quietly and gone to the kitchen to write a long letter to Carnett, all about the various possibilities: no doubt he was sword-cursed, but he had reason to believe that he was less likely to be a killer than one of the sword-keepers, or manipulators, somebody who pressed buttons to send people like Old Joe out to kill strangers chosen at random . . . Or were they chosen at random? He would find out.

The sole was finished, he really didn't care for dessert or coffee. And as for Gloria, who had hardly cut her veal . . .

They looked at each other and he almost told her how he felt, but instead he swallowed and said, "I might as well go. Wish me luck."

"You know I do." Her eyes were glistening with tears all of a sudden. She smiled and reached out to grasp his hand, hard, as he stood up. "I'll pay. All right? Good luck—and I'll call you in half an hour, and later, if necessary." She bit her lip. "I love you."

"I love you, too." He bent down to kiss her.

Walking out, a trifle self-consciously, he felt oddly lightheaded, a feeling that persisted as he walked east on McMillan before his first turn to the right.

Vestiges of that feeling persisted while George was

176

fishing out his door keys. Now, then. Feeling like a hero, even a doomed hero, had been fine; but he'd better watch his step inside and stick to plans he'd worked out listening to Gloria's even breathing, alternately taking pleasure in that peaceful sleepy sound and then resenting it.

As he put his key in the lock he thought of Norman castles à la Robin Hood movies; as the door swung in, he visualized guns poking out of bunkers in Korea and he kept his mind on those bunkers as he walked in, clutching his gun. He turned, closed the door, exhaled. Fine, so far. Nothing had changed in the room, the toddy mugs were still on the bookcase next to the sword, exactly where he had dropped it.

He felt a strange revulsion as he leaned over for a closer look.

Up close, the Seeking Sword didn't look particularly impressive. Carnett had said that no self-respecting weapons designer would let anything that crude out of the shop. George could see why. The sword's dark sides were marred by countless hills and valleys. The point was actually bent. The strips of ancient rawhide around the hilt looked petrified and were covered with nicks and stains, while the weapon conveyed a curious impression of, well, wholeness.

Words from the *Somnium* rang through his mind: "Some say that, even though prayers and relics avail not at all in this regard, there are men whose very presence, by grace of the LORD, can cause a slumber to overcome the steely eyelids of the aforesaid Tautewoimateyn, who speaks with those of the sword-cursed who allow him to . . ." Later on, the author had mentioned that "thinking of walls crumbling has brought the voice of the aforesaid demon to the ears of some who put their precious immortal souls in danger thereby."

Well, he could probably keep up his defenses for some time, but what would happen after he fell asleep? Seppius had been described in the *Somnium* as a "thief in the night." That might be a metaphor.

But he might as well get it over with. He'd feel like an idiot if nothing had happened by the time of Gloria's call.

So-o-o, go to it, man. Open your mind. But first, how about a drink?

Why not?

He filled a coffee cup with whiskey and forced himself to walk slowly—most slowly, feet most unwilling—back to the living room, where he slumped down in his armchair. Such memories, associated with the chair, starting with him and Betsy in Columbus, their first apartment, and then Evelyn, Mrs. Thorne, Lenore before she met Sherm, Gloria . . . The past was a wall behind one and memories were cracks in the wall and—

He quickly shut his eyes and then clamped both hands to his ears, even grinding his knuckles against his temples—to no avail.

As John Lambert had said, there was no stopping the torrent of sound, a stream of noises inside the skull, sometimes distinguishable and sometimes not. Roars, screams, screeches, whispers, whimpers, thuds, thumps—however many words connoting sounds there were in English, there they were, all of them, phonemes and tonemes, from highest-pitched scream to lowest-sounding *thonk,* all crowded into his mind and pushing in all directions. Some of them reminded him of words. He tried to think of a prayer, to remember what he'd done with the revolver, *tried* because it was so hard to think in terms of words with this hurricane of roaring syllables sweeping through his mind. STOP! Ahhh . . . The level of noise decreased, almost palpably. Yes, he'd left his gun on the kitchen table.

He tried to stand up but the muscles in the backs of his thighs wouldn't function. He dug his knuckles into his eyes, hoping the sparks would break the spell and distract his attention from the hellish hypnotic din—din, moreover, that now seemed to be definitely resolving itself into distinct sounds, phonemes, words. Until, with a sort of click, the sounds began falling in place, to fit together. All of a sudden most of the noise, except for a slight television-like background hum, died away, leaving in his mind the words, alien and clear and utterly indisputable:

Kinsman . . . welcome . . .

29

November 27, 1971

Kinsman . . . welcome . . . much . . .

So. He'd been right. He *was* descended from a long line of rotten, murderous super-shamans.

Kinsman . . . welcome . . . much . . . time . . .

Time? He hoped there would still be time to blow his brains out.

Again, George tried to stand up—without result. If only he hadn't left his gun in the kitchen! He forced his tensed-up muscles to relax in preparation for another desperate attempt.

Suddenly, by a supreme effort, he heaved himself erect. Sweat burst out over his body, he felt itchy all over—including inside his skull—and, after another click, a barrier seemed to dissolve and more words flooded into his consciousness. He had had no sensation that might be likened to walls collapsing; rather, his impressions had been of . . . well, water, red water, soaking into a sponge, inevitably.

Regardless of that, he'd better get his gun. He swallowed, and forced his feet, one step at a time, to bear him toward the kitchen table, while more and more words sounded through his mind. Now they were beginning to form a pattern:

Kinsman, welcome . . .
Much time has passed, from the last time . . .
we, kinsmen, were gathered together, for feasting . . .

179

George had a mental image of a typewriter carriage, moving from right to left, skipping several spaces after "welcome." While that was happening he took another step, with less effort and also less determination.

. . . together, for feasting. . . .

Much time, much doing, many cold white winters. . . .

Hail, kinsman . . .

The recorded message had reached that point when he grasped the gun and stood, wondering. So far, there had been nothing sinister about the message. In fact, the overtones had been friendly . . . or rather concerned, warm, solicitous:

. . . Hail, kinsman! All hail! May your suns ever be warm the right ways. . . . May your pit traps never fail to catch meat, lean or fat, for the feasting. . . . May your spear shafts never break, your arrows never miss, no one else's dog reach the prey first, your women drop children aright . . .

The words were English—at least George perceived them thus—but their pattern did not seem to fit English at all. For a moment, he wished he had paid more attention in that required Anglo-Saxon course—not that this was likely to help.

Oh, shit!

A sudden feeling of disgust, actually overriding the continuing message, made him literally reel on his feet. He reached for the bottle of old Jack and tipped it up. Ahhh . . . The taste of good whiskey washed the distaste from his mind, but the words rolled on and on, hoping he would do well in dozens of activities he had never seriously considered—and then, without warning, the message ended with a triply emphasized *"Hail, kinsman!"*

George blinked and turned around to look at the electric alarm clock on the filing cabinet. Yes, here, now, at 1:15 P.M., he was still alive and in his right mind, several minutes before Gloria was due to call. And—hail, what?

Hail to thee, kinsman!

All he could do was gape.

When kinsman meets kinsman, greetings are ever in order.

180

No shit?

Another wave of distaste, disgust—stronger than the first—at his own words and mental processes now swept through George's mind. *Greetings are no occasion for speaking, of . . . unclean, of vile substances.*

What the hell?

He sat on a kitchen chair and tried to find the gun again, even while part of his mind found that particular preoccupation totally incongruous. Anyway, what was the problem?

Thoughts of dung are for dung.

Most incongruously, a bit of almost-forgotten high school lore flitted through George's mind, to the effect that "Class will tell and shit will smell."

That is most true.

The swiftness—rather, instantaneousness—of the response was too much, and incompatible with the idea that this might be a recorded message. Although, considering what people said about computers these days, who could tell? Still, somehow, George felt he could sense a personality immediately behind the words, those he had heard and the new words:

The smell of dung . . . of heedless kinsmen in the encampment of kinsmen, the smell of the remains of past prey . . . the smells . . . frighten off skittish deer, even elk, from afar off.

Weird. The whole thing. Everything about the Seeking Sword, Kill-thinkers, super-shamans . . . Sweat broke out on George's forehead. He had braced himself for a recruiting pitch, maybe a hypnotist's spiel with flickering klieg lights and all—and here he sat, bottle in hand, staring at his feet and listening to a lecture about the advantages of proper camp hygiene.

He reached for the bottle, wondering whether his hand would obey him. It did. Whiskey tasted the same, too, delicious and then tingly on the back of the tongue and all the way down.

He took a deep breath, because, as W. C. Fields used to say, sometimes a man simply had to grasp the bull by the tail and face the issue. He gritted his teeth and asked, aloud: "Who are you?"

I am I.

181

The naturalness, serenity, and the tolerant, half-humored disdain at the stupidity that would allow anybody even to ask, was overwhelming; George felt glad he was seated. He blinked, swallowed, and yelled at the top of his voice: "Let's get this over with!"

For a moment—probably five seconds, but it seemed a lot longer—his mind was blissfully, restfully empty. Then:

It is only a matter of kinsman greeting kinsman, after long years.

What kin?

I and you.

Somehow George knew that "I" referred to the sword, and nothing but. Only how could he be akin to a piece of ancient, crudely forged iron?

Yes—how?

It is a story . . . a long story.

The words halted, then continued:

Listen, now . . .

A pause, long enough to make George wonder what would come next, and the stream of words resumed. The last few statements had been, well, conversational in tone, if this made any sense, but now the words were formal, self-conscious, almost sacerdotal, with a stylized opening that recalled the *Hail, kinsman.* George missed a few words as the narrative began.

. . . coldest winter all but the oldest of Men could remember. . . . Bleak bright lights streaked the sky, Moon wept tears of ice that glimmered about it in rings, Great Bitter Water froze, shore to shore. No way to fish properly because the ice was too thick to break, but Men harpooned seal, even smoked bears from their lairs, suffering little, through having laid up firewood, for the Greedy Warmer-Devourer. Then was it that Worker-with-things-and-spirits-for-Men became aware of summoning: COME! COME! COME! All about it resounded, but being wise, he found which way to go, through looking at all six directions, seeking counsel from drum and drum-spirits, from the holy innards-scalding ash broths, of birchwood, larchwood, oakwood, the six holy herbs, mouth bleeding, insides heaving, gasping for true counsel from Sun, Bear, Seal, Elk, Pike . . .

There was more of it, much more, and as the strange recital continued George could see it: dark pine trees crowding close to beaches that ringed the ice plain glistening in wan wintry sunlight, with dust devils of fine snow chasing around jagged reefs and islands lost in haze—and then—cut!—the gnarled, white-bearded man making final inventory. Bow, ten arrows, two spears, an ax of green slate, about the size and shape of a spread-out hand, two knife-like scrapers, one of gray flint, the other of sparkly quartz. He bound on skates made of the shoulder blades of elk, hobbled across rough ice close to shore and set off, muttering in frost-stiff whiskers, using the spears as poles at first and then gliding smoothly toward where Sun, setting, was turning the overcast sky luridly pink.

In a way, this resembled visions George had seen during Seeking Sword murders. It had the same emphasis on detail: the flaking of flint blades, exact configurations of knots, the shape of every ridge and furrow frozen into the beach sand. At the same time, everything felt formal, preordained, almost like a work of art; in any case, totally without those qualities of immediacy and spontaneousness that had accompanied the murders. No feelings of fierce joy or duty well fulfilled. Instead, the . . . well, atmosphere surrounding the journey of Worker-with-things-and-spirits-for-Men to the Island-of-Flame-Eggs was almost one of boredom. The narrator had lived with the tale a long time. It was important to him. But he had told it many times and George thought he could detect occasional stirrings of emotion—nuances were becoming easier and easier to spot—but most of the time the "voice" remained curiously flat and unemotional.

The lack of feeling was noticeable more in some places than in others. For instance, there were the scenes where Workers-with-things-and-spirits-for-Men arrived on the island after seven days and nights on the ice. First, he saw a thread of smoke on the horizon. This became thicker; he saw a sort of hump; he kept going, never looking right or left because now, the sound in his head was deafeningly loud and this was obviously the place. The snow on the island lay

183

waist-deep. Worker-with took off his skates, dropped his bundle of provisions—dried flounder, dried berries, smoked elk meat and aurochs' tongue—and started wading to where:

> . . . pinelings' branches were blackened, and snow had turned to slush, for warm was the ground, warm to a Man's touch, the bared-to-the-sky pine needles smoldering for a spear shaft from where lay the Flame-Eggs, dark red, shimmering, sizzling, smoking on black ground, bare to winter sky amid snow on the ice-clasped island . . .

This seemed to call for something extra—maybe heavier rhetoric or an explanation or at least, the very least, a change of tone. But Worker-with glanced at the Flame-Eggs, nodded, and began looking for a campsite. He found one not far away, under the roots of a large fallen pine, fetched his gear, and gathered branches for a fire, kindled from the Flame-Eggs. That night, as he toasted his bare feet and chewed the tough meat strips, he only felt contentment at having reached the island, having read the signs right; not a trace of wonder or speculation about the Flame-Eggs seemed to cross his mind—at least not according to the narrator's version of events.

All in all, the narrator seemed to take a lot for granted, and he did not take kindly to interruptions. *Tales are told, questions answered, each in its own time.*

George gave up after several futile attempts to find out more about the Flame-Eggs. They had been mentioned in the *Somnium*. So what were they? Parts of a meteorite? Something flung up by a volcanic eruption? Something supernatural? Maybe the narrator—he still could not think of the sword in that role—would get to it in his own good time.

That hope died, slowly, as Worker-with waited for the Flame-Eggs to cool, a process that took many days, during which the old shaman hunted, resharpened his skates, chipped himself more arrowheads, and spent what seemed many hours in crooning to himself and staring at the Flame-Eggs or his own little fire. Occasionally he worried whether winter would last long enough; no Man had ever crossed Great

Bitter Water by dugout canoe and it would take long to make one, all by himself. The Flame-Eggs grew darker, day by day, and whenever new snow fell the circle of bare earth around them was smaller. Still, Worker-with chose an ash tree, felled it with his green flint ax, and stripped off the branches. The process of felling the tree was a lot faster than George would have expected.

One day, however, when the ice still seemed firm, the Flame-Eggs no longer caused chips of dry wood to burst into flame. The old shaman was ready. He packed the Flame-Eggs—about a dozen chunks, weighing perhaps ten pounds in all—in a skin bag. Putting out his fire, he tied on his skates and set off in what George judged to be a southeasterly direction.

The return voyage was as epic as the outward journey, because the ice was beginning to break up. But in the end, Worker-with reached the shore not far from the beach where he had set forth, now gaunt and wind-burned, bone-weary, but content at a job well done. Apparently it had been all part of a day's work, and that was how he referred to it by the roaring campfire in the encampment of Men by the River of Salmon, half a day's trudge through the snow-laden forests from where he had reached shore. A burly man called Knows-where-elk-are-plentiful asked what Flame-Eggs were good for. Worker-with answered:

"As a stone is thrown further with a sling, and harder, so the Flame-Eggs lend power to the words of the singers, the craftsmen of words, the Workers-with-things-and-spirits-for-Men."

This was good enough for the Men.

At this point George called for a break. Curtain time! It was after 3 P.M. His legs and back hurt, his bladder was killing him, his head ached . . . He lit a cigarette with shaky fingers, struggled to his feet, and staggered to the bathroom.

Cold water on his face felt wonderful, driving the pain into some remoter recesses of his mind, but the burning of his eyes remained, along with a faint ringing in his ears. He wondered if he would be able to stand the rest. The pronouncement about the Flame-Eggs had clearly marked the end of a section of the

Saga of the Flame-Eggs. Many of the "runes" of *Kalevala* ended with similar pronouncements, usually by Wainamoinen, the wise old shaman-hero. The first section had brought the story from—5000 B.C. to 4999 B.C.? How many sections were there?

He needed a drink. His cup was half full; he tossed it off, went to the kitchen and refilled, spilling a good deal, then drank two glasses of tap water, barely aware some of it was running down his chin. The world was a strange place. A few hours ago he'd marched into Galway Place, head high, heart in mouth, grimly determined to resist the recruitment pitch with all his ability. But, instead of a recruiter, the sword—or person behind it—had turned out to be, well, a garrulous old man. Or so it seemed; a lot of things still didn't make sense.

The phone rang. Gloria.

Forgetting the whiskey, he dashed back, picked up the phone on the fourth ring, and sank into the armchair.

"George!" She sounded frantic. "George, is that you?"

"Hi," he began, feeling rather foolish. "I'm sorry, I—"

"Have you been outside, or something?"

"Outside? No . . . Why?"

"I've been trying to get you every fifteen minutes for the last hour and a half." She had been worried; now she was starting to sound angry. "At least you could have let me know."

He almost laughed out loud, but managed to retain control; or so he thought until, before he could say anything, Gloria wanted to know what was so damned funny.

"I'm sorry," he said. "I should have called you. I —I just got carried away, I guess."

"So what did the super-shamans have to say?" He could tell she was still angry, but also relieved. "That's what got you carried away, right?"

"Uh-uh."

He was not sure how to answer the question. It was nice of her to call, to worry—he appreciated it. But how could he tell her when he hadn't heard the end of the saga? As a narrative, it was fascinating, but its point eluded him. He half-expected a disapproving roar in his mind; but there was none. Instead, he heard Gloria take a deep breath. "Uh-uh, what?"

"I don't know yet," he said, stung by the sharpness of her tone. "Look—it's a lot more complicated than I expected, and I'm still trying to figure it out."

"Maybe you need some help?" she suggested, sharp and solicitous at the same time. Worried, too. "Or, how about a drive, while you sort things out?" After a long pause, she added, "You *can* go for a drive, can't you?"

"Me? Sure."

What did she think he was—a prisoner bound to a chair? A ventriloquist's dummy? Of course, she was right to worry. He had not called. He must have failed to notice the phone ringing. Suddenly, he felt shaky, and sweat broke out all over his body yet again.

The scenarios he'd built up in advance had been all wrong. Obviously he had underestimated the sophistication of the super-shaman(s). The Saga of the Flame-Eggs could serve the purpose of distracting him, providing him with things to remember while more sinister messages were implanted or imprinted in his mind, monstrous seeds that would germinate some day.

Maybe. That could be. But he found it hard to believe, because it would not fit the voice, or personality behind the voice, or whatever. On the other hand, anybody vicious enough to be a Kill-thinker would be capable of any pretense—as Carnett insisted.

George swallowed and looked up at the shelf where the sword lay.

Gloria's voice called him back to the present. From the way she sounded, she must have repeated her question several times already. "George? George! . . . How about going for that drive?"

Drive? Yes. "Maybe later," he said. "Right now, there are too many things I have to work out."

"What's there to work out?" She sounded exasperated.

"Look. I can't explain just yet." Damn it, why couldn't she understand? "I'll call you back in a couple of hours. Okay?" She started to say something but he cut her short: "Look, I'm all right. Nobody's trying to brainwash me, or anything."

"George—"

"I'll call you later. Please— Oh, goddammit!"

She had started to say something; he slammed down the phone and walked to the kitchen for his whiskey cup. The phone started ringing before he had it halfway to his mouth. He let it ring, walked back slowly, sat down. Finally it stopped. He dialed her number.

"Look, I love you, and I appreciate your concern, but I want to work this out first. I'm fine and I think you were right about me and Sir Minferth." He was not entirely sure of that, but it should help calm her down. "I'll call you later—say, about seven. Okay?"

"Are you sure you're all right?"

"Yeah."

"How about . . . if I came over anyway?" She had sounded tentative; now a more positive tone came into her voice: "There's no danger—right?"

Of course not; and of course she would do her best not to distract him; but, damn it, this was his show and he did not want to share these moments with anybody. Not yet, anyway. He liked to show off as much as anybody, but to every thing there is a season, and . . . He shook his head. "There is no danger," he said in a voice that sounded oddly gentle to his own ears. "No danger, you can believe me, for me or you or anybody. I just have to be alone a while longer. I want to be alone."

"I want to be with you."

"Gloria, I want to be with you too, but not now. Okay?"

He did not wait for her answer before hanging up, but he did not pick up the cup until he was sure the phone was not going to ring again. It didn't.

Scarcely five minutes had passed, though this was hard to accept. Anyway, thinking of a theater curtain had been enough to stop the narration.

George lit a cigarette, thought of the curtain rising, and said: "Here I am."

Yes, kinsman.

A chilliness was in the words, but also an undertone

of warmth—almost as if proper behavior could not always be expected.

"The story was very interesting," George said diplomatically, "but there are some questions I'd like to ask before you continue."

No answer; but he had the feeling that Whatever was prepared to answer.

"Do you have a name?"

Yes. For some reason, the question had been amusing.

George felt blood rush to his face. What was the name and what was funny about his asking?

Men have different names, at different times of life, and true names that never are told. . . . No Man would properly ask a question like yours. There was an amused pause. *But I know why you asked that way.*

George decided to swallow his irritation. "All right, what was the last name by which other Men [his mind supplied the capital letter] called you?" If he was a kinsman, goddammit, he should have a right to know!

True. There was a pause, and a burst of sounds—ten or twelve syllables that made no sense to George, who thought he detected a "sepp" or "zepp" sound about halfway.

Of course: whatever language the Men had spoken would be long dead.

He took a deep breath. "This name. Would it have meant Worker-with-things-and-spirits-for-Men?"

The reply—an affirmative monosyllable—had clear overtones of patience finally rewarded.

Okay. Now, had the kinsman also been referred to as Seppius?

By some, sometimes.

Aha! The feeling that he was at last on to something long hidden sent a strange thrill up and down George's back. One more point, now: what about the Kill-thinkers? Or should he say, super-shamans?

Your words, kinsman, are nothing.

Did that mean . . . ? George let images of the Kill-thinkers, as he had pictured them, flit through his mind, aware of the danger in which he might be placing himself and others, but certain there was no such danger.

Indeed. There was an overtone of approval, super-imposed over feelings of disdain and amusement.

George reached for his cup, took a sip, and asked, aloud, "How did . . . Seppius become the Seeking Sword?"

The answer had overtones of exasperation: *I have been trying to tell you this, but there is an order to which tales are told.*

Maybe so, but he was primarily interested in—

Tales are told, questions answered, each in its own time.

Seppius' tone brooked no argument. Okay. Since he had no choice, George lit a cigarette and settled back, allowing the stilted, oddly formalistic narrative to sweep through his mind, conjuring up images of Men going about their business, which seemed much like those of such forest Indians as the Hurons and Iroquois, except that these Men raised no crops at all. They hunted and fished, and the women and children picked berries and mushrooms. Hunting was generally good, because the population was thinly spread—and Worker-with-things-and-spirits-for-Men soon found a practical use for the Flame-Eggs. Looking at them, and thinking of game—say, red deer by a certain carefully visualized lightning-blasted tree—caused the animals to come there.

Hah! George sat up, blinking; the images evoked by Seppius' narration faded. Only the words remained, droning on and on with a distinct touch of irritation about them. He raised his hand, feeling silly.

Yes?

The schoolmasterish overtones of the monosyllable made George grate his teeth. Okay. Were the Flame-Eggs raw material for the Seeking Sword? Why had it been made?

Tales are told, questions answered, each in its own time.

Why couldn't there be an exception, just this once?

What is proper is proper.

George yielded. "Go on, Seppius," he said, aloud. "I hope you don't mind my calling you Seppius."

Men no longer speak properly. The "voice" carried a sort of overtone of good-natured disdain, as if it was not George's fault.

Okay. There was no arguing with Seppius, on points of procedure at any rate. George had a sip of whiskey, relaxed, and let the sword, if that was all there was to it, take over, recounting how the old Workers-with only used their new talisman in times of need because there were many things most Men, not to mention Others, should not deal with. A hunter was better off knowing how to stalk game; the women must find hazelnut trees, raspberry patches, and mushroom grounds with no new-fangled assistance. Thus the Keepers had meant it to be.

Keepers? Hell, no doubt they would be mentioned again. Let it pass.

Seppius continued. Old Worker-with—Seppius I? —eventually died and passed his job and the Flame-Eggs on to the husband of his second daughter. The Flame-Eggs still felt warm, but George got the impression the sensation was psychological rather than physical.

This part of the narrative was really dull. Men, male and female—as far as Seppius was concerned, "Men" was strictly generic, and George wondered whether it would have come across in his mind as "People" if his upbringing had been any different—were born, lived, mated, brought forth young, died, and were left lying in their tepee-like lodges in summer; when snow blanketed the ground Men lived in caves, dugouts, and similar structures and dying Men were borne to die in the open, under a sky filled with fantastic bright stars, wind howling in the trees. It was much quicker this way. And, winter or summer, memorial feasts were the biggest celebrations Men had, with everybody contributing meat and drink, a sort of chewed-berry wine or a kind of mead: fermented honey flavored with herbs.

Nothing much happened in a historical sense. From time to time a disaster occurred—epidemic, forest fire, unusually cold winter; and occasionally, when their number increased beyond ninety, one-third of the Men left the encampment. This might be accompanied by unpleasantness, even murder, but usually the parting was friendly, with one departee, man or woman, receiving part of the Flame-Eggs. Generation succeeded generation, with George wondering about chronology: What year B.C. had Seppius I picked up the Flame-Eggs? How many years passed from his return from Great Bitter Water to the late-winter day when Hates-cry-of-thin-legged-curlews returned from a long, long trip southeast?

Hates-cry brought Men a firsthand report on short and sharp-nosed people, definitely Others because their speech was incomprehensible.

To Seppius, groups of Men who departed apparently remained Men for a few generations, a century or so; after that they would be referred to as People. Others . . . well, they resembled People in some ways, but their speech was strange, and these new Others did amazingly little hunting. Furthermore, they did not move from one place to another according to the two seasons, and during coming-summer they would go around a treeless place, tossing about grass seed. A strange grass it was, growing thigh-high. And after cutting off the heads of the grass stalks in late summer, the Others beat the seeds out of them, boiled the seeds, and . . . *ate* them.

Grass seeds? Seppius was so good at communicating shock and distaste that it took George thirty seconds to realize he was getting a neolithic hunter's view of agriculture.

So maybe the author of the *Somnium* was not so far off, talking about a feud that lasted seventy times seven generations.

George had questions he ached to ask now, but didn't. It wasn't so much the words in which his questions would be dismissed—hackneyed enough and insulting—but the telepathic overtones, scornful and superior, were more than he cared to face. Drowsiness crept over him. The history of Men, told thus, in terms of one generation succeeding another, full of long names he could never hope to remember, was pretty dull—something like the history of the Cincinnati Gas & Electric Company, or of one of the downtown banks, sticking to cash flow with all the scandalous stuff decently omitted. Seppius seemed to be concerned with birth rather than conception, and some of the descriptions of difficult births were enough to turn a man's stomach. Not many people could read a dozen Annual Reports, one after another; and that was exactly what this part of the Saga sounded like, with an occasional diversion like the description of the strange Others' long, half-subterranean houses divided into six, seven and more hearth-rooms, or some of the accounts of journeys from This World to Yonder World to set things right or bring back souls that had strayed. All in all, it was what one might expect a shaman's version of history to be like. And that, in a way, was a disappointment.

Listening wearied you, so I halted. The narrator was both amused and slightly solicitous of George's welfare.

He rubbed his eyes, feeling very strange. He must have dozed off. Well, he'd been weary with worry when he walked in and—

There is nothing wrong with fearing and wondering about what one knows not.

Okay. Hard to argue with that. George stood up, and wondered what Gloria was doing. Calling Carnett? Fat chance. He picked up his cup. Empty! He went to the kitchen, wondering whether to call to extend the deadline to, say, 9 P.M. and decided against it. The narrative had to reach some kind of climax, so he might as well get it over with. A drink to that!

He refilled his cup and started back. On the way, his eyes fell on the sword, exactly where he had put it—how many hours ago?—and the way the rough, dark metal reflected light. So Seppius was in there, eh? Or was Seppius the sword? In either case . . .

He was about to pour some of the good sour-mash whiskey on the ancient weapon and whoever or whatever inhabited it, but a sudden thought caused him to stay his hand.

Well meant you this, kinsman, and thanks be to you therefor. Something about the tone threatened to bring tears to George's eyes. *It is not needed. Other kinsmen, however, many of them older and more experienced, have still done far less to make their guest feel welcomed.*

"I hope you feel welcome," George said, trying to sound formal; a moment later, sitting down, he added: "Kinsman." The word felt strange but did not seem at all ridiculous in this context. He tried to ignore the stab of fear in the back of his mind because Part III would be getting down to the brass tacks; instead he raised the cup to the sword. "Anyway, here's to you, kinsman, and let's continue the story."

He forced himself not to think as he reached down for the gun, slipped off the safety, and straightened up in his seat as Seppius began:

This is the tale of how the sword came to be made.

George's hands tightened on cup and gun. Hah! The action should start soon, and Seppius' tone bore this out.

Instead of the long, leisurely, Longfellowish cadences of the tale of the generations of Men the narrative was becoming a jumble of quick-moving images, all but superimposed on each other. Men kept wandering from river to river. Some Man committed an awful no-no, killing two bear cubs and their mother; bears could only be killed properly in winter, save in self-defense. For a while Men lived close to a long house of Others, with some intermarriage—at least George chose to think of it thus—before scarcity of elk—or moose?—and red deer forced Men to move some distance away, to a fairly narrow river flowing northward. Then, several winters later, came word that the grass-eating Others were no more. A band of Others of different type, tall, burly, with glossy red and yellow hair worn in braids, had come from the direction of Two-tailed Beaver Swamp. The narrative was full of place names like this.

One of the grass-eating Others, a haggard male coughing blood because his ribs had been smashed, gasped out the tale: The burly ones had arrived with women and children and belongings heaped in wooden boxes mounted on round slabs of wood that turned with loud shrieking; Seppius gave George to understand he had seen such things often, but unnatural was unnatural. The newcomers also prodded along puny aurochs with closely set, forward-pointing horns; the dying bringer-of-tidings demonstrated with

194

his hands. A short time later, a dispute arose—Men never understood why—and the newcomers wiped out the grass-eating Others. Here Seppius' narrative became choppy, the imagery a jumble of waving spears, flailing arms, clubs, axes, bows twanging, men falling ending with the longhouses a mass of flames against a darkening sky while the newcomers rolled on the ground, wrestling with the women of the grass-eating Other—those who had not been killed—even though the act of begetting, properly, should be performed in the greenwood with only the eyes of the Keepers upon each couple. Still, the ways of Others were strange, in any case, because the grass-eating Others had the habit of copulating together in their grass field at the start of coming-summer with Moonfull.

Others were not Men; that was all. Seppius' pronouncement carried a note of finality. George got the impression that Seppius had spent years and years— God, how many years?—watching the doings of Others and still found them as incomprehensible as ever. More wearisome, naturally—the freshness was off the bloom, so to speak.

The killing of the grass-eating Others made no difference, really, to Men; actually, for a while, game became more plentiful because the newcomers lacked skill as hunters; furthermore, they killed wolves with a single-mindedness appropriate to persons whose souls had been stolen and set to certain tasks in Yonder World while their bodies still had the ability to move around.

"They acted like people under a curse, then?" George asked.

Under a curse . . . spellbound . . . those are words of Others, for the situation.

The tale continued. The newcomers lived in tents of aurochs' hide set up close to formations of sharpened stakes. The heads of the grass-eating Others, after being soaked in a wooden tub filled with salty herb broth, were stuck on the stakes. None of the heads were ever used for divination or any other sensible purposes; they were there only for show. The newcomers seemed totally unaware how good brains tasted—or even marrow—although some of them had sneaked off into the greenwood to eat the livers of dead grass-eaters—raw, of course. This much they *did* know. The newcomers Men called Cowdung-covered-knees, or Shitfeet, because they penned up their puny aurochs close to their dwellings until a Man could smell the encampment from afar, upwind or downwind. They raised eating-grass too, and spread dung all over low-lying fields and scraped it in the ground with sticks. A disgusting act.

Their speech was not unlike the barking of dogs, although less melodious; but in time—while several Workers-with died, some of old age and one from a tree falling on him—Shitfeet and Men reached a sort of accommodation. The numbers of Shitfeet increased faster than those of Men—an overtone of bitterness accompanied this statement—and they built another encampment, and another, and another, even though they were also very prone to kill each other and frequently experienced all sorts of misfortunes out of ignorance and willfulness. The Keepers, who often assume bear's shape, did not like to see bears killed without due ceremony, but some among the Shitfeet made a practice of bear murder, bragged of it, and were honored for it. Some of them would take beaver and other animals from Men's traps; this could lead to altercation and killing. As somebody said: Shitfeet had no souls, being born without, because the Keepers took their souls from them while in the womb and handed these to a mad shaman in Yonder World to whom a favor was owed.

Likely enough. Otherwise—since they looked like Men—why would they live as they did?

George stirred uneasily. "Hey," he started to say, "what about the world we live in now?"

It is no world for Men.

The supercilious tone—with no hint, even, of a sneer in acknowledgment that Seppius had seriously considered the alternatives—annoyed George. He took a sip of whiskey. The Men had had nothing like this; they hadn't had houses worthy of the name . . . Hell, he preferred the present.

You know no better.

What the hell was that supposed to mean?

You were born into a world of stone, rather than trees or grass. Stone has long been taking the place of grasses, and trees, and animals. Stone has a way of being, like everything, but Men like grass better.

Okay. George took another sip, lit a cigarette, contemplated the smoke rising as the words inside his mind took him back to the world of Men and Others.

The elm tree fell on Seppius XXXVII—or XLV, or whatever; he was succeeded by his son, a graybeard with two grown sons and several grandchildren. Now the images were even more vivid, the statement about grandchildren accompanied by glimpses of gurgling babies, drooling, yowling, grinning, with silky white furs wrapped around them, only plump-cheeked faces showing; then, other images, of boys practicing with bows and little girls making awful faces as they chewed deerhide and elk sinew; a swirl of faces, all somewhat alike in having flattened noses tilted upward, high cheekbones, shining eyes and lank hair, whitish, brown, and black.

Suddenly, George felt himself awash in tenderness (Yecch!) at successive views of a young girl, brown-haired and slim-bodied, clad in a smock of plaited plant fibers dyed red with madder juice, a garment her father had traded for with Shitfeet. Her name was Swift-as-ermine-with-running-brook-laughter, a phrase that conveyed only the feeblest indication of the associated feelings and images: first, ermines—mink-like, frolicking in a forest clearing, both in brownish summer fur and rich white winter pelts; and then the Brook—not any brook, but the stream flowing in a loop around Men's encampment, a clear, merrily burbling stream sprouting from the heart of the world, holy, fiery, pure, eventually mingling with Great Bitter Water, also holy, but bitter due to receiving all the waters of This World wherein soul-equipped beings, Men and birch trees, bears and eagles and oak trees, People and pike fish, Others, sorrel, thyme and foxglove and wolfsbane, wolves and honeybees and elk, aurochs, deer and foxes, hares and hawks, perch and catfish, crayfish and frogs and water lilies and pine trees—they, all of them, all the soul-equipped of This World lived by devouring or ingesting parts of passing souls. Thus, in a way, the pretty grand-daughter's name and its implications amounted to an animistic creed, more compact than the Nicene but not without certain parallels thereto.

George wrestled his thoughts away from contemplation of the various implications, deaths and rebirths and all that, and forced his attention back to Seppius' narrative, which now had taken a lyrical turn, about a certain late afternoon with Moon's bow bent to the right, just before true-summer. The grass was green, new leaves were bursting from buds, and gnats were dancing in stillness redolent with wood smoke and meat cooking in clumsy clay pots with coals heaped up around them.

He—the narrator, really, but the boundary between selves, with "self" defined as the basis of perceptions, was growing fuzzier and fuzzier—was leaning against an oak tree. Not any oak tree, but Oak tree, the tree at whose roots other Workers-with had laid down offerings to the Keepers.

An unexpressed question brought the reply that Keepers were Keepers, and might manifest themselves in a tree—any tree—or stone, cloud, frolicking bear cub, venturesome tadpole, unusually quacky duck . . .

Seppius made it clear that this was hardly the time to wonder about final purposes even though the lazy, mellow evening seemed to be meant for contemplation, because—because, all of a sudden came a frantic shout from the direction where Brook came close to the clearing occupied by Men's encampment.

George had hardly noticed it, the encampment, presumably because it was all too familiar to Seppius. There were eighteen lodges made of deerskins stretched over long poles, some of them plain and others adorned with designs in brown and white clay, soot, and bright madder-red; a dozen cooking fires burned. Women and children wandered about. Most of the hunters were still out, while Older-son (Walks-heavily-in-night-amid-campfires is the name by which everybody in the encampment knew him. To his father and mother he remained Older-son. His wife may or may not have called him Walks-heavily-in-night-amid-campfires, probably not) and his younger brother had

gone north to trade for new dogs with another group of
People. The Men's dogs had died of sickness during
fading-winter. The current Seppius did not yet know
why, and this was one reason he had stayed—to make
offerings at various places where Keepers had manifested themselves.

Keepers . . . Men must have offended them, dreadfully, somehow, because ten heartbeats after a yell,
Always-whittles-too-deeply came running out of the
thicket of alder trees and willows. A spear flew over
his shoulder; he almost stumbled over it, but managed to keep going. A figure appeared between the
foremost alder trees. It was clad in plaited fibers, dyed
red!

But what of the hunters? The winter had been
hard; many had died, men, women, and children; but
this morning ten grown men and four boys had gone
forth toward the encampment of Shitfeet over which
Murkhosteri gennu held sway as Big Man . . .

The answer to the old man's agonized, unspoken
question came in a swirling chaos of images. First,
at the place where the new footpath passed the
slope named Blackberries-like-it-here, with a thicket at
bottom; there lay the hunters, dead, spear-pierced
and ax-mauled—even the sharpest stone blade did not
always break the skin—along with five Shitfeet, dead,
and a sixth, Big Man's nephew, sitting against a
maple tree, trying to hold his guts in place, gasping
and wailing as he tried to sing his death song. Such
was the custom of Shitfeet; Men died silently, teeth
clenched together.

The hunters must have walked into an ambush on
their way home. An elk's corpse, legs tied to a pole,
lay among the fallen.

The old man's hand continued to rest on Oak tree.
George could feel the roughness of the tree's bark
against the palm of the old man's hand, but at the
same time the succession of emotions sweeping
through Seppius' mind—baffled amazement, desolation,
sorrow, rage, hatred—made him glad he was firmly
planted in his armchair. Then, a moment later, he lost
track of these considerations because too many things
were happening too fast.

Five Shitfeet now ran into the clearing, baying loudly, their leader barely twenty steps behind Always-whittles-too-deeply. Laughs-dropping-children-in-fading-winter, who lived with Noisy-coughing-but-catches-many-fish, picked a brand from the fire and thrust it in a Shitfoot's face. He fell back, screaming, but one of his companions drove his short fighting spear into the woman's middle. She doubled over. Fisher, still weak from winter sickness, emerged from his lodge, ax in hand. Two Shitfeet headed for him.

Seppius stopped leaning on Oak tree. His long-bow was by him; he set arrow to the sinewy string, drew back. *Whisshhht!* A gray-feathered shaft sprouted from one Shitfoot's left kidney. The man bent backward, mouth wide open, screaming. His companion turned to look, and Fisher's ax thwacked on his right shoulder. He dropped his spear. An awful grin came on Fisher's thin face as he swung the ax, two-handed, against the Shitfoot's left temple!

Knows-where-bears-sleep had also been left behind; he had been sleeping in bushes west of the clearing, as usual. Now he was standing there, rubbing his eyes, and his little son, six winters in This World, was headed his way, dragging three good longspears. Four more Shitfeet burst into view. The spears of two of them almost grated together inside Knows-where-bears-sleep; the third sank his boat-shaped ax on the boy's head; the fourth, about to spear the boy, screamed loudly as one of the old man's arrows sprouted from his left eye, where it had gone in a whole hand's breadth. The Shitfoot fell on the fresh green grass, kicking, and howling horribly.

The old man was in despair. If only his sons were here! Swift-as-ermine-with-running-brook-laughter was swinging an ax at a red-bearded Shitfoot; he grabbed her ax handle, dropped his own ax, reached for her . . .

Seppius fitted another arrow to his bow, but then noticed a hint of movement twenty steps away, swung, and let go.

Aye. It was Murkhosteri gennu, Big Man, whom Men called Hates-his-own-dogs. The arrow entered

200

his right side. Good. To cough up blood until he died, many days hence, was for Big Man fitting and proper.

Meanwhile, Seppius fitted another arrow to string, aiming at the Shitfoot group on top of Always-whittles-too-deeply, at the madly flailing arms and legs. He let go, watched his gray-feathered shaft sail through air, heard footsteps behind and to the left, started to turn—

The last thing he saw was Big Man on one knee, leaning on a hide-covered wickerwork shield, and then something smashed against the old man's head.

Next thing he knew, he was facedown in dirt, arms and legs spread painfully wide apart. His head hurt. His stomach and chest, too. In fact, every breath he took hurt. Some of his ribs must be broken.

The air was heavy with the smell of smoke, burned flesh, and honey.

Honey—of course! He could feel the tiny feet and jaws of the ants. As he stirred, flies rose up, buzzing angrily. The Cowdung-covered-knees had been afraid to kill him and had staked him out among the shambles, smeared with honey all over so the Littlest Ones would loosen his soul from body.

That was their mistake. This Worker-with-things-and-spirits-for-Men was mild-tempered, befittingly so; but now they would be sorry, sorry, sorry, sorry . . .

He opened his eyes and moved his head, painfully, side to side. He could see corpses, in profile, here and there, among broken cooking pots and ashes. Fisher's headless body lay two steps to his left, a stake pounded through his liver region; just beyond was the corpse of a woman, also headless and staked to the ground. He strained at his bonds but they would not give.

After a while, he stopped tugging and trying to thrash around and lay still, weeping with pain and rage. He must get loose! Had to. Had to. Otherwise, long before Older-son and Younger-son returned, the Littlest Ones would be stripping the last shreds of flesh from his bones. Even now, they were beginning to crawl up along his sides and arms.

The Flame-Eggs! The Shitfeet might not have

known where to look—under the holy right rear corner of his lodge. Perhaps they had been afraid to look.

Spread-eagled, face down, he could not perform the ritual aright, with proper gestures, but it might work. He fixed his mind on the rough, reddish stones in their age-old leather sack, first on the sack and then on every individual Flame-Egg fragment.

Hah! His eyes moistened at the first remembered twingings in the back of his mind and then throughout his head. His aches and pains seemed to fade; it was no longer of any importance that he was tied facedown against the ground and that the Shitfeet were leading their captives—yes, Swift-as-ermine among them, her face badly bruised and eyes red from weeping—along a path near Little Dark-Water Lake. That glimpse in his mind caused the old man to dash his face against the dirt.

Hot tears burst from his eyes. He had failed to give warning! Men had been killed. But the Shitfeet would be sorry, sorry, so sorry.

Ahh! His imperfect ritual had worked. He raised his face and smiled grimly as flies buzzed up from him and ants scampered away. He lay a long time, relaxed now, savoring his release from the threat of being eaten, bit by tiny bit, by the Littlest Ones. He could sense wolves in the alder trees; they did not trouble him, because the meat of dead Men would suffice the gray hunters, and despite absence of laying-out platforms this was proper. Darkness spread over the clearing and he fell asleep. Occasionally, half-wakened by some night sound, his thoughts went to the Flame-Eggs, but no one bothered him, although some foxes, and a pair of wolves, came to feed. The wolf bitch was badly in need of meat for her milk; the sounds of chewing and swallowing were pleasant to the old man's ears, a sign the world was as it had been: the dead Men, Fisher and the others, had killed and eaten and were being eaten in turn, even if the proper rites could not be performed.

He woke just before dawn. Soft rain was falling, washing his wounds, laving his aching limbs. Light-headed and feverish, he thought of the rain drops as somebody's fingers, many winters ago—but only briefly. All of a sudden, memories flooded back and he strained painfully at his bonds. Then, smiling grimly, he licked the wet earth before starting to tug, very, very deliberately, at his softening rawhide bonds. The Shitfeet had used good, firm knots, but this was a long and friendly rain; and he had nothing else to do, in any case.

He finished freeing himself in mid-afternoon.

For a long time, he continued to lie there in the continuing rain. It had been agony. His left arm was broken, his left leg was broken, several ribs must be broken; but at least he could move. The pain—he bit down on his lip—did not matter. He gritted his teeth. Even if no Man was near, crying out in pain was not proper for an initiated hunter. He crawled to the nearest broken food pot. Much later, crawling painfully to Brook, he grinned with grim satisfaction, sure now that he would make the Cowdung-covered-knees regret their doings.

Strips of rawhide would keep the splints in place on his broken limbs. Fortunately there were enough broken, half-burned lodge poles and spear shafts lying around. In a few days his sons would return . . . It would hurt, of course, hurt dreadfully . . . He did what must be done, splinting his leg and arm, chewing his lips; and then he crawled under the bushes near Brook.

He never knew how long he slept. Maybe the next day—gray and chilly—he woke, stiff and acheful all over, no longer light-headed but rather sodden in mind, full of dreadful sorrow. Still, he was alive. He devoured some meat scraps, fell asleep . . . woke, wolfed more dried venison, wept, slept . . . slept to wake and stare in a wolf's questioning eyes while trying to fix his thoughts on the Flame-Eggs. He heard chewing sounds in the clearing. He slid back into sleep. Next time he awoke, he felt stronger, strong enough to remain sitting against an alder tree after drinking from Brook. He watched the afternoon sunlight shift across the clearing where Men's chewed bones were becoming soil now, properly so, and wondered when his sons would return. Sun set, gnats came to dance on the air, a round-faced Moon peered over the treetops. Dogs and wolves challenged Moon, so white and round-faced.

That cold, white light made Men sleep uneasily. But Others . . . Others, even the now-gone grass-eaters, did strange things in the light of the round-faced Moon. He had seen them, with the help of the Flame-Eggs. Yes, he was strong enough to watch to-night.

George wondered, vaguely, about the technical details of this experience. He had felt the old shaman's every ache and pain and had set his own teeth at the sound of bone grating on bone, without losing awareness of his own room and chair. Had anybody devised a technical vocabulary to cope with such experiences . . . ?

The Shitfeet had built a huge bonfire in their encampment. George realized he was wrinkling his nose. Murkhosteri gennu, Big Man, Hates-his-own-dogs, was lying on a heap of fine peltry by the fire, his hands shaking as he drank fermented honey flavored with herbs from a large bowl, coughing up globs of blood every now and then. Hah! The arrow had flown aright, and it was proper Big Man should die slowly. All the other Shitfeet were there now, dancing and whooping and screaming. Eleven of them were raping captive women—*Men!*—and, yes, one of the captives was Swift-as-ermine-with-running-brook-laughter, clawing and biting.

The old man set his teeth, fighting down his rage, forcing himself to watch: memory would strengthen him later, when strength would be needed. The captives were naked, covered with bruises, each with one ankle tied to a heavy wooden block. The Shitfoot women were prancing around the bonfire, as were their extra men; from time to time a warrior would take a kinsman's place with the captives and, every now and then the wounded chieftain would put his bowl down and roar aloud. Thereat, several Shitfeet would whoop and drag a captive over to be fondled by the death-marked Big Man with a sort of desperate roughness, while the dancing picked up speed and everybody yelped more and more loudly.

It was all supposed to make the food grass thrive and the females, of Shitfeet and their domestic or captive animals, to bear more young more easily. Proper enough, for *them*.

Now they were taking Never-stops-chattering, knee-high brother to Swift-as-ermine, and tearing him limb from limb. Some of the red-dripping chunks were carried away in the dark night to be buried in the eating-grass fields and under odorous byres, while his head was set aside, probably destined for some sharpened stake; but most of the boy was tossed in a large, brightly colored cooking pot. All the Shitfeet rested then, for a while, allowing bubbles to burst and steam to arise, giving the captives an opportunity to weep without interruption, while a gray-bearded man with a bad left leg—his name was Thammi-tunnégandhur—strummed on a three-stringed bow chanting:

"Glory! Glory and blessings! Oh glory
Unto the hero, eagle-eyed, fiery-hearted destroyer
    of dark sorceries!
The buxomest doe-eyed wood damsels, plump-
    haunched and squealing, in fetters, fattest
    morsels of flank meat and foamiest mead—
Matching the gore he made flow forth over wide
    pastures—
All are the conqueror's due, aye, but far grander
    than these is the glory!
Glory of Big Man, bravest in battle, most all-
    knowing in council, sagest, selecting the best
    site,
The site where valorous warriors, laughing in
    fierce joy, launched their fierce, all-smashing
    onslaught,
Slashing to shreds the darkling shroud, sorcerous,
    land-overshadowing,
Laving the wide pastureland with rivers of wood
    skulkers' gore,
Smashing spells, the spells that rot grain in the
    field, kill kine in their byres, smother babes in
    the womb.

No more are those spells now. So great is the
glory of Big Man and valorous warriors!
Glory! Glory! Glory and blessings upon all . . ."

Thammitunnégandhur's paean went on and on. Despite his gray beard, the man appeared entirely unaware of the unseemliness of bragging in behalf of
another. The old man's lip rose in scorn, as Murkhosteri gennu smiled painfully, with some effort, on his
pile of furs. After a while, but before the paean had
ended, old Shitfoot women began to dip bowls into
the broth and carry these around; those captives who
refused to participate in the meal were beaten until
blood flowed; that, too, would be a thing to remember.

So many things to remember, the old man thought
wearily, staring at dark treetops outlined against the
sky. So many . . . He fell asleep, seated, fists clenched
by his sides.

Gradually the scene faded from George's mind. He
sat up. Yes, his fists were clenched too, so tightly
the knuckles were white. He shook his head, but the
memories, unbelievably vivid and detailed, stayed in
his mind; he could almost whistle the tune of the
paean. The fertility rites of primitive agricultural people were pretty raw, from either a modern man's or
a Stone Age hunter's point of view, though there were
also certain revolting things about the hunters—such
as the way they disposed of their dead.

*Listening to long tales can be as wearying as their
telling.* The words had definite overtones of sympathy.
You were becoming weary.

"That's all right," said George, looking at his hands,
wondering whether Seppius' fingerprints—he could
almost see the gnarled fingers superimposed over his
own—had been anything like his. Not that it made
any difference. He was tired, his mind wandering. He
had told Gloria he would call her . . .

What time was it?

The alarm clock said 5:40. He turned and started
to dial Gloria's number with shaky fingers.

Gloria picked up the phone midway in the first
ring. "George?"

"Yeah. Listen, I'm fine, but this is taking me longer

206

than I expected." She inhaled sharply; he added: "I'm all right. Don't worry about me."

"Are you still listening to the sword's message?" She sounded incredulous.

He said yes; she demanded to know what it was.

He gulped. "That's hard to explain. And besides, I haven't heard the end of it yet."

"I see." She sounded annoyed. "How much longer is it going to take?"

"I don't know. Maybe a couple of hours."

"Sure of that?"

"Sure of what?"

"That you really don't want me to come over so we can go and get something to eat and . . . compare notes." Her voice was rising on the last words; her concern seemed to be overcoming her exasperation. He hoped she would not start to cry.

Neither of them said anything for a long moment.

"Look, I'll call you when it's over," he resumed, trying to be persuasive. "We can go out then. I'll be okay. It's just that—that I don't want to stop now, halfway."

She did not answer but he could hear her breathing into the phone. "I'll talk to you later about everything," she said after a while, and hung up.

Now what?

That is for her to tell you, herself.

For a moment, there, he had almost forgotten Seppius. So he could read minds from two miles away.

Yes. The tone was matter-of-fact, and then, as the implications began to sink in, Seppius added: *Listening to Others is improper, and among kinsmen it is not seemly at all. . . . But there is no way not to hear when, close by, two speak to each other.*

"I see." George shook his head, lit a cigarette, and sat down, wondering why Gloria's being upset should seem so important now, this minute, and obviously even to Seppius.

You are old to be living and sleeping by yourself. The words carried a hint of reproof.

George took a deep breath. Maybe he liked living alone. Besides, it was none of Seppius' business.

Man, or woman, lives as part of kindred. Gnarled

*are pine trees sprouting lonesomely from sand dunes
by the seashore.*

Yeah. Sure. George had a vision of Betsy—and what
might she have said about this situation? Actually,
Gloria probably felt the same way, but . . .

*You were going to see her. She would be glad to
see you.*

"I hope so," he said without thinking.

This seemed to please Seppius, because a feeling
of happy tenderness that was positively cloying—something like that associated with thoughts of Swift-as-
ermine—flooded George's mind. Fortunately it was
wordless. George bit his lip. Now the tone was becoming chilly; he must have hurt Seppius' feelings.

George had to bite his lip again—and think of biting
his lip, hard—to keep from laughing out of relief and
at the incongruity of it: George Quinterus worrying about the feelings of the Seeking Sword! At the
same time, he genuinely regretted offending the old
man. No, the old kinsman. A strange, quaint, archaic
phrase, but it fit the situation.

He ground out his cigarette, wondering what Seppius thought of the habit, nodded toward the sword's
shelf, and said aloud, "I am not used to sharing my
feelings, because I have been living alone. That is why
I reacted the way I did." He paused. "I am sorry."

The ways Men live and think change. The tone was
grudging, definitely disapproving. *Some things do not
change, however, and this is proper.*

George set his teeth; for a moment he had the distinct impression that Seppius was about to tell him
what he ought to do (!), but in the end—he could almost hear the sigh—the old shaman merely said that
the tale was already many winters old, and its telling
could wait.

"I'm sure of that," George responded, trying to keep
his voice steady and wondering whether Seppius
found this amusing.

Still, he had come this far; he'd annoyed her, sure,
but in a way tonight was the culmination of years of
hard work—and he'd better see it through. Going to
see Gloria now would be like yelling "Hold every-

thing until I call Carnett, the television people, and everybody."

No. It had started out his crazy show, and he might as well keep it that way. He'd talk to Gloria later and . . . Shit! Could he ever be alone with her now?

"Let's hear the story." Somehow speaking out loud felt more normal.

It is a long tale from the attack on the encampment of Men to the night I came to this dwelling. An undertone of censoriousness rang through the next phrase. *Thoughts of dung are for dung.*

Dung? What the hell did the old bas—kinsman mean, taking off like this? George half got to his feet, took a deep breath, and sank down at Seppius' response.

After thinking of dung, you wanted to be alone with your thoughts—and properly so, since the thoughts were of you and her. A pause. *The name Gloria is not to my liking, but no one has asked her, in accordance with the customs of uninitiated Men these days, and neither did her parents know any better. That is, her foster parents, those who raised her and named her.*

George had not really doubted Seppius' telepathic powers and this was more evidence in their favor. The Barrs had adopted Gloria and had never told her who her parents were. That is, if they knew; George was inclined to doubt this, because by the time she was twelve, old Raymond Barr would have thrown any unflattering background info in her face. This was beside the point; the important thing was that Seppius was no eavesdropper when he lowered the curtain. Curtain, down!

That was good. And they could talk man to man—man to sword—when he wanted. George smiled; the hell with semantics, proprieties, whatever. But he'd better get the curain up if he waned to hang on to his ancient kinsman's goodwill. Okay, curtain up!

Perhaps it was his imagination, but suddenly he could sense somebody else's presence in the room, or rather, in the back of his mind. For a long moment, he sat, studying his stretched-out feet. Now then—his relationship with Gloria was their business, and any time they wanted advice they would ask for it. Period. Enough said?

He could sense Seppius' approval in the form of— almost—a chuckle, followed by: *It is a long tale.*

"I can take a hint."

George got up, went to the kitchen and looked at the half-empty bottle. No, he'd had enough. Then he turned to the refrigerator for a beer.

On the way back, he paused for another look at the sword. A thin film of gray dust covered the walnut-stained shelf, but the dark blade and handle were spotless; Bernie Kratzel's file mark was distinctly lighter—the sword's most noticeable feature.

He turned away and flung himself on the chair. "Kinsman, tell me how the sword was actually made." He lit a cigarette.

Actually made? No Man would say that.

George almost smiled at the suggestion of *harrumph!* before Seppius picked up where he had left off:

Already, at the time of the spring feast, the old man had known what must be done: the Others must die. But how? He went to sleep with the question on his mind, and one morning—a bright, warm, radiant morning loud with the trilling of dozens of birds for whom George's city-bred mind had no names—the old man knew the Flame-Eggs would provide the answer.

Here Seppius broke into a long, incoherent chant about pureness of fires, fiery snakes, and sky-fires— aurora borealis?—and how no death could stop a Man from doing what ought to be done. George puffed on his cigarette and sipped beer.

The chant ended with a flat statement that Older-son and Younger-son, with that little prattler and prancer, Flints-break-in-his-hand, had arrived near Brook. They had brought no dogs, but the little boy was carrying a cock capercaillie—his first—that he had killed with a throwing club. Apparently several days had passed since the morning loud with birdsong.

Seppius' chant had kept George from becoming so immersed in the tale that he could see through the old man's eyes, but now the scene was acquiring more detail, however this worked. Both the old man's sons had children of their own and had killed many bears, not to mention deer and elk. They were burly, tow-haired, with Karl Marx–type beards, and their wives had called them by other names; but to their father they would always remain Older-son and Younger-son. They showed little surprise or emotion, properly, at the news of the raid. Younger-son turned around and went back in the forest to hunt, while Older-son reset his father's broken arm and leg. That hurt, horribly, though the old man kept his mind on the Flame-Eggs and some red deer who should be near Weedy Pond, the place where Younger-son was headed with his own boy. A man must needs eat his fill to do what ought to be done.

The roasted venison that night was the best thing the old man had ever eaten, even though the raw white meat of the capercaillie had also been delicious. Capercaillie were a kind of large grouse. After eating, the old man explained what must be done and the initiated Men bore patiently with the endless prattling and questions of little Flints-break-in-his-hand. Some of the boy's questions were very painful to the old man's ears.

What ought to be done was simple enough. There were at least fifty male Shitfeet, full-grown, and alto-gether they numbered close to three hundred. They'd had ill luck in the past, due to offending the Keepers, but Men could not rely on this—especially since the Keepers also seemed angry at Men. No doubt there was a reason; but this was no time to worry about that. So, then: the Men could try and kill the Shit-feet one by one, but it was unlikely the four of them could accomplish this. They all agreed the Shitfeet must die for what had been done. That was only proper. It was unlikely that any other groups of Men, or People, would join in a fight that did not really concern them. Also, even if they found new wives, it would take generations before they were strong enough for a return raid on the Shitfeet, who would also have been increasing in numbers. In the mean-time, however, a weapon might be made of the Flame-Eggs.

Next morning, the Men began with their task.

First, they moved their encampment two days' journey—very painful for a hobbling oldster—to a fine stand of pine trees and elm trees near the stream called Black Deep Water. Older-son and Younger-son and, after a while, their father felled trees, many of them, split the trunks and hacked these limb from limb —a task that lasted well into winter. The younger Men never went far to hunt. Whenever food was needed, the old man used the Flame-Eggs to call game in close, and never did that take longer than half a day—an indication that the Keepers were back on the side of Men. The weather proved that, too: the rains held off so the wood could dry, and necessary herbs sprouted forth in great abundance, even in places where they might not be expected to thrive.

Hah! These were not everyday times.

When all was ready, and the signs right, the three grown Men put the Flame-Eggs on flat stones surrounded by piled-up firewood. The old man made fire with two sticks and a bowstring of sinew from a doe's left hind leg, using the proper kind of dried pith—George's mind had no name for the reed-like plant from which the pith came. For days the fire blazed, the greatest fire ever made by Men; and after five days—sweaty, choky days spent in arranging chunks of wood and toiling in smoke—the Flame-Eggs became dark-red and soft, ready at last.

The bed of flat stone slabs extended beyond the fire's edge. The outermost stones were smooth, like the side of a good ax, close to the pit that it had taken Older-son eleven days to dig and prepare—a pit so deep a tall Man could barely reach its rim with upstretched hand, lined with good white river clay, hardened by a fire they had burned on the bottom.

Now, on the sixth day, with the rising sun red beyond the smoke, Men pushed the Flame-Eggs, so soft they tended to stick together, out on the flat stones with long poles that would catch fire after a few tens of heartbeats.

Gritting his teeth, a piece of dripping deerskin over his face, the old man knelt upon wetted deerhide on his bad leg, his thigh throbbing with pain, braving the heat and smoke and sparks to go to work, pounding

Flame-Eggs into proper shape with the blunt end of Younger-son's ax.

Only part of the Flame-Eggs, the yolks, so to speak, would serve his purpose; it was hot, strenuous work to separate these, but he did it, somehow, gasping for breath, sweat running into aching eyes over his blistering forehead. From time to time, his sons would push the tacky red mass back among the flames while the old man staggered to the far side of the clearing and lay down, shaking. Then Flints-break-in-his-hands, whose name they had just changed to Claps-hands-at-big-fire, doused him with water. It had been improper, really, to change the boy's name; he would not be ready for his manhood rites—which he would go through all alone—for seven winters; but still, with everything improper and in disarray, the new name was pleasant to the man's ears. Older-son had suggested it, sadly; he had not smiled since learning the fate of his daughter, Swift-as-ermine-with-running-brook-laughter.

After the sun had started to set, Older-son and Younger-son began carrying water into the clay-lined pit. The old man returned to his task.

Thrice he had to fall back, to be revived by Claps-hands-at-big-fire, very serious and purposeful. But at last the weapon was almost done, not unlike a *koikhienethekonnan,* or flint dagger, but larger, pointed, with sharp cutting edge. It would serve Men well.

Yes, indeed, he mused as he staggered away from the fire for the last time and lay, smiling while Older-son began tumbling hot stones into the water-filled pit.

The last time? He was not altogether sure of that. There were no precedents for what he was about to do, as far as he knew. Still . . . He looked up at the cloud-flecked sky, with the constellation Men called Bird's Nest and the nine Spear-stars close to the top of the curved sky-vault; the three Wolves were skulking behind a cloud, but the Bear's Eye, the motionless star far up in the north, twinkled, seemingly amused by Men's doings.

He lay there, stretched out on a deerskin, savoring every bit of feeling: that clump of stiffish hairs beneath the small of his back . . . the joy of being able to stretch a leg too long bent . . . the kiss of the breeze, warm from the great fire, on his naked chest. He would go on—not as he was, but somehow. The way to Yonder World was familiar to him and it made no sense worrying about the unknown. He looked up at the stars; and then, as his grandson's footsteps came closer, he closed his eyes before the cold water splashed all over him. That, too, was a pleasure he might never feel again.

"Thank you, son's son," he said, trying to keep his voice even.

After a while, he returned to the task. The pit was now full and Younger-son kept pushing red-hot stones into it; the rising steam hurt the old man's bare feet as he put some finishing touches on the weapon. He closed his eyes, opened them, looked at it—yes, it was done. He made a gesture to Older-son, who came forward with an armful of herbs, mumbled something, and dumped the fragrant dried herbs in the hot bubbling water—

The steam almost made the old man jump up and flee. He didn't. How could he? He crouched on the hot stones, fixing his mind on the weapon, on Yonder World, the paths leading up to it and into it, and on hot, red Shitfoot blood aspurting.

Younger-son had stepped back. Worker-with-things-and-spirits-for-Men clutched his grandson close, hugged him, wishing him well in behalf of Men present and past, and Keepers; he pushed Claps-hands back, stood up slowly and painfully and looked around the clearing one last time, fixing all its details in his mind: dirt, stumps, stones, sere ferns under a clump of yews, sere brown grass, crows on branches, clouds in the darkening sky, stars, his sons' faces and figures.

A shift in wind sent smoke swirling low, hiding everything in murky haze. The old man reached for the weapon, folding a rabbit skin around the hammered-out tang that would form its handle. *Sizzle . . . sizzle! . . . sizzle.* The sound made him flinch, but it didn't matter, because of what was ahead. A crow flew over the clearing, cawing loudly, like a Keeper. Hah! A good omen.

One . . . two . . . three . . . four steps—and there

he was, on the edge of the pit full of steaming, bubbling hot water, trying desperately to fix his every thought on Flame-Eggs and the scorching hot weapon in his hand, and yet wondering . . . Wise Men, Men of power and skill, had sent their souls into standing stones, or elm trees or birch trees—but for some days only. In his case, it could be many winters before he might rest.

He must do what ought to be done. He lifted his crippled left leg, warming the toes in the steam; took one deep breath, his last; bowed from the waist and plunged, head first, into the steaming water.

The bubbling surface came closer . . . closer . . . closer—and how long could such a short dive take, anyway? Searing, scorching heat passed over his scalp, face, shoulders and back, like a red-hot knife. Then came waves of agony, horrible pain, and dreadful anguish. What if this was the wrong, improper thing? He saw a flash of long hallways with smooth, shiny, whitish walls, a glimpse of what George might have called a three-dimensional system of intersecting corridors; and then a new feeling swept away the pain— a feeling of neither hot nor cold, nor anything in between, but of rightness, duly arriving in these bright halls, a prospect of well-earned rest, someday, on a comfortable heap of furs, by a good fire, in pleasant company—

The phone started ringing and George reached for it with a grunt of exasperation. It would be Gloria, of course.

Oh, hell. It was time he took a break and he could use some dinner. And maybe she was entitled to learn what he had discovered.

"All right," he said into the phone. "Where shall we eat?"

30

November 27, 1971

"NOTHING EVER HAPPENS over Thanksgiving weekend, anyway," Joseph Carnett said to his wife. "I think I'll skip the news and go to bed."

"Okay," said Helen, looking up from her book. "I'll let you know if there's anything exciting."

He had just finished brushing his teeth when the phone rang. Helen picked it up after four rings, listened a moment, and called for him.

He went back into the living room, almost stumbling over the coffee table. This damned house took a long time getting used to. "Who's that?" he asked.

"It's a young woman," Helen said, her hand over the mouthpiece. "She sounds excited."

"Perhaps you ought to listen in," suggested Carnett, trying to make light of the situation.

Helen smiled and gestured toward the television set. Carnett nodded: he would take the call in his study.

As he picked up the phone, wondering about the call and wishing he'd brought along his pipe and fixings, he heard Helen hang up the phone downstairs.

"Carnett, here."

An explosive release of breath. "I hope you're happy now!"

"I beg your pardon." The response was automatic, even as Carnett's mind ran over the possibilities. George Quinterus' girlfriend, Gloria? The words had been screamed into the phone, she was furious, Midwestern—most likely Ohioan—and her voice had held definite overtones of fear and desperation.

"I think they got George."

"You're . . . Miss Barr, right?"

"Right," she said, took a deep breath, and exploded:

"Well, you and George together stuck him out on the limb, and he's in it now . . . I think," she added a moment later, in a smaller voice.

"What happened?" Carnett hooked a chair with his foot, pulled it over, and sat down. His hand holding the phone trembled. No, God, please, he uttered in silent prayer, and never mind the futility of that sort of belated effort.

"Oh." Evidently she had expected him to know, or hadn't considered that he might not know. "Oh. Hell. George got hold of the sword, and the whoozis—whatever they are—are getting hold of him."

"Really?" He was glad he'd sat down; sorry he had not brought his pipe.

"Really," she mimicked his voice. "Look, that's easy for you to say, whether it does any goddamned good or not." Carnett flinched at the fury of her voice. Anger began to rise in him, but he choked it back. She probably had cause to be furious and frightened. A moment later, he heard her swallow, and then she said in a considerably less agitated tone: "I—I guess I'd forgotten you wouldn't know what happened. He hasn't called you, has he?"

"No. What happened?"

She started to cry. He listened, silently and risked a quick dash to the side table where he'd set up one of the pipe racks. Yes . . . She was still sobbing, and from the sound of it had put down the phone—even if she had addressed him while he was gone, she would try again. He tucked the phone under his chin and began filling the old briar pipe he no longer smoked in public. The pipe was lit and going well by the time she was ready to resume the conversation.

"I'm sorry," she said, after blowing her nose loudly. "I—I just flew off my handle, I guess." Carnett made reassuring sounds. She sniffed—he could almost see her shake her head angrily—but after a pause she said: "What happened is, the man who's been committing the murders came and dumped the sword on George's doorstep Thursday night and took off—even though George had his gun. He . . . said getting shot would be an act of mercy."

She almost started to cry again, but regained control

217

in mid-sentence, and related the story: George's determination to solve the mystery by himself, his visit to the Catholic church and hearty lunch, her own desperate, repeated phone calls; and then, after she had pried him out of the house for dinner, they'd had a bitter argument an hour ago over what had happened and whether George knew what he was doing.

That started Gloria crying again, and Carnett wondered for a moment whether she could afford the long-distance call. Librarians did not make much money. He could hear Helen moving about, and at 11:24 she came up with one of the large brandy snifters, half full.

He nodded his thanks and whispered, "Seeking Sword." Her eyes widened.

At that moment, Gloria regained control of herself. "I think he started with the idea it was his show, and that he didn't need any help," she said. "That's how he felt last night, and today, and up to—hell, up to the time I went to get the car. My car. He must have walked or he took a cab."

"You said he's bought . . . this Seppius' story," said Carnett. "What is it?"

"It's something like the *Somnium*," said Gloria. "Remember that booklet the creep in L.A. took him on? About this sorcerer called Seppius who went to hell because he'd been avenging his family for fourteen thousand years, and the sword he'd cursed, and people like—like a Sir Minferth, whose presence sort of neutralized the sword. Well, George thinks he's one of these . . . 'sword-keepers,' he calls them!" Her voice rose in pitch.

Carnett nodded, to himself and to Helen, who had lingered in the room, looking curious. He pointed to the phone and Helen nodded, smiling. Her feet were still sounding on the stairs a moment later when Carnett asked Gloria to go ahead with Seppius' story. He hated to personalize the sword: it was like giving in to evil, like yielding the devil that proverbial first inch.

Gloria's voice was grim. "He hasn't heard the end of it yet . . ." she said. "But the way George tells it, there were these two Stone Age tribes somewhere in Europe. Call them A and B. There were other people then too, of course, but they don't come into the story." Her voice became more animated, as though she was becoming fascinated despite herself. "The witch doctor of the A's found some weird stones he called Flame-Eggs. These were a kind of telepathic transmitter—anyway, they could be used to tell deer to go to certain places and so forth." She paused. "He has no idea when this discovery happened, but it must have been way before 2000 B.C. Anyway, generations later, the B's came along and massacred the A's—all of them, except the witch doctor and some of his sons.

"The witch doctor made the Seeking Sword out of the Flame-Eggs, imprinted his personality on it, and he's still in there—or so George says. He's got all kinds of telepathic powers, and he can spot B's and A's. And whenever he finds a B, he starts looking for an A. Then he persuades the A to kill the B. I guess John Lambert was an A, and the kid, whatever his name was, a B," she added after a short pause. "That's about all, except that he can also order the rest of us around—I guess you and I would be C's. Only, George says Seppius doesn't like to drag strangers into family problems." She gave a short, bitter laugh. "To hear George tell it, the witch doctor is a gentleman— doesn't kill women or children, never hurts outsiders when he doesn't have to. Crap!"

The implications of what she had said were appalling, and George's sticking up for . . . whatever . . . was a bad sign. All of a sudden Carnett recalled George saying, back in April, that he knew the sword would never harm him. At the time, it had sounded like blather, but maybe *they* had already been probing at George's mind?

Carnett shuddered, took a sip of brandy—Californian, not the best, but good enough—and asked Gloria what George thought now about the various theories.

Another bitter laugh. "He says it's just the sword. There never were any Kill-thinkers, or super-shamans —and there are no proficiency tests, just murders at Seppius' command." Real hatred came out in Gloria's voice. "Why can't the old bastard stay dead, like he ought to?"

"You mean you believe all this?"

Carnett could not quite bring himself to do so. A centuries-old, secret European-American order of assassins was sort of barely conceivable; but an ancient sword imprinted with a Stone Age witch doctor's personality, or haunted by a shaman, or—hell—a *living* sword . . . well, that was too much. He believed in good and evil, sure, and not just as bloodless Unitarian abstract concepts; and furthermore, there were plenty of instruments of evil in the world; Hitler had been one, Stalin another, and present-day Eurasia was full of the bastards from Mao to Park to Brezhnev. But evil incarnated as a sword? No. Repeat: no. The idea was incredible, impossible, sickening, altogether too allegorical, a goddamned abomination. It had to be a lie, part of the deception practiced by the assassins or super-shamans, to cover their loathsome tracks.

In his reverie, he had missed most of Gloria's reply and asked her to repeat it.

"What's wrong—run out of tape or something?" she demanded.

All right. It helped her to blow off steam. But still . . . He bit his lip and said, "I'm sorry. I was just thinking, and I didn't hear you."

"I hope you were thinking about your part in all this."

"My part?"

"Yeah."

"What do you mean?" Sometimes Carnett was surprised at his own defensiveness. Sometimes he regretted he had ever got mixed up in this, regardless of the rights and wrongs. Evidently he was more regretful than he'd thought.

"You encouraged him."

"Encouraged him? How?"

"By taking him seriously. Oh, crap, I was going to say I was trying to talk him out of it, and Jim too, in his way, and if it had worked we'd never be having this conversation and George wouldn't be in . . . in whatever condition he's in." She paused. "Damn you— I mean Seppius." She paused. "But you, too."

All this left Carnett quite dizzy. If Quinterus had never called him up, Gloria and Jim Whatsisname would have talked Quinterus into giving up his quest. And the murders would have gone on and on. But that would have been all right, because Quinterus would not be involved . . . He asked her whether that was what she meant.

"Oh, hell!" She was dangerously close to crying point again. "Of course I don't mean that. Of course murder is murder—as you people in government should know." Her voice kept rising.

Carnett thought he could hear Helen take a deep breath.

He forestalled her. "Forget the politics. All right? The point is: regardless of those people who blew up the building at Wisconsin, and—and, all right, the Ohio National Guard, and so forth—the sword is worse. It's got to be stopped. Right?" Even if witch doctors are a persecuted minority, he added in his mind.

"Okay," she said doubtfully.

"I really admire George for setting out to stop the Kill-thinkers. After all, they weren't after him. He was just trying to do the right thing."

"I know. I know . . . He's that sort of guy."

Something about her tone made Carnett wonder. Right now, however, George's relationship with Gloria was beside the point.

"He is," Carnett said in a soothing voice, listening for Helen exhaling. Yes. He must be doing all right. "He is one hell of a guy, and he's got himself into a fix, and we'll have to get him out." He hoped he sounded less fatuous to her than he did to himself. "We've got to get him out," he said again, continuing his pep talk to himself. Go, team, go; blood, sweat, tears! Rah-rah-rah! At the same time, he was appalled at being annoyed—and at George, for going out and getting himself in trouble, so that now Joseph Carnett was expected to go save the man, and get himself killed, while Helen and the kids . . .

Carnett ground his left knuckle viciously against the side of his stubbly jaw. That wasn't fair. As he'd just been saying, George Quinterus was one hell of a guy; and he himself had been in it for some time now, also of his own free will. He'd have to do whatever he could—even if George's cause had been less worthy.

There had to be more to it than this all-too-pat story of the Stone Age shaman's revenge, right out of the old-time B movies. Real life was more complicated, without solitary heroes or villains taking on the world on a continuing basis. It was hard enough to swallow one Oswald or Sirhan, once.

He had again lost track of what the girl was saying, but he did not want to ask it again. It was something about how she had tried to reason with George and failed. "He always thought a lot of *your* opinion, and so there's a chance, just a chance, that you might make him snap out of it." A pause, and then: "Excuse me. I can't stand it anymore." Another pause, during which she seemed to swallow, and click the back of her tongue against the roof of her mouth.

"I . . ." he began, not quite sure how he would finish the sentence.

"Forget it," she interrupted him. "I mean—I'm sorry, but good luck. If it works, he'll call me, and if not—" She slammed the phone down, hard.

People like her! He slammed the phone down, too, his mind racing back to their previous encounter, her ideas about secret weapons, the way she looked at him—and at George Quinterus, whenever George paid any attention to what he had said.

The hell with her. People like her gave him a pain.

That was hardly the point, however. The point was that something had happened to George and she was extremely upset—and he'd damn well better find out, for everybody's sake.

31

November 28, 1971

ITEM: GLORIA MIGHT be right; the Kill-thinkers had taken over George's mind and he'd told them all he knew—and nothing Joseph Carnett might do would make any difference. The only unanswered question was whether it was worth their trouble to kill all who knew about them.

Item: The Kill-thinkers had made a zombie out of George without picking his brains. Unlikely.

Item: The Kill-thinkers had taken over George and knew all, but didn't care because centuries of success had made them overconfident like thousands of villains, from Achilles to Sauron. An unwarrantably optimistic assumption. Right should triumph in the end, but no man could expect to live long enough to take the truly long view.

Item: She might have gotten on George's nerves and panicked when he told her to get lost. A pleasing thought, but not one to be taken seriously.

Item: Every hypothesis they had come up with was wrong. Perhaps.

Item: George's story was right. Unlikely.

So then—he'd better call George, listen carefully, and take precautions whenever the doorbell rang. He should have brought the hunting rifles along from Marbury and should buy Helen a .25 pistol and . . .

All these possibilities passed through Carnett's mind as he walked down the still uncarpeted steps of the rented house. Then, as he turned left at the bottom of the stairs, the sight of Helen sitting on the sofa next to the phone, with Dick Cavett—whose show she really liked, as he did, too—turned very low and Krazy sprawled by her right hip caused a wave of tenderness to sweep all over him.

Helen looked up. "Well, Joe?"

"I don't know." He remembered he'd left the pipe upstairs in an ashtray. "I just don't know," he said, marching over to the sofa and sitting down heavily, trying to sort out his options again.

Since Gloria had hung up only a minute ago, there must be at least a half-dozen he had not thought of yet. He knew his limitations.

Helen smiled. "I think she really loves him." She paused. "She's also very worried."

Carnett blinked. "It's as simple as that?"

"I didn't say that." She sounded amused; only slightly amused, because her voice carried an undertone of worry and she knew what this was all about.

"What do you mean?" he wanted to know.

She looked him in the eye for a long, long moment. "I mean that Gloria probably never took him seriously before, and now she's upset. Of course, she has cause. She's also blaming you somewhat illogically, and . . ." She smiled, somewhat impishly. "I think she sounds like a girl I'd like to know better."

"Oh?"

"They both sound like people I'd like to know better."

"Really?" He was rather dumfounded.

Helen nodded. "Like we always agreed suburbs are kind of unreal," she said. "Only, who wants to live in a high-rise hotel? Anyway, you wouldn't find these two in either place—though you just might find them in Marbury."

"Or around most campuses."

She nodded. "Yes."

They looked at each other, and she was the one to break the suddenly heavy silence. "What will you say to him?"

"I don't know. Really." He paused, thought it over. "I don't know, but I'd better make up my mind, hadn't I?"

She nodded. He thought it over for a while. "Like to listen in?" he asked then.

"If you want me to."

"My pipe is upstairs."

They looked at each other; he shook his head. There

224

was plenty of brandy left in the glass, and while he might want a long drink later, this was not the proper time for it. He got up, blew her a kiss and headed for the stairs.

Back in the study, he sat and puffed on the briar for a minute before he hit the floor with his left heel. He picked up the phone and dialed George's number.

The phone rang eight times before a sleepy voice said hello.

"George Quinterus? Joseph Carnett, here."

"Oh. Hi." A pause, and then: "She called you, did she?"

"Yes." Carnett thought he could hear Helen breathing on the extension.

"Well?" Quinterus asked after a pause.

"Well, what?" He intended to feel the man out, but George wasn't making it easy.

"Do I sound like a goddamned zombie, or something?"

This was a question Carnett had not expected. He shook his head. No. George sounded just as he'd expect him to, this time of night.

"Well?" demanded George, a note of annoyance creeping into his voice.

"You sound like yourself." Carnett hoped he was not sounding too doubtful.

"Yeah."

Carnett picked up his pipe during the ensuing pause. "Yeah, what?" he asked, at last.

"I hope you're satisfied, or whatever. Excuse me, now."

Carnett heard the sound of George drinking—probably beer from a can.

"Were you listening to more . . . of the sword's story?"

"Yeah."

"What do you think of it?" He wondered whether that was the right question.

George thought it over. "It doesn't matter what I think of it."

His voice trailed off, and Carnett again heard the sound of drinking. Now what? Suddenly he wondered whether the sword—the thing—could tune in on his mind over the phone, by way of George's mind. He sniffed. He was getting upset. But then, he had reason to be. Right? Maybe so. But he also had a job to do.

He cleared his throat, loudly, and George said he was still there, listening. Carnett asked him for his version of what had happened. "After all, you haven't been sending in any reports," he said. "I was getting concerned. She just called me before I had a chance to call you, and I wish it hadn't turned out this way."

"Yeah." Another pause, and then: "Look, I haven't been trying to hide anything. There's nothing to hide. I mailed a report this morning on how Paytna brought me the sword, and since then I've been busy listening to Seppius."

"Just what does that word refer to, anyway?"

"Oh." The writer chuckled; the sound sent shivers down Carnett's spine. A moment later, George said Seppius was a proper name, a contraction for something like Worker-with-things-and-spirits-for-Men.

"Worker-with what?"

Gloria's account had prepared Carnett somewhat. But this—and George's matter-of-fact tone—were a lot to ask any man to swallow.

"Sorry. Hell, let me tell you the story." Carnett must have gasped, because George hastened to add: "No, I'm not trying to recruit you, or turn your mind, or anything. I couldn't do anything like that and you're most likely out of it, anyway—a Group C type, to use Gloria's terminology." He hesitated. "She explained this, didn't she? I mean, I'm not talking about blood groups, but when I was trying to explain about Men and People, and Shitfeet, she said why not call them A, B, and C—only Men and People both were A's. Are A's, I guess."

"All right, all right." For a moment Carnett was afraid this would end it; that's how fed up George sounded. "She told me, and she told me about the other terms, too."

As it turned out, George had not quite decided about terminology, but his story was pretty close to Gloria's account. The way he kept referring to the

Seeking Sword, or Seppius, bothered Carnett, though —not so much the words as the tone of voice. In the beginning, this was understandable; after all, the old shaman had suffered a terrible wrong in a time when there were no means of legal redress. But George's sympathies remained apparently unchanged, even when the blood feud continued into times when no one knew what it was all about.

Carnett could see why Gloria had said the Killthinkers might be getting hold of George's mind, and as he listened to the Sword's story, which he still couldn't accept, he found himself looking for possible clues.

The story was simple enough, even though Carnett didn't know much about prehistory. George was glad to help out. First, there had been the glaciers. These were in retreat about 15,000 B.C. The French cave paintings were dated to that period in time. By 8000 B.C. hunters had followed reindeer and other game animals as far north as Finland. About that same time—8000 B.C.—people in the Middle East were beginning to raise wheat or barley, but it took thousands of years for this so-called Neolithic Revolution to spread into Northern Europe, which remained a happy hunting ground of . . . all right, call them A's. After all, they had been there first.

The massacre of the A's would have occurred somewhere near the Baltic coast of Germany or Poland. George wasn't sure; he was more explicit about the date. The first agricultural settlements near the Baltic Sea dated from before 3000 B.C. According to archeologists, these people, sometimes called Danubians, because their settlements were first excavated in Hungary, lived in large wooden houses divided into separate rooms, usually with one hearth per room. The Danubians had some kind of fertility cult, coexisted with the hunters in some places, and presumably corresponded to the first group of Others, or C's. Scholars disagreed violently on whether or not they spoke an "Indo-European" language. Centuries later, another and very different people arrived in northern Europe from the southeast. These newcomers were tall and raw-boned, raised crops but seemed more dependent on cattle-raising, and buried their dead in single graves—the men often with finely-polished axes unsuited for chopping down trees. In fact, these beautiful, canoe-shaped axes gave these people their name—the Boat-Ax People, in archeological texts. Most scholars agreed that these people's language had been Indo-European.

"Seppius calls them Shitfeet, or Cowdung-covered-knees," George informed Carnett. "Gloria called them the B's."

"I see," said Carnett.

"Some scholars say these people, our own ancestors, by the way, introduced the warrior ethic to Europe," George went on, trying to make his erudition sound light, but without much success. He paused for more beer, and Carnett used the time to relight his pipe. "Now, there had been plenty of bloodshed in ancient Egypt and in the Near East already. Besides that, different clans of People fought over hunting grounds, and I'm sure the hunters and Danubians didn't always get along either. It's just that the battle-axes are supposedly the oldest stone implement found in Northern Europe that could not have been used for anything except show, or for fighting."

"You aren't taking Seppius' word for all this, are you?"

"He's not really talking about that. I've read a lot lately . . . but now, let me tell you the rest."

There was a simple, remorseless, utterly horrible logic to it, especially as recounted in George's matter-of-fact tones. The B's had killed the A's, and dragged the surviving women into captivity. The survivors, seeing their only chance to get even, made the Seeking Sword and the shaman's self-immolation somehow imbued the weapon with his coldly vengeful personality. Carnett decided to let that pass for now. The remaining A's attacked the B's, and were hunted down and killed. The B's celebrated the victory with an epic mead-drinking bout and much barbarous chanting, while the sword was set up as a trophy in front of a wooden idol.

Some years passed; and then, after many of the sons of the captured women had reached maturity, all the

B men were slaughtered one night after a feast by the half-A boys and, apparently, slaves, who must have been of either C or A origin. The sword's part in the slaughter was unclear, as George admitted freely. In any case, the victors burned the standing grain, butchered the livestock for a feast, and reverted to the hunters' way of life, sort of under the direction of Seppius' granddaughter, named Swift-as-ermine-with-running-brook-laughter. Shades of Longfellow and Laughing Water! Still . . . in a way, the name was vivid, and must have lost something in— how many?—translations.

Being either A or B was apparently a recessively inherited characteristic and probably depended on more than a single gene. Both A's and B's, or at least the two clans directly involved, must have constituted breeding populations with certain specific characteristics, like strains of laboratory rats and rabbits, while the rest of the human race—the C's—apparently lacked these particular genes that very likely had something to do with brain-wave patterns and—

All of a sudden, Carnett felt slightly ill.

George kept droning on while he regained his composure with the help of the pipe. The original massacre, George was saying, must have happened around 2500 B.C. Each new generation contained both A's and B's and the sword kept busy, until the hunters couldn't endure it any longer. Around 2350 B.C., their clan—which apparently had moved further north and east—broke up and the sword was left buried deep under the ashes of a dead fire. The forests for a day's journey around were declared taboo: too dangerous to hunt in. This did no good, of course, besides insulting Seppius to the depths of his—iron?— heart; from his point of view, the A's had forsaken their own cause, as defined for all time by those A's living at the time the sword was made. In any case, a few generations later, say around 2200 B.C., a man —an A, or more A than B—happened to pass through the forbidden area; he soon felt an urge to dig, found the sword, wondered about it, camped in the clearing, and that night Seppius made his first previously ignorant convert. The young man, whose name was

Yllevenenne something, or "lynx-like," because of the cast of his eyes, turned west instead of north, and two days later he killed a hunter named something like Elthenessury, who was more B than A—in George's words. Yllevenenne had never heard of Elthenessury, or his clan, but as he slashed the other man to death he was sure this was the proper thing to do.

"The cuts and thrusts are kind of ritual," George remarked at this point. "They really haven't changed at all, and the victim doesn't know what is going to happen—and doesn't believe his own eyes."

"I see," Carnett said. "Say, does it just go on like this?"

He could almost see George nod. The writer's voice sounded weary. "I guess so. We haven't got to the end yet. He was just telling me about the doings of Kills-many-tens, sometime around 1900 B.C."

Around 1900 B.C. . . . that would be around the time of Hammurabi, the Babylonian king and law-giver, half a millennium before Moses led the Jews out of Egypt. Carnett permitted himself to shudder —both at the story, and at the ordeal still ahead of George, for all his apparent sympathy toward the monster, or monsters, that operated the sword. This, in itself, was baffling. How could Quinterus feel that way?

"George," he said after a long pause, very carefully, wondering what Helen might think of his approach. "George, what do you think is going to happen?"

"To me, you mean? Hell, nothing." There came the sound of drinking from a half-empty beer can. "Remember what the *Somnium* said about sword-keepers? Well, it looks like I'm one, too."

"Indeed?"

"Yeah. That means no more killings as long as I keep the sword with me." George paused, and added in a conversational tone: "I hope I'll have time to make Seppius see the light. He's not such a bad guy. Only sort of, well, circumscribed."

Carnett put his pipe down and reached for the brandy, wondering whether the liquor would persuade him that this—the whole conversation—was for real.

Back to the fray! Carnett shook his head and asked why the hell George thought he could trust the bastards?

The writer laughed. "Can't get the Kill-thinkers out of your mind, can you? Look, there aren't any—only Seppius, the shaman who sent his soul into the sword, or whatever technical term you want to use. It's been him, all along; a goddamned one-man operation going on for over four thousand years." He repeated the last phrase, his voice full of awe. "Four thousand years! As I read him, Seppius is the type who does his duty, but every so often even he gets tired. Ready for some R & R—as we used to say in Korea. Then, since he's sentimental, he finds himself a fireside—as I gather it, with some particular A who is especially congenial for some reason." A note of pride crept into George's voice. "I guess I'm the current sword-keeper."

"I still don't see how you can trust—his—word," Carnett insisted.

"Two reasons," said George in a slightly aggrieved voice. "First of all, neither Lambert nor any other killer ever had these . . . well, leaked visions, like I did. None of them mentioned the kind of relationship with Seppius that I've got. Secondly, telepathy is a two-way street. You can shut the other guy out, but you can't lie; the emotions come across along with the words." He finished off the beer in the can. "Civilization would never work if telepathy was more prevalent," he announced in ringing tones. "Excuse me, now. I'm still dry."

So telepathy was a matter of the words and the music, both.

Carnett ground his knuckle against the left side of his jaw. He'd better avoid digressions; this was too serious. Fine. Levity, all levity . . .

He finished his brandy before George picked up the phone again, with a cheery: "Well, here I am."

"I suppose I should congratulate you," said Carnett.

"Thanks." George sounded puzzled. "What for?"

"If you're the sword-keeper, you've stopped the

bloodshed for our time, right?" The writer grunted. Carnett heard Helen inhale sharply as he started his next question. "What did Gloria say to all this?"

A touch of embarrassment tinged the writer's voice. "She . . . well, she told me to shove it. The sword, I mean."

"Did Seppius have anything to say to this?" Carnett could not resist asking.

"Yeah, he did," George said after a long, tense silence. "Only I don't see where it's any of your business. I've never asked how Mrs. Carnett looks at your little hobby, have I?"

Carnett bit his lip. *"Touché."*

"You did raise a good point, though."

Now what was the right answer to that? Carnett suffered through a good minute by the wall clock before George said: "She really hates the sword. I tried to reason with her but that just doesn't work."

"She really cares for you," Helen broke in. A moment of strained silence followed; then she added: "I hope you don't mind my listening in, Mr. Quinterus. But don't worry about Gloria. She may say things you don't care for, but she's on your side and I'd very much like to meet her."

"I'm glad to hear that," George said in a small, toneless, preoccupied voice. "Well, I guess this conversation has gone on long enough. I don't want to run up your phone bill too much." He paused. "Good night."

Carnett sat, shaking his head, staring at the phone and absent-mindedly puffing on the now dead briar pipe. Yes, he had his own problems. But even if the phone was tapped—McCullough, over in Engineering, claimed most of theirs were—the troubles of Joseph Carnett were as nothing compared to George's, who had got himself in a real win, lose, or draw sort of situation. Perhaps Helen had been right about Gloria; but even so, Carnett could not see any future for them. He got up to go downstairs to join his wife. Thank God for her. And God help George Quinterus and Gloria—all of them, in fact!

32

December 1, 1971

THE SKY WAS gray. The cold rain had let up a bit, but the trees in the back yard were still dripping as George staggered into the kitchen to fix some instant coffee.

All of a sudden, he felt ravenous; while the hot water was running, he started frying eggs. Talk about sounds of music! Sometimes nothing could compare with a sizzle. He fried two more while eating the first pair, with some cinnamon toast; he also started some real coffee, and took a full mug to his armchair.

God, he was tired! He looked almost resentfully at the sword, so shiny and clean, without a speck of dust. How did Seppius do it, and why?

Dust tickles.

Oh? He should be getting used to this, but the beginnings of conversations still seemed unreal, even after four days, and the same was true of receiving answers to unspoken questions.

Dust feels like ants crawling up the legs and arms. No doubt. As George sat down and put the mug next to his right ankle, he wondered vaguely what "feels" might be like from Seppius' point of view. That was only one of thousands of questions he had thought of while being imprinted with the seemingly endless recital of how A slew B. Gloria's stark, unemotional terms were best; they even suited Seppius (who considered alphabetization something for Others), because the proper ordering of things should be a matter of course.

You enjoyed eating the eggs scorched, on hot metal and in fat. I felt pleasure at my kinsman's enjoyment.

Okay. That made sense.

233

You, kinsman, are learning. The words carried strong overtones of approval, but gradually the tone changed to utter loathing, as so many times before: *Men are not what they used to be, and ought to be as Men. They live among Others and learn the ways of Others and forget the ways of Men.*

The bitterness of the next words was like a knife thrust: *Men even forget that they have forgotten.*

George blinked. "Sorry," he muttered, reaching for a cigarette.

This has been happening for many tens of years. You were just born.

The patronizing tone made George bridle. "Look here," he said aloud, "as far as the Men are concerned, they had a pretty idyllic way of life, but there's no way it could have lasted." Silent dialogue didn't feel right, but as always his thoughts began to race ahead of his tongue; in another second he gave up the struggle.

Okay. The hunters had been happy in their way, but that way of life had been doomed even while Seppius I was fetching the Flame-Eggs, well over a thousand years before the raid on the encampment of Men. In any case there was nothing Seppius-in-the-sword or anybody else could have done about it. Some hunting people like Lapps and Samoyeds, Chuckchi, and Eskimo and Athapascan Indians of the Canadian Barrens had maintained their ancient way of life until the twentieth century; but even they had succumbed to modern civilization. As far as Seppius' band of Men were concerned, the final act began when the first grass-eating Others started hoeing their barley fields within a hundred miles of the Baltic in . . . 3200 B.C.? The exact date wasn't important. From then on, it had been only a matter of time. Even if Seppius' encampment had never been attacked, sooner or later, peaceably or not, his descendants would have started farming, because agriculture was a more reliable way to fill the belly than hunting. With game getting scarcer and scarcer, as it was bound to do, even the most stubborn of Men would have had to change their life-style.

It would have been wrong.

George had expected some vehemence, but there was none. Seppius was merely stating a fact.

"I don't see where right or wrong has anything to do with it."

The ways of Others are right for Others, not for Men.

"It's not that simple. Life is not static. Things change, and so do life-styles." George realized he hadn't lit his cigarette; he did, and observed: "Not all change is for the worse."

It is hard for you, kinsman, to stop being one of the Others—in your mind. This was patronizing; then Seppius changed to his schoolmasterly tone, with a hint of patience sorely tried. *The last thing you said is true. Not all changes are for worse, or better. The clouds in the sky are never the same on two different days. Leaves that grow from the same branch of a birch tree arrange themselves differently from one summer to another. Seasons change, in truth, and so do faces of Men in the circle around a feasting-fire, from year to year, because some have died of disease or in childbirth or in the hunt, and others have joined the circle, by birth, or adoption, or coming to live in the encampment.*

"That's not the kind of change I meant," argued George. "I meant changes in life-style." For instance, cigarettes had only been around since the 1800s, and canned beer . . . Hell, life in 1971 was a lot different from life in Seppius' day, with warm houses instead of smoke-filled tepees, an assured supply of food, cities, cars, planes . . . Yeah, and Hiroshima, napalm raining on Vietnamese jungles, chain-reaction crashes, smog, highway detours, starvation in India, Biafra, the slums of—well, Cincinnati, any major city. Sometimes a man couldn't help but wonder about progress, but turning the clock back was clearly impossible.

Many Men have said the same thing after saying I was wrong.

Once again, George thought of skin-clad Men huddling around their fires, the pale blue skies of early spring when grown hunters would eat the last morsels and go forth—because if they brought in no meat, no one would live to eat the summer berries, roots, and mushrooms. It had been a harsh, cruel time, while nowadays—

Men are living the way Others live. The words dripped contempt. *You were thinking, kinsman, of many hundreds of persons, persons living like those Others you call Danubians, dying, starving in a land where no grouse or deer live anymore, a treeless land, without eating-grass even, only dust and scorching sunshine.*

George bit his lip. Oh shit!

Thoughts of dung are for dung.

He took a deep breath before another try. "You can't just condemn the whole modern world as simply as that."

The kinsman's words mean nothing. Seppius had stated one of his facts; now he reverted to schoolmasterly tones: *Men have been learning the ways of Others. Others were always fond of names, and words they themselves did not understand.*

George felt the blood rush to his face. Obstreperous old bastard! All right, score that point for Seppius. But the real world was the here and now, while the world of Seppius' Men—and their mores—was gone forever.

World. The overtones were distinctly disdainful. *What is that?*

"Oh." Composing his answer, George let the images flood his mind: the little globe with pencil-sharpener base he'd had as a child, achingly beautiful astronauts' photos in *Life,* a copperplate engraving of Galileo, and figures—diameter of 7,927 miles, surface area of approximately 197 million square miles, total mass—

Kinsman, it is hard for you to stop thinking like one of the Others. Seppius sounded sympathetic.

Seppius wasn't trying to deny he was part of the —well, physical—world, was he?

I am here, if that is what you are wondering about. A pause. *Here.*

So?

I am here. You are here. You are my kinsman. A hint of amusement accompanied the next sentence. *Let Others worry about the meaning of the words of which they are so fond. That is not proper for Men.*

Oh, sure. George took a long drag on his cigarette. That would be far too simple, though, because "here" had to be at an identifiable locus, where such-and-such coordinates on a map were intersected by a temporal.

His line of thought was interrupted by the telepathic equivalent of a guffaw. *I am here!* There was a sort of bubbling quality about Seppius' words. *Here. Here is where I am, and all else is darkness, full of fires representing trees and many, many, that represent grass, and some representing what Others call animals and persons, different persons, Men, People, Others, Cowdung-covered-knees.*

George leaned forward. So all living things appeared to Seppius as fires in darkness? He'd thought as much. *True.* The bleak overtones made George's eyes feel moist.

Unless a kinsman is with me, Seppius added a moment later. The overtones suggested such cozy warmth, pleasure, affection, loneliness put aside and out of mind that George started to feel embarrassed. (Curtain, down!) That was the trouble with Seppius. He sort of grew on you, like a friendly tumor, as Gloria had said. (Up, curtain!) George reached for the half-forgotten cigarette, inhaling deeply, as the old shaman continued: *Being with a kinsman is like living-through, rather than knowing. When I am with a kinsman, I see with him as he sees and hear with him as he hears, feel with him as he feels and smell with him as he smells—meat cooking, and the wind off flooded meadows by the river in coming-summer.* A note of wistfulness had crept in; George could almost sense Seppius swallowing. *I felt the wind and rain in the face of the kinsman who brought me to this dwelling, and I sensed his relief though he was still worried and full of regrets as he went to his own dwelling far from here. He, too, thought the way of the Others, but he was less degenerate than most Men now.* The last statement had simultaneous overtones of condescension, regret, and disgust—and "degenerate" was a feeble, pallid term for the image in Seppius' mind: something like carrion hobbling on three twisted legs, smelling to high heaven.

George took a deep breath and kneaded the back of his neck. The image had been sickening—so why hang around people he found nauseating?

It is proper for Men to sit by the fire in an encampment where kinsmen live.

Even if the kinsmen are disgusting? And, moreover, want to be left alone?

Kinship is kinship. It is something that cannot be denied. Seppius was stating incontrovertible facts, but the overtones were becoming softer, almost cloying: *A Man belongs with kinsmen, and it does not matter if the kinsman's feelings would cause me to throw up, had I still stomach, gullet, and liver.* George could sense the effort by which the old shaman kept his feelings under control. Now he relaxed; the overtones changed to wry amusement: *Having no stomach, or colon, can be for the best, after seeing the fiftieth winter's snows melt and run down-stream.*

This sounded like a proverb. Seppius continued with a hint of wistfulness: *Many are the things to be missed: eyes, ears, tongue, penis, hands and feet . . . stretches of skin to feel the wind's caresses, ears to hear proper talking of Men, eyes to see blueness of sky and the sea's ever-shifting waves, and greenness in summer. Aged Men talked much about their problems in voiding, so it may be well I have no colon. Earlier you asked about dust, which I can cause to shift and I do not let settle on me because I have no limbs and cannot scratch.* Seppius was sounding both wry and wistful. *It is proper to avoid irksome things when it is impossible to have the pleasure of getting rid of what irks one.*

He had finished on a really poignant note, with a hint of the woman called Everbright-eyes-as-she-spots-berries in the background. She had died years before the raid. Just what did Seppius miss most, anyway?

To this there is no answer.

George took another long drag on his cigarette.

When all things are gone, a Man can only wonder. Sometimes it may be the touch of a dear hand, or a glimpse of the moon. A hint of embarrassment accompanied the next words: *It may be being able to stretch, to scratch, to shout at the top of the voice . . . or to taste strawberries.*

"Strawberries?" George hadn't expected that.

Yes. Especially strawberries that are ripe and not oversized, berries the size of the little finger's tip— wild strawberries, obviously—*that have grown on a southward slope in a clearing filled by sunlight.* Seppius paused, savoring. *Strawberries are the best thing to eat on a hot day of summer.*

George was still trying to think of an answer, when the old shaman added: *Would that I could taste strawberries again.*

He felt a wave of sympathy for the old shaman. This kinship business really seemed to be getting to him. What if he took the sword along to Europe, to some of its old haunts?

I am as I am.

The bleak overtones almost brought tears to George's eyes. "I'm sorry," he said after a while.

You cannot do anything about it. The all too familiar note of resolution was back, eclipsing the lapse into self-pity. *Feelings, tastings are gone. All that is left are memories and reminders, stronger reminders whenever a kinsman is near.* Seppius was sounding bleak again. *But that is better than wondering . . . Wondering . . . Shall there be another coming-summer like that before all was killed and burned?*

George wiped his eyes, feeling ridiculous. But worse was to come, because—he got the impression of absent-minded rambling—Seppius was describing ice breaking up on the Brook and ducks returning from the south; *hyuyillahasettenet* (white flowers) blossoming beside the last patches of snow, flowers whose fragrance was overwhelming; and how Seppius felt about these memories that he seemed to have kept apart from all later impressions . . .

Long last days in the long, white, lonesome halls
Far from the bustling of Men's encampments,
Far from dark pools, where stark pike stalk their
    prey . . .
With no new tidings from the rain-drenched earth,

Wet brown earth, seething, panting, with the win-
ter past,
Soft brown earth whence green grass shall soon
be sprouting . . .
With no new glimpses, of gangly elk calves
prancing,
Awkwardly, on slopes deep with snow no more . . .

Seppius stopped, painfully embarrassed. What on
earth for? Trying to comfort the old shaman—maybe
he was finally grasping the meaning of kinship—
George said: "Next spring, I'll . . ."

There seemed to be nothing sensible to say, so he
let the images sweep through his mind: hills along
the Ohio River in fresh green spring finery . . .
what the marshes by Lake Erie must look like in
April . . . the unbelievable flowers blooming on shell-
plowed hillsides along the Korean DMZ.

True. Summer will come. Seppius seemed to have
regained control of himself.

"I . . . we, we'll drive around the country and you
can see coming-summer through my eyes." George
wiped his eyes with the back of his hand, basking in
Seppius' approval.

*The offer is proper, what kinsmen do for each
other, but it is one thing to see coming-summer, and
another to know it through a kinsman.* The overtones
were as bleak as any George had experienced. He felt
his eyes become wet again, trying to think of . . . well,
every winter must end, pots of gold at the ends of rain-
bows, spring following fall. *Nach jedem September,
kommt wieder ein Mai.*

When the task is done there will be time for sleep.
Seppius sounded embarrassed again, and suddenly
George realized the old shaman begrudged himself
these periods of rest and recreation, maudlin meander-
ings by Men's firesides. So should he swell with pride
at being a swordkeeper, a recipient of four-thousand-
year-old confidences? He shook himself. Duty was
duty and all there was, no doubt; and properly
initiated hunters should feel no elation at doing what
was proper. But perhaps—just perhaps—these R & R
periods had another purpose, inseparable from duty, to

make sure the stock of B's would have a chance to replenish itself? After all, what if Seppius was not ready to sleep yet?

It is hard for you to stop thinking like one of the Others. Mild enough, with overtones of contempt, increasing in intensity, and an image of what must be the great-granddaddy of all winter storms. George felt glad to be sitting down, before his mind was blown blank by the force of: *MEN DO THINGS BECAUSE THEY ARE PROPER.*

33

December 1, 1971

WHEN GEORGE GOT a chance, about an hour later, he asked about the second verse that described elk calves and springtime. He half expected a violent outburst, but Seppius was only startled.

Why ask?

"I liked it and I just wanted to know," said George, smiling at the mixed emotions accompanying Seppius' response. As for his own reasons, there was no point trying to hide them. He had liked the poem, and he was getting (Down, curtain!) tired of how, over and over, unwilling Men, who had learned the ways of Others, still did the proper thing at the old shaman's "urging."

By now, Wednesday afternoon, the Saga of the Shaman's Revenge had reached the eighteenth century, with the score 33,887 to 4000; only *approximately* four thousand, because Seppius did not care what happened to *"bad kinsmen who never wished to do the proper thing"* once they had finally cut the throat of their particular Shitfoot.

As for worshipers, like the benighted peasants of

Assachwenmaege, he was even less understanding and more scornful than George.

The murders had a good deal of variety. Sometimes stranger killed stranger, as Yllevenenne slew Elthenessury. John Bendersen and Olav Dagne knew each other; and that was true in hundreds of other cases. Sometimes the killer never realized, or admitted to himself, what was happening, as in the case of Sir Walter the Crusader and the Bailiff of Notzem. Or the killers—Hervör, Mirilae, Vuzalep, or Akutte—had known all about their destiny; and sometimes the victims—like poor Erich Goelst—had, too. Endless variety in details went hand in hand with terrible, numbing sameness: Seppius spots another virulent "fire in the dark" and rises up high, "seeking round about"— another of many expressions never explained to George's satisfaction—before persuading the nearest Man, usually successfully, to go and kill. All this was recounted in a sort of rhythmic news-report style, in a more animated tone than Part Two of the saga, with everybody's name, features, age, and a few hundred words on the . . . well, description of stalking, chase, whatever, followed by a coldly gleeful account of the throat-slashing.

Sickening. And that was not the worst of it. Somehow—George would never be able to explain—he knew that Seppius' narrative was being imprinted on his mind so that he could recall every incident, word, expression, gesture, and detail down to the length of candles guttering on the alchemist's workbench next to the large bowl of acid. George shuddered at what had happened that day in Pagedi. He could also recall the mismatched buttons on poor Erich's patched blue coat, the skyline of Hammaburg before Danes burned it in the 860s and of Jomsburg when Bue the Stout saw it for the first time in the 970s, not to mention the jovial bantering words between Klaus Störtebecker and Gödiche Michael, and the expression on Johann Röde's face when he saw the branding iron, or Lyvo Peter's smile as he whetted his knives . . .

George Quinterus was not altogether sure he wanted to be able to remember all these things.

Still—and this had occurred to him during brunch

—listening to Seppius was making him the world's foremost expert on North European history. It was like looking through a keyhole—but at real, live people in real-life situations. He could even listen to a philologist pronounce words as he thought they should have been and say: "Yes," "No," "How about *oeo* instead of *ieo,* with a twist of the mouth?" In time he might get Seppius to open up on other things.

Gradually, he became aware of a gentle knocking or scratching at the back of his mind. Oh. (Yeah. Up, curtain!) In the instant before Seppius' words came flooding in, George wondered about the old shaman hovering around outside—if that was the right word—waiting, knocking . . . The writer shuddered.

New things take a moon to get used to.

Of course. How did Seppius know when to depart and when to return?

When a kinsman stands up and walks away from the campfire into the dark woods, tagging along would be improper since he wants to be by himself.

All right, but there was no fireplace at 659 Galway Place and, anyway—George tried to repress the thought—Seppius was on the shelf of a bookcase in the living room while George lay stretched out in bed.

There is a fire, spreading warmth, whenever two or more kinsmen are together. The feelings associated with the words were reverential, familiar, warm, cloyingly so, with undertones of schoolmasterly exasperation. After all, Seppius and George had gone over this before. George set his teeth for what would surely follow, as it did: *Men who live among Others and learn the ways of Others often forget the ways of Men proper unto them.*

Yeah. Well, he couldn't help it, being born late in a degenerate age—and, furthermore, what about the elk calves?

Seppius sounded almost coy. *As for that verse, that is something to pass time with during long, dark silences. Beside the tale of the doings of Men, that is nothing—birch-tree leaves rustling while the Man-carrying eagle flew over the clearing.*

There was no help for it, then. George raised himself on one elbow and lit a cigarette, wondering about the weather. Still wet? Hard to tell, since the shade was down. Maybe he should call Gloria at work—or later, maybe.

Not all things ripen with more time. Some spoil.

The fatherly, concerned tone made George grit his teeth. "I'll call her, damn it," he said. "I'll call her when I want to—and I'd appreciate it if you didn't listen in." That would hurt the old bastard's feelings. It did.

Snoops are smashed on the snout, and properly so.

Seppius was still aggrieved as he added: *A kinsman's doings concern all kinsmen, because of the love they have for each other—else how could enough hunters be gathered together to stalk the bear in his lair, or aurochs in summery glade?*

All right. George's own parents had been like that, too, and he could sympathize with them, now; even with Seppius. But some things remained private.

True.

Okay. Now that they'd established the point, Seppius might as well continue his tale.

A guest's welcome may differ, several times the same day. This had been just another proverb, but the next phrase made the back of George's neck tingle, momentarily. *Keepers, too, have been known to vary in their moods.*

Yeah. Keepers. One of many subjects on which he could use more information. The Flame-Eggs were another. And so were the exact manner in which Seppius spotted virulent bonfires, and his explanation of the laws of inheritance governing the descent of Men and Cowdung-covered-knees, and the precise mechanism of Seppius' telepathy. Just how had he imprinted his personality on the Seeking Sword . . .

Kinsman, you keep asking questions that have no meaning, Keepers are Keepers.

Seppius was being patient. Oh, hell! George sat up on the bed, threw his cigarette on the floor, reached for a shoe to grind it out—there! Silly and futile as it was, the gesture made him feel better.

Once kinsmen have heard enough, and talked over things enough, they generally come to know, and to know what has been talked about.

Oh sure. George rubbed his eyes. Hell, the truth

was, he had been cooped up with Seppius too long now and needed somebody—not Gloria, just now—to talk to; or he could go for a walk, regardless of sleet, and—

The phone rang.

Incredible, the speed at which he moved to answer a call from Gloria—or Carnett. After all, who else would be calling at this hour?

"Yeah. Hello?"

"George?" A vaguely familiar voice.

"Yeah . . . Who is this?"

"Jim. Jim Stanfield."

Stanfield. He'd got a grant to go to Göttingen and read the letters of long-forgotten German Romantic poets. Good for him. Lucky man—no one would have given George Quinterus a grant for work of much greater significance. But what was he doing back in Cincinnati? Grants did not expire at Thanksgiving, did they?

"What are you doing back in town?" George asked.

"I had to come back for my father's funeral. He died last Saturday, and the funeral was yesterday."

"Oh." George had a vague image of old Mr. Stanfield, tiny and bald, with wire-framed glasses, an ex-brakeman for the L & N Railroad (Louisville & Nashville—a monument to long-dead daring mayors of the 1870s). "Oh. I'm sorry to hear about that," he said, trying to sound properly condolent.

"It's all right. He'd been sick for years, with cancer of the prostate, and the doctors said it was probably just as well he went quickly—he'd only been in the hospital three weeks."

"Oh." What else could one say?

"I got back Monday night. I thought of calling you up, but Gloria asked me not to—not till after the funeral." Jim paused. His voice was different, more tentative, as he added: "How about joining me for a drink? I'm getting sick and tired of everybody going over the arrangements Dad and I made last summer, and cousins calling up to ask if he left a will." His tone became more emphatic. "Funerals are a bunch of crap."

"Yeah," George agreed, recalling the scenes after

245

the Staszewski kid plowed into the side of his parents' car six years before.

"Are you free right now?"

"Hell, yes." George forced a laugh. "Just what did Gloria tell you about my . . . possession, anyway?"

"Only that you got hold of the sword and that you were . . . very, preoccupied with getting its message down."

"That's all?"

"Well . . . yes." Jim sounded wary. "She— Hell, she's worried sick about you. She doesn't want you to become a zombie. Also, she'd like you to call her."

"I see." He'd been hoping she would feel that way. A couple of times, during breaks, he'd found himself composing apologetic speeches, but they always sounded too ridiculous.

He wondered if Seppius was listening; probably, because the old shaman had said he couldn't help but overhear conversations close by. So what? He was the one who kept urging George to get together with Gloria.

"How about a beer somewhere?" Jim was saying. "You can call her later—but please call her, because she really cares about you."

"Oh." George felt his eyes grow moist and a lump rise in his throat. A long moment later, after he felt he had regained control of his voice, he said: "How about Smyser's? That okay with you?"

34

December 1, 1971

JIM'S BEING IN town was a real piece of luck, because, hell, he'd spent too many days with Seppius, and George was not yet ready for another round with Gloria. Too bad about old Mr. Stanfield, though,

George said to himself as he walked down the cement steps.

It is proper for hunting companions to share grief and joy, because they may become kinsmen.

Oh, no! He closed his eyes, as if shutting out the bleakness of the afternoon would also rid him of Seppius' censorious presence. In a way it did. He felt the old shaman's mind withdraw, and caught a suggestion of injured dignity and annoyance at being falsely accused.

It's all right, Seppius, he said silently. It's all right, and I'm sorry I snapped at you. But as I told you before, some things ARE private—

"I said, I hope that's the end of the rain."

Unh? George looked wildly about. One of the old ladies who lived at 646 Galway Place—Mrs. Walters—was looking at him curiously.

"Are you all right, Mr. Quinterus?" she asked, just as Seppius' reply began:

Whenever you wish to be by yourself, all you need do is say so. Loud words never settled anything, and it is improper to make accusations without thinking over the matter first.

All George could do was nod. One nod could serve both Seppius and Mrs. Walters, who repeated her weather remark while Seppius continued his discourse about propriety. As far as the old shaman was concerned, there was no difference between etiquette and ethics. He had said so many times already, though not in so few words.

"You had the strangest expression on your face," Mrs. Walters was saying in a concerned tone that set George's teeth on edge.

"I'm sorry . . . I, uh, thought I heard a siren," George lied, hoping Seppius was finished. Two conversations at one time were too much. He even wondered if he had been moving his lips. "I've got to meet somebody at three," he said.

Good thing his car was only twenty feet away, even if he did have to pass her first. Thank God for Henry Ford, he thought as he started the car.

Men were better off going places on their own feet.

247

Sure. Only in this situation, the car had been a life-saver.

Kinsman, you worry too much about the opinions of Others.

"I'm not about to resign from the human race, just yet!"

He bit his lip; damned if he was going to apologize. Instead, he jammed his foot down on the gas pedal.

There was a suggestion of hesitation about the beginning of the reply: *Men who live among Others may learn to act the way Others act, but they are still Men. I can see this. They have forgotten the proper ways to behave, and I am not surprised, because their mothers and fathers have forgotten even that there is something to forget. Many winters has it been thus, but that does not make it right and proper.*

George wished the old shaman would get to the point. An odd idea flashed through his mind: Seppius, like Atlas of old, carrying the burden of the world or—worse yet—Seppius self-sacrificed for men, bearer of guilts . . .

Too much.

I have been telling you, you have learned too many of the ways of Others. Seppius sounded scornful. *The Others were ever fond of using strange names, strange word, words they themselves did not understand.*

"Anything you say." George made a right turn—and there was the modest red neon sign of Smyser's and, wonder of wonders, a space in the tiny parking lot. He sat a minute in his car, surprised at the shaking of his hands. That beer would sure taste good.

Seppius continued the discourse about Men and Others. If Carnett could hear him now, no one could blame him for considering Seppius a recorded message. Anyway— He sat up with a start, trying to *feel* in the back of his mind for Seppius' presence on the other side of the barrier, however that worked.

No trace of the old shaman. He was alone. Alone!

He stretched, bumping his knuckles against the car ceiling, and wiped his sweaty forehead before getting out in the cold; he stretched again, luxuriously.

Inside, Lennie Smyser put down the cigar he'd

248

been using to make a point and nodded. "Hi there, Mr. Q. Long time no see."

"I just got back in town."

"What the hell for? To get your throat cut?" Lennie must have seen something in George's eyes, because he hastened to add: "We been having a lot of nut murders lately and the last one happened in a friend of mine's place."

"I heard." Of course the remark had been because of Stone's Grill in Silverton. But it made a man wonder, George mused, as he ordered a beer and took it to one of the booths.

Lennie looked at him a moment and turned back to Mr. Brehms, the skinny retired shoe-store manager with thin hair and wire-rimmed glasses. Lennie himself weighed about 270 pounds and had a broken nose and a cast in his left eye. The nose was a souvenir of Golden Gloves days; the eye provided the occasion for frequent and lengthy discussions, of cataracts, detached retinas, Mongols, and related subjects. Right now, the topic was lasers.

Neither Lennie nor Mr. Brehms knew much about lasers. That was all right—George could hardly tell laser from death ray himself. But looking at them, and overhearing an occasional phrase, made it clear that the world was unchanged. For him, the world might never be the same, but 99.99 plus percent of the people had no idea anything was different. He could get on a soap box and they'd just lock him up. In a way, they'd be right, everybody had enough troubles already, and in four thousand years Seppius had caused a lot fewer deaths than many properly chosen politicians did in a few hours.

Still, that was no way to look at it. George Washington would be ashamed of his namesake, for Christ's sake! For all his sermons about right and proper, Seppius was just plain wrong. An honest man, but incredibly narrow-minded, possibly senile, or mad—and what did madness mean in this context?

Just thinking about this made George feel ill at ease. Suppose he'd never looked at MacKenzie's book. So what? For hundreds of years, Seppius had been dealing mostly with people who had never heard of the Seeking Sword. Forewarned did not mean fore-armed. In a way, it was enough to make a man believe in fate, predestination, being riveted to the escape-ment of astrological clockwork—all that crap. George smiled. Seppius had put him in his place about big words and great meanings.

Jim's voice broke into his thoughts. "Hey, cheer up. I got caught in traffic."

Jim didn't look nearly as cheerful as he sounded. There were new lines on his face and dark shadows under his eyes, but his handshake was firm as ever and he'd picked up two beers at the bar.

"I wasn't worrying about you," George said. "I was just thinking—hell, trying to make up my mind on where I stand in all this."

Jim looked sympathetic and said nothing. Instead, he reached out and put his hand on George's left shoulder.

They stared at each other. Jim stopped himself from speaking at the last moment, several times. "Any-thing I can do?" he asked at last.

"Anything? What do you mean?" George was puz-zled.

"I mean, just what the hell happened?"

"You really want to know?"

Jim nodded. George thought he looked a bit ap-prehensive, but what the hell. After all, when the man went to Europe, George was still chasing Kill-thinkers. Anyway, he was someone to talk to.

"I know all about the midnight delivery," said Jim, trying to sound nonchalant. "Just tell me what hap-pened later, and how you feel about it."

"Okay," George said, lighting another cigarette. Twenty minutes later he finished with Seppius' final assessment of the personality of Old Joe Paytna even though somehow speech could not do justice to the old shaman's words and overtones of approval, dis-taste, and perplexity. *It is not proper to avoid doing what is proper, but being ashamed of doing well what is proper is a way of behavior for which Men have no word. I had thought of staying with him. But every time he put out a fire, he first felt proud of evading the pursuing Others. Then he began talk-*

ing to himself in meaningless words, and would kneel by his sleeping place, weeping and calling for help from persons he thought lived on top of the clouds. There are no Keepers or persons, Men or Others, on the clouds, as I told him. He would flee and come back, even when I did not call him. I only had true difficulty with him once. These comments, out of the chronological sequence, had come after Seppius' account of a Bronze Age murder.

Jim stared at George, wide-eyed when the writer had finished. "Good grief!" he said, wincing at his own words. "What do you suppose it is?" Jim's voice had dropped to a near-whisper.

"A sword with an old shaman's personality imprinted upon its molecules, or on some of them." Sometimes the words of Others came right handy.

"Oh, come on."

"Come on, what? I don't believe in ghosts!"

For some reason this made Jim laugh out loud, but it only took him an instant to become serious again. "I'm sorry," he said. "I really am. But most people would say that describes you to a T. After all, one could call Seppius a ghost haunting the sword, right?"

"I suppose so," George conceded. "Still, if he's a ghost, he wouldn't be there anymore."

"Oh?"

"The sword has been exorcised at least seventeen times, including three times in major churches."

Jim said nothing. Instead, he fetched two more beers. On his return, he asked how George could believe in exorcisms—and, presumably, demons—without believing in ghosts.

"I don't. It's just that ghosts, demons, exorcists—that whole bunch all belong together. They're all parts of the same continuum, and I don't buy any of that because it's as Seppius says: there are no persons living on top of the clouds."

"But there are things like the Seeking Sword here on earth?"

George nodded. Of course—but what was the point of arguing about metaphysics? He'd wanted a recess from Seppius' presence and, perhaps, a sounding board for ideas—like how he might persuade the old shaman to call off the blood feud, not to argue whether the Seeking Sword existed or how to define it!

"All right," said Jim, gesticulating with his cigar. "The sword is. How did it get here?"

George shrugged. "I told you. A Stone Age shaman found some strange stones. A few thousand years later his descendants made the sword."

"And that's all?"

George shrugged irritably. "I guess so." He was starting to feel talked out. Some people . . . ! What did they know, anyway? He wondered whether other Sword-keepers had had this problem, trying to explain the situation to uncomprehending Others.

Others? Cold sweat broke out on George's back. Others? Was he beginning to identify with Seppius? Oh, God! He looked up at the smoke-darkened ceiling.

The bad moment passed and he managed to smile while telling Jim he felt fine. Sure. Everything was all right, even if he and Gloria had some problems. But these could be worked out; he would call her. The book was selling and he would go on next week's autographing tour as scheduled. After all, he had to make a living—right?

Jim nodded, only partially reassured. "Of course," he said, adding, after a long moment: "Another round?"

"Okay." Jim's trip to the bar gave George a chance to collect his thoughts. Let's see now . . . there had been some things Jim was more interested in than others. Yeah. "Remember when you wrote me about possible connections between the sword and wishing rings?"

Jim put the bottles on the table. "Yes. What about them?" He sounded more preoccupied than interested.

"The rings are also made from the Flame-Eggs," George explained. "When the original A's split up, before the massacre, their shamans would take along bits and pieces of the material. Seppius figures that only Men—or rather, People, those with the genes of the original Men—are entitled to use Flame-Eggs,

252

and only for proper purposes, of course." He drank some beer. "That's only a sideline, of course."

"You're one of these Men?"

George nodded, and Jim wondered aloud whether he was one, too.

"I don't know," said George. "I could ask."

He closed his eyes (Barriers, down!) and tried to phrase the question in his mind. The old shaman's words were undiminished in strength: *One of the Others.*

Thank you, sir, and we'll now resume our private discussion. Aloud, he said: "You're safe. He couldn't care less about you—and actually, everybody is safe now."

Jim shook his head in wonder. "If I ever find any Flame-Eggs, I'll leave them be," he said feebly. "By the way, what are they?"

A reasonable question that had no answer, since four discussions of the subject had ended with bitter words about mutual misunderstanding—even if George and Seppius enjoyed the advantages of telepathic communication, with every nuance and connotation transmitted exactly as intended.

Any reasonable, sensible question deserved an honest answer. "I've tried to find out. Several times." George shook his head. "It doesn't work because Seppius won't think in our terms—or maybe he can't. I don't know."

"What do you mean?"

"I asked him if the Flame-Eggs fell from another world, and he said world was a meaningless expression. So then I tried to explain the solar system to him and from there we got into atomic theory." He picked up the beer and drank deeply. "Hell. It's no use. He doesn't think like we do, and knows it all—or so he says."

"Reminds me of my mother-in-law." Jim toyed with his cigar.

George nodded. "Reminds me of a lot of people, but he's the most extreme case I know of. It's really weird, though. I've lived alone half my adult life, and usually I've liked it that way—but now, all of a sudden, I'm part of a clan or something . . . and

253

I'm not sure how I feel about that." A note of wonder had crept into his voice. "Sometimes I feel . . . like I'm stuck on flypaper. And other times . . . other times it feels warm, cozy, *safe*."

"Safe?" Jim sounded incredulous. "Gloria says just thinking about the things you told her gives her the creeps."

"I suppose so."

George lit another cigarette, partly to avoid saying anything. The problems of other sword-keepers, his predecessors, came to his mind. No wonder so many of them tried to get rid of the sword. Having it around the house was something only a shaman or an eccentric millionaire could get away with. Suppose Gloria called the police and the detectives came to take Seppius to headquarters and grilled George about the murders.

"Well?" Jim asked, and George wondered whether he had seen his shudder and misunderstood its cause.

"Oh. You mean about feeling safe? Well, it is safe —and as long as Seppius stays in my place, everybody is." He proceeded to explain about the old shaman's need for rest and recuperation. "I think he may actually be slowing down a little," he added. "First, he went a thousand years without a break, but since 1400 his R & R breaks have been getting more and more frequent. He's also coming across occasional Men who won't listen. On the other hand, maybe there's just more of my type around now."

"You really believe him?"

"Yeah. It's like I said—you can't lie with two-way telepathy. I know that's hard to accept." George crushed his cigarette in the cheap glass ashtray. "Believe me, I wouldn't have, either, a week ago. But, goddamm it, I'm not hypnotized, I'm not possessed, I'm not under a spell!"

"Shhh." Jim put a finger to his lips. "Not so loud."

"I'm sorry. It's just . . . it's just that I've only had it a few days and already I'm getting tired of explaining. So when I think of a lifetime of that—"

"What do you mean, a lifetime?"

"Well, what would you suggest?" He lit another cigarette. "Don't say anything about going to the authorities. What the hell could they do? I don't think Seppius would stand still for being tested; and as for me, I'd rather not get locked up. I'd rather go underground, and with Seppius' help that should be easy."

"Oh, really?" The way Jim practically recoiled made George wonder.

"I didn't mean I'd kill anybody," he tried to explain. "That wouldn't work anyway, because no one tells Seppius what to do—and I mean no one. It's been tried. I meant I'd wash dishes or drive a laundry truck, and write stories about the Seeking Sword's past in my spare time."

"I see." Jim was still edgy and suspicious—justifiably, considering the history of the Seeking Sword.

Seeking Sword: strange, thinking of Seppius that way, George mused. Of course, he had himself done so, but until recently he had not known any better.

In a way, now, he could understand the killers' compulsion to explain why they'd put out the fire, and their strange conviction that they would be applauded. The killers' memories began fading as soon as they had completed their tasks. *I do it this way because these bad kinsmen's memories were to them so painful,* Seppius had said. *True, they did not want to do the proper thing; but in the end they did it, and it is proper for kinsmen to be forgiving and kind to each other. I also found that the whole tale would only make them more unhappy.*

Poor fellows; they didn't have a chance. Nobody did, except possibly the world's greatest storyteller, and George knew that wasn't he—he couldn't even make up stories, he had to adapt from real life. He hadn't even got *Thoughts That Kill* off the ground until after the trip to Marbury. Now, at least, he had this total, or total-plus recall of Seppius' experiences.

Jim cleared his throat, interrupting George's train of thought. "So you think you'll be able to make a living off it?"

George shrugged. "I hope so. In a way, I'm doing so already. But that's only part of it. As I was saying, everybody, all the B's, are safe while Seppius is with me." He smiled. "And while there's life, there's hope.

I should be able to talk him out of this . . . this blood feud."

"You really think you can?"

"Hell, I hope I can. I'm not sure I know anything, anymore." He leaned forward and lowered his voice. "To tell you the truth, when I came in here I was kind of shocked—both pleased and shocked—that the rest of the world was going on as usual."

Jim thought this over. "I think I see what you mean," he said. "Yes. I think I know what you mean." A slight smile crossed his face. "At the same time, you shouldn't take it for granted nothing has changed—Gloria, for instance. Maybe you ought to give her a call?"

Yes. Gloria. George glanced at his wristwatch. 4:22. He got up and went to the public telephone between the doors of the two rest rooms.

Mrs. Ehmig, who answered the phone after the fourth ring, said Gloria had left the library five minutes ago. Yes, she had mentioned shopping.

Oh, hell!

"I just missed her," he told Jim as he returned to the booth. "I'll try again later."

35

December 5, 1971

PARKING ON MOUNT Adams always had been a pain; in the end, George squeezed the Ford into a space overlooking the sunken-level school yard on Monastery Street and walked two blocks. He'd driven past Gloria's place twice, but she had not come out. Okay. Maybe she hadn't seen the car, and she certainly had cause for annoyance.

A raw northwest wind tore at the Victorian buildings and chased torn bits of cloud across the gray sky. Last night it had snowed—not much, enough to make the slopes treacherous for the Sunday tourists' big cars. George grimaced as another gust of wind tore at him; on days like this, Los Angeles didn't seem half bad.

He rang the bell and stood, hands jammed in the pockets of his plaid jacket. An old mutt, mostly white but with black face and tail, wandered past. Gloria came down, bundled up in her big fake-fur coat, a red wool cap pulled over her ears.

"Hi!" she said, sounding brisk and cheerful. She looked up and down the street.

"Over by the school."

They started uphill. George, feeling very tender, kept sneaking looks at her. She had put on pale pink lipstick and some mascara, and her eyes looked brighter than usual. They talked about Christmas hucksterism, the latest inadequate and idiotic welfare proposals out of Washington, the dirty war—subjects on which agreement was inevitable. It was nice to agree; the disagreements would come soon enough.

In a way, George was surprised at her readiness in accepting the invitation for a drive and brunch. She had been cool and distant when he'd called Wednesday evening, after a few beers with Jim. Thursday had been much the same—he'd gone downtown and offered to take her to lunch, but she already had plans, or so she said; and he'd gone home and got in a violent argument with Seppius, about right and wrong, the morality of blood revenge, and how it was unfair to ruin Men's lives and then cast the poor slobs aside because they had not willingly cooperated in their own destruction in a cause that had lost all meaning . . .

Kinsman, you are thinking as one of the Others, Seppius had replied patiently. *Men decided what must be done, and while there are Men it is only proper to keep carrying out the decision. . . . Any man can question the wisdom of the decision, but only a bad kinsman would piss on the council fire, and turn his back on everybody.*

There was no arguing with Seppius: he had a proverb for everything, knew everything—in a way, he was a thousand times worse to have around than Betsy had been because George had been at least able to feel superior to her, while with Seppius . . . Shit!

Thoughts of dung, are for dung, had been the shaman's reply.

He'd stormed out of the house, got drunk at Smyser's, and returned to the apartment about 7 P.M. After he woke, around midnight, Seppius had blandly resumed the Saga of the Seeking Sword, finally reaching the present century. That session had continued until 4 A.M. Friday, ending with Andrew Grauman's slaying in Stone's Grill in Silverton on November 24, 1971. When George woke up, just before noon, he had called Gloria at work and suggested the Sunday outing; and ever since, he'd been wondering about his gladness over her accepting the invitation. Seppius' approving comments had been totally unappreciated.

He felt comfortable around Gloria. The saga of Seppius was important and interesting—but, damn it, he had been looking forward to spending some time with her. Cocktail-party conquests, one-night stands with literary groupies—these were gratifying to a man's ego, an old dream come true. But he might as well face it; this had started as a no-strings-attached relationship between two adults, and a connection had developed. God knew why or how, but he was glad of it, and . . . well, here they were. He held the car door for her, she made a little joke about gallant male chauvinists, and they drove off.

Neither of them said much as the car chugged east, past Hyde Park and out into Clermont County, with occasional glimpses of the placid brown Ohio River beyond snow-flecked fields and stands of bare trees.

"Trying to get out of Great-granddaddy's range?" she asked once, as they crossed the creek at Pleasant Point, the marker arrow pointing left to U.S. Grant's birthplace under the huge maples. In summer, the little house was almost invisible from U.S. 52; it was being maintained as a museum. Maybe next summer . . . "You think we're still in range?" she repeated.

He shrugged. "I've tried to pin him down, but"—he raised his right hand—"he has no concept of miles, or anything except spans and steps—and days' journeys."

The memory of that discussion made him smile. Seppius agreed that the amount of distance covered in a day differed among persons, but he wouldn't, or couldn't, comprehend the need for a standard day's journey.

"Why the smile?" Gloria wanted to know.

"Just thinking about our argument about why miles are necessary."

A half-minute later she asked him about the length of a span. He told her: the distance from tip of thumb to tip of forefinger, spread out as far as possible.

"Didn't he realize that varies, too?"

"Sure. He said each of the Men has his, or her, own span; and since everybody in the encampment knows everybody else, there is no reason to worry about misunderstanding."

"Oh."

He hadn't been able to think of a rejoinder, either.

She started hunting for a station that was not broadcasting religious music. Shortly after she found one —it came in weak, with a lot of static—he pulled into the parking lot of the big motel on the north side of the road. The motel was several years old, and the builders had left some of the trees, but it still looked out of place.

As George and Gloria got out, they could see the roofs of Moscow, Ohio, across the fields that used to be flooded every few years before the big new dam went in on the river. Moscow wasn't much of a town: a few hundred roofs, surrounded by trees, red-brick schoolhouse, a couple of church spires. In the 1960s, the Ohio had occasionally still come right into the streets, so Cassidy & Schenck put their Motor Inn on high ground, what was then empty land between New U.S. 52 and the hills to the north. Now the fields were no longer empty. For a mile or more, there was the standard string of cinderblock structures with neon signs: hamburger joints, DariDelites, chain chicken places, a drive-in discount store, one gas station after another. The C & S Motor Inn had been one of the first and age was beginning to endow it with a certain tacky dignity as its prim striped curtains—scarlet and orange, dark green and navy blue—started to fade.

The Paddlewheeler Room was open and already doing a moderate brunch business. George and Gloria found a booth with a view of the merrily burning electric logs in a fireplace with a shiny replica musket above it. George leaned back—the seat was none too soft—and stretched, craning his neck. The river was out of sight; all he could see was restless gray sky, some treetops, occasional trucks lumbering by, east to Portsmouth or west to Cincinnati. He and Gloria did not say anything until the waitress came for their orders.

George felt ravenous. Gloria smiled as he ordered three fried eggs, Kentucky ham, genuine home fries, toast, and coffee; all she wanted was the Number Two: French toast, two strips of bacon, and coffee.

He lit a cigarette; she studied his face, still smiling. "Looks like you've lost some weight," she remarked.

"You don't seem to approve. I thought I was supposed to be too fat," he said, trying to match her gently chiding tone.

It was nice to sit across the table from her. She looked good, in one of her wild print dresses with flowers and leaves in red, orange, and gold on dark green, and she was wearing the silver-and-turquoise bracelet he'd bought her.

"You should lose weight, but you should go on a regular diet. It's no good eating less and still drinking the same amount."

"I think I'm drinking less," he said. "I've cut down on smoking, too."

"Don't tell me Great-granddaddy disapproves." She made a face.

"I'm not sure about that." The Men had drunk mead, and a kind of wine made from berry juice, but they certainly had not known anything like tobacco.

All of a sudden, so abruptly it almost frightened him, Gloria's face lost its carefully controlled expression. She leaned forward, her voice halfway between a hiss and a scream. "Are we safe here, or aren't we?"

Now what? He looked around; no, nobody seemed to have noticed. "Of course we're safe."

"Are you *sure?*"

"Sure. Look. We're in no danger. Seppius doesn't—"

"I wish you wouldn't refer to that thing as if it were a person."

"What do you mean?" Of course Seppius was a person. He had a personality. Shouldn't that count for more than number of limbs, shape, color, whatever?

"I don't see how you can stand being around it." Gloria shuddered, so violently that he wondered whether it was for show. "I couldn't stand being in the same room with it for five minutes." He looked at her. "Not if you gave me a million dollars," she said defiantly, eyes flashing and jaw thrust forward. Her hands were nervously tearing up a paper napkin.

He was still trying to think of something appropriate and sensible when she took a deep breath. "I don't understand," she declared. "I mean . . . it's a murder weapon—worse than any other murder weapon —and I don't understand how you could stand being around it unless it's got hold of you somehow." She paused. "I won't say 'hypnotized.' We went over that already and you're right; hypnotism is too limited an idea for . . . for *this.*" She dropped the napkin shreds.

"For Christ's sake, Gloria!" He tried to keep his voice down. "Look—I'm not hypnotized, I'm not possessed, I'm not taken over or any of that nonsense."

"You used to hate and fear Kill-thinkers. You don't, anymore."

"There never were any Kill-thinkers."

"How do you know? Just because you've been fed this goddamned line and—" She looked around the room, wildly. "There's that couple over there. They just came in." She inclined her head toward the pair, about to sit down next to the fireplace, the woman tall and thin, with sharp nose and pale purple hair— more silvery, actually—and the man medium height, beefy, with jowly red face and a few strands of light brown hair.

"What about them?" George wondered.

"They might have been following us."

261

"Oh, for Christ's sake!"

She glared at him. "Remember that crime-story writer—yes, Sleighton. And what happened to him?"

"Oh, hell!" This was poetic justice, his old paranoia come back to haunt him, and maybe someday he'd be able to laugh about it; but right now it was an awful pain in the neck. "Look," he ventured, "if I'm in for it, wouldn't it be easier to kill me at my place?"

"Auto accidents are supposed to attract the least suspicion."

"Oh, hell."

"All right," she said, with an obvious effort not to quarrel. "I've got to go to the ladies' room. Excuse me."

"Don't worry. I won't turn into a werewolf while you're gone."

"Of course not." She laughed, almost convincingly. "There's no moon out."

And she was gone, leaving him glaring at his cigarette smoldering in the glass ashtray, wondering, trying to figure out how to persuade her his aims were unchanged, even if he had changed tactics because the Seeking Sword had turned out to be something different from what he'd expected. The task was now to convince Seppius he was wrong, rather than to get a fix on the hideout of non-existent Kill-thinkers. He was still wondering, when the food arrived. He was cutting up his ham when Gloria returned, very calm but still breathing fast.

The way he shoveled it in made her smile again, and when they had finished eating it no longer seemed appropriate to pick up where they had left off. Instead, he lit another Winston—for some reason, he couldn't finish a cigarette today—and watched her sip coffee. How should he start? Not with protestations of goodwill and innocence, and how he cared for her; hell, if she couldn't grant that, what was the point in talking at all?

She put her cup down. Okay. Time to talk. "You can't understand why I'm not as antagonistic to Seppius as you are. Right?" he asked.

She nodded, picking up another paper napkin.

"Okay. You just look at him—sorry, it—as a sort of movie monster. Right?"

She nodded.

Fair enough. He picked up his cigarette and put it down again. "Well, in a way you're right. But that's only part of it. I'm not sure it's fair to judge Seppius by modern standards; it's like trying Cochise according to white man's law. More so, actually, because Seppius is more lawman than killer, the way he and his people see it."

"His people? What do you mean his people?" She sounded incredulous; her voice rose in pitch. "Who? You, yourself, maybe?" Suddenly her eyes appeared moist, and her voice broke as she said: "George . . . if you really are hooked, or under control, or whatever, I wish you'd realize I want to help you. How, I don't know. But if there is something, anything . . ." She paused. "Please."

He felt very humble, gazing at her. He should be so lucky. But what could he say that she would be willing to accept? The whole situation was ironic, in God knows how many ways, and someday they would look back and laugh about their respective predicaments. But meanwhile . . . what the hell could he say?

"George?" Her voice was almost pleading, but he thought he could also detect a calculating undertone. Nothing wrong with that; he too liked to think things through and sometimes to construct elaborate scenarios.

"George. What is it?" She was sounding more and more deliberate, more and more insistent.

"Look. I'm not under any control." Feeble, but the best he could do. "I'm still trying to stop the murders; only the job is different from what I thought. I know this sounds silly, but I figured I'd find the hideout, and we'd call in the cops, FBI, Marines, somebody—bang, bang. Come out with your hands up. And then I'd write my book and we'd get married and retire to Big Sur, or someplace."

He hadn't intended to mention marriage—he'd more or less just visualized them living together—but now that the words had slipped out they didn't sound half bad.

The words seemed to have passed right by her.

He tried to explain his strategy again, but this didn't work too well, either.

"Are you sure that's what you're trying to do?" she asked after a while. "It's more as though you're trying to make excuses for it." Her pronunciation of "it" made it clear her flesh crawled at the thought of Seppius.

"Seppius isn't a mad robot in a movie," George protested. "You can't just press a button and turn him off —he has no buttons."

"Don't shout."

"Shout?" he asked, puzzled.

"I didn't know you could show anger against it." She appeared intrigued.

He rubbed his temple. True, she wouldn't know; she'd never given him a chance to describe his arguments with the old shaman. And now that the Saga of the Seeking Sword was told there would be more and increasingly angry arguments.

"Listen to me . . ." He started trying to explain about the old man and his loneliness, his grim devotion to duty, his sentimental feelings. She let him talk, and after the waitress had refilled their cups, she asked whether he felt like a recruit to the clan.

"Clan? Oh, you mean do I feel like a descendant of the Men?"

Now they were getting somewhere. Of course he was one of the Men; and accepting that, somewhat unwillingly to be sure, had given him a much firmer, more comfortable feeling of belonging, being part of something—in this case a long, long line stretching back through the centuries. This was another thing Seppius had never explained to his satisfaction, but somehow the old shaman could "see" who a given Man's forebears had been. He could not "see" them all, of course. George had not even learned any new information about his great-grandfather and great-great-grandfather. But Seppius had told him how the name originated. In the 1590s, a schoolmaster in the town of Plön had Latinized his last name from Kinter to Quinterus. He'd had five sons. Only one of them lived, and he became a master shoemaker in Preetz, a pretty little Holstein town between two lakes of which people said: *"Jede drüdde Mann dar ist ein Schoster,"* or Every third man there is a shoemaker.

He tried to explain this to Gloria, his voice choking up as he described how Master Reinold Quinterus' grandson Hans killed Bernard Ehricke with the Seeking Sword while working as a journeyman shoe-maker in Lübeck. Hans Quinterus had just arrived in town; Ehricke was an apprentice in a ship chandler's shop. Hans never tried to flee, and was hanged twenty days after the slaying. Seppius did not know what happened to Master Reinold, or to Reinold's son Gert, who traveled to Lübeck to testify to his own son's good character.

Gloria had appeared more and more interested as the story progressed. "I see I was wrong about one thing," she said, while George was drinking his now luke-warm coffee. "You're not a recruit—just somebody carried away by his goddamned royal descent." She took a deep breath. "And now, speaking of descendants—how do you feel about having some?"

What was she talking about? He set his cup down. "You mean Rita? She's cute, and I guess I love her. But what do you mean?"

"I wasn't talking about her. I mean . . . you're going to have— Oh, the hell with that!" She swallowed, then stuck her jaw forward. "I'm pregnant."

"Are you sure?"

She nodded.

"You're absolutely sure?"

Now she flared up. "I should know!"

He reached for the cigarette smoldering in the ashtray, trying to collect his thoughts. It had been quite a wrench, from Seppius to this . . . what most people would call real life. But wasn't everything inextricably mixed up? Seppius, George Quinterus, A's and B's, fires, Gloria?

Gloria—pregnant! A flash of exaltation: the seed, nay, genes of Quinterus (and Men, or at least one strain of Men) shall not perish from this earth! This was followed by . . . well, oozy feelings of doubt. He'd been gone most of the fall, there was that slimy painter called Fechner, and she had dated some other guys as well . . . Damn Lenore MacDonough and her catty remarks about girls who lived on Mount Adams. The point was . . . But hell, he wasn't trying to weasel his way out now, was he? Quinteruses didn't do that sort of thing. The point was, Gloria was pregnant. By him.

Hip, hip, hooray!

Seppius would be pleased. So what?

On the other hand, why now? She had been on the Pill and wasn't likely to forget, at least not through oversight, though there was that failure rate of one percent, or whatever. Okay. It hadn't been accidental. She loved him, wanted to bear his child. He just managed to keep from looking smug. Even if, unbelievable as it was, she was after his money—well, there were many less pleasurable ways to spend the loot than on her and George Junior. He reached across the table, took her hand, and gently extracted the napkin shreds from between her fingers.

"I love you," he said. His voice sounded firmer than he had expected it to.

A minute or more passed, with neither of them saying anything, until Gloria's hand stirred in his. Such a small, slight, fine-boned hand. He let go, but she didn't take her hand away; she just let it lie there.

"Say something, George. Anything," she said eventually. Her voice was calm, too, but her hand was trembling—and so was his.

"I don't know what to say." He felt humble and yet not ill at ease. Everything was going to be all right.

She smiled. "This is a new situation. Usually the problem is how to get you to shut up."

"Uh-huh." Some of his old doubts returned. Also, they were in a public place. He looked around surreptitiously. No one seemed to be paying any attention. "Gloria," he said, "this . . . this is a new situation for me, too. Even though I have been through it before," he added hurriedly. "By that, I mean, I've been a father before . . . But then, everything was different. No, I don't mean that. I mean—"

"You mean, the other time you were married."

Her voice was very calm. He felt a shiver go down his back. Yes, the other time, before Rita's birth, when he had been married. But that was not the point;

the 1950s had been a different ball game, with different rules. The main point concerned Seppius.

Weird, jumbled images whirled through his mind: killings; birthings, vivid scenes of births in medieval cottages with knife, ax blade, or horseshoe, something iron under the bed to ward off Evil; babies and swords— No. That was a bunch of crap, that whole line of thought. Life was too real and serious for allegorizing and moralizing. Besides . . .

He shook his head vigorously. The situation did not call for murky philosophizing but rather for something clear—a clear statement of George Quinterus' feelings and intentions. Gloria knew this, too; otherwise, why would she be sitting there that way, leaning back, a half-smile on her lips and her eyes, clear gray now and sparkly, fixed on some point above and to the left of his head?

He picked up his cup, finished the cold coffee, put it down. All right, how did he feel? When Betsy announced her pregnancy, he had been stunned, overwhelmed, glad, surprised, worried about the responsibilities—all the usual things. This was different. A moment ago he had yelled hooray in his mind—almost aloud, in fact. If he had, he could imagine the confusion, ending in smiles and claps on the back after he'd explained that his wife—

Wife? He blinked, looked at their intertwined hands, and raised his head.

"George," she said, smiling. "You don't have to propose."

"Uhhh . . . what do you mean?"

"I'm a big girl. Grown up. Able to take care of myself." There was a tinkling sound to her voice.

He nodded. Damn it, he should be getting used to having his mind read, but it was still disconcerting as all hell. "You mean, you could see right through me?"

She shook her head, serious now. "Actually, you aren't transparent, just consistent."

"I see."

She smiled again. "You've got two questions on top of your mind . . . but I don't know their order. One: Will I keep the baby or, rather, allow it to be born? Two: When is she due?"

He'd been thinking of a boy, but it didn't matter. He nodded, feeling sheepish, allowing the grin to spread over his face.

"The answers are Yes, I think so, and sometime in June or early July."

"I see." Yes, he had meant to ask about that, but . . . "I'm glad, really glad," he said. "And now, would you mind answering a few more questions?"

"That depends." She tried to match his tone of mock severity, but he could tell she was not as much at ease as she tried to appear.

"Okay. Will you marry me?"

"I'll think about it."

He hadn't expected that; in fact, he'd been all set to ask why she had not told him sooner; she must have known for a month. He blinked and demanded what there was to think about.

"Several things." She was very serious again. "For one: How long are you going to stay in your knight suit?" A moment later, she said: "It's part of that expression you just had—like ain't-I-grand-for-doing-the-right-thing-for-her." She stuck out her tongue. "No, you don't look that way now." She laughed, her tinkly, silvery laugh. "You're back to human."

"Oh . . . Okay." He had that coming, no doubt. Now what?

"The next question is: Your place or mine?"

"What difference does that make? I mean, we both have—"

"Maybe. But maybe I don't like being rushed into long-term commitments." All of a sudden, she looked very roguish. "After all, when we started out, this was supposed to be a no-strings relationship between two consenting adults—right? Remember? Well, marrying you isn't the only option open to me at this point in time."

"Oh, God."

Her jaw was thrust forward again; she was obviously enjoying this. But why? He asked.

"I'm trying to make you mad."

"Mad, like insane; or mad, like angry?" He was getting angry, himself.

"Mad, like angry."

"What for?"

"So I can get some straight answers." She leaned back and folded her arms across her breasts.

"Look, goddammit, I meant it about the damned proposal." He *was* getting angry.

"I forgot to thank you." She smiled. Her voice was warm, a bit tremulous, as she continued. "Thank you. I do appreciate it, very much. You're a nice man and I love you, and I think I'd love being with you the rest of our lives." She hesitated; when she spoke again, she sounded apologetic but determined. "And now, if you think I'm being bitchy, I'm sorry—but there are a couple of things I want to clear up."

What was she trying to do—bargain after the agreement? But no. She hadn't agreed to anything, and he knew why.

"All right," he said, swallowing. This took care of half the lump in his throat, but only half. "Okay. You want to know where the sword fits in. Right?"

"Right." Her voice was low, quiet, and inexorable. She thrust her jaw forward again, leaning across the table. "I always thought those princesses who let their husbands put a sword between them in bed would have been better off with the frogs," she told him. "Well, your Seeking Sword is worse—much worse."

"But I told you—" he began.

"I know you did."

"Then—"

"It's disgusting and I can't stand being around it!" Her voice rose to a near-screech; some of the brunchers looked up, but at that moment the first contingent of the churchgoers arrived. Gloria forced a halfhearted smile. "I know it's got a personality, and tells great stories, and all that," she said. "I don't care."

Goddammit all, why did everything have to be so complicated? He tried to explain again—the way he'd tried with Jim—but she shook her head. "Don't make this into a me-or-the-sword deal," he ended up pleading. After a long pause, he finished his cigarette, while Gloria shredded a napkin.

"It already is that kind of a situation." Her voice was calm and low.

"Oh, hell!" He wished he could get a drink—damned blue laws—but that wouldn't solve anything, even if it made him feel better. "Look, love," he began, "look, I'll think of something. We won't move in together this afternoon anyway, and next week I've got to go and sign books in New England, and—"

"Are you taking it along?" she wanted to know.

"No . . . I guess not." Actually, he'd been looking forward to being alone again, even watching television in hotel rooms and reading . . . Hell, anything. He suddenly realized he had not even bought a newspaper for almost a week.

"You're sure you can tear yourself away from it—and me, too?" The hint of amusement in her voice caused him to wonder.

On a sudden inspiration, he said: "Hey—how about coming along? My treat. After all, I'm the rich one now."

She made a great show of considering the invitation. "Where to?"

Let's see. Wednesday, December 8—Hartford. Thursday—Providence. Friday—Worcester. Saturday—Lexington. Nothing on Sunday except taping a local talk show in Boston, then two days around Boston and on to Portland and then Albany. He was due home Tuesday, December 21, and on January 10 he was supposed to report back to Los Angeles. He'd just proposed, but when was he going to find time—literally—to get married?

Gloria asked again. He said he would be in Lexington on Saturday.

"I always wanted to see Lexington and Concord," she said. "Suppose I fly out Friday night. I'll rent a car and see the rude bridge while you sign your books, and then we'll drive to Boston. I haven't been there for years," she added.

"Okay," he agreed, and recited the rest of his schedule.

She was unperturbed. "We can get married after Christmas—and I don't care where, as long as it's not a Newport justice of the peace."

"Once an Ohio girl, always an Ohio girl?"

She smiled. "Don't try too hard," she said, and squeezed his hand as they got up.

He left a $10 bill to cover the tab. What the hell. It was an occasion to celebrate. And as far as Seppius was concerned, he'd think of something. Of course he would.

36

December 12, 1971

NOT A BAD-LOOKING couple, Joseph Carnett said to himself as he spotted Gloria in the back of the seafood restaurant in Boston. She and George had obviously been here for some time. She had cut her hair short, her suit was bright orange, and, with her face animated as it was, she looked enchanting. George's back was toward Carnett; the writer was dressing better, even if he had let his hair grow out some. But then the man had a lot on his mind these days, Carnett thought.

Carnett was glad they were getting married. A man living by himself was not a whole man and that was equally true of women. He had been luckier than most.

He banished the smirk from his face as he made his way to the writer's table, rehearsing the important points in his mind:

Item: George Quinterus. Carnett did not like the writer's sudden change of mind about the Seeking Swords' nature. The explanations had been unsatisfactory. He might not be hypnotized or possessed—the idea made Carnett wince—but there was something unhealthy and ominous about the situation.

Item: The weapon. George insisted there were no Kill-thinkers. Perhaps; George was certainly in a position to know. And yet the alternative explanation was worse. Kill-thinkers and super-shamans had been bad enough, but a living sword . . . ? The very idea was a blasphemous obscenity. All the adjectives that kids and peaceniks were applying to the administration's Southeast Asian policy really fit that kind of Seeking Sword.

Item: Helen. Fortunately she approved, both in principle and inasmuch it affected Joseph W. Carnett, fifty-three-year-old government lawyer who had decided to put his ass on the line in a situation where he would be lucky to end up looking like a moron. Boy! Wouldn't the columnists love it: "Hick GOP Lawyer Goes Off Deep End After Reading EXORCIST." That's what they'd say, and too bad—because there wasn't a thing he could do about it. The sword, whatever it was, must be stopped. Period. Joseph Carnett might curse his fate but he could not duck out on it.

Item: Gloria. Fine girl, basically, but he couldn't help wondering about her. She was marrying George regardless of her almost physical reaction to the sword. How could she expect it to last unless George got rid of the sword? And where would that leave George? She had nutty ideas about politics, but she was no gold digger. Nor was she old or ugly enough to be desperate.

Helen had said there must be more to the marriage than met the eye. Perhaps he should have brought her along. He must remember to ask Gloria where she liked to shop; Helen had agreed a $100 gift certificate would be right, and—

All of a sudden Gloria looked up. "Hi, there!"

"Hello," Carnett said, as George turned around, half scowling.

The writer looked tired, with dark circles under his eyes. He had also lost weight; the jowls were disappearing and his collar looked loose. So did the dark brown tweed jacket.

On second thought, it probably hadn't been a half-scowl. George was just tired, and perhaps annoyed because of Carnett's arrival at this particular moment. Gloria had obviously forewarned him about meeting here, presumably well beyond the Seeking Sword's range.

Now George was on his feet. They shook hands; there was a certain nervousness about the writer's grip and he seemed generally unhappy, being no doubt tired of talking about the sword. Fortunately there had been a waitress right on Carnett's heels. She asked if he would like anything from the bar before he'd had a chance to fumble his opening lines. He ordered a beer.

George took a swallow from his glass. "I suppose you've got some bright ideas on how to dispose of it," he said without further preliminaries.

Carnett had half expected something of the sort. "No, not really."

"Then why go to all this trouble?" The writer made an elaborate production of looking furtively around the restaurant. "I feel like a character in a goddamned spy movie." He knit his brows. "Hey, man, got the Ipcress File on you?" he asked in a stage whisper.

"Take it easy, George," said Gloria.

"All this rigmarole." George spread his hands. "We could have met anywhere. It wouldn't make any difference if it was Cincinnati, because Seppius doesn't eavesdrop."

Evidently he and Gloria had been talking about the super-shaman, because the girl flared up.

"Sure. That's what you say, but how do you know? All you've got is his—I mean, its—word." She put a lot of loathing in it.

George shook his head, looking fed up. He lit another cigarette; Carnett noted three half-smoked, crumpled butts in the ashtray.

Gloria looked at the writer with real concern. Then, with a quick glance at Carnett, she said: "All right, George. You can feel the other mind, or whatever, withdraw. You're sure that's what happens—but how can you know?"

"Seppius is not a liar."

You couldn't argue a point like this, but Carnett felt he should make an effort. "He doesn't seem like a liar to you, but how can you be sure that he—they

273

—haven't developed all sorts of techniques of deception?"

The writer shook his head again. "I told you. Both of you. There is no way to lie by telepathy."

Too bad that wasn't true of human speech. It would eliminate a lot of lawyers' jobs, but . . .

They discussed this until the waitress returned for their orders: lobster for George, crabmeat salad for Gloria, the land-and-sea combination for Carnett. Then the discussion resumed, ranging from personalities to genetics.

Carnett let George do most of the talking. (In a way, this was his show.) Then, as the waitress brought a third round of beer, the lawyer excused himself.

Yes. There was a pay phone outside the men's room. "Helen?"

"I thought it might be you," she said, her voice betraying her concern. "How is it going?"

"Not bad, but I haven't got much time."

She laughed out loud as he explained the situation, made a joke about the size of his bladder, and said she had a pad ready to take down what had been said, point by point:

Item: George did not appear to be possessed, hypnotized, or whatever, but his enthusiasm for Seppius was hard to take. Also hard to comprehend.

Item: Yes, they really seemed to be in love. But he really couldn't make any forecast about the Quinteruses' future happiness. Insufficient evidence. However, he was sorry for saying that Gloria might have staged a big offensive to distract George from his preoccupation with the sword. She wouldn't have, and he wouldn't have fallen for it if she had. And yes, Gloria liked Pogue's.

Item: As for the sword, George kept describing Seppius as a murderously sentimental grandfather type, sort of a Victorian parent who'd never heard of Hell and who maintained that propriety—his kind—was its own reward.

Item: Yes. George felt sorry for Seppius. Too much so.

Item: No. Seppius wasn't anything like the Pongos and Cetrulias and Kardecs, and all the other so-called spirits of mediumistic blather. And not jut due to different methodology. Seppius didn't give a damn about stages of perfection; in fact, when George had brought up that point, Seppius said it was a bunch of crap. He —sorry, it—was only concerned with completing a not too enjoyable and seemingly endless chore. Of course, that could be camouflage.

Item: "I was wrong about the blood-lust bit. Apparently grim dedication to abstractions is enough to keep somebody on an unpleasant job for thousands of years—unless it's all a clever lie, as I think it is. Of course, if it is true, what other options does Seppius have?"

Item: How does it work? Well, apparently Seppius could detect patterns of brain waves. These patterns of consciousness, or whatever, appeared to Seppius in the form of fires. At least that was the descriptive term it used, presumably due to its primitive mentality, or the primitive vocabulary of the "Men," or whatever. The reason for George's using the term "consciousness" was that he said Seppius also saw the "fires" of plants—and even if a plant could somehow sense the direction of the sun, that did not mean the plant's sensory system should be called a brain.

Helen said: "All right. What next?"

"Well, to get back to the A's and B's, from Seppius' point of view there is an obvious difference. George thinks that whatever causes these differences is inheritable, but not in the strictly Mendelian sense."

"Yes," said Helen. "I know about Mendel's peas."

"All right, from Seppius' point of view it's not a matter of A's and B's as such, but rather a continuum stretching from A to B. Some cases are obvious, but every so often a super-shaman has to make really close decisions. And whichever gland controls the brain waves, it's activated at puberty—and only in males. Some of the Seeking Sword killers happened to be psychopaths, George said, and some even tried to use the Seeking Sword as a crutch—if you can believe that."

"I think I can," said Helen.

"And then—"

All of a sudden, Carnett noticed George Quinterus lurching toward the men's room.

He looked rather unfriendly, and the sight of Carnett on the phone did not seem to surprise him in the least. His mouth twisted into a scowl. "Tell K-3 Q-1 is on a leak," he growled.

"Look, I was just telling Helen I had arrived safely."

"Yeah." George paused and turned, very deliberately, composing his features into a sneer.

Oh, hell. Carnett held out the phone. "You've met Helen. How about saying hello to her?"

George looked at him for a long moment, reaching for the instrument and then allowing his hand to drop to his side. He shrugged, turned, and opened the door.

When the door had closed behind the writer, Carnett finished his call quickly.

Back at the table, Gloria looked at him with curiosity. "Well?"

"Helen wishes you well. George walked in on me while I was talking to her." A sudden impulse made him add: "That's absolutely the truth."

She relented a bit. "Your wife sounded nice over the phone."

"She would like to meet you." Carnett drank thirstily from his glass. "But that's neither here nor there. When this is over, we'll all get together and celebrate. But meanwhile, what were you discussing while I was gone?"

"This and that."

She looked glum. Carnett could see her point: this was bad, but the FBI or CIA would be much worse. Also, she had probably been called to task, explaining why this particular confrontation had seemed advisable, here and now.

"I'm sorry," Carnett said after a while, filling his pipe. "Actually, sorry is not the right word. I was doing what seemed to be the most advisable thing, under the circumstances."

"Sure." She meant it.

"I'm really glad that's how you feel." He paused, deciding not to light the pipe yet. "He'll be back—and what will we be talking about?"

"How to persuade Seppius to stop killing people," she said tonelessly.

The waitress arrived with the dishes. Gloria kept a fixed smile on her face for a while; and then, after the waitress' departure, she began describing the discussion, especially about one occasion when Seppius was persuaded to depart from its straight-and-narrow policy of not being used in current affairs.

Indeed?

"He says it happens every so often," Gloria went on. "This particular occasion was in East Prussia, around the time of Chaucer. That's the region where amber used to wash ashore after storms, and the government claimed it all. The serfs had to go out after storms to pick amber, and government officials could hang anybody on the spot who they said was trying to steal some." She paused.

Carnett nodded. "I know amber is a fossil resin."

"Just checking. Well, in the 1380s, an innkeeper called Paul Saeppaine happened to be the sword-keeper—or so George says—and a local official called Balkratzen was making a real pig of himself, raping women and framing anyone who made a fuss." She grimaced. "It was really grim. There's an old play that George discovered, where a masked Teutonic Knight kills the villain, but apparently that was all wrong. The Teutonic Knights were in charge and the Grand Master couldn't have cared less as long as the coins came rolling in." She looked over her shoulder, toward the men's room. "To make a long story short, a girl called Marya asked Saeppaine to help her, and Seppius killed the pig—or rather, caused one of Werner Balkratzen's own men to do the job."

"How?"

"Just gentle persuasion, I guess. Nobody *tells* Seppius what to do." She looked over her shoulder again and picked up her fork. "Seppius is an honorable man. Bunk!" She dug into her crabmeat salad and a moment later looked up and said brightly, "Here's George now. He can tell you all about it."

"All about what?" the writer wanted to know.

"Great-granddad, of course." George forced a

smile and Gloria said, still brightly: "I was telling Joe, here, about one time he made an exception."

"Which one?"

She said it was the one involving the pig Balkratzen. George nodded and sat down. Carnett suggested that maybe they should concentrate on the food; Seppius could wait. No one objected. He could almost feel the tension relax.

After a while, George asked how far Gloria had got with the story.

"I see," he said when she explained. "Now, then— the innkeeper told his wife stories, interminable stories, like the stories Seppius himself tells. He and Seppius got on very well, especially since Mrs. Saeppaine would never dream of contradicting her husband about anything." He smiled. "Seppius doesn't think much of her, but that's beside the point, which is that somehow, by a combination of reasoning and appeals based on the mutual obligations of kinsmen, Seppius was persuaded to take care of the Balkratzen, who, incidentally, was a sort of justice of the peace with one hell of an extensive jurisdiction."

Carnett nodded. "That's always dangerous," he said, and held up his hand. "Let's lay off present politics. I gather you're saying the sword can be persuaded to change its behavior?"

"I've tried," George admitted. "I haven't done so well." He took a deep draught of his beer. "The point is, I'm no good as a debater. I get mad and he comes up with something like 'Loud words never settled any disagreements, only causing spears to shed blood'; and from there on it's all downhill." He looked hard at Carnett. "You. You're supposed to be an expert at persuasion—that's how lawyers make a living. Right?"

"That's one way to put it."

"So, maybe you ought to give it a try." George looked at Gloria, and Carnett could not decide whether the writer looked truculent or regretful. "In any case, I'm getting nowhere at it."

"You mean, stand there in your living room, arguing with it?" A preposterous idea, but also appealing. *And in this corner, Mr. Carnett, in behalf of humanity, justice, and motherhood!* He suppressed a smile.

278

George had been watching him intently. "Yes. Why not?"

Why not, indeed? He would certainly do a better job of it than the writer. After a moment, he nodded. It might turn out to be a mistake; but for the moment . . . Frankly, he was curious to feel what telepathy was like.

"All right," he said. "I'll do it. I always wanted to debate a fanatic."

George lit another cigarette. "Fanatic," he said. "Yeah. He sure is one—narrow-minded, arrogant, knows everything because he's been around about forty-six hundred years." He looked sheepish. "He's basically a decent guy, but he was narrow-minded even back then."

"A *nice* fanatic, in other words," said Gloria.

George shook his head; a note of wonder came into his voice: "Even so, I like him. Yeah. He's potentially dangerous, sure, and murder is murder. But I feel sorry for him, and I like him too. He sticks to his principles and he isn't vicious. He hates torture, and destruction for its own sake."

"I see."

In a way, this Seppius was not unlike many people Carnett had known. Some had been ministers; others, judges, policemen, politicians, Navy officers. He nodded. He had by no means accepted George's latest theory; but even so, Seppius' character traits—if that were the right term—might give them useful clues. For instance, its sentimentality, strangely chivalrous attitude toward women, feelings about ecology, pollution, and the oneness of man and nature . . . The Kill-thinkers had put a lot of work in their monster.

A pity. All that effort could have been spent in a better cause. At the same time, Carnett could understand the reasons for George's obvious fascination.

"Basically, then, you think the old shaman's personality is unchanged?" he asked when the writer paused to light his eighth cigarette.

"More or less. I think he was a pretty rigid type to start with, and he's become worse." Another pause, while George toyed with the match. "Sometimes I think he's mad, but, hell, I'm not a psychiatrist. And

I'm not at all sure we can judge a person from another culture by our Western standards."

"You mean, except in day-to-day matters?"

In one of his last letters, just before he stepped on the mine, Joe Junior had written from Vietnam: "I think they are all crazy, from our viewpoint, and once you accept this you can at least have a basis to guess what might come next. Only don't ask me, please, whether they are born that way or whether this is a learned pattern of behavior; and in a way, isn't that true of us all? We each wave our arms on a hilltop and none of us uses exactly the same semaphore code as anybody else."

George had shrugged at Carnett's question. The lawyer swallowed, hard, and told them about the letter.

Gloria looked down at her plate while George squashed his cigarette. "I guess so," he said. "Anyway, as far as that goes, Seppius is not without his weak points, and if we find a way to use these—hell, if we can get him to call off the feud . . ." He paused. A dreamy look came to his eyes. "There is so much he could tell us about ancient life."

"Sure."

The idea—sword on lectern, with eager students taking notes from . . . what? A loudspeaker? Each from his own mental voice? Carnett bit his lip to avert a smile. Certain aspects were intriguing, however: how were trials really conducted among ancient Angles and Saxons? And did trial by jury really go back that far?

He banished the beguiling thought from his mind. Later—if ever. Right now, other things were far more important, such as possible weak points.

George confessed he really didn't know what these were, but Seppius was obviously sentimental, with strong feelings about reciprocal obligations among kinsmen. He might resent an invasion of his privacy by one of the Others. He was proud of his consistency, but might not take kindly to tricky syllogisms, though he was unlikely to resort to violence.

"He just doesn't care about any systems except his own," the writer concluded.

"A pity."

"All the more of a challenge—right?" The writer's smile was crafty.

George Quinterus was definitely not a hard man to dislike. And yet he had cause to act this way. Carnett picked up his pipe. It had gone out. Good. Fiddling with it provided time for thought. All sorts of possibilities, some truly mad, went swirling through his mind. Pulling it off would be a real coup and the incongruity of it appealed to him even more. Arguing with a ghost, or whatever, would be some precedent, regardless of where—and looking at Gloria he was sure it wouldn't be in the Quinteruses' living room.

"We're working out a compromise," she said, sweetly.

37

January 5, 1972

IT WAS A ridiculous compromise, but it worked. Since George and Gloria now lived on Galway Place, George had buried the sword under the roots of a large maple in a park. She was still working; this gave George plenty of time to commune with Seppius, and in a few days he would leave for Los Angeles, taking the sword along.

"At least it'll keep me away from bad company," he told Carnett with a forced, nervous smile.

Carnett said nothing. The writer seemed barely able to control his excitement; he had even whistled a tune after picking up Carnett at the airport on the Kentucky side of the river. They were on the way to Winton Woods Park now, and Carnett found the overcast sky depressing as they sped north between hillsides where dark trees stood guard in patches of snow among clusters of houses.

George chuckled as he turned on Hamilton Road. "I almost buried the sword here, in Spring Grove Cemetery. It would have been closer but—hell, can you imagine what might have happened?"

Carnett had to smile at the idea. "Would Seppius have minded?"

George shook his head. "Not really. He thinks death is natural, like breathing. I've tried to tell him he's the proof to the contrary, but he says I don't understand."

Carnett repressed a shudder. What had he let himself in for? he wondered, for the tenth time. They had driven only a few miles, but airport, civilization, and twentieth century seemed far, far away as they proceeded on this weird errand a little further on among snowy, wooded hills under a dark gray sky.

No! This was no way to prepare for the struggle ahead. He banished the doubts from his mind and started filling his pipe.

"So the big thing is to settle the matter of the definitions from the start," he said.

"Yeah." George looked rueful. "That's where I—I mean, I've tried. And in the end, I start yelling about the meaning of justice and he comes out with the line about loud words."

"I see." Carnett could see Seppius' point. Neither man said anything for long dismal minutes, until the car had crossed the Mill Creek Bridge and entered the deserted parking area. Two other vehicles were there: a battered blue Volkswagen and green Chevy pickup truck. Bare trees stood in dense ranks on the snowy hillside, starting a few steps beyond the edge of the concrete. No one was in sight, just the yellow trash barrels, drinking fountain coated with ice, and a forlorn cement-block building that contained the rest rooms.

George pointed to the glove compartment. "Care for a drink?"

Carnett forced a smile and shook his head. "Later, perhaps. Are you sure Seppius will even talk to me?" he asked, getting out.

If not, that might be for the best. It would also be a damned cop-out. It took him a long moment to realize that George's shrug was in response to his question; the writer reminded him of the agreed-on sign: the instant he "heard" Seppius, he would blink rapidly several times and raise his left hand.

They started out on a trodden path under the trees. The writer pointed at a tall maple a hundred yards downhill and nodded.

Carnett was trying to concentrate on the incongruousness of the situation. Boy, wouldn't Jack Anderson have fun with this one? And not only he, but Buchwald, Wicker, Hoppe, all the rest, even Kilpatrick and Buckley.

Sure. So it would be his last government job, and he might have trouble in private practice; but that was too bad. Washington was becoming tiresome anyway, and the re-election campaign would be a Roman circus, regardless of who the Democratic candidate would be.

He set his jaw.

George stopped and turned, blinking, raising his hand—there! "Seppius says hello," the writer said, his voice shaking as he pointed to a stump. "Have a seat. It's kind of rough at first, while he's working out the neural pathways in a new mind."

Carnett nodded. George had told him about this. He stepped sideways, toward the stump, and brushed off some snow with his leather gloves, trying to make his mind blank; relax—relax even when the berserk locomotive started bellowing inside his skull. He clamped his teeth on the pipestem. Come on, you can take it, he kept telling himself, trying to ignore the violent itching, tingling sensations, until the sound gradually changed, running the gamut from low, angry, surf-like roar to opera singer's high C, with faint sibilant whisperings thrown in—and also thunderous rumbles, buzzes, mechanical-sounding clicks in the sequence in which, all of a sudden, inexplicably, he started hearing—feeling? perceiving? no, hearing—syllables and words. He wondered whether he would hear the long greeting and felt . . . the impropriety of that: there was no kinship between them. Them? Were they already in communication?

We are.

There was a suggestion of amusement and smugness about the words that irritated Carnett as he thrilled to the realization of having taken a step, the first all-important step. (For all mankind? Come off it!) The quality of light seemed to change, the dark tree trunks ceased to look sinister. Everything was going to be all right.

Only, there was a wordless, inarticulable sensation of amusement in the back of his mind. Not his own amusement. He could not explain, even to himself, how he could tell; but it was unmistakable, and he could understand why George claimed to know things he could not explain.

Many a kinsman has taken longer to hear, and to speak back, without using the tongue in his mouth. The overtones of amusement remained, but the main impressions were sincere approval and benevolence. All of a sudden, Carnett realized he was smiling. Smiling! Grinning like a goddamned buffoon at praise from a murderous old maniac. (The feelings associated with Seppius' presence somehow made it inconceivable that he—yes, he—might be a mere instrument.)

Carnett took the pipe from his mouth, saw it had gone out and reached for his lighter, halting in midmovement.

The ways of Men are not the ways of Others. Seppius' overtones were not hostile, only indifferent, unconcerned . . . Something about them made Carnett wonder about the possible reactions of ocean tides to the publication of Newton's celestial mechanics. Put a sun here, put a moon there . . .

The response was immediate, chilling, seemingly allowing no appeal: *The Others have ever been fond of using names, and strange words, that they themselves do not understand.*

"Sorry about that," Carnett said aloud, surprised at his flippancy. Still . . . why not? Levity might not help, probably nothing would; but the solemnity, utter, deadly solemnity, of Seppius' statements was worse than anything he had encountered in a lifetime spent mostly among people who took themselves too seriously.

"Could you hear me?" George's voice seemed to come from very far away.

Strange. The writer was standing with his back against an oak, arms crossed, a puzzled expression on his face. As Carnett turned toward him, George closed his eyes, but the lawyer saw a suggestion of movement about his lips.

Yes. I will make it possible for you to hear each other. Seppius was being indulgent, reminding Carnett of the way Helen's brother, Bill, used to talk to their children at Christmas. Carnett bit his lip; then, remembering his pipe, he bent to an oddly comforting task—perhaps because it belonged to the real, everyday world?

Carnett? There it was, in his mind, without having passed through his ears. He thought he could sense a hint of concern, but of that he could not be sure, because, unlike Seppius' statements, this had a flat, repeated, mechanical quality. Carnett shook his head, looking at the writer. "George!" he shouted. "George! No!"

"Yeah." Quinterus looked at him, nodded. "Okay. I'll speak out loud."

"Yes. Thank you, George." Carnett put the pipe back in his mouth. A small thing, this. Not a step anywhere. Merely a declaration of independence and solidarity on the part of two humans in the presence of . . . a monster that Carnett could still hardly admit to himself existed, a monster without slavering fangs or talons dripping blood—childish stage effects to frighten simple men. But a monster all the same—and worse, much worse, for all its unassuming appearance and simple, straightforward, self-limiting ways. After all, Dracula operating by daylight wouldn't be the same, either.

He had forgotten Seppius could hear his thoughts. No matter; he had nothing to be ashamed of except the casual way he had regarded John Lambert's weapon during that long-ago trial.

So you are the champion. The last word sounded

somehow out of context, as if it were no part of Seppius' normal vocabulary, while the total absence of accompanying overtones seemed perfectly natural. Carnett blinked, staring at the rough old tree trunk. Funny, the way he seemed to take such terms as Seppius' vocabulary and Seppius' kindred for granted all of a sudden.

He wondered, abruptly, where he fit into Seppius' scheme of things.

The response was immediate, with very faint overtones of approval. *You are of the Others, but it is proper to ask whether you have a place by the campfire.*

"I see." That was just as well.

True.

This was still approving, but Seppius sounded more distant as he added: *Thrust with your spear, champion.*

Carnett and George exchanged glances, the lawyer trying to remember what he had read about ritual combats in New Guinea.

Unthought-over excitement was ever the way of the Others. Men, too, have now learned to behave improperly.

"Maybe that's because we haven't got centuries, like some people." The words escaped almost without thinking, in response; he could understand now what George meant about Seppius' superciliousness.

Possibly. The overtones left no doubt that Seppius was being courteous, despite an implication—coming across as a faint visual image—of unworthy kinsmen as people who would sharpen the spear of the champion from the other side of the river.

Now what? Carnett dared not look at George, so he turned back to his pipe, struck a light. The first long pull really felt good, but he did not have a chance to enjoy it, because of the challenge: *Thrust away, champion.*

The tone was worse than the words. Carnett had expected hostility and defensiveness, respect rather than—it galled him to admit it, even to himself—this indulgent curiosity, like Miss Eaton in the second grade saying: "Yes, Joey, tell me the answer, what was it the lollipop said to the wrapper?"

You want me to stop what I have been doing because you do not regard it as proper. You are one of the Others and thus it is proper for you to feel so. My kinsman was brought up among Others.

A pitying tone became apparent. *And thus, he feels the way you feel.* After a pause, Seppius added: *Is this so?*

Carnett nodded; then he said aloud: "Basically yes. But you are wrong."

I said, thrust away.

All right. Carnett took a deep breath, sticking out his chest, and took the pipe from his mouth, trying to ignore the thought that he must be looking silly. "George has told me about your blood feud, and I sympathize with you. Big Man's people were wrong. They deserved to be killed, and I don't care if their way of life represented a step forward from the way of life of . . . of the Men to our way of life. That is beside the point because murder is murder. But by the same token, this blood feud you have been carrying on for hundreds of years is just as wrong—perhaps even more wrong than what they did."

He paused and looked at George. The writer nodded in approval.

Blood feud is a term of Others, a term without meaning.

"It may have been a term of the people you call Others, but it has meaning," argued Carnett. Of course it had meaning, a meaning that must go clear back to Seppius' own neolithic time, when people believed blood was the vehicle of life-force and that if somebody disrupted the harmony of the universe, at least locally, by shedding blood and dissipating some of the life-force without due ceremony, the way to balance matters was, as the Bible had put it: He who draws the sword shall perish by the sword. He who sows storm reaps the whirlwind. Anyway, Carnett realized he had not spoken aloud and George must be feeling left out.

Seppius' reply was calm and even, a statement of fact with no overtones of any kind:

Your words are only many attempts to wander as far as possible from the flickering campfire, while keeping its glow in view, instead of walking up to it.

"What?"

Seppius obviously had made this point many times: *Harmony is one of the Others' words, for when all are behaving properly. When somebody behaves improperly, that is wrong, and certain things must be done to set things right. Somebody may have to shed blood, to set souls free.* Seppius' regret was unquestionable; then, overtones of disdain began to echo, accompanied by a note of, well, lonely steadfastness: *What matters is setting things right, doing so properly. Men must do this without fretting about the words of Others, who look at one spot on the ladybug's back, who all winter long argue about one word that should mean many things, the word that should settle always which of ten should wade in freezing water to place a log from bank to bank. Such words are not worth worrying over while resting in between doing proper things.*

The argument was full of holes; but even so, Carnett was left feeling like a scolded schoolboy. Telepathy—God, was it powerful!

Let's see now. Primitive men had regarded the world as a place of ritual and mindless violence, rather than the arena for competition between potential alternatives dreamed up by philosophers: a place for antitheses to butt horns together and come forth as synthesis, the beast with two fused heads and two pairs of hind legs kicking in different directions (each antithesis being not unlike a Rocky Mountain goat). Ditto for dialectics, a portmanteau word . . . with said suitcase full of fighting-mad baby dragons hissing like teakettles.

Others have ever been fond of using names and strange words that they themselves do not understand. Seppius' tone was automatic, reflexive, with just a hint of smiling forbearance.

Somehow, the conversation had taken a turn very different from the high-minded debate Carnett had primed himself for. He had come to argue about principles. Strike that, he said to himself, before Seppius could come up with another demeaning proverb. A feeling of the merest ghost of a sympathetic smile spread through the back of his mind. Goddammit!

He puffed furiously on his pipe, trying to think of some way to turn Seppius' flank—a hopeless task, clearly, given the unequalness of the situation since Seppius (ugly name) could read his mind.

I did not seek you out.

"That's irrelevant." This time, he remembered to speak aloud for George's benefit.

There would have been no talk like this, had you not come here.

Fair enough. Still . . .

I am doing what is proper for Men. I have been doing that and shall do that. A pause. *You have come to tell me why I should cease, but I have heard no reason why I should.* Seppius sounded bored.

"It's not just a matter of my coming here."

No response; only a suggestion of doubt.

George spoke up. "I've been arguing the same points."

You, kinsman, have learned to think like one of the Others.

All right. Time for another tack. Carnett took a deep breath before asking: "Proper procedure—that is an important part of things, isn't it?"

True.

"Are you following proper procedure?"

I am.

"How?" Maybe this was getting somewhere!

Only four of the Men were left, when my sons and Claps-hands-at-big-fire sat down, back from their errand. We talked over things that had happened, and all Men agreed what would be done. Seppius' tone left no doubt of the propriety of this.

"All right. So isn't there a proper procedure for . . . calling a halt?"

True.

"And what would that be?" he asked, hoping for a reasonable answer.

All the Men agreed on what would be done. All the Men can agree on what should be done.

"Oh no!" Seppius' tone had been matter-of-fact and that was why Carnett was startled by George's

289

reaction. The writer looked aghast as he shouted: "Do you realize what that means? Every one of the Men—myself, Neumann, Old Joe, God knows who —we'd all have to give our formal approval."

To Carnett it sounded unreasonable, but surely there must be some way. A quorum . . . Carnett could not conceive any twentieth-century men wanting to continue this monstrous blood feud.

A word without meaning.

Quorum? Blood feud?

No Man may speak for another except by previous agreement, as in settling boundaries of hunting grounds.

"But they did have representatives entitled to speak in their behalf." Somehow Carnett had always assumed so; the primitive hunters who had survived long enough to be interviewed by anthropologists had had their spokesmen.

True. Seppius' tone was stern; now it became even grimmer. *An encampment might send one or two Men to speak for all; but if these agreed to give away too much, or involved the rest in fighting against their wills, they were driven from the circle of lodges with blows of spear butts.* He paused. *Sometimes their women followed. Sometimes the for-speakers were women and their mates might follow.*

So?

It would be improper to assume that any of the Men could speak for the rest.

"But that is possible?" inquired George.

True. But a Man cannot say he can do so; he must have been told so by the rest of the Men, meeting together in the middle of the encampment.

"Under present-day conditions, what would the encampment consist of?"

The middle of wherever Men live. Seppius' tone was again matter-of-fact, unconcerned, almost that of a bored schoolmaster.

Carnett was surprised to notice he was sweating. He wiped his face with his sleeve. Let's see, now: Seppius did not, could not, mean that he and George should call an assembly of the A's alive today, to discuss whether or not it was time to end the feud? Something about the sheer unreasonableness of it appealed to his sense of the ludicrous. Why—

You are not of the Men, champion. Seppius might have been a court clerk reciting names of jurymen. *You have no place in an assembly of the Men.*

That stung, like a whiplash. Why, the—!

You are one of the Others, champion. Seppius spoke with just a hint of weariness.

"Who named you the judge?" demanded Carnett.

A word without meaning. Now Seppius seemed amused. Then he became serious once more. *Do not tell me about the Others and how they live, and how they need some to order the rest of them around. This was not the proper way of Men.* He paused, and the tone became more contemptuous as he continued.

All you have told me and my kinsman before you, and more kinsmen before him, is that you do not approve of what I do. . . . But as I have told my kinsman, again and again, the ways of the Others are not the ways of Men.

"In other words, you do only what you want to?" Carnett had almost used the phrase "law unto yourself," but that would no doubt have caused another remark about meaningless words. Funny how quickly he was becoming conditioned to think in Seppius' terms.

I do what is proper for one of the Men to do. The Men decided what I must do. The Men can decide whether I should do something different.

"That is what we're trying to do: to find out how."

You are not one of the Men. This is no concern of yours.

Carnett saw George's sympathetic smile. Yes; the writer had gone this route. But, goddammit, there had to be some way!

"It is my concern, because I'm concerned with the welfare of all people," Carnett said, choosing his words carefully. "Haven't you ever heard of the greatest good of the greatest number?"

The greatest number are the little six-legged ones skittering over the ground, and those of various sizes, that are rooted in earth. I do not think you are speaking of them, champion, or of the eyeless, limbless, hard-surfaced ones who are hard to disturb even by chipping, although that happened when the Flame-Eggs were made into the weapon. You are not speaking of them. There came a pause, heavy with condescending contempt, before Seppius said: *You are only concerned with the Others.*

Not just Others, goddammit! Men, too, because they are the same, part of the same society.

A word without meaning.

"You, the Men—and other men, the People—you were a society, too," George interjected.

We were Men or People. Seppius was unperturbed. *Men have no need to think of themselves in the words of the Others. The Cowdung-covered-knees may have thought thusly because they thought they had been set apart, doomed never to learn proper behavior and to wander about restlessly, never at home in the shadow of the ancient trees.* A note almost of pity infused the next words. *You fret about these things, too, and there is nothing you can do about it, champion, being one of the Others.*

The pity—that hurt. What did Seppius think he was?

But before Carnett could say anything, George spoke up. "The Men were set apart, too, Seppius."

The Men lived by groups in encampments, but Men were part of all else.

Carnett swallowed. Let that pass. They had drifted off target enough as it was. Back to the main point. How were they going to assemble this great council of Men . . . and how were they going to find the Men in the first place?

That is a task, champion, that you and my kinsman are taking upon yourselves.

"You're right, there," Carnett said loudly, righteous anger rising in him.

No response.

A moment passed, during which Carnett became angrier, though he tried to fight it because of the monster's smug, complacent, insulting indifference. Then George asked, loudly and yet apprehensively: "Will you help us find the Men, to tell them? For instance, what if I carried you from land to land—?"

No.

"Why not?" demanded Carnett, more and more appalled at the magnitude of the task, because even if they could identify Men, they would have to explain to every single one what this was all about and why they should assemble somewhere. And who would pay the fares? And what about new Men ~~reaching puberty?~~

I am not dissatisfied with things as they are.

A hint of amusement there—a sign of hope?

"You may not have changed in four thousand years," Carnett said, "but the Men, your relatives out in the real world, they have changed. I can understand you and your sons making your decision four thousand years ago—but I doubt any of today's Men would agree with it."

They have not told me so. A pause; and then: *You will tell me the Men no longer remember, and that makes everything different. It does not. Proper behavior is proper behavior.*

Somehow, Seppius' words conveyed an idea of propriety as timeless and unchanging, but at the same time constantly in motion—like fire, or waves of the sea.

Carnett was still trying to think of a reply, something to the effect that Seppius had kept his eyes shut tight because he might find no place in a changed world, when the old shaman said: *Indeed, the world is changed. My kinsmen have told me so many times; and you are about to tell me about shelters ten times taller than any tree, about better foods, with nothing that contains a soul coming under the teeth, thereby saving the eaters much worry, about boxes with wings that can fly above clouds, and throwing stones that burst into splinters, killing thousands, and boxes on round things that scamper about on stone laid on top of what used to be good grass on which elk fed.*

The shaman paused, while Carnett wondered wildly what—and how—the monster thought of the war and the Christmas air raids on Hanoi. George had said he had no conception of states, or religion, or philosophy; and that explanations were useless. But

Seppius' next words were a surprise: *Then, also, there now is a round thing with horns, going in circles around that which all breathe, and a person can speak through that thing to all by means of the boxes on whose front sides shadows come and go to accompaniment of sound.*

Seppius paused again; he seemed amused. *Surely you could speak to Men this way, explaining why they should meet, and where and when.*

Oh, sure. Carnett could see himself going to the directors of the communications satellite company, explaining their desperate need for time. And how should the message be phrased, and what about Men who didn't watch Channel X, or didn't care, or didn't even have a television set or radio?

If this was a joke, it was in one hell of a poor taste. He shook his head, barely hearing George say, "Oh, shit," and the response:

Thoughts of dung are for dung.

Sure. As he raised his hand to wipe his face, he suddenly thought of one possible chink in the smug old bastard's armor which they had discussed in the Boston restaurant a few weeks ago: "About all Men getting together—did you ask them about Balkratzen when you did that?"

He could sense the old shaman's puzzlement, and smiled. Hah!

That? The sword-keeper Saeppaine and the daughter of his friend, and the person who ordered Others about on the sea's shore. Seppius' tone was calm, almost indifferent. *True. He died though his fire was not baleful. But I raised myself up, seeking round about, and saw that he would have sons whose fires must be put out.* Seppius paused.

And that was all there had been to it?

True. Seppius seemed surprised at Carnett's expectations.

"It didn't make any difference that Balkratzen was a rotten bastard?" George asked.

He acted the way you would expect one of the Cowdung-covered-knees to act, one giving orders. Seppius might as well have added: What else is new?

The all-encompassing slur and the bland arrogance

of the old shaman—Carnett bit his lip. Temper. Temper! Now, then—regardless of Balkratzen's vices, he had not been a B, a Shitfoot, whom Seppius considered it his duty to kill, so had he consulted the Men?

True. . . . I have wondered about that on other occasions—whether it was proper for me to heed Paul Saeppaine out of the lovingkindness a Man has for his kindred. Seppius' tone was thoughtful, but not greatly concerned. *Besides, Werner Balkratzen might have had no sons and many daughters.*

The tone of unctuous regret, Carnett mused, illustrated by a half-glimpse of a medieval family by their fireside, was almost too much from one who obviously had no understanding of right and wrong.

Words without meaning, much loved of the Others.

"What?" Carnett could feel his control starting to slip.

Seppius' tone was utterly indifferent: *I did not ask my kinsman to bring you here, champion. You do not pass my time pleasantly. Rather would I learn Wind's songs in the strange trees hereabouts, and listen to birds and squirrels and watch little six-legged ones, their feet folded together, dreaming of coming-summer as they lie in frozen earth or savor the seeds' expectations of soon sprouting forth . . .*

The tone, with its implications of aggrieved patience and forbearance, was even more aggravating than the blather and syrupy feelings about seeds and bugs. Bugs, for God's sake! Carnett jumped up, suddenly furious. He stamped on the ground and roared: "You bastard! Rotten, stinking bastard!"

Loud words never settled a dispute, not even over nothing.

The old devil would have made a fine preacher! But the hell with that. Carnett kicked the tree; then, hot tears springing to his eyes, he ground his heel on the spot between two knee-like roots from where Seppius' words seemed to rise, while yelling at the top of his voice: "You . . . goddamned old hypocrite! Murderer, murderer who went crazy in the sword! Crazy, I tell you! Mad, full of hate for the whole human race. And the nerve to preach about pure earth and ecology! Go to hell!" He kicked the tree again. "Go to hell, you—"

He stopped cursing, appalled, because his right foot swerved suddenly to the left, missing a sapling growing between the roots, and crashed against the maple with an inexplicable force that sent pain flashing up to his knee—enough agony almost to make him shut out the wind-like howling, derisive sound that had quickly sprung up all about him.

The howling ceased.

Carnett raised his foot again and paused, suddenly wondering whether his tantrum had attracted attention. No. George was the only human being in sight. The writer looked pained. Well, Carnett knew that losing his temper had been a stupid childish thing to do. Perhaps he should apologize. After all, he had come here to debate principles.

It is the way Others can be expected to behave.

Carnett had the impression the words were not directed at him; George must have made some silent comment. He was about to ask but was forestalled. *I spoke with him only out of the lovingkindness a Man should have even toward a bad kinsman.* The impact, even to Carnett, was like a heavy club striking both kneecaps; George appeared literally to crumple against the tree, while Seppius continued in the same indifferent tone: *Men have been forgetting the ways of Men, and trying to behave like Others, even to calling on champions from beyond the river to speak for them in discussion with kinsmen whose meat is cooked on the same fire. Still, Men are Men. Even the worst of bad kinsmen can have a son who is of the true Men, in pursuit relentless and steadfast when closing with the elk. And this shall be true when trees have their leaves once more.*

After a brief pause, Seppius said in a tone both consoling and triumphant: *Kinsman, rejoice! Your son will be a true Man, who will put out fires without number, gladly, knowing what is proper for Men to do.*

38

January 5, 1972

GEORGE QUINTERUS FELT completely numb. The words of congratulation—congratulation!—kept reverberating in his mind. Yes. Should tell Gloria. Would tell Gloria. And then?

He was mildly surprised to find himself seated by the car, with Carnett two steps away, and looking rather foolish with his long face all red and the dead pipe in his hand.

"Suppose I drive?" the lawyer said.

George nodded. He could walk all right, but a twenty-mile drive might prove too much. He handed over the keys and stood, his feet starting to feel cold, his mind awhirl with damnably vivid pictures of a son who would put out many fires gladly, rejoicing in doing the right thing.

He shuddered. Carnett opened the door. He climbed in.

"Where to?"

It was an effort to think, but in the end George managed to come up with directions for Lebanon, Ohio. Gloria had taken time off and driven there to see the relics of the Shakers' things in the Warren County Museum. She had also got a motel room—they had decided to spend a few days away from Cincinnati and would meet in the Golden Lamb about 5:30.

She was not expecting much from the confrontation in the park. Carnett had not expected much either, at least not from the first encounter. George had gotten his hopes high, and . . . *Hail, Mary, full of grace* . . . He closed his eyes. Prayer wouldn't help, even if he

297

felt better. Men—in the human sense; not Seppius'—had prayed before to be rid of the sword's evil, sacrificed to it, had tried to exorcise Seppius, had cast the sword into sea and fire. Once, about 200 B.C., the sons of Wennegaso had plunged the weapon into a porpoise's back and released the animal to take the curse from their shores. The porpoise swam straight out for half a mile, swung back, and lay on a sandbank that was barely awash, within sight of the despairing crowd; the sword worked its way out in a couple of hours, and the porpoise swam off into a sunset while the people debated what to do next.

Saints had tried and failed; Seppius regarded St. Anscar, back in the ninth century, as a courteous listener and persuasive arguer, while St. Vicelin, in the early 1100s, struck him as arrogant and narrow-minded. The shaman considered exorcism ceremonies, particularly those performed in churches, impressive, interesting from a professional point of view—pretty good for Others to have thought up and carried out, though overly elaborate like most things done by Others.

After a time, George opened his eyes. Darkness was closing in, the rolling hills were becoming lost in the distance, with lights coming on in farmhouses surrounded by snowy fields.

"About six more miles," said Carnett. His pipe was going. "I think I remember the way, though it's been a while. Helen and I had one of our anniversary dinners there," he said in an absentminded voice. "Our sixteenth. Joe Junior was in high school, and JFK was going to get the country moving again after the Bay of Pigs . . . What a bunch of crap." He half turned to look at George. "Say, do you suppose that's why the longhairs started calling policemen pigs?"

"I'm not sure." George did not want to talk: what was there to say? He knew about Carnett's son dying in Vietnam. The war was wrong, a moral abomination born of official lies; but that did not mean Joseph Junior might not have been a nice-enough guy. Anyway, he was safe and dead. Dead and safe, while George's own son—God, how he'd hoped for one!—was unborn and already doomed to a fate worse than death.

He really couldn't blame Gloria if she wanted an abortion. Couldn't blame her; she was bearing the kid. But he had a stake here too, and, anyway . . .

He sank back into reveries about the debate in the park. It had been all wrong. All wrong. Just because Carnett had done well before judges and juries didn't mean he could do anything arguing with the sword.

He thought about it a while, until a glimmer of hope appeared on the horizon. Somehow, the two —Seppius and the sword—did not seem the same. The sword was cold, harsh, deadly, inexorable, upright in its mean and cruel way. Seppius had the same characteristics, but he was also sentimental, a grandfather, an old man who sometimes mourned that he could no longer taste food or feel the caress of wind on his skin. A man could reason and appeal to him. It had been done, and not just once, for all the sword's talk of single-minded propriety. George was a Man, of Seppius' kin, so he should be able to make Seppius understand, better than Carnett could hope to, marshaling arguments and points of law. Not that he'd ever got around to those. *Some champion!* The Men of Seppius' time had had no law in that sense, so Carnett's arguments naturally could only irritate the old shaman.

He looked at the lawyer with mounting resentment. Neither Carnett nor Gloria really knew anything, so how could they expect to deal with Seppius? As for himself, he had been an idiot. Just because he hadn't succeeded immediately, he had gone running for outside help. No wonder Seppius had called him a bad kinsman! All he could hope now was to undo the damage.

Next week, in Los Angeles, there would be plenty of time, and in the end Seppius would come around. Seppius was still human, so how could he fail to see that the blood feud no longer served any purpose? True, other sword-keepers had tried and failed. But they had been uneducated, or unbelieving, or unduly pessimistic.

Carnett had not said anything since the silly question about pigs. Just as well. Now, after two trucks whooshed by, the lawyer cleared his throat.

George sat up. "Unhh?"

"I've been thinking . . . I need a drink."

George reached for the glove compartment, but the lawyer shook his head. "No. Not that. I could drop you at the Golden Lamb and go have a martini and come join you about six." Carnett shook his head again. "I have to get off by myself to collect my thoughts. I'm really not much of a champion, I guess."

"Okay with me," said George. Suddenly he realized he had been wondering how he would break the news with Carnett standing around. "Sure," he said. "And thanks. We—I'll think of something yet."

Later, George was still confident as he walked up to the restaurant's door, but his earlier feelings of apprehension were beginning to return. What would Gloria do? And what could he tell her to calm her down? He had faith in Seppius' benevolence toward kinsmen, but he had not been able to convince her of this—and what could he say to her now?

Bringing in Carnett to argue with the old shaman had been a mistake, the worst mistake of his life. Worse than getting interested in the Seeking Sword in the first place? Well, his path might have crossed Seppius' anyway, and at least he no longer had to scrimp for a month to afford dinner for two and a night in a nice motel.

But Seppius had a forgiving nature where kinsmen were concerned—the Saga of the Seeking Sword contained many instances of this—so nothing was lost, only time. It was just as well Gloria had not wanted to come to Los Angeles.

He took a deep breath, squared his shoulders, and opened the door.

There was a sort of waiting room on the left as one entered the Golden Lamb, with huge fireplace, magazine racks, and chairs and settees, both over-stuffed and Shaker-style—uncushioned, functional, and yet pleasingly shaped. The dining-room walls were decorated with Shaker implements, everything from churns

300

to the chairs which the Shakers hung on wooden pegs when not in use.

She was wearing her orange pantsuit, relaxing on a settee, staring at the fire. In her lap lay an old *Life* magazine. She looked up, saw him, and smiled.

"Gloria . . ."

He didn't know how to continue, but one of the motherly waitresses spotted them at precisely that moment. "Ready for dinner, sir?"

"There were supposed to be three of us," said Gloria.

"That's all right. How about a table just inside the door, where you can see the other party come in?"

The waitress pointed to the right. George nodded. Gloria stood up and he took her hand—small and warm, with long, fine fingers.

The waitress said her name was Mrs. Bolton, and she took George's plaid jacket while he held the chair for Gloria. An instant later, Mrs. Bolton asked whether they wanted anything from the bar.

"Yes. A double Jack Daniel's, black label, on the rocks."

Gloria had brought along her Manhattan.

He hoped she would not ask anything until his drink arrived, and she didn't, even though her expression became more and more puzzled as he sat in glum silence. When he put his glass down after a long swig— God, did that feel good!—she leaned forward and put her hand on his.

"What's wrong?" Her voice was soft and her eyes dangerously moist. "Is everything all right?"

"We . . . well, we didn't convince Seppius. I think it was a mistake." He looked at the glass, then shook his head, taking a deep, deep breath: "Gloria, darling, he—he—said our baby is going to be a son, and . . . one of the killers." A lump had formed in his throat; tears started in his eyes, her image became blurred. "George Junior . . . doomed. Doomed to commit murder after I am gone."

Gloria's mouth was half open. He couldn't be sure, with his fuzzy vision and the subdued light, but all color seemed to have left her face. For a long minute she said nothing, but her hand tightened on his; she put her left hand on the table, too, sort of clawing at the white tablecloth. He found himself staring at the thin loop of gold they had picked out together two weeks ago.

"I'm sorry," he said, feeling both foolish and reprehensible. Seppius might—would—have found him anyway, but Gloria would not have become involved without him. "I'm sorry. I wish . . . Hell, that's no use. Anyway, I thought you had the right to know."

He had been afraid his voice would break in midsentence, but it didn't.

"It's better to know," she said mechanically and shook her head; then she shook her head again, hard, as if trying to wake up.

She must feel trapped in a nightmare, naturally enough, and he wouldn't blame her for exploding. But instead, she clasped both hands in front of her face, lowered her head, and started to sob—first softly, then more strongly. Then, to his surprise, George realized he was sobbing, too.

A fine spectacle they must be making. Surreptitiously, he stole a look around. They were still early for the suburban Cincinnati–Hamilton–Middletown dining crowd, and this was Wednesday; there were only a few diners, mildly interested, but since both man and woman were bawling, obviously no one felt entitled to interfere. It would be improper. Even Mrs. Bolton plainly felt that way; she was pretending not to notice anything.

Nice of them. Damn! George swallowed and reached for his drink, hoping their tears would be gone when Carnett arrived. He kicked his left ankle savagely, hard enough to make him bite his lip. Snap out of it, for God's sake, Quinterus. Are you man or crybaby?

He should have kept his mouth shut, but it would have come out anyway, and it was best to get it over with. Even if— No, he could not be absolutely sure he could talk sense into Seppius. At any rate, that would take time, and he did not want to be separated from her forever. Any way he looked at it, something was wrong. George swallowed and rubbed his eyes. Gloria was blowing her nose into a little white handkerchief.

He half rose, shifted the chair so it almost touched hers, and put his right arm around her shoulders. She looked at him, and at that moment he felt very protective. Tender toward her, angry at himself, Seppius, Carnett, the whole world . . . Still, angrier at himself than anybody else. He had gotten her pregnant. The pregnancy—he glanced at her, her breasts and belly, but there were no visible signs yet—the pregnancy was complicating matters enormously.

Gloria was sobbing again, but less loudly, and just as George finished his drink she blew her nose again, wadded up the handkerchief, dropped it on the table, and looked at him.

"Sorry about the crying act," she said, her voice quite calm—not at all as he had expected.

He said nothing, just gave her shoulder a squeeze and thought he saw Mrs. Bolton nod in approval. That nod, glimpsed from the corner of his eye, made him feel a lot better.

"What happened to Mr. Carnett?" asked Gloria, suddenly concerned.

"He decided to have a drink before joining us."

"I see. Now, then . . . I think I had better go and get my face together." She pushed back her chair and stood up. "Excuse me." Grabbing her purse, she set off for the restroom with firm, even steps.

George lit a cigarette, glad she was taking it so well. Damned well, in fact, making everything easier. But still it was one hell of a mess.

"Well, just take a look around, sir," he heard one of the waitresses say.

Carnett must have arrived.

He had, and was looking around the dining room like an inspector general. (His mannerisms probably had not helped him with Seppius.)

George ground out his cigarette and reached for his glass. Mrs. Bolton would be at the table right on Carnett's heels.

Carnett was still in mid-nod after hearing from George that Gloria had gone to the ladies' room, when Mrs. Bolton appeared to ask whether he would like something from the bar.

"Beefeater martini, double, with a twist."

"Yessir," she said. "Anything else?"

"A menu, please."

"How about a refill for me?" George asked. "And for the lady, too."

"Yes, sir."

She was off. Carnett sat down. He and George exchanged a long, hard look and George nodded, hoping his face did not betray too much.

Carnett nodded, too. "I can imagine how hard it must have been for both of you." He paused. "But it's probably best this way, in the long run."

"She took it a lot better than I expected. She cried, but that's . . . well, natural. I ended up bawling myself. Still, she took it a lot better than I had expected."

Carnett said nothing. The drinks arrived, he took a sip and put his glass down again. George lit a cigarette. The waitress brought three menus, and a busboy appeared with butter and hot, fresh rolls.

"Gloria is all right," Carnett said after a while, pensively. "She is all wrong about some things—politics for instance—but she's basically all right."

"Don't patronize her, goddammit!" George suddenly felt ready to lash out in any direction—and especially at this so-called champion from across the river.

Carnett narrowed his eyes. "I'm not patronizing her," he said thoughtfully, after a while. "You are. I never wondered how she would take it." He reached for his glass. "You don't owe me any explanation, so let's drop the subject. Is that all right?"

"Okay by me," said George grudgingly. He puffed hard on his cigarette, thinking. Hell, they were all under a lot of tension, and had been. Carnett knew that. Still, he'd better watch himself, because Gloria and Carnett might not see that everybody's best chance lay in his persuading Seppius, Man to Man, possibly over a lengthy period. But then, he was practically on his way to Los Angeles right now, and surely Gloria would prefer his taking the sword far away.

He was still trying to decide on the best way to bring up the subject when Carnett abruptly got to his feet. "Hello," he said, solicitously. "I hope you are feeling better."

304

"I am."

George jumped up to pull out Gloria's chair. She sounded normal; looked it, too, except for being somewhat pale. She sat down, nodded, and picked up a menu. "Have you decided what you're going to order yet? I'm about starved."

Mrs. Bolton returned, hovering protectively near Gloria's elbow. She looked curious and just a little disappointed when no one said anything except to order dinner: steak for George, country ham for Gloria, and chicken pot pie for Carnett. As she walked away, Gloria looked first at George and then Carnett.

"Suppose we don't talk business until after dinner?" she said, forcing a half-smile. Now there was a slight tremor in her voice, and her eyes were a little too bright; in fact she looked ready to burst into tears.

Carnett nodded. George followed suit. Just as well —he'd have more time to think things out now.

Gloria asked Carnett if the Nixon crowd was getting worried now that the truth was out about the government's tilts in India and Pakistan. The lawyer shrugged and said Jack Anderson's columns were a passing thing—a truck rumbling past in the night. The main thing was that Hanoi was back at the conference table. It was a pity, though, that the only way to get them there was by bombing hell out of them, because none of these people needed to die. It was such a waste, really, and—

This touched off an argument that lasted halfway through the meal.

39

January 5, 1972

JOSEPH CARNETT WAS still seething as he followed the Quinteruses out of the Golden Lamb, walking to the ridiculously named Forty-One Winks Motel after two hours of talking, mostly about diddly-squat. He had managed to make it sound funny when he recounted how he kicked Seppius' tree, but his foot was still sore and he tried to keep his mind off it by thinking of other snowy evenings, long past, when he and Helen had gone for hand-in-hand walks on her dad's place.

Oh, well. He spat against the cinder-block wall of the drugstore on the corner. The way things were going, he might well be home before next Christmas! All his life, from fourteen on, anyway, he had prided himself on his intelligence, with nought but scorn for scabrous courthouse hangers-on—partly, because of their stupidity—and, later, for the venal operators hanging around the legislature. But the stupidest of those dumb, dumb bastards would never have got into the bind Joseph Carnett was in now.

He shook his head. It was a mess, all right. But even with full foreknowledge there was no way he could honorably have acted in a different fashion after George Quinterus stepped into his office. And so here he was, bright, experienced, sophisticated, a man who had seen some things and read or heard about the rest, trudging down a snowy street in Lebanon, Ohio, and trying to think his way out of one of the most god-awful problems in the history of the world. A melodramatic way of looking at things, perhaps, but justified under the circumstances, and—

the thought cheered him considerably even if it was malicious and unworthy—the man who had got him into this was not having an easy time of it either.

The Quinteruses had been arguing almost from the moment they left the Golden Lamb. Carnett had stayed far enough back not to eavesdrop, but he couldn't help wondering whether the argument was going along lines that had crossed his own mind:

Item: George Quinterus, his hopes and plans. The writer thought he could persuade Seppius if only they'd let him. He might, but it seemed unlikely; it would be out of character for Seppius to abandon his life's work, and the best they could reasonably hope for was that Seppius would remain quiescent until George died, around 2015 A.D., provided he lost weight and started exercising regularly.

Item: Seppius insisted this was rest time—so nothing would be lost, from an objective point of view, by George's trying. And more power to him.

Item: Gloria Barr Quinterus. A smart, good-looking young lady. Carnett smiled wryly; his mother, or Helen's, would never have agreed with this usage and they might have had a point; the way the Quinteruses were quarreling in low voices, holding hands and staying as far apart as possible, eight days after their wedding, was as good an argument as any he could think of against the modern practice of routine cohabitation before marriage. Apart from this, she obviously had her doubts about George's chances of success; and regardless of the fate of humanity, if George brought the monster home she would walk out. The effect of that on the writer was a matter of conjecture, though he might well stick with Seppius, who, after all, was a persuasive individual in his own right.

Item: George would be very upset hearing all this, for many reasons, ranging from his human dislike of being proved wrong to, well, morbid fascination—moldy old term, but expressive—for his ancient kinsman.

Item: Seppius, or the Seeking Sword. Lived up to prior advertisements. Carnett had sort of expected this, half-fearfully, but the experience had still been a shock.

Item: Seppius' fate, in the sense of ultimate disposition of the case. The subject had already come up in Boston, and left each of them frustrated and annoyed: George because he did not want the sword destroyed; Gloria because she didn't like her husband's hunt for alternatives, which she called excuses; and Carnett because every alternative had its shortcomings—one reason he had looked forward to the encounter in the park as a sort of reconnaissance mission.

Item: The reconnaissance mission. What had he learned? Not too damned much. He was definitely not an invincible champion, even if his heart was pure. George hadn't been making up stories. The Seeking Sword was real, and the ghost, or whatever, that made it go had a definite personality. Good-bye, Killthinkers!

Item: It was unlikely Seppius could be persuaded by logic or any appeal except to emotions. Apparently he had swerved from his insane straight-and-narrow in the past, but only—here was the rub—temporarily. He must have lost face in his own eyes each time. As a result, George's idea wouldn't work, though it might gain them—Carnett, really, because Gloria was in no position to do much—time to set up something.

Set up what? Why, some method to destroy the sword, of course.

Item: Fire? No go, according to what George had said. Seppius had been cast into flames many times, most recently in the 1680s and for the first time around 1500 B.C., when the priests and other wise men of the Upaterenchunnen—that's how the tribal name had sounded in George's mouth—bound the Seeking Sword between two voluptuous teen-aged virgins and set fire to the heap of wood under them. It had been a gigantic pyre, burning for two days and three nights. It had had no effect on Seppius, who considered it disgusting and said that he'd helped one girl, distantly akin, to die immediately. All in all, what else could one expect from Others and Shitfeet?

More specifically, iron melted at 2800 degrees Fahrenheit and boiled at twice that temperature. This, naturally, was true of ordinary metal. No one had ever thought about the effects of possible sentience, not to mention willpower; even humans had endured temperatures of well over 200 degrees for several hours as long as they could sip liquids to replenish their body fluids.

Item: Water? That, too, had been tried. From the eighteenth century B.C. to the 1890s, people had thrown the sword into lakes, rivers, or seas. Always, it would re-emerge—sometimes in a few months, sometimes after many years. Seppius had also learned from experience. His forebears had controlled game by means of the Flame-Eggs—wishing rings could allegedly still do this—but in any case Seppius could tell fish or sea crabs to push the sword along the bottom. Time meant little to him; both A's and B's would multiply, in any case, while he was out of action; and the reappearances of the sword were marked by hideous massacres.

Once, soon after 300 A.D., the sword emerged on a beach in the autumn and was then buried ten feet deep beneath a wandering dune. It took Seppius thirty-seven years to reach the surface, patiently moving grains of sand a few at a time—and the mid-fourth century had been a time of unparalleled bloodshed.

Back in Boston, Gloria had suggested throwing the sword in various places: the Mindanao Trench in the Pacific, some deep place in the Antarctic or off the east coast of Greenland, around Spitzbergen or Jan Mayen Island. Still, entirely apart from how they would accomplish that, they had no guarantee Seppius might not return, slavering for prey at any time from—this was 1972—say, after 1980.

Brighter than a thousand suns, etcetera, glory hallelujah? All right, a nuclear explosion would vaporize even the most acutely conscious, determined, cool piece of metal; but this method had its own fearful drawback.

George said the Seeking Sword appeared to be conscious all over, that it had no sense organs or specialized areas. Apparently every molecule was equally purposeful and capable of trying to attain the sword's purposes. It was weird, against all reason, it should not be. But there it was, and walking away with a shake of the head was just another, easily defendable, way to chicken out. In this connection, however, Carnett had wondered about smuggling the Seeking Sword to the site of a French nuclear test in the Pacific.

George's answer had been matter-of-fact and chilling: "I assume the explosion would scatter the molecules and it would take them thousands of years to reassemble by chance, if they ever did—but since they are conscious and probably light enough to float in air, they might reassemble in a few months, or—" George had stopped, looking distressed. When Gloria coaxed him to speak again, he'd said: "Seppius' feelings can be hurt rather easily, since he considers himself the instrument of justice. He was really mad when his tribesmen scattered and left him buried under the fire pit. After being blown apart . . . well, he might decide one sword is not enough and we could end up with a hundred Seeking Daggers instead of one Seeking Sword!"

Far out, to use Debbie's jargon.

Far out!

The thought caused Carnett to put his foot down painfully hard, because it was all so pat with him working for NASA. Put the sword in a spaceship, shoot it off. Not to the moon—that was too close; or Mars, because people might go there someday. But to the sun, or past Jupiter or Saturn into interstellar space. Even a spacecraft passing Mercury to fall into the sun would actually be irresponsible, like smuggling the sword to a French test site, in view of the solar wind. Streams of energized particles poured out from the sun, propelled by that immense thermonuclear reaction; sentient molecules could easily hitch a ride back to earth that way. Obviously the sun was a no-no.

Carnett smiled, glad of the darkness and empty streets. He really should try to be more serious, though, and look up Frank McCullough as soon as he got a chance. The black scientist was working on a rocket called Pathseeker, scheduled to blast off on April 7, shortly after the Pioneer rocket, which would carry an inscribed aluminum plaque on its endless journey past Jupiter and on out of the solar system. The plaque would be inscribed with the figures of a man and woman and various mathematical symbols so that any eight-eyed folks from Arcturus might be able to determine, millennia from now, where that primitive rocket had come from and what its makers had looked like. That, at any rate, had been a loud assertion of Dr. August Jesselson, head of the Pathseeker team. Dr. Jesselson had predicted in a press conference eight days ago that Pathseeker, which would give man his first close-up look at Saturn in 1979, would also serve as the monument to interstellar communication. He, himself, was designing the plaque; and since the rocket had some extra weight-boosting capability, the payload might as well include a collection of artifacts that would give the folks from Arcturus a real idea of humans and their way of life.

Now, then. Presumably the security watch over the collection of tools, or whatever, would not be overly tight; and the Seeking Sword, in any case, was more representative of human pursuits than any set of metric socket wrenches, an idea that should appeal to Frank McCullough's sense of humor. Carnett was not sure it could be done; but any hope—no matter how faint—was better than none at all.

He smiled again, at the louder, more assured sound of his shoes striking the sidewalk. The Quinteruses had turned left moments earlier; the red neon sign of the Forty-One Winks was blazing straight ahead.

How long would it take Seppius to start feeling lonely and forsaken in the emptiness beyond the orbit of Pluto?

40

January 5, 1972

ROOM 228 WAS at the end of the uncarpeted corridor to the right of the Forty-One Winks' lobby, where the elderly desk clerk had bitterly resented the interruption of his study of *Playboy*. Joseph Carnett was last in line—still in the doorway, in fact, when Gloria disappeared into the bathroom. George tossed his plaid jacket on the double bed and said he'd better get some ice.

"Fine," said Carnett, wondering if he would get to talk to Gloria and whether this would be a good idea.

Yes, he decided, unbuttoning his topcoat. People like George Quinterus, would-be intellectuals who had not got their theories published yet, tended to underestimate other people, understandably enough, and especially women. Most people were tolerably intelligent about their own concerns; most statements about general stupidity had been made by unappreciated intellectuals.

The thought actually made him smile as he hung up the coat in the open closet across from the lavatory. He looked around, muttering a silent prayer, for a moment deriving entirely irrational comfort from the probable presence of a Gideon Bible somewhere close by. "Help me, Lord," he half prayed, "because even though I am going to lie and deceive, and provoke to anger with ulterior motive, I do not expect to profit from it. I am doing it to help and save others." After a pause, he added "Amen," under his breath as he sank onto a chair.

Carnett had not heard the toilet flush; now Gloria

312

was coming through the doorway with her mouth set in a thin line.

"Something seems to be troubling you, sir," she said, attempting to smile, her voice calm, with an undertone suggesting it might not take much to cause her to break.

Carnett got up and nodded.

She sat on the bed, kicked off her shoes, looked at him doubtfully. "Well?"

"Two things." He decided not to bother about choosing words, modulating the voice, all that. "Two things. First, there may be a way to get rid of Seppius by shooting him off into space."

He wondered whether he could finish before George returned with ice, and hurried through a description of the rocket—and the importance of allowing George to think he would have another chance to convert Seppius. Not that he was likely to succeed in that undertaking.

Gloria frowned. "I see your point," she said. "I can't understand how he still . . . But he wants to take the sword with him anyway, and I've got to sort things out in my own mind." She paused; her fine eyes looked perilously moist. "Okay. We work out the space-shot thing, while George entertains himself with *that*. I agree we must keep it from him because there's no way he could hide it from Seppius." She pronounced the name with loathing. "It's unfair but okay. Maybe it will start killing people anyway and maybe it won't, but there's nothing we can do about that. I suppose I'll be able to stand it."

She wiped her face with a wad of pink Kleenex and gave Carnett a dangerously bright-eyed look. "Sure —" All of a sudden, her voice broke. "I mean, it's weird, really freakish, and I can't understand it. I used to tell myself that whenever a situation didn't make sense any more, that was the time to get the hell out. It worked once, but here I am; he didn't make sense two years ago, but I'm still hanging around. Hell, it's right out of the damned soaps, my getting tied up—and pregnant, for God's sake—with this guy who keeps saying trust me, everything's gonna be all right. Crap!"

313

She turned her head away. Carnett started to get up again. But this was no time to get caught in the act of comforting the heroine. The situation was too much like a Grade B movie already.

He went to the bathroom and closed the door behind him firmly.

When he emerged there was still no sign of George —Carnett looked out the door to make sure. Gloria had regained control and repaired most of the damage to her face.

"I'm sorry," she said. "I guess I haven't had too much practice at handling emotional upheavals." All of a sudden she grinned. "Secret intrigue is something else I have no practice at, but it sounds exciting. Now, then—we have covered all the points, haven't we?"

"More or less."

"More or less?"

Carnett was still trying to decide on the proper terminology, when he thought he heard footsteps. "I was . . . wondering whether we'd have the, well, *moral* right just to go and destroy Seppius." He raised his voice. "That is, if George can't make the old bastard see the light."

"Of course I can!" George's booming voice was much too hearty. He marched in, plopped the white plastic bucket on the dresser, and asked Gloria where the bottle was.

"Top drawer." She and Carnett exchanged glances. All systems go.

George started pouring whiskey into the plastic glasses. "I take it you both have your doubts about my sanity," he said, attempting to sound cheerful even though his underlying mood was clearly one of glum determination not unlike Carnett's. He dropped in the ice cubes one by one, gently, with exaggerated delicacy. "Here, darling. Both gesture and phrase were somehow awkward, and she smiled, too brightly. He nodded and handed a glass to Carnett, who half rose to accept it, murmuring thanks. George took a healthy swig, refilled his glass, and sank in the other armchair.

"Well, what's the decision of the brain trust?"

Carnett had not quite decided on the reply, when

Gloria said: "We can't see how you can say you trust that—*thing*."

"He's never lied to me yet." The response was quick, automatic, but George's tone was quite different an instant later. "I realize you've had a shock and that you're almost allergic. But that doesn't really change anything." He added, after a pause: "Give me a chance. Please."

"You're absolutely sure?" Carnett was really curious.

George turned to face him, but at that moment Gloria burst out: "You don't have to sound so damn proud of being a sword-keeper, the monster's best friend! Crap!"

Carnett had thought she would start crying. She didn't. Instead she leaned forward, chin thrust out, eyes blazing with anger—trite phrase, certainly, but descriptive.

George looked at her a while before replying in a low voice. "I understand how you feel, but, goddammit, I'm trapped too. I don't like the murders. And, hell, I can't blame Seppius either. So I've got to convince him, that's all. Please trust me—I just need some time." His voice was now earnest, almost wheedling. "Some time—during which nobody is killed. I can do it, and anyway, I'll be leaving for L.A. By the time I come back everything should be okay."

"What makes you think so?" she asked in a stony voice.

"I've got more to fight for." George grinned; it looked horribly incongruous. "It used to be mankind, an abstraction at best. But now there's George Junior, too."

"I see."

"Today was a disaster." He paused. "I never should have brought an outsider into a family dispute." George's voice made Carnett shiver. The writer took a sip of whiskey and added: "I know it's been hard on us all. But this isn't the end, and I'm sure I can put things right with Seppius."

"Goody for the two of you. What about me?"

"Uhmh?" Gloria's reaction dumbfounded George; he muttered something about sorry, this was hard for them all, but he was trying to straighten things out . . .

"Lots of luck!" Carnett put in, trying to sound as sarcastic as possible.

"This is none of your goddamned business," George declared.

"You dragged me in, so now you're stuck with me!"

Thinking back to the debate could be really infuriating. Carnett had hardly thought of his tantrum and hurt dignity in the car and had not even mentioned it over the phone to Helen, but now . . .

George looked at him. "I'm sorry," he said, shrugging, and a harsh note crept into his voice. "Damn, I'm sorry about everything. But what the hell do you want to do? Sit here and cry on each other's shoulders about the rotten old bastard? What good is that going to do?"

"We might figure out some way to destroy it, or get rid of it," said Gloria.

Oh, no! Carnett cast her a warning glance.

But she knew what she was about. "We should have an alternative, just in case your apologies aren't enough."

"I don't think there is any other way," George declared. "I also think it would be a mistake to try."

"Mankind deserves him, eh?" In the heat of the argument she had slipped into using the personal pronoun, but her intonation was unaltered.

"Oh, hell." George turned aside, disgusted.

Carnett decided to step in again. "I don't think we're accomplishing very much," he said, carefully trying to maintain the proper tone of dignified concern. "Maybe we should—"

"Oh, the hell with that," George exploded. "Look —we all want to see an end to the murders and I happen to think the peaceful solution is best. You can't hold Seppius legally responsible, and there's no way to imprison or execute him anyway. So our best hope is for me to persuade him; and I just might be able to do that, even if you don't like the idea. I don't give a damn why—whether it's prejudice, or whatever." He clamped his mouth shut, red-faced, and glared at Carnett.

Gloria's angry, cold, and yet tremulous voice

caused George to turn his head sharply. "All right, if that's how you feel," she said.

They frowned at each other for a long moment—at least thirty seconds by Carnett's wristwatch—before George looked aside, muttering under his breath.

"Sorry to be such a bitch," said Gloria, not a whit less defiant.

Carnett tried to stand up; this was getting too rough, regardless of the fate of all mankind. "Maybe I should take a walk, or check out my room upstairs," he said, bitterly ashamed even though this argument probably would have proceeded along similar lines without his presence in the Cincinnati area.

Now what? The writer wasn't going to start a brawl, was he? He'd jumped to his feet, barring Carnett's way with outspread arms.

"Allow me," George was saying, with the same over-elaboration of courtesy as when he was pouring drinks; he actually bowed from the waist and threw his half-empty plastic glass on the floor. "I can tell when I'm not wanted!" His foot crunched down. "This started out a halfway civilized discussion, I thought, but you both just want to curse and weep, so maybe I should go have a beer—or, better yet, take off. Yeah. I could take the Saab, since Mister Carnett's suitcase is in the Ford, and tomorrow we can get together for brunch and you can tell me what I should do to save civilization and all that crap."

He reached for his jacket on the bed.

"Stop it!"

Her tone made George flinch. "Look," he said, in an almost calm voice. "I'm not implying a goddamned thing, but I'm obviously an uncivilizing influence in this assembly. So I'll get out, for everybody's good!" He grimaced. "I trust this is okay?"

She began to clap her hands, vigorously, her eyes half shut and teeth clamped down visibly on her lower lip. Carnett tried to think of something, anything, as George glared at her, then finally stormed out, slamming the door. There was something pathetic about that gesture, as well as something admirably defiant and irrelevant, too, all at the same time.

317

Gloria clapped her hands eight more times after the door slammed.

She and Carnett looked at each other; he walked to the door and looked up and down the corridor, with special attention to doorways. Apparently the coast was clear. He frowned and turned back.

Gloria Quinterus was lying face down on the pale blue bedspread, sobbing. She gave no sign of having heard him and he stood in the doorway for a seemingly endless minute, wondering whether he should go to room 309 now. Then he tiptoed back to his chair, where he sat down quietly and relit his pipe. As he watched her, his eyes stung; and rubbing them, no matter how hard, did not help in the slightest.

Poor, poor Gloria! A few hours ago, Helen had wept about her plight, and had wished for some way of conveying her sympathy. Sitting here now, watching Gloria's shoulders heave and twitch, Carnett tried to imagine how she might feel about her situation and the new life quickening inside her womb, blind, unthinking, doubtless unaware of anything except vague well-being as nutrients were absorbed and duly metabolized. Helen and he had discussed this long ago, before the births of Joe Junior, Roger, and Debbie, respectively, but the circumstances had been altogether different. For the Quinteruses, everything was much tougher, because Gloria could not but feel ambivalent, to some degree, about her unborn son—not to mention George, with his doubts and mixed feelings, and the whole goddamned mess they were in.

Gloria seemed to be breathing more evenly; she was probably falling asleep at last—well-earned sleep after a truly hellish evening. Carnett sipped his whiskey and smiled, trying to picture himself as the bullman in Picasso's assorted versions of *Watcher over Sleeping Beauty*. Hmm. Years ago, Smallett and Olferth and some other professors of law had warned him he might be dealing with raw life as well as points of order. He had never doubted them, but he had not realized the possible implications until now.

When his wrist watch said 9:38, she was fully asleep, head turned to one side, breathing slowly and evenly with a slight smile on her lips. Well, any pleasant dreams she might have she had earned. Carnett felt very paternalistic, and it didn't make a damned bit of difference what anybody might think of his state of mind. Whether or not romantics were born or made, nowadays, there was no cure for the condition except, possibly, the firing squad.

Smiling, he tiptoed out of 228, leaving a note on the sink. "Call me. 309. About cars. Carnett."

41

January 6, 1972

Br-rrr-ring!

George Quinterus became aware of the hideous noise only gradually, and at first he just lay, rubbing his eyes, wondering why Gloria wasn't answering the phone. Maybe she'd gone to work already? No, this was Thursday, supposedly part of her vacation, their honeymoon, and—

God! Memories of yesterday poured into his mind: picking up Carnett at the airport, driving him to the park, making small talk, followed by the farce and the painful, stupid, idiotic scenes until he finally stormed out, got in her car, and drove home.

The phone kept ringing.

He almost got up on the fifth ring but managed to restrain himself. According to wire-service mythology, you hung up after the seventh ring because no one could resist Mr. Bell's siren song that long.

The phone rang on and on, and when this transpired for the eleventh time, George decided it must be Gloria. She'd purchased more than a dime's worth of sheer annoyance out of Mr. Bell's invention on several occasions.

Brrrr-RRRR-innnnGGG!

Twelve. George sat up. Yeah, he had come home in the Saab while she stayed at—not the Golden Lamb, the other place—screeching that he should be ashamed about Seppius and all that crap.

Okay. Maybe Seppius was not the nicest . . . well, person, in the world. But what did she want him to do? Jump up and down, yelling curses, while she sat looking aggrieved in ladylike fashion and Carnett made inane remarks about being reasonable, and lower your voices, ple-ease?

He got out of bed and began moving toward the living room, trying to decide how to answer. Too bad he hadn't had any coffee. Last night he'd just sat up too long, drinking, thinking whether, when, and how they would kiss and make up. No problem, as long as she didn't start yammering about swords and triangles.

He picked up the phone on the fourteenth ring. "Hello?" Might as well sound as amiable as possible.

"My, but you're in a pleasant mood this morning." She sounded defiant, but not quite sure of herself; she had made up her mind not to back down, but would be happy if the issue did not arise.

Okay. Still, she had no call to wake him this early. She should have known better. Where were the cigarettes?

"George?" Her voice was still firm.

"Yeah."

"Mad at me?"

"Yeah." He had been, thinking of her sitting in the motel room, phone in hand, especially if Carnett was anywhere in range. For a moment, he'd thought of them on that pool-cue chalk bedspread, but the image just wouldn't hold together. She wouldn't; and with all his faults, Carnett wasn't the type either. But it would still be irritating as all hell if they'd had breakfast, discussing options and strategies and how much they could safely tell him.

She had started to say she was sorry, but her next words had slipped past him. Right now, though, she was saying there was no doubt he knew more about the sword than anybody and just might be right.

320

"Why do you keep calling Seppius the sword?" he wanted to know.

"Oh? *Why?*" She sounded a bit put out over the interruption. "What else should I call it?"

"What's wrong with Seppius?"

"It's too . . . too humanizing. Oh, I know that's a bunch of semantics, because the old shaman was alive once. I suppose a science-fiction writer would call the sword a cyborg or something." She continued in a more animated voice: "It doesn't really make any difference to me. If you can talk sense to it, fine— only I still don't see how you can stand it. I'd rather be shot."

He bit his lip and kicked his ankle. Goddammit, even if he succeeded—after he'd succeeded, rather— they would still be fighting about Seppius every day and night of their lives. But how could he persuade Seppius—mostly on the basis of how-can-you-do-this-to-your-own-kinsman?—and then walk out after the old shaman agreed? Seppius' reaction—and George couldn't really blame him—might well be to get back to work, then. And where would that leave George Junior? Besides, walking out would be a dirty trick to play on a kinsman.

Of course, maybe he didn't have a chance and it would come down to whatever Carnett and Gloria might dream up.

Maybe. Only he hated to think so. It just wasn't fair.

"George!"

He heard more edge to her voice now, and it made him feel tearful. He'd wondered about that before, this strange hold she seemed to have on him.

Right now, he'd better answer her. "Sure. I'm still here."

"Say something, then." A pause; then she asked: "Have you dug it up yet?"

He said no. She said that was good; he told her he was glad of her approval.

"I don't approve of misplaced sarcasm." She was starting to sound exasperated.

Okay. It didn't matter; he drew back his shoulders and took a deep breath. "Let's get to the point," he said. "The point is, we don't need to go over it all again, but basically I think I can persuade Seppius. You believe that's impossible, or unlikely, but you need some time to set up whatever the two of you came up with. Okay?"

He paused; Gloria said nothing but he could hear her exhale after a loud, deep breath. He bit his lip. He'd regret what was coming enough without kicking himself for it now.

"Maybe you're right and maybe I'm right," he continued, starting to feel ridiculously melodramatic. "Only we'll never know unless I try. You can see that, can't you? I'm not mad at you anymore, but you know I can't just quit now."

He waited fearfully for her reply, but when it came it was subdued and soft-voiced. "Good luck. You're basically a nice guy and I want to trust you."

Now what could he say to that?

She spared him the trouble. "I still can't understand what you see in it." Her tone set George's teeth on edge; she really loathed Seppius. "Still," she added, "I hope you succeed."

"And what happens then?"

He bit his lip again. Forgiveness was always hard as hell to accomplish; protestations of it were seldom even convincing, let alone for real. So if George Quinterus saved humanity, how would it pay off at home? He held his breath.

"It will be damned hard," said Gloria without a moment's hesitation. "I can't stand it, but I suppose I may have to learn. Woman's lot, right?" she concluded wearily.

"I wish you wouldn't take it that way."

"I don't like it, either."

Too bad this wasn't a telepathic conversation. Too bad about the baby. Without him, they could have their fight and go their own ways. Too bad about a lot of things.

"Good luck," said Gloria, her voice suddenly soft. "Let me know how things go."

She hung up before he could answer, leaving him sitting phone in hand, staring at his bare toes.

Damnation! He stood up, stretched, and went to

run hot water for instant coffee. The clock said 10:35. A lot of his things were in California already, so there wouldn't be much to pack; but he'd better go and pick up Seppius as soon as possible, before he even called the airline to change his reservation. Fortunately this was a dark, cold, gloomy day—suiting his mood—a day that would keep people out of the park. He wondered how Seppius was feeling.

Knowledge of coldness is not unlike feeling the cold.

He'd known, of course, that Seppius had remained within range. The compromise had been for Gloria's sake and he had made his trips to the park because sitting in the armchair and conversing with Seppius would have been ridiculous. Seppius had understood, as a result of past experiences.

"I'll be out soon, and we'll go to California," George said aloud. "It's warm there." He let his mind dwell on images of Los Angeles: hills, beaches, the sea, dusty palm trees, smog, cars, oil pumpers . . .

The sea. Are you planning to throw me into the sea, kinsman? There was a tone of weariness about the words. *Being in the sea can be restful as well.*

"No!" George was surprised at the violence of his response. And, yes, sorry about yesterday and—

All Men have made their mistakes. Seppius paused and asked: *Will Gloria come with us?*

"No, but she may change her mind later." George lit a cigarette. "At least I hope so."

It is not good for you and her to be apart before the child is born. Strange thoughts often come at times such as these.

"We'll get together again."

You are not sure of it. That is to be deplored. Seppius' solicitude flowed through George's mind and the old shaman began to tell him how the wife of Speared-two-salmon-at-once became ill and died in childbirth while—or because—he stayed too long on a hunting trip.

George smiled as he began looking under the bed for his shoes.

42

January 15, 1972

Los Angeles was warm, all right, but working on the script was a real pain as far as George was concerned. The evenings and late afternoons were fine, because even though he might never feel completely the same about Seppius again, the old shaman regarded the situation as normal enough. He had many stories about past sword-keepers to prove his point; only three of the whole throng had kept the sword without major domestic difficulties. He also refused to call off the blood feud as a personal favor to George, or George Junior, though he listened with great patience to the various arguments the writer brought up.

They still think of ways, to destroy me, do they not?

Seppius asked this one evening while some ex-jock was discussing the Miami Dolphins' chances in the 1972 Super Bowl.

"Yeah," said George. Why deny the obvious? After all, he wondered about it often enough. It would probably have something to do with the space program, but he doubted that Carnett would come up with anything workable.

The champion has been interested in me for long time. Seppius paused. *Why is he so eager to see his spear tip dipped in blood? None of the Cowdung-covered-knees to die, of late, has been of his kindred.*

George put down his cigarette. "He is concerned about laws, codes of conduct—and according to our laws you have committed murder. That is one point on which we agree."

I am doing what is proper for a Man to be doing.

"Hardly any of the Men living now would agree with you."

It would be proper for them to agree.

George sighed. How many times had they gone over this?

Men have learned too many of the ways of the Others. Still, they have, for the most part, done the proper thing after I made it clear what should be done. Most of them didn't want to, being bad kinsmen, but they did it.

Maybe both Men and Others had changed, to the point where it was improper of Seppius to continue to expect the same responses?

The answer was immediate and uncompromising. *Men have not turned into Others, even if there have been changes of hue in the fires.*

Didn't they have the right to change their feelings to match the new fires?

Kinsman, your question is, yet again, without meaning.

Oh hell. George gnawed his lip. "The point I was going to bring up is—and you've told me before and I've asked you before—but the sons of Swift-as-ermine were each other's kinsmen, though some were Men and some were not, and kinsmen should never harm each other. So wasn't it improper of them to kill each other? I ask the question only because I care about you." The odd thing was, he really did care.

Seppius' answer was full of proper, cloying appreciation of a kinsman's concern: *It is hard to explain to one who cannot see the hues in the fires. They who look alike are not the same, nor yet always they who come from the same womb; because when one in a litter of whelps has six legs or two heads, that one is no dog even if the mother is a properly trained bitch good at driving in deer in the greenwood.*

Oh sure. And next would come "No elk ever turned himself to a hawk because she had grown weary of running in the grass."

Kinsman, you are learning and learning properly. First, words and then the meanings of words.

George went to get a beer, wondering when

325

he would hear from Gloria—and which of them would call the other first.

She did.

Her voice had a little trill as she asked how he was and added that everything was fine with her, and, as far as she and the doctor could say, George Junior as well. "Really, you worry too much," she added. "The big day is still many months away."

"I know, but that's the way I am."

"You're sweet," she said, with a laugh. "And now, the business part. How's the script going?"

"Not so well, but I'm told that's normal here."

"I suppose . . ." she said.

"How about Carnett's great plan?" he asked.

"What plan?"

"You mean he gave up on the whole thing?"

"Look, I don't care to discuss these things," she said stiffly, and changed the subject to comparing January in Cincinnati and Southern California. After a while, the conversation became quite pleasant.

43

February 16, 1972

ON FEBRUARY 16, 1972, Gloria Quinterus was scheduled to call some time after 8 P.M. to report on her latest conversation with George. Joseph Carnett was glad they were getting along so well. George would throw a tantrum when Seppius was blown off the earth, but that was too far ahead to worry about now. Even Helen thought the Quinteruses had a chance, and she certainly ought to know.

Thinking of Helen downstairs, trying to read a magazine while waiting for the phone, made Carnett feel warm inside. Helen and Gloria had become quite friendly in January, when Helen stayed at the Galway Place apartment for a few days, right after George left for Los Angeles. The visit had done Gloria a lot of good, even if it hadn't stopped her arguing about politics. She would start off with some crack about Mr. Nixon's trip to China, which was easy to defend, or—and this would be more troublesome —the Berrigan and girlfriend trial. That was bad, because it looked too much like a frame-up and the only bright spot in that whole dismal scene was that John Mitchell was resigning to run the President's re-election campaign. The wise men had almost screwed up in '68, but this year, after the China trip and peace —even if not "peace with honor"—the election would be a landslide, with all possible help from the Democrats.

The phone rang. Carnett put down his pipe and picked it up, bracing his shoulders as he did so. "Carnett, here."

"Hi."

They heard a click as Helen picked up the extension.

She and Gloria exchanged greetings and Carnett said: "Business before pleasure. How is everything?"

"I'm paying for this call," Gloria insisted. "Anyway, unless you can tell me why that stinker shouldn't be impeached—" She paused, chuckled, and added: "George is fine. He's unhappy with what they're doing to poor Sally, because the book was honest schlock and not straight porn, but he's enjoying the weather and the company. I guess."

"He'll get over it," said Helen.

"I know. It's weird . . . he never mentions Seppius unless I ask, but I can tell it's always in the back of his mind, and I'm not sure which way would bother me more."

"Is he making progress?"

"He says so, but when I ask for details he turns vague. Today he even tried to change the subject." She hesitated. "He's got an idea for a novel, a kind of spy thriller about secret agents trying to get hold of the Seeking Sword. In the end they do—and that's it, for them. George says something like it actually happened."

"I wouldn't be surprised," said Carnett. "What about the Florida trip?"

"I told him I may go to Florida sometime during April. I'll be getting huge by then, and March in Cincinnati is depressing. He asked if you're finally ready to kill the sword," she added with a nervous little laugh. "I told him you were still racking your brains, and blackmailing people to run off things on computers. Anyhow, I said my stepmother's sister, Mrs. Altman, had invited me to stay with her there. She's been thinking of selling her house and finding something smaller, because her husband died in November. Meanwhile she would like some company." Gloria paused. "She's nice. My favorite aunt, I guess."

"You mentioned her before," said Carnett. "Where does she live, anyway?"

"A development called Frenchman's Creek, near Lakeland. They moved there fifteen years ago, before land prices went out of sight."

While Helen asked about the Altmans, Carnett visualized a map of Florida: Canaveral—Cape Kennedy had never sounded right—was due east of Orlando; Lakeland would be southwest of Orlando, about halfway to Tampa. Thirty miles from Orlando to Canaveral, and fifty from Orlando to Lakeland . . .

It ought to work out. So many things could go wrong—at their end and on the launching pad. It wasn't often a space probe went off exactly on schedule, and if Seppius had too much time . . . Still, Pathseeker's ARA—assemblage of representative artifacts—was their best bet.

Helen and Gloria had finished their discussion of Mr. Altman, who had sold life insurance for thirty-seven years, with time out for service in World War I. Gloria asked if there was anything new at Carnett's end.

"There's not much we can do ahead of time, now that Frank McCullough has agreed to help. We'll just have to play it by ear."

"I've got an idea," said Gloria. "I'll tell George I'd like to be alone with him a while. We can reserve rooms near the airport. I could leave a note, or call, and ask George to come somewhere else while Frank gets the sword."

"How is George going to get somewhere else?" The idea had possibilities.

"My Saab can be right outside. He's got the keys to it."

"Do you think he'll leave the sword in his room?" Carnett wanted to know.

"He knows how I feel about it." She laughed harshly. "He'd better—anyway, let's hope he will leave it. You don't have any strong-arm men standing by, do you?"

"Of course not." Hiring a couple of goons might be easier, actually, than the arrangements had been to substitute the sword for a large file in the ARA. Even though no one was particularly concerned about ARA security, there would still be people around and Dr. Jesselson planned to have the container placed aboard Pathseeker during a little televised ceremony while he made a speech. That would show the Pioneer people, even if the Jupiter space probe was scheduled to blast off sooner.

"Okay," said Gloria. "I wouldn't want to be an accessory to a mugging. Anyway, I've been telling George that since we let him try things his way, the least he can do is give us a chance. I know it's not a logical argument, but I keep pointing out you could have sent the FBI after him because he's withholding evidence."

"What does he say?"

She laughed, less nervous now. "He grumbles a lot, but I really think he'll go along, because he's getting worried too. He doesn't want George Junior to end up being lobotomized, or filled up with tranquilizers." Carnett heard a brittle sound to her laugh.

"Does he know about Mrs. Altman?"

"Sure. She sent us an electric skillet as a wedding gift, and called up. He talked to her."

"That's good. You seem to have everything under control."

"Good," said Helen. "Why don't you get off the line, dear, because we've got things to talk about."

44

April 6, 1972

GEORGE QUINTERUS STILL wasn't sure whether the invitation was on the level or not. True, he knew Mrs. Altman, and it all made sense, but . . . He glared at the baggage carousel in the Orlando airport. Here he was, ready or not—and where was the suitcase?

It will come down the moving slope in eighty heartbeats.

A friend like Seppius could be helpful in many unexpected ways.

Should I look up and around, to see why she is not here to welcome you?

No, thanks, George thought back at Seppius, who had made the trip packed among his T-shirts. Journeys by air were nothing new to Seppius, who had flown from Copenhagen to Berlin in 1937 and had crossed the Atlantic several times. *Sometimes it really helps to move rapidly,* he had observed. *It is, however, proper for Men to look for the tracks of elk and wolf as they travel, and to feel the dirt underneath their soles.*

Seppius did not even approve of riding on horseback. In fact, he was a devil to please, as in the matter of the $20 sheath George had found in a Burbank craft shop. He'd been unimpressed. *It is of deerskin, adorned with markings much like those that the Men used; but the bearded youth of the Others who traced the lines in the leather knew not what the markings stand for and could not have killed a deer, as is proper for one of the Men before undertaking to fashion something from the leather his woman has chewed on, and put to soak to make pliable and soft.*

Just as George had been about to rage properly, Seppius had added: *Still, a leather sheath is better than many. Wood is proper, also, but some have been made of wood and metal with pegs inserted to keep a Man from doing what is proper. Be thanked, kinsman.*

George had meant buying the sheath to be a joyous occasion. It had not been so, and the memories still hurt after three weeks.

But, what the hell, here he was. And where was Gloria?

The last time she had called, she'd said a week at her aunt's place was plenty—and why didn't he come down to see her? They would not have to stay at Mrs. Altman's. She would get a room at the Lafayette Motor Lodge, close to the airport.

No use wondering—it was enough that she had invited him. But maybe she had ulterior motives. The Pioneer rocket with its aluminum plaque was gone, but there would be another probe in a few days, and then Apollo 16 a week from Sunday. However, she had not even mentioned Seppius.

Most likely, right now, she was setting up some kind of surprise. A pleasant thought. She would be very pregnant, but beautiful and—

It is very pleasurable that you will again be together. A son should know his father, from his earliest glances around this world, and a father should know his son, to teach him the things that are proper for Men.

Sure. He could almost see Seppius beaming.

And there was the suitcase. George squeezed in between a fat, fiftyish man in gaudy shirt and burnt-orange slacks and a purple-haired woman with huge sunglasses and violet slacks that bulged spectacularly. He picked up the suitcase, shook his head at the old black skycap, worked his way out to the taxi stand.

It wasn't often that he got out of the terminal ahead of the crowd. It seemed only a minute until he was in a cab on his way to the Lafayette, puffing on a cigarette. There was nothing to look at; here in the East it was dark already. He smiled in the dark, wondering about the surprise. Gloria had been sounding really

331

friendly and hopeful in recent weeks, since mid-March.

The women of most sword-keepers have feared me and loathed me, and some of them never ceased to feel that way. Being Others, they could not understand. Gloria is one of the Men, in some ways much like Swift-as-ermine-with-running-brook-laughter, though never has she laughed in my presence.

George squashed his cigarette in the ashtray.

She may try to throw me into Great Bitter Water, or the champion may do it for her. Or they may throw me into fire, or into a hole. Seppius' tone was resigned, with a suggestion of wry amusement. *She believes this would be best for the son she is bearing underneath her heart, but it would not be proper for one of the Men. She has learned to think as Others do. That is because too many Men, over the years, have failed to act in the proper fashion, and have not taught their sons and daughters what is proper for Men. It would be the same were I to go to another kinsman's dwelling.*

George said nothing, and tried to blank out his mind. Seppius could be a dreadful bore.

A word of blame that strikes to the heart is always painful. After a pause, Seppius continued. *It is all the same. Being under the dirt is restful, and being under the bitter water is restful. I would not see the passage of seasons. Yet I would miss seeing one of the true Men growing up from squalling suckling to silent hunter. . . . How to make tools, how to get in spear reach—every hunter must learn these first. . . . Striking hard, when close enough, is simple.*

The changes of tone—wistful to gloating to pedantic—set George's teeth on edge.

And then here they were, halting under a red neon sign. The cabbie had the suitcase ready as George arrived at the rear of the cab on feet that suddenly felt heavy. Goddammit, he had not realized how much he'd looked forward to seeing Gloria again. And the old bastard had spoiled it all!

I spoke because we may not have occasion to be together for some time.

Seppius was offended.

As George counted out change, he projected the thought that he understood, was sorry; but he would appreciate being alone until morning. Don't call me, I'll call you . . . Walking into the brightly lit lobby, he felt the old shaman withdrawing, and smiled.

The dark-haired girl at the registration counter smiled back. "Good evening. sir. Do you have a reservation?"

"I believe my wife checked in earlier today." Suddenly aware of how some people might take this, he tried to look proper and dignified. "The name is Quinterus. George Quinterus."

She looked at her file and nodded. "Yes. I see." She turned, and George wondered whether she had wiggled her behind more than necessary. It was too large, but nicely rounded. "The room is 355," she announced, handing him the key. "You'll be staying the week, sir, is that correct? And will you need any help with your luggage?"

"No. Not really." He looked at the key. "Thank you."

"The elevator is that way, sir."

She pointed left, and he saw the elevator doors just this side of the Lounge d'Egalité. Either Gloria was in the room; or, if not, he could leave a note and come down for a cold beer. He smiled again.

He took one last look around. She might be hiding behind a potted palm, giggling as she watched him. He hoped very much she might be.

No such luck. Several middle-aged businessman types staring at newspapers, a well-built blond matron, a slim black man with a mustache reading a science-fiction magazine . . . Too bad.

She was not in the room either, but her red suitcase was on the luggage stand, four maternity dresses—suddenly he felt a lump in his throat—were hanging in the closet, and some of the toilet articles looked familiar, as he noticed while washing his hands. He was not certain whether to be alarmed or annoyed, but this surely wasn't his idea of a warm welcome. He looked around, annoyed now, and saw the note taped to the television screen. Hah! Playing games, eh?

*Motel room's no place for a reunion. You agree?
So I got somebody, a friend of my aunt's, to lend
us a beach cottage temporarily. You were already airborne when it went through. There's a
map on the other side of this, and the Saab is in
Lot B. Keys are in top dresser drawer. Sorry
you'll have to drive, so I got an extra magnum of
Mumm's.*

Love, Gloria

"Sorry, love," he said aloud. "I thought— Never
mind."

He felt the corners of his mouth pull upward. Let's
see, now . . .

The cottage (marked with a red X) was on Ponce
de Leon Inlet and he should take U.S. 17/92 north
to Sanford (18 miles), east on Florida 415 (22 miles)
to Florida 44, which would take him (12 miles) to
New Smyrna Beach; and there he should turn north
on U.S. 1 and drive 3 miles toward Port Orange before turning off on a local road across from the Shell
station. Fifty-five miles in all.

Hell.

He looked at his wristwatch, calculating differences
in time. Okay. By the time he reached Second Honeymoon—hah!—Cottage it would be almost 9 P.M.,
provided he did not get lost, run out of gas, or something like that. Gloria and her sense of humor, not to
mention the romantic, could be a real pain. She had
even left a phone number, in case he was too tired or
—no doubt—too drunk.

Oh well, maybe he was being too hard on the poor
girl. She meant well—and must have put up with a lot
of yack to land the cottage, which was bound to be a
more suitable place for a reunion than this thoroughly
ordinary room. He took the map, put her keys in his
pocket—he already had a set—and took his toilet kit
from the suitcase, which he left lying on the bed.

All systems go for the drive to "The Shellsides"
near New Smyrna Beach, and she who had laid all
this upon him could damned well sit and wonder until
he arrived there.

Swinging his arms as he marched into the Lounge

d'Egalité, which would likely charge 75¢ for a glass of draft, George noticed the black man still reading his science-fiction magazine. Boy, could he tell the man a weird story!

He was starting to look forward to the cottage, even if it would take more than an hour on strange roads in the dark. But first, the beer.

45

April 6, 1972

A LOT OF space-agency employees lived in the development on Ponce de Leon Inlet and the house marked on Gloria's map belonged to Alton Partinger, a fuel composition analyst who had taken his wife on a Caribbean vacation after the Pioneer shot went off like clockwork.

That had been a stroke of luck. Frank McCullough lived next door to Partinger, they played squash and tennis together, Frank had keys to the house—a real relief, because none of them had seen how George could be fooled by McCullough's place. He wouldn't buy the idea that a friend of Mrs. Altman would have a house full of African statuary.

Right now, though, Joseph Carnett sat in McCullough's house, wondering whether that had been their last stroke of luck. George was overdue: they had figured it would take him ninety minutes, and almost two hours had passed since Frank's phone call at 8:03. Moreover, suppose Seppius did not care to be handled by a stranger? From everything Carnett knew about the old shaman, it was inconceivable he would not suspect something—and suppose George had the sword in his car? Carnett could not conceive of doing something like that, but the writer had done a lot of things he would never have done. Furthermore . . . suppose his own nerve failed him when he had to let himself into the house next door and sit there, gun in hand, waiting for George to come out of the bedroom. Successful criminals usually started earlier in life. What if the writer charged him, or Seppius caused him to freeze or drop dead, or . . .

He shook his head. This was no way to prepare for battle. Instead, he reached for his pipe and tried to picture things going well. By now, Frank should be passing through the Canaveral checkpoints. He had every right to be there, even late at night, just before the Pathseeker blast-off. In a way, it was lucky about August L. Jesselson, Ph.D., and his mania for speeches: the ARA would be in the control building, a lot easier to get at than it would be inside the spacecraft itself. There would be people around, and that could be a problem, but Frank would bring it off if anybody could. They might be wrong about Seppius having more trouble with the minds of blacks. But it seemed logical.

Carnett shook his head again. Here he was, worrying, at 9:57, after a whole evening of telling Gloria and Helen their troubles would soon be over. Suddenly, he froze. A car was coming up the driveway. It sounded like the Saab.

46

April 7, 1972

IT HAD BEEN a good night's sleep.

George yawned; then he lay still and listened to the birds and the sound of Gloria's even breathing. God, he had missed her! Memories of the homecoming whirled through his mind; it had been even better than he'd hoped for. She could be awfully sweet.

He had tried to tell her how sorry he was about everything, but she had told him not to worry. He'd said he wasn't making much progress with Seppius; and she'd said they should try and forget the sword this one night.

He raised up on one elbow and studied her sleeping face, turned to the right, with a slight smile on the full lips. A wave of tenderness swept through him. After all he had put her through, there must be some way he could make up for it. When he had finished the damned script and collected his pay, they would take a long vacation, the two of them and George Junior.

And what about Seppius? Well, he could shift for himself for a while. Kinsmen owed a certain amount of consideration to each other. Speaking of that, he wondered about Seppius in the suitcase he'd left on a bed at the Lafayette. Let's see, now, would that still be within range?

He closed his eyes and waited, at first impatient, then wondering, and finally alarmed as the scene, faint and strangely distorted, came before his mind: a room with fluorescent lights and barred windows, cement-block walls, and ceiling painted institutional green. Several desks were in the room, metal desks and metal chairs, and everything seemed to rock and sway as if—yes, as if somebody were walking with Seppius held in a kind of briefcase, and the old shaman had not made a full contact with the person's mind. George knit his brows as he sensed Seppius feeling his way along strange neuronal pathways, working out the patterns. He got the impression that Seppius found the task strangely difficult, that he had not become interested until recently. After all— George cringed at the impact of a thought that was not even directed at him—the tricks of bad kinsmen should be ignored because of the loving-kindness that kinsmen owed to each other, and Others had been used before to carry Seppius from one place to another in behalf of various Men.

Good God!

George sat up, appalled. Clenching his eyes tightly shut made the image slightly more distinct, but Seppius was not responding to his agonized calls. Bad kinsman!—even that would have been welcome. Any sign that the old shaman acknowledged his existence, their relationship, the good intentions on both sides . . .

I did not know for sure that this was a trick, Seppius, he pleaded silently. I had my suspicions at times, but I did not know. They had told me to go ahead and try to persuade you. Why wouldn't you listen to reason?

He bit his lip, bracing himself for the reply, about how the ways of Men are not the ways of Others. For a moment, he thought the words were forming in his mind, very faintly. No, not really.

The scene before his mind was changing. Evidently the person had put the briefcase down and was opening its clasps. The surface where the case lay looked like a terrarium lid covering a metal tray filled with various objects. He could not tell what they were, but it didn't matter. Or did it? Now the person was taking Seppius from the briefcase.

George caught a glimpse of dark skin, coveralls, a shiny plastic badge—the science-fiction fan from the lobby? Well, why not?

He remembered something else. There had been a lot of news stories about space shots: the Apollo flight, the Pioneer flight, and the Pathseeker flight. One would carry men to the moon, the other would carry a plaque past Jupiter and on to interstellar space, and the third would also end up out there after passing by Saturn. It would be carrying something called an Assemblage of Representative Artifacts, or ARA for short.

So that was it!

Sure, he could see it—from Seppius' point of view: a maze of geometric shapes, round and polygonal, a bottle clamped down, a saw, a book that looked like a child's primer, something that might be a transistor radio . . . He could see several open clamps coming closer, and a moment later he shivered at the faraway touch of cold metal against Seppius' surface—a faint sensation of wonder and curiosity. Men and Others had made more than ninety attempts to get rid of the sword, but this was a new way.

The shimmering overhead that must mean the plastic lid was coming down on the ARA, with Seppius serenely starting to explore his new surroundings, was too much. Too damned much!

"Watch out, Seppius!"

He jumped out of bed, hearing Gloria cry out in sleep, and headed for the living-room door. Who had closed it? On the way, he grabbed his clothes from a chair, and as he opened the door he involuntarily covered his genitals with the clothes because Carnett was sitting next to the phone table.

The phone was gone, but a large-caliber automatic lay on the table. An uncapped thermos sat on the floor next to the lawyer's right foot.

"Good morning," said Carnett. "Why don't you get dressed and sit down—there."

47

April 7, 1972

DR. AUGUST L. JESSELSON, the project head for Pathseeker, had been predictably orotund in the press conference that opened with the ARA's insertion into the sleek rocket. This called for a special interruption of the countdown, but Jesselson had arranged it easily.

An ass, yes, but a fine-looking spokesman. His appearance helped, of course: six feet one, heavy-set but not fat, fine jutting jaw, and shaggy mane of iron-gray hair not unlike the late Senator Dirksen's. There was also a mellifluous quality to his voice.

". . . We have no idea, of course, whether or not any intelligent beings will ever look upon this assemblage of representative artifacts aboard Pathseeker," he said. "Perhaps men like ourselves, centuries from

339

now, will find our primitive space probe still beating its course toward the star we know as Arcturus; and if they do, I hope they will drink a toast to us in the Scotch we have included in the capsule. It is good now, and will be good centuries from now." His hand swept up, over his head, and ended by pointing at the sky. "We do not even know whether there are any other intelligent beings in this vast universe. At the same time, it seems unlikely that life should have developed only upon earth, and that the development of intelligence similar to ours should be a unique event, something that has happened only once in the multi-billion-year history of our galaxy."

Jesselson paused, and brought his hand down. The camera panned past him for a view of Pathseeker on its launching pad, and then the control room with its long line of technicians peering at screens and dials.

Goddamned bastards! George could just picture what would happen if he reached a phone and told NASA somebody had put a bomb on the rocket and five billion dollars of the taxpayers' money would go up in a puff of smoke at— He bit his lip. The wall clock said 10:26, the countdown had about eight minutes to go.

Suppose Carnett had to go to the toilet and left his wife holding the .45 and he tackled her after diverting her attention somehow, got hold of the gun, and called—add another minute to get the number . . . Of course the bastard might have a second gun. Damn it, suppose he had to tackle Gloria for the gun?

He braced himself for Seppius' reproof. There was none. Would be none, ever, regardless of what he might do or not do. He'd wondered about that and he'd been right about the feeling of utter desolation mixed with relief, resentment, regret, and other emotions that he would be hard put to name.

For the ten thousandth time, he let his eyes rove around the tidy living room, from the grim-faced, tense Carnett to the hopeful, desperately smiling Mrs. Carnett . . . to Gloria. Gloria Barr Quinterus. Pale, slightly disheveled, her face covered with red splotches from crying, uneasily perched in an armchair well out of his reach. Mostly, she stared at her feet or at the handkerchief she kept twisting with her fingers. Once in a while, she would look at him, defiant and appealing at the same time.

He could read the message all right: not, "Try to understand me;" but rather, "You ought to understand me."

Yeah. He could understand her, and he couldn't really be angry at her for what had happened. At the same time, understanding did not mean agreement, not by a long shot. He had told her—them—and told them, again and again, that it would take time. What they had decided to do showed what they thought of him and his opinion of his own abilities. They harped about Seppius and how narrow-minded he was, but he didn't see where they were any better. Gloria had made up her mind from the beginning. When disbelief and ridicule, galling and condescending in themselves, were clearly no longer appropriate, she had switched to a more basic emotion: plain hatred, hatred almost to the point of physical reaction. She had cursed, connived, plotted, lied, deceived—and yet he was sure that last night had not been all make-believe, or even that there had been any significant portion of make-believe in it. That was a humbling realization.

Furthermore—he swallowed, watching the countdown continue—she had other reasons, some of the most powerful that had ever been known. He stole a look at her, her sad face turned to the window for the moment; he swallowed again and stared at his bare feet. She had wanted George Junior, or Annie. There was no doubt about that, even though she'd never explained her reasons very clearly. That didn't matter now. He could see it. From her point of view, she had a choice about whether or not her child would be born doomed to something worse than cancer or Tay-Sachs disease. So, from her point of view it was a simple problem and she could have no doubts about her decision.

Of course, she'd had a lot of help in reaching her decision—not that she'd really needed it. Carnett had taken care of that. George glared at him, the arrogant, stuffy bastard with the gun. He could just see the lawyer spouting forth spite after his humiliation in the park. Memories of that encounter made George feel uncomfortable. It had been a bad scene in every respect, but most of the fault was his because he had involved one of the Others in a disagreement between Men. To that extent, even Carnett had been a victim of circumstances; but he'd naturally refused to face the reality that not even his kind could solve every problem in the world, that others might have answers too and that the right answers might be unpalatable from the Carnetts' point of view. It was all of a piece with Vietnam, where the same message was now being crammed down those same throats—a point on which he and Gloria could agree.

Sure, but that was not the issue. She had her principles, to a sometimes tiresome degree, but obviously they had not prevented her from joining Carnett in this, yet another scheme to improve the world. George smiled grimly; in a way, this could even be regarded as yet another attempt to make the world safer for representative democracy.

By the way they were all looking at him, everybody must have noticed the smile. He stared back, first at Mrs. Carnett, then at her husband, and finally Gloria. She looked ready to start crying again. In fact she had cried, sobbing loudly and unashamedly, for several hours after he had waked to find himself a prisoner. Or kidnap victim. Or victim of unlawful restraint, as he'd pointed out to the bastard with the gun while Mrs. Carnett comforted Gloria in the bedroom. In a way, it was distressing to see her so much at her ease around the Carnetts now, after breaking down the way she had.

He met his wife's look without flinching. *One, two, three . . . thirty, thirty-one*— There she'd had enough. She looked away and rubbed her eyes. Carnett took a deep breath.

George turned to face him. "Let the sermon begin."

Carnett shrugged. "Never mind." The lawyer turned his eyes back toward the television, but George could tell he remained under close surveillance.

Apparently there was some kind of a hitch,

because Control had called a hold. The countdown had stopped. For a moment, George wondered— But no, mechanical things meant nothing to Seppius. They were strictly for Others; he could recall innumerable pronouncements on that subject.

The hold seemed to distress Carnett. Good! Let ~~him stew, let him suffer, let him worry; it was only~~ fair, in return for all the plotting and conniving. He could just see it, starting with the night he had walked out on the weep-and-curse session in Lebanon—if not before that, since Carnett had never granted Seppius the least particle of goodwill or honor.

George shook his head angrily. Maybe he'd file charges yet, or maybe he'd let Gloria talk him out of it . . . Yes, that would be better. Hell, he'd made his share of mistakes, but the worst had been going to see Carnett. John Lambert had been no help at all. He would have been better off never setting foot in Marbury, because there was no way he could have prevented the murders committed by Joe Paytna or Lewis Neumann. But Bernie Kratzel's death and Al Robinson's ruined life . . . these would be on his conscience forever, and the burden was even worse because Carnett had been dragged into his life as a result.

He shook his head again, even angrier now. That was not true. It was stupid. Spilt milk was spilt milk, and all of them—everybody in this room and everybody else, all the way back to the beginnings—had always tried to do things for the best.

Damn. He glared at his hands, his fingers clenching and unclenching. If only Carnett didn't have the gun. He stared at the barrel, visualizing the metal shaft stretching on and on . . .

But shouldn't it be grooved—because of the rifling? And why should he see shadows suggesting a ladder?

Ladder? His head jerked up.

Yes. The image was faint, seeming to fade in and out; a pang of regret flashed through George's mind; but—his heart beat faster—the Seeking Sword was no longer in the ARA case!

He sensed the nearness of a person—one of the technicians sent in to repair the trouble? Apparently

343

the sword was now in a tool kit, because it swayed and occasionally George sensed the thud and clatter as the kit banged against the side of Bob—yes, Bob Mollinson, Robert T. Mollinson—as the thirty-year-old technician climbed down the ladder. Mollinson was muttering to himself, wondering how he would get this—he didn't know what to call it—to his car without attracting suspicion.

Hah!

George almost yelled in triumph. Carnett had failed! He could just see their faces, the lawyer's and Gloria's and Mrs. Carnett's. All it would take was three words, and there wasn't a thing they could do about it!

Mollinson was talking with other technicians, walking away from the rocket. The countdown had resumed.

Carnett accepted another cup of coffee from his wife. George closed his eyes and buried his face in his hands. He did not want to see Gloria right now, or face any of them. Not until he'd got this worked out.

Seppius had implied he might find another sword-keeper, and this could be a young man, somebody who would live for many years and perhaps even succeed where George Quinterus had failed. That was unlikely. The new sword-keeper might outlive George Junior. But more likely, the new sword-keeper would be somebody George's age and when George Junior was in his thirties he'd have to face the problem Sir Walter faced after he cut down, in line of duty, the heathen priest who happened to be sword-keeper in the 1200s.

Sir Walter had been one of the Men, too. He'd known he came from *saxeverdammte* stock; he was strong-minded and devout in a way modern men—except maybe some Communists—would find hard to credit. But even so, he had not been able to bend Seppius to his will—no one could, including an alchemist who thought he could control demons. But quite a few Men had held out against the old shaman, starting with Oyennokheapaine back in the Bronze age.

Oyennokheapaine had been a shaman—and in that, George could see some cause for hope. According to scholars, a person became a shaman because he was summoned by the spirits, presumably something like the Keepers, whom Seppius never had explained to George's satisfaction. By all accounts, it was a very impressive summons, not unlike being called by the Lord, and George was glad he'd never had the experience. Furthermore, those who resisted the summons usually got sick and died unless they obeyed the spirits, or at least that had been the case among various nineteenth-century people, Eskimos as well as Eurasians. The scholars had naturally been more interested in the persons who had become shamans. The men and women who resisted were passed over in a few sentences, much as Seppius passed over the bad kinsmen—the term still hurt— who refused to kill Shitfeet. Furthermore, George had not been particularly interested—then. But he was now.

He'd find out how some Men resisted successfully, even if he had to learn new languages, Finnish and Hungarian, Magyar, Yukaghir—whatever might give him a clue as to how George Junior could defend himself against the worst. Assuming he and Gloria stayed together—as he devoutly hoped—and that there were no more Seeking Sword murders, he would have until the middle 1980s to do his homework, hoping that the answer didn't involve doing something totally unreasonable.

Totally unreasonable? He could see Carnett chuckle at this use of the words. The hell with him.

George stole a peek in between his fingers, no longer really hoping for a chance to grab the .45. Carnett was putting down his coffee cup. Gloria was looking hopeful. Mrs. Carnett was outside his line of vision. The countdown was nearing its end, as the white numerals in the corner of the television screen showed only seconds remaining.

He dropped his hands and leaned back, savoring the moment when Carnett leaned forward with eager eyes and face as the base of the rocket was momentarily obscured by a dense cloud of smoke. The tension was visibly draining out of the lawyer's face, even though he was just as liable to a charge of unlawful restraint as he'd ever been.

George grinned. No one seemed to notice: Gloria was actually smiling, a bit uncertainly, her eyes glued to the image of the Pathseeker rising slowly on its fireball. George stole a glance at the television. Yeah, the rocket was off the pad, streaking away through the sky, en route to Saturn and Altair, or whatever.

Out of the corner of his eye he saw Carnett put the pistol on the floor and stand up, no doubt to uncork the bottle of California champagne he had mentioned earlier. A few little words would wipe the smile from the man's smug face: "Call up NASA, tell them they left the VIP behind!" But then there was Gloria.

Gloria! He looked at her. She was beaming, glowing, literally radiating happiness and relief in all directions.

He bit his lip. Gloria was due for some rest and relaxation, even if they never managed to patch things up again. They would, though; he was sure of that. Anyway, Carnett didn't matter; and his relief was no skin off George's back even if he died without ever knowing that he had failed. But destroying Gloria's happiness right now, when a single word would do it, was more than George could bear to do.

There was the plop! and then the sound of the champagne cork hitting the ceiling of the kitchenette to his left. In a moment Carnet would enter the room with the foaming magnum in his hand. Mrs. Carnett had already set a tray with four glasses on the table. The next scene was all up to him.

The lawyer walked straight to the table, filled the four glasses, put the bottle down, picked up a glass and walked over to where George was sitting. Without a word, George accepted the glass. He did not look at it, or at the rising bubbles, while Carnett handed glasses of champagne to the women and then raised the fourth glass.

"To better days."

"I'll drink to that," said George, wondering whether—or how long—he would be able to keep his secret.

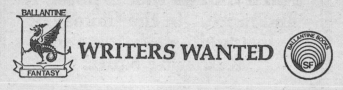

WRITERS WANTED

Every writer who has ever succeeded in science fiction or fantasy was once unpublished. Some editor somewhere discovered that first book in a pile of unsolicited manuscripts and loved it and published it—and the rest is history.

Ballantine has been a leading publisher of science fiction and fantasy for more than 20 years. And we still read all those unsolicited manuscripts with great anticipation—hoping to find the next star.

It could be you—but only if you send us your manuscript.

We're looking for *good* stories—well told—with *interesting* characters involved in all kinds of *well-developed situations*.

In essence, we're looking for the same kind of book that you look for every month when you head for your local bookstore. The kind of book you're damned glad you've read and may even want to read again sometime!

Don't be shy...we can be very friendly to those who send us promising books. The rewards can be substantial.

So do keep us in mind...

Ballantine Books
Science Fiction/Fantasy
Dept. U.B.I.
201 East 50th Street
New York, New York 10022

L-69

You'll find all that is possible and more...in the fantasy of Evangeline Walton and Katherine Kurtz.